TWELVE LABOURS OF LOVE

LAURA STEWART

ALSO BY LAURA STEWART

The Murderous Affair at Stone Manor

Mistletoe and Murder

To my wonderful family.

GLASGOW – VALENTINE'S DAY

*M*allory Caine jumped up and down, pulling her woolly cardigan tighter around her body as an icy draught whistled down the hallway of her flat.

Shivering, Mallory was currently barred from entering her own lounge which had the only reliable heat source in the guise of a real fire, and slightly more importantly, the television.

Mallory's best friend and flatmate, Caz Lovatt, stood blocking her entry.

'Just give me two more minutes, I'm planning a surprise. I promise you; it'll be worth it.' And before Mallory could protest, Caz darted back into the lounge and closed the door.

With the loose-knit acrylic blend of Mallory's cardigan not offering much respite, Mallory also jammed on her woolly beret and mittens.

When viewing the flat a few months earlier, the cavernous rooms and high ornate ceilings were impressive enough for her to overlook the more dated design statements of the period blonde sandstone tenement. But Mallory thought she'd gladly swap her 'original stained-glass feature windows', which rattled in their frames whenever the number four bus trundled past on its regular, twenty-minute service, for a more modest-sized, low-ceilinged, double-glazed flat that didn't rely on clanking temperamental radiators for warmth on what had turned out to be one of the stormiest February days on record.

Stomping into the kitchen, Mallory flicked on the overhead strip light, illuminating the dated pine cupboards and beige glazed tiles with barley ears and windmill motifs. She and Caz had disguised as much of the décor as possible with a wide array of fairy lights and it was these very lights Mallory switched on and stood next to hoping they'd release some warmth. She briefly considered switching on the oven and standing in front of it, but it was so ancient there was a jolly good chance she'd end up gassing herself. Instead, she switched on the kettle and spooned some coffee into a mug and mused over what kind of surprise Caz had in mind.

Since meeting Caz on their first day at art school ten years earlier, Mallory had been the recipient of many Caz surprises and they ranged from the nice to the dubious, to the downright awful. Mallory had loved the surprise party for her last birthday. The 'lucky dip' auctioneers box full of Europop singles and taxidermied birds was strange, but amusing. However, the 'digital detox' weekend Caz had booked for them had been torturous from start to finish. Not content with switching off their smartphones and leaving their laptops behind, the organisers insisted everyone also forgo electricity, running water and their own comfortable beds by pitching tents in woods miles from civilisation. Not a natural camper, Mallory had never had a more uncomfortable night's sleep, terrified creepy crawlies would find their way into her sleeping bag.

And so, Mallory felt more than a little trepidation at what was going on behind the firmly shut lounge door, especially as she could hear hammering coming from inside despite Caz's attempts at drowning it out by playing her Tibetan monk chants playlist at full volume.

As the kettle came to the boil and switched off, Mallory became aware of someone joining in the cacophony of noise by pounding on the front door. No doubt it would be their busybody neighbour with the low noise tolerance and high meddling factor, Mallory thought with a sigh, watching as her breath misted in front of her. But instead of the purse-lipped Mrs McClusky on her doorstep clutching her yappy Yorkshire terrier, she discovered her friend Oliver Walsh; doubled over and gasping for air.

He thumped his chest with his fist, coughed then looked up at her through his mop of sandy blond hair and rain-splattered tortoiseshell glasses. 'I ran… all the way.'

'Um… why?' Laid back to the point of horizontal, Olly, in all the years Mallory had known him, had never run for anything and she wasn't sure whether to congratulate him or call for ambulance assistance.

He straightened up, looking puzzled. 'I just got a call from Caz to say there was an emergency and I had to get round here pronto.'

On cue, the lounge door opened a crack.

'Okay! You can come in now,' Caz whispered dramatically.

Exchanging a wary glance with Olly, Mallory opened the door further only to be engulfed in a heady cloud of rose and sandalwood incense.

'Quick! We can't have any energy escaping.' Caz ushered them in and slammed the door behind them.

'Seems all the oxygen has!' Mallory gasped, choking on the thickly perfumed air. Then, as the fug cleared slightly, Mallory was able to see the full scale of the horror, turning 360 degrees to take it all in. 'Oh my God, Caz! What have you done?'

Everything had been covered in pink satin.

Caz had managed to bunch the material in the middle of the ceiling, nailing it in place so it hung down the walls giving the effect of being inside a very camp Bedouin tent. She'd also draped the satin over all the furniture on which she'd then dotted dozens of blazing pink tea lights in sequinned and bejewelled holders which glinted and reflected off the shiny fabric.

'Oh my!' Olly exclaimed, not even attempting to hide his amusement as he dried his glasses on the bottom of his shirt. 'I can see the emergency; you now seem to be living in Barbie's harem.'

'Caz…' Mallory said carefully, looking closely at Caz, wondering if her friend had flipped completely. 'I know you've obviously worked hard, but I don't think this is terribly practical,' she said as tactfully as possible, eyeing up the pink scatter cushions and lumps of rose quartz littering the floor. Having her home turned into a shiny bubblegum-pink temple of a fire hazard was indeed a surprise, but not a very welcome one, especially when such an outré makeover would mean waving goodbye to their flat deposit.

'Oh no, it's not permanent!' Caz laughed, her berry brown eyes glittering. 'It's just for tonight. And now we're all here we can begin.'

'Begin what?' Mallory pushed back a strip of fabric which was wafting dangerously close to a naked flame.

But Caz merely smiled enigmatically and handed her and Olly a pink candle each. 'What day is it today?'

'Tuesday,' Olly suggested.

'And?'

'Oh God! St Valentine's Day,' Mallory said miserably, noticing a large pink papier mâché love heart suspended from the ceiling like a piñata.

'Correct! But more importantly than that, in a few minutes' time the planet Venus makes an auspicious conjunction to Mercury,' Caz explained.

Mallory looked blankly back at her. Over time she'd grown accustomed to Caz's dabbling with the spiritual; she'd been happy to be her Reiki guinea pig, had accompanied her in some tree hugging in the park at the summer solstice, and she didn't mind listening to all the meditation music (although the Tibetan monk chanting had started to get a bit creepy), but this time Mallory had no idea what Caz was on about.

'Planet of love? Planet of communication?' Caz sighed in disappointment at her ignorance. She held up a red leather-bound book, her sparkly fuchsia-painted fingernail tapping the gold curlicues of the title: *Ask the Universe*. 'According to this, tonight is the perfect time to ask the heavens for help with our love lives.'

Olly backed towards the door, hands up in surrender. 'My love life's fine, so I'll be leaving you lovely ladies to it.' With ninja-like reflexes, Caz grabbed onto the front of his shirt and held fast. 'You don't *have* a love life.' She pulled him back towards her. 'We all need help.'

Olly waved a piece of pink marabou about in disdain. 'Judging by all this frou-frou nonsense, I don't think it's *us* that needs the help, Caz.'

'Pink enhances the energy to channel love.'

'I don't *want* to be love-channelled, thank you very much.'

Not wanting a full-scale argument to break out between her two best friends, Mallory removed Olly's shirt from Caz's grip and lowered the piece of marabou he wielded.

'I'm willing to admit we could do with a bit of celestial assistance. Come on, Olly, you've been single for aeons now and the last few guys I've gone out with have been awful.' Caz turned to Mallory. 'And you *definitely* need help.'

'Me?'

'Yes, you! Aphrodite, the goddess of love, deals with all aspects of the condition, including mending broken hearts. You've got to do something. When did you and Don split up? I mean *properly* properly, not including the weeks when he mucked you around with his selfish indecision.'

Mallory opened her mouth, so used to leaping to Don's

defence, but quickly shut it again, knowing she'd be shouted down; Olly and Caz were not her ex's biggest fans. 'A while ago,' she hedged.

'Four months.'

It was really three and a half, but Mallory thought it best not to correct Caz in case she and Olly thought she'd been keeping a close eye on the calendar, mentally marking off the days since she'd been Don-less. Which she hadn't. Not really.

'You've got to halt your spiral of misery and move on,' Caz said.

'My spiral of misery? Come on, I'm not that bad.' Mallory laughed. 'Am I?' She looked at Olly for back-up but he'd become engrossed in studying his shoes.

'Sorry, but I have to agree with Caz,' he mumbled, finally allowing his hazel eyes to meet hers.

Mallory couldn't believe it! She thought she'd coped admirably since Don had buggered off to America. As one of Britain's hottest artists he'd been lured by the bright lights, big city and even bigger bucks of the New York art scene and the promise of a one-man show in a cutting-edge gallery, but before he'd even reached the end of his road in a taxi Don had decided he wasn't cut out for long-distance relationships and had broken up with Mallory.

Despite her heartache Mallory had soldiered on, keeping it together through all his wee-small-hours-of-the-morning phone calls when he was full of remorse and whisky in equal measures. And she'd not even resorted to hibernating under the duvet when he'd kept changing his mind, one minute telling her he couldn't be without her but before she could call easyJet to book a one-way ticket he'd call back to say that it was better they were apart after all.

She thought she'd been a rock; stoic throughout.

'I know it's been tough,' Olly continued, 'but it's as if you've lost your spark. You never go out anymore.'

'Of course I do! I'm at the gallery every day,' she protested, miffed they were rounding on her.

'That's work,' Olly said. 'You don't seem to socialise anymore. You've lost your Mallory mojo,' he added, kindly.

'You've lost a bit of direction, that's all,' Caz said gently. 'You need to have some fun and move on. When was the last time you picked up a paintbrush?'

Mallory chipped at the candle with her thumbnail unable to argue back; annoyingly, they had a point. She'd been putting in extra hours at the gallery, in her part-time role as assistant, but had been using her tiredness as an excuse to leave her own paintings on the back-burner, but even throwing everything into her job hadn't managed to fill the emotional vacuum. At risk of never being allowed to join a Germaine Greer-inspired empowering feminist group, she had to admit that without Don she'd been feeling at a loose end.

Caz carried on. 'In fact, we *all* need to have fun. Don't you think it's terrible that on the most romantic night of the year we're all here, date free, with only a microwaveable meal and the new *Midsomer Murders* to look forward to?'

'St Valentine's Day is a load of hyped-up nonsense,' Olly said.

'St Valentine's Day might be, but *love* isn't,' Caz pleaded with them. 'The book says that the sky tonight is in the perfect alignment for the heavens to receive incoming calls. All we need to do is ask the universe, Venus, Aphrodite, who*ever*, up there, for help. What have you got to lose?'

'Dignity?' Olly said, holding the pink candle aloft.

Caz turned to Mallory. 'Humour me. Suspend disbelief for five minutes. Imagine if it *does* work...'

Mallory, who'd been looking forward to her Marks and Spencer's Chicken Kyiv and seeing what imaginative murders Detective Barnaby would be solving, just wanted her lounge back but knew from experience the sooner they did Caz's bidding, the sooner they'd be finished.

'Heaven forbid if we come between you and your auspicious conjunction. Okay, count me in.'

Caz clapped her hands in delight. She turned to Olly. 'Come on! Say yes too, these things always work better in triumvirates!'

'Oh, all right, you witchy wench,' Olly grumbled, giving Mallory a *why did you agree to this* look.

'Sit!' Caz commanded.

They sat, cross-legged, on top of the floor cushions.

Caz wriggled into a more comfortable position and closed her eyes.

'I, Caz Lovatt, request that the goddess Aphrodite look down from the heavens and bless me with her help. Please let me meet The One. Soon.' She opened her eyes and lit her pink candle, then nodded at Olly.

He cleared his throat. 'I, Olly Walsh, would like to ask for help from Aphrodite to… um… I can't believe I'm doing this.'

'You have to be completely open and say what's in your heart or it won't work,' Caz whispered.

He raised a sceptical eyebrow but nonetheless threw back his head and screwed up his eyes. 'I would love to have the courage to seize the day.' He opened an eye. 'That do?'

'Ooh! Very obscure, care to elaborate?' Caz asked.

'Nope.' He lit his candle.

They both turned to Mallory.

She took a deep breath. 'I, Mallory Caine, ask the goddess Aphrodite for help to…' She closed her eyes. What did she want? She wasn't sure she wanted love at all. She'd been there before and it had caused her nothing but pain and misery. Did she really want to go through it again… although, what they were doing was *obviously* complete nonsense – as if the goddess Aphrodite existed!

Mallory should just say what Caz wanted to hear, that she too, wanted to meet The One… But the words froze in her throat. Did

8

she really want to tempt fate...? What if maybe, just *maybe* there was something in this conjunction business.

What was she thinking! Of course there wasn't, and anyway, she'd been under the misapprehension that Don was The One.

What if she asked to meet The One and Aphrodite *was* listening and Don had been The One and he came back into her life... would she want that? She really didn't think she did as she remembered his less-than-adorable traits, like his mood swings and the sulking if he didn't get his way. Oh yes, and his inability to commit. Could she be that specific? Would that be too much information to get across? Was it like Twitter and she had a restricted word count?

She realised she was taking an awfully long time to speak. She peeked at Caz who was watching her expectantly. She had to say something...

Deciding to avoid the Don issue entirely she thought she'd ask for something a little more general. 'I would like to ask for help to be happy.'

'That's a bit on the vague side,' Caz said in disappointment. 'Add a bit more.'

Mallory rolled the pink candle between her palms for a moment then shut her eyes again. 'Aphrodite? Hello, it's still me, Mallory. As well as being happy, or at least a lot happier than I am at the moment, I'd um... I'd like to have a bit more direction in my life. Ow!' Caz's elbow dug into her rib. 'Okay! Aphrodite? I'd really like to start having fun and to get out more.'

'Mallory! You sound as if you're a geriatric wanting to have a last jolly to Skegness before you shuffle off this mortal coil. And at least *try* to make it love-related!' Caz grumbled.

Mallory took a deep breath to start again. Caz hadn't given Olly such a hard time over his *courage to seize the day* and to Mallory that had sounded incredibly lame.

'Don't you want to meet a guy?' Caz pressed.

Mallory supposed she did, eventually. Once she'd completely

gotten over Don. She'd never been quite as willing as Caz seemed to be to kiss a barrel full of frogs just on the off-chance a prince was hiding among them. Yes, she knew she was picky, *discerning*, she'd be inclined to say, but really, more than anything, Mallory wanted to get on with her evening, for Caz to get off her back and to stop being the focus of attention.

'Aphrodite? Sorry, I know you'll be busy tonight so I'll get on with it. I'd really love to be happy and to have more fun and excitement in my life. And I'd love to meet a fabulous guy; someone handsome and passionate and fun-loving.'

Caz smiled in approval.

'What do we do now?' Mallory asked, lighting her candle.

'We wait.'

'For what?'

'For the candle to burn down. We keep repeating our requests to ourselves until we enter a sort of meditative state and continue like that until the wax has melted away into the ether completely. That way we know Aphrodite will have heard us.'

'Heard us?' Olly said with a groan. 'Caz, she'll be sick of the sound of our voices.' He held up the pack of candles, tapping his index finger underneath the words *burns for five hours*.

CHAPTER 1

*J*uly in Glasgow. For the city's inhabitants, summer usually meant grey clouds and rain that was marginally warmer than in March. Yet this year Glasgow had pulled out all the stops and for over a week had been giving a damn good impersonation of the sun-soaked South of France. Minus the beaches. And without nearly as many sexy French people.

With the mercury levels rising as morning changed to midday, Mallory decided to make the most of the sunshine – as well as begin the fitness regime she kept promising herself she'd start – and carry her latest submission to the gallery where she worked and regularly exhibited.

Mallory started off gung-ho, loving the warmth of the sun beating down on her back through her sundress; a new purchase to herald the good weather. She never usually went for dresses, far preferring jeans and a shirt, but she couldn't resist the cheerful orange and yellow floral print with the 1950's influenced nipped-in waist and full, swinging skirt that was straight out of a Doris Day musical.

Had she not been carrying such a large painting Mallory

would have been sorely tempted to skip along singing a few bars of 'Que Sera, Sera', but after just a few hundred yards the four foot by four foot bubble-wrapped canvas seemed to increase in weight and awkwardness with each step she took and she ended up half carrying, half dragging it through Kelvingrove Park.

Huffing and puffing past all the chilled-out groups of friends sprawled on the grass, sipping iced coffees and reading books, Mallory's arms ached and her hands smarted from where the string cut into her palms from carrying such a weight. Then her shoulders began to burn from her negligence at sun protection. Worse still, she was being followed by a gigantic bee, buzzing in lazy zigzags round her head, no doubt attracted by her florally inviting dress and new perfume, a heady mix of jasmine and orange blossom.

Eventually, Mallory arrived at the Reiss Gallery and she dragged the painting through the doors before slumping against the cool plasterwork, feeling a little faint from the heat and exertion. Although Mallory loved the summer, it didn't return the favour: it wasn't a benevolent season for pale-skinned, auburn-haired Celts.

Looking down at her chest she saw her exposed skin had started to turn an unbecoming shade of lobster (which clashed horribly with her orange dress) and a smattering of freckles had appeared on her shoulders.

Johan Reiss poked his head out from the back office, smiling widely when he saw her. 'How's my favourite artist?'

'Worried I'll get sunstroke. And I think I've dislocated something.' Mallory winced as she experimented with a shoulder roll.

The octogenarian limped over to greet her. 'Why didn't you call me? I would have sent the van to get it,' he chastised lightly.

She blew a lock of damp hair from her eyes. 'I thought I could do with the exercise, work up a bit of a sweat.'

'Horses sweat, men perspire and women *glow*!' Johan chuckled as he ripped away the protective wrap from the painting.

'Glow? I'm glowing enough to power a small nuclear reactor!' She fanned herself with her hand as Johan freed the painting of its confines. He took a step back, his deep-set eyes, almost entirely hidden by wayward bushy white eyebrows, scrutinising her work.

From first meeting Johan at a Christmas party five years earlier when they'd enjoyed a lively debate on the merits of Pop Art over some hot buttered rum and mince pies, Mallory had become a regular exhibitor at his gallery and then became his part-time assistant as their friendship grew.

'It is absolutely stunning, my dear. As always,' he said of the landscape, full of vibrant colours and broad brush-strokes.

'Thank you, I'm quite pleased with it.'

'Quite pleased?' he said then gave a chuckle. 'You really need to stop being so modest about your work. There is no need. Especially when people are already talking about the interior design of the cocktail bar you've been working on.'

'They are?' Mallory said, so surprised she stopped counting the freckles on her arms. She'd only just finished the commission of the décor for Bizbar. She normally stuck to fine art but when a friend of a friend was keen to get her involved to work on the interior design, Mallory had jumped at the new challenge and change of direction.

It had pushed her out of her comfort zone, but she'd loved the ambitious project, transforming the interior of the bar to embody the decadence of the bootleg speakeasies of twenties' New York. The pièce de résistance was the huge mural she'd painted on the back wall; a sexy scene of faded glamour and shadowy assignations of gangsters and their molls.

Johan laughed, leaning forward on his stick. 'From what I've heard, it's spectacular.'

'From what you've heard?'

'Oh, you know how I like to keep my ear to the ground,' he said evasively.

'Johan!' Mallory warned him. He loved nothing better than to eke out a good story for dramatic effect.

'A young man I know happened to see it and was, what was the phrase he used… *blown away*, yes, that was it. He was blown away by your work. Now, it so happens this young man is also on the lookout for a talented artist to help him with a similar new venture.'

'What? Who?' Mallory asked, thrilled that she'd had such a great reaction to her work, doubled by the prospect there might be another job on the back of it.

'It's my godson. You've heard of Alex Claremont?'

There was only one Alex Claremont that Mallory had heard of; the party-loving playboy son of the renowned Scottish business tycoon, James Claremont. *That* Alex Claremont was frequently cited as one of Britain's most 'eligible bachelors' that every society magazine wanted for the middle-page party spread and whom every society gal wanted to spread for at a party. Surely he couldn't be the godson of sweet, reserved, slightly fuddy-duddy Johan?

'The Alex Claremont who is always in the tabloids?'

She obviously hadn't kept the scepticism out of her voice as Johan laughed.

'You sound surprised. But, yes, that's the Alex I'm referring to. His father James and I were good friends once.' Johan shrugged. 'We don't see each other that often now, but I've always stayed in touch with Alex. There's quite a bit more to him than the press would like you to believe.'

Mallory wasn't so sure. From the articles she'd read about him in the magazines Caz left littered about, she'd gleaned he was rich as Croesus, thanks to his father, had done some part-time modelling and was most often to be found leaving glamorous parties with a model or actress, sometimes both.

Johan was watching Mallory with amusement. 'I really don't think he's as bad as the press portrays him.' He chuckled. 'He has a very good eye.'

'For the ladies?'

'For art. But I'll say no more about him. He's up from London for a few days and you can meet him yourself.'

'I doubt it would come to anything as I don't plan on moving to London anytime soon for *any* job.'

'Ah, well, this venture will be in Glasgow, that's why he's here, but I'll let you ask him about it yourself. I told him to call in here this afternoon to see your latest submission and I've photographs of all your previous work. I really do believe your star is on the ascendant, my dear. And this venture of his is bound to be high profile. It could really make you, especially if you're just starting out in interiors. I've told him about you and he can't wait to meet you. I was going to give him a copy of your CV, but I can't seem to find it...'

Johan's woeful filing was one of the reasons he'd hired Mallory as his assistant. 'Would you be able to bring in a copy, an up-to-date one?'

'Of course.'

'Good, good. Now I will go and make us a nice cup of tea. I have a new Earl Grey to open.' Johan got up and went into the back office, leaving Mallory with her thoughts.

Career-wise, it would be foolish to rule out any job, especially as she had so recently changed her focus to the more commercial world of interior design. And, Johan was right, if Alex Claremont was involved, it would garner a lot of attention.

She'd never thought of herself as terribly ambitious, but with the possibility of an exciting job within her grasp, she'd be an idiot to not try to get it.

CHAPTER 2

*F*our hours later, Mallory sat in the middle of her living-room floor, slathered in after-sun, staring at her laptop.

Who'd have thought writing a CV could be so difficult?

The professional part of her résumé was no problem at all, in fact it was fairly impressive, but it was the 'other interest' section she found to be problematic.

She wound her long hair into a bun, tucking the odd stray curl behind her ears and focussed on the page in front of her, racking her brain for any hobbies or pastimes she could put down that could set her above the rest in terms of being an appealing, well-rounded candidate.

There was her interest, verging on unhealthy obsession, for reality television and an in-depth researched knowledge of the Cadbury chocolate collection, but she didn't think either of those was worth a mention.

But she hadn't exactly lived a life on the knife-edge of excitement lately. Or ever, for that matter.

She was still staring at the screen a few minutes later when Caz walked in and plonked herself onto the sofa, blowing the black fringe of her latest asymmetric, geometric, gravity-defying haircut out of her eyes. 'What's up?' she asked, delving behind a cushion and producing a handful of Roses chocolates.

Helping herself to a praline, Mallory filled Caz in on her lacking CV.

'It can't be *that* bad.' Caz unwrapped a strawberry cream.

'Caz, my main hobby is watching reality television.'

'There's more to you than that.'

'Oh yeah, I can also eat my own body weight in chocolate and drink an impressive amount of wine without falling over. Go me!'

'Speaking of which…' Caz unearthed a bottle of wine from behind the sofa and jiggled it invitingly.

'You see?' Mallory despaired. 'Don't get me wrong, I like my life, but it's hardly *eventful*,' she said, ramming a chocolate caramel into her mouth. She tapped her laptop. 'I'm dull.'

'You're not dull!'

'I want people to read about me and think I'm fun and adventurous, but in reality I'm little better than a recluse!' Miserably, she picked at the caramel welded onto her back molar.

'What about the modern dance shows you went to? And you were always going off to watch those jazz things.'

Mallory gave an involuntary shudder. Those had been Don's hobbies. He'd always dragged her along to contemporary dance performances and obscure jazz festivals and she'd quietly suffered through them all, hoping that something would suddenly click into place and she'd be able to appreciate them.

Surely, she'd thought, with enough exposure they'd end up growing on her. It had happened that way with olives and Gordon Ramsay. But no, to her, most modern dance looked like someone having a tantrum with all that floor thumping and tortured angst, and scat always made her want to laugh with the 'dooby dooby doobing'. She'd take indie rock over a revered ageing bluegrass guitarist any day.

'Those were things Don wanted to do. I just went along with it and the tragic thing is now I have no idea what *I* like doing!'

'You've just needed a little time to readjust to single life, that's all. *Now* is the moment to seize the opportunity and start living for *yourself*.' Caz pulled a corkscrew out from behind a cushion and opened the wine. 'You're a film fanatic; you love going to the cinema.' With a flourish she pulled out the cork with a satisfying *pop*. 'And reading!'

Mallory wasn't sure devouring the latest Marian Keyes novel was worth mentioning on a CV.

'Hang on! I've got an idea!' Caz bounced up and down on the sofa, the springs protesting at her exuberance. 'We'll write your dream CV, putting down all the things you've ever wanted to do.'

'But I can't lie! Especially not to Johan!'

'No, I don't mean to give *him* the made-up one. Just give him your old CV, whether you think it's dull or not. Print it off.' Mallory duly did.

'Hold on a minute!' Caz jumped up and bounded into the kitchen, returning a couple of minutes later with two wine glasses.

She settled herself back on the sofa and reached over to lift up Mallory's laptop. 'We can make up a CV of the person you'd like to be. It's something a lot of the self-help books cover; projection, or something like that. And then all you need to do is tackle them one by one and gradually you become that person.' She flexed her fingers. 'Now then, Ms Caine, what would you like your CV to say?'

Mallory sat back, leaning on her hands, warming to the idea. 'I need to cover everything. Sport, adventure, music...' She pondered for a moment. 'You know, I've always had a notion to play the guitar...'

Mallory refilled their glasses. 'It would be nice to know a little more about this stuff too.' She studied the back label on the bottle of wine.

'Hold on.' Caz frowned. 'How'd you spell 'connoisseur'?'

'And I'd love to be able to speak Italian,' Mallory said wistfully, remembering the amazing time she'd had at the end of her first year of art school when she'd bought a Euro Saver rail ticket and backpacked around Italy for a couple of months. Ever since, she'd had a vague notion of learning the language, but the only Italian she'd picked up was courtesy of the menu from the nearby trattoria and Eurovision Song Contest entrants.

'I would love to be fitter. I need to learn a sport.'

Caz duly typed the information. 'What kind? Tennis?'

Mallory shook her head and thought for a moment. 'Something harder and faster.'

'Shinty!'

'Not that hard and fast. More like squash. Yes, make it squash. And something spiritual to balance.'

'Tai Chi? Yoga?'

'Oh, yes – yoga. I'd love to be more supple.' Mallory stretched her arms up, wincing as her shoulder cracked.

'Y-O-G-A, Yoga!'

'And something challenging, something skilled.'

'Chess?'

Mallory shook her head. 'Too prepubescent geeky. Something more glamorous like, like... I know! Dancing!'

'I thought you didn't like dancing.'

'Not modern dancing, I mean some sexy, fun dancing, like salsa!'

Caz typed. 'Cool!'

'Ooh! And something a bit daredevil. Rally driving!' Mallory's eyes lit up.

Caz laughed. 'You'll have to learn to drive first.'

'I can drive!' And she could. *Sort of.*

'When was your last lesson?'

'A few months ago.' Okay, so she was no Lewis Hamilton. 'Put down rally driving, this is my fantasy self, remember. Ooh! And abseiling! It always seemed cool when they did it on *Blue Peter*. And definitely for charity, I'd like to have more of a social conscience'.

Caz skim-read what she'd just written. 'Okay, husband? Kids?'

'Certainly not,' Mallory said adamantly.

'You never know...'

Mallory bristled. 'I don't need a man in my life. I'm better off single. I've been focussing on my work which has gone so well and–'

'*Being independent and rediscovering myself and burning my bra and blah, blah, blah,*' Caz mimicked. 'I love the fact you don't want to be defined by a man, but you can still date one. I know you're scared of getting hurt, but at some point you'll have to dip your toe in the great big love puddle of testosterone.'

'You make it sound so appealing!'

'I'm putting down that you're engaged. There! That's a compromise. You know I've got loads of very nice, good-looking male friends, any of which would be delighted to–'

'Caz...' Mallory interrupted Caz's well-meaning attempts to get her in the dating loop again.

Caz smiled benevolently at her. 'You don't fool me. You're still a romantic. You can recite the entire script of *Sleepless in Seattle*...'

'I'm a film fanatic, remember? It's a classic of the genre.'

'Face it, Mallory, you're a die-hard romantic.'

'*Was* a die-hard romantic,' Mallory corrected.

'I know you thought it at the time, but Don obviously wasn't The One.'

'Nooooooo.' Mallory wailed in mock horror, putting her hands over her ears. 'Not *the* The One speech! Anything but that! I'll repent, I'll repent.'

Caz gave Mallory an old-fashioned look. 'Cynicism produces a lot of negativity, you know. Anyway, back to your CV...'

Mallory drained her glass and unwrapped another chocolate truffle. 'So, what have we got?'

'Hold on, it's still printing.' Caz stood a little unsteadily, knocking over the empty bottle of wine as she plucked the paper from the printer. She cleared her throat.

'"After graduating from Glasgow School of Art with a first-class degree, Mallory Caine spent a few months travelling, gleaning artistic inspiration from various countries and cultures, which is apparent in her work". And then we have page after page of your exhibits and commissions, etc, etc. Here we go... "Since travelling around Italy as a student, Mallory has always felt a kinship for this part of the world and she recently took time out of her busy schedule to horse-trek around Tuscany, combining her equine skills with her natural flair for the Italian language".'

Mallory burst out laughing but Caz hushed her down with a wave of her hand, before continuing. '"Highly musical, she plays the guitar and sings in an up-and-coming band and regularly performs DJ sets, but her sense of rhythm doesn't stop there as she's also recently taken up salsa dancing.

"Playing squash keeps Mallory fit and she loves nothing better than to partake in action-packed weekends, from Munro bagging to rally driving, zip slides to rock climbing. She loves anything which gets the adrenaline pumping and involves time spent in the great outdoors! Though not all her time is spent in the fast lane; Mallory is also an advocate of the spiritual and physical benefits of yoga. And as a film fanatic she loves a relaxing evening in, watching romantic classics.

"At the weekend Mallory loves to socialise and is a keen amateur gourmet cook and wine connoisseur. She lives in Glasgow and is engaged. Her most recent achievement was completing an abseil for an art therapy charity".'

'Oh my God! If I met someone like this I would probably hate them!' Mallory laughed.

'These are all things you *want* to be able to do,' Caz reminded her.

'I know.' She spun the empty bottle of wine on the carpet. 'Apart from the travelling and being a film buff, the rest are lies.'

Caz flapped the printout at her. 'They're not lies, they're just things you've not done yet.'

'But can you actually see me ever doing them?' Mallory said doubtfully.

'YES! The whole point of this exercise is to start to be like this person. You need to focus on each one at a time then achieve it. Focus and achieve is your new mantra. Remember back in February when we asked Aphrodite for help?'

Mallory wasn't given a chance to forget. Every day she had to listen to Caz bemoaning the fact she *still* hadn't met The One.

'You said you wanted to have more fun and get out more. This is your chance! And I think we should go out and celebrate the beginning of your new, fun-filled, adventurous life right now!'

'Why not, it's not as if I've got a gymkhana first thing in the morning, is it?' Mallory laughed and stood up. Then she suddenly remembered why they'd started the exercise in the first place. 'I still need to drop my actual CV in to Johan.'

Caz reached over and picked it up. 'Here we go! It's nowhere near as exciting as your new one, but it'll have to do. Johan lives not far from here, doesn't he? Why don't we make the most of such a beautiful evening and go for a walk and we can pop it through his letterbox on the way.'

CHAPTER 3

*N*ext morning, Mallory padded into the kitchen to make breakfast, finding Caz already sitting at their table, chatting to Olly.

'Hey,' Olly said with a smile. 'Thought I'd pop in for a coffee before heading round to the studio. Are you there this morning?'

Mallory shared a studio with a couple of other artists, Olly being one of them, where he did his illustration commissions. Being in high demand for children's books, he'd made enough money and bought a much bigger flat with plenty of space and could easily work from home, but he insisted on keeping his place on at the studio as he liked the camaraderie and he often said he'd just end up wasting his day watching Netflix if left on his own.

'Not today, I said I'd pop in to help Johan.' Mallory searched through the cupboards for something she could make for breakfast.

She really fancied bacon and eggs but because Caz was on another of her diets, all meat and dairy products had been confiscated leaving nothing more tantalising than rice cakes and meal replacement shakes. Closing the cupboards Mallory joined her friends at the table with a mug and poured herself a coffee.

'I needed to get up early to start my new business plan,' Caz said as she dived under the table and came back up holding a doll's head aloft by its golden curls, like Perseus brandishing the decapitated head of Medusa. 'What do you think?'

'Um…'

Caz back-combed the nylon tresses. 'I managed to get hold of twenty of them from various charity shops, I'm going to stick them on spikes and use them to show off my new range of jewellery in the window.'

'Spikes, eh? Nice.' Mallory looked to Olly but he merely smiled and took a sip of his coffee. Mallory reached over and squeezed Caz's hand knowing how much her friend struggled to stay afloat. Caz rented a little unit in an arcade in the west end where she made and sold jewellery but business was so slow she'd taken on a part-time job in a pub to cover expenses, and each week it seemed she had more and more shifts. Caz had put everything into her business but, although incredibly talented, she never seemed to get it off the ground, growing more despondent as the months rolled on and she barely broke even.

Caz sat back in her chair nursing her mug. 'I need something that grabs people's attention and I think this could be what I need,' she said, her chocolate-brown eyes twinkling impishly as she rooted around the table for an indelible black pen.

'I love it!' Mallory said, honestly. It was totally bonkers, but then, so was Caz.

Holding the head down and removing the pen top with her teeth, Caz drew on thick black eyeliner Cleopatra would have been proud of.

'Oh, Mallory, I almost forgot!' Caz said after spitting the pen top onto the table. 'Your phone rang while you were in the shower. It was Johan wanting to thank you for the CV and he said he had spare tickets for tonight's exhibition opening and offered them to us all. He's such a sweetheart! *And* he mentioned someone else who'd be there.'

'Who?'

'Three words. Alex. Sexy. Claremont,' she trilled.

'Please don't start this again,' Mallory warned. The previous night Caz had been banging on about how dreamy Alex was and how perfect he'd be for Mallory to have a rebound fling with.

'What's this?' Olly said, looking up from his phone.

'I've not even met the man yet!' Mallory said defensively. 'He's a potential employer. He's got a new venture starting up and said to Johan he'd be interested in meeting me to hear my ideas.'

Caz opened up the magazine beside her. 'And there he is…' She sighed like a teenager with her first crush on a pop star.

Mallory looked at the photograph Caz slid round to her. Alex Claremont *was* a very good-looking man, there was no denying it. He had the classic tall, dark and handsome hat trick, with just a bit of edgy rogue thrown in.

'Look! There's the obligatory blonde beside him,' Mallory pointed out scathingly. 'Oh, and is that France they're in? Yes, I do believe it's Nice, how terribly unoriginal. He's celebrating his thirtieth birthday. And it looks as if he's just walked off that.' She pointed at the huge sleek yacht behind them. She scanned the article. 'Listen up, "I know I have a reputation but I can't help chatting up every woman I meet. What can say, I have a high sex drive". He sounds such an ass!'

Caz whisked the magazine back to her. 'Johan also wanted me to tell you that Alex dropped in to look at your work and he loved your paintings. But seeing that you don't care…'

'Of course I care about him liking my paintings. Work is work. I don't have to like someone to work for them and I can't be that picky at the moment, unlike some folk around here who are wealthy enough and successful enough to be able to pick and choose their commissions,' Mallory teased, looking over at Olly.

He took another sip of his coffee, his face reddening.

'Aren't you even slightly excited?' Caz enthused. 'You might be working with one of the sexiest men on the planet.'

Mallory loved Caz's enthusiasm and optimism that she already had the job in the bag, but Mallory wasn't convinced. She had a sneaky feeling Alex Claremont was probably only doing Johan a favour by agreeing to see her.

❧

That evening's exhibition was taking place in a converted warehouse with the vast area having been sectioned off into four rooms, each themed loosely around one of the four astrological elements. Mallory was keen to make a beeline for 'air' in the hope there would be some discernible ventilation or air conditioning to counteract the hot bodies pressed against each other on the sweltering summer evening.

'God, it's hot in here. I feel a bit faint,' Caz whispered to Mallory as they pressed into the crowds standing in front of the large sculpture installations which took up most of the floor space in the first of the four rooms.

Mallory turned to see her friend start to sway slightly, her balance not being helped by the six-inch leather stilettos she was wearing.

'Have you eaten today?' Mallory asked as she gave her arm as a support.

'No, I made such a pig of myself with all those chocolates last night I couldn't risk not fitting into these.' Caz slapped her black PVC trouser-clad thigh.

'Maybe your corset's too tight.'

'I don't want it coming loose.' Caz looked down at her ample cleavage spilling out the top like two scoops of vanilla ice cream in a sundae glass. 'Maybe you'd better double bow it for me, just in case,' she said, turning around for Mallory to grasp the two leather thongs.

Mallory obliged. 'Can you still breathe?'

'Breathing's overrated. Pride knows... no pain.' Caz gasped. 'Right then, where is he?' She scanned the sea of heads before them.

'Olly? Don't know, I haven't seen him.'

Caz gave Mallory a meaningful smile. 'I meant Alex, you dummy. Although it might take you all night to find him as it looks like half of Glasgow's here. Oh God, art luvvie alert. Honestly, I swear they just come for the free booze!'

Mallory turned to where Caz nodded and recognised the group who turned up to every gallery opening, an insufferable mix of people they'd long ago learned to body-swerve.

A waiter squeezed past them laden with glasses of sparkling wine and Caz swooped in, securing the two fullest. She passed one to Mallory.

'You know,' Caz said, after knocking back a mouthful, 'you probably haven't even noticed, but there are some *very* nice-looking men here tonight. There's a guy at your three o'clock, standing by the pillar. Utterly divine. What d'you think?'

Mallory didn't even bother to glance over. 'They're all yours, Caz.'

'It won't hurt to take a look.'

Mallory shrugged. 'I'm not interested.'

'You know, it's not...' Caz broke off, sniffing the air, her attention caught by a waiter walking past her with a tray of canapés. 'Oh bugger! They've got hot prawn wasabi filo pastry thingies. I will not eat; I will *not eat.*' She turned away from the temptation, fanning herself with a gallery leaflet. 'Okay. Let's go look at art.'

❧

The heat continued to soar as more people piled in. The indecipherable chatter echoed round the rafters as Mallory wandered through the rooms, one eye on the paintings and one eye on the lookout for Alex Claremont. Despite telling Caz she wasn't in the least bothered about meeting him, Mallory did have a couple of butterflies taking up residence in her stomach since, after all, there was the potential of her getting another job and although she'd never admit it to Caz she was more than a little intrigued to see what Alex was like in the flesh.

Caz's well-meant meddling had finally worn Mallory down and she'd found herself agreeing to allow her best friend to have a hand in helping her get ready. Mallory had been banned from throwing on her usual skinny jeans and top and having her hair tumble about in its normal untamed corkscrew curl state and instead had to endure a painstakingly lengthy session with some hair straighteners. Though she had to admit she felt good in the pale-green floaty summer dress Caz had insisted she wear. Even her skin looked more sun-kissed than sunburned after she'd brushed on some bronzer.

With the sparkling wine already having turned flat and warm, Mallory helped herself to a glass of red and made her way through to the next room.

And stopped dead.

Directly in front of her, on the largest wall, hung a massive painting.

Of herself.

And she didn't need to check the signature to know who painted it.

Don Marsden.

As if reeled in by an invisible magnetic force she slowly walked towards it, battling against the natural instinct to reach out and touch the canvas, wanting to feel the rough raised edges of the paint against her fingertips.

It's just a painting, she told herself, wiping her suddenly clammy hands on her thighs.

Just a painting.

Mallory tried to look at the painting dispassionately. There was no denying the painter's skilled technique. Don had captured her perfectly; auburn hair fanning across the pillow of their bed in the villa they'd rented for three months on the outskirts of Florence three years earlier.

The strips of early morning sunlight breaking through the slats of the half-closed shutters fell on the bed where she slept. Her skin was luminously pale, almost as white as the lace bedspread loosely draped over her, barely covering her naked body. The same lace bedspread she and Don had bought together in the local market the previous day.

Her stomach twisted at the memory.

'Is that you?' A middle-aged woman in a deep-magenta sundress asked, standing beside her.

'Uh, um, yes,' Mallory mumbled, wishing the painting wasn't quite so big or so prominently placed. Or had her quite so naked.

'Thought so. Your hair. *Love Lost.*'

'Excuse me?'

The woman pointed at a small plaque. 'It's the name of the painting. Are you all right, dear?'

'I'm fine,' Mallory whispered. Truth was she felt slightly sick at the shock of seeing herself.

'It's a very… intimate painting,' the woman said tactfully. 'You must know Marsden well.'

Mallory swallowed. 'Knew.'

'I hear he's doing very well over in New York. Good on him, I say.'

Mallory said nothing.

'Doesn't totally fit in with the element theme, but I suppose they wouldn't want to pass up the opportunity of having one of his here. He's quite the draw. This, here, is one of ten limited edition prints. I read that he's holding onto the original, doesn't want to sell it, evidently.' She looked at Mallory, obviously waiting on some more gossip, which wasn't forthcoming. 'This one got snapped up pretty quickly.'

There was a red dot stuck to the wall beside it indicating it was already sold.

The woman smiled at Mallory before wandering off.

Although Mallory was also desperate to walk away, the painting kept her mesmerised.

She'd loved that holiday in Italy. The villa had been a haven where she and Don had escaped reality for twelve glorious weeks. Lazy mornings were punctuated with grappa-laced espressos as they people-watched in the local trattoria.

Each afternoon Don would disappear into the makeshift studio he'd created, leaving Mallory to roam the hills at the back of the villa. Sometimes to sketch, but more often than not she would be content to sit back in the grass, looking up at the rolling, ever-changing sky.

One morning she'd woken to find Don painting her; cigarette dangling from the corner of his mouth, every cantankerous sinew of his frame poised over the canvas as he worked. She'd been happy to lie there, basking in the warmth as the sun crept round the building, reaching into the bedroom.

And now the same painting hung on the wall of the gallery, dominating and commanding attention.

Just like the artist.

But instead of feeling flattered, Mallory felt violated. When Don had painted it, they'd been very much in love, but now she'd been bought by someone willing to pay for a hand-embellished, one of ten limited edition prints no doubt for no more of a meaningful reason than the colours matched a coffee table and sofa.

And what the hell was he doing calling it *Love Lost*? Their love hadn't got *lost*, as in *whoops, where did I put it again?* – Don hadn't returned it.

Feeling long-suppressed anger and resentment stir inside her like a dormant volcano waking, she took a deep breath and reminded herself she was far stronger now. She was fully prepared to admit that like all cheesy pop songs, the first cut of love was the deepest, but it didn't mean she should bleed to death for him.

A few more people had stopped and were staring at Mallory, whispering to each other. She needed to escape, and fast.

She turned to bolt for the nearest exit.

And slammed directly into another body.

Helplessly, she watched her red wine vacate its glass and splatter down the front of a man's white cotton shirt.

Without a moment's hesitation she dropped her bag and grabbed the glass of white wine the man was holding and threw it over the stain, remembering reading that it was meant to help.

It didn't.

Very slowly her eyes travelled from the shirt to his face.

The extremely handsome, and instantly recognisable, face of Alex Claremont.

CHAPTER 4

'Ohmigod! I'm so sorry.' Mallory gasped, staring at the spreading stain on Alex's shirt. 'It's completely ruined.'

'You know, I think you might be right.'

'I wasn't looking where I was going. It's so crowded and I needed to get air...' She trailed off, wanting to kick herself for her clumsiness. Of all the people she could have done that to, it had to have been him; a potential employer. She couldn't have had a worse first meeting if she'd tried.

He was still staring down at the stain and she hoped that he wasn't hugely pissed off, or would threaten to sue for emotional damages or have a hissy fit in a spoilt *do you know who I am* way. But when he looked back up, the corner of his mouth was curling into a half smile.

'I'm impressed. It normally takes at least twenty minutes' conversation before someone wants to throw a glass of wine over me.' He gave her an easy smile. 'You've broken a record. Let me get you another,' he said, gently prising the empty glasses of wine from her white-knuckled grip, giving both the empty glasses to a waiter who had materialised at their side. Picking up two full glasses he handed her one.

'Don't suppose you've got a spare gent's shirt in there.' He nodded at the bag which still lay at her feet. 'Size fifteen collar?'

'Damn, I just gave away my last one,' she said, relieved he seemed to be taking it so well and not calling for security to have her removed. 'Oh, hold on!' Remembering she had a tissue in her pocket, she pulled it out, and although slightly crumpled, it was clean. 'This might help.'

'I don't think it will fit,' he deadpanned.

She dabbed at the stain, becoming a little flustered to feel his chest so hard and muscular beneath the fabric. He looked at her with a bemused expression as she realised she was fussing like a mother cleaning up a messy child. 'Uh, why don't you do it.' She held the tissue out to him. 'Was it expensive?'

'Horribly so,' he said as he attempted to clean the stain, but within a few seconds it became woefully apparent the tissue wouldn't rise to the occasion.

'I'll buy you a new one.'

'There's no need.'

'No, I insist. Or at least let me pay for the dry cleaning.'

'Really.' He laughed, looking back up at her. 'It's just a shirt. Anyway, I should really stop sneaking up on people.' He gave her a look which suggested he had no plans to do any such thing. 'Sorry, I'm being so rude; I'm Alex Claremont.'

'I, uh, I know.' She didn't think there was much point in her pretending not to know who he was.

'Damn! My reputation precedes me!' He gave her a mock rueful look as he ran his hand through his thick wavy black hair, a stubborn lock immediately bouncing back onto his forehead. He lowered his head to hers conspiratorially. 'Don't believe a word of it, unless of course, it's good, and then you can safely assume it's true.'

'I'll keep an open mind.'

Mallory took a sip of her wine deciding Alex Claremont was nothing at all like the man she'd expected. Rather than the vain, self-obsessed Lothario he came across as in print, in person Alex was all twinkling charm and bonhomie. As well as incredibly forgiving about his shirt.

And Mallory was prepared to admit Alex Claremont really *was* astoundingly good-looking; far better in real life than any photograph could do justice to. With his heavy dark brows accentuating the pale smokiness of his eyes, an indefinable shade between grey and blue, and expressive mouth with full sculpted lips that seemed permanently on the brink of breaking into a wide smile, his looks went beyond the tick-box trinity of tall, dark and handsome.

Realising she was staring unabashed at him Mallory looked away quickly, aware of a flush starting at the base of her throat, spreading to her face.

'I have to say, it's been a long time since I've been in the situation of seeing a woman naked without knowing her name first.'

'Excuse me?' Mallory started, thinking she'd misheard him over the noise in the gallery.

He cocked his head to the side and winked. 'Call me old-fashioned, but I always prefer to know a woman's name *before* seeing her naked.'

'I…' She stared at him. Just what the hell was he implying? She could feel her face reddening even further, but this time in anger as she recalled the article she'd read earlier where he'd admitted to chatting up every woman he met. Well, she wasn't just any woman! She pulled herself up to her full height of five foot nine, though even with her heels, she still came a few inches short of him.

'If that's your attempt at a chat-up line, you've got the wrong audience, Mr Claremont.'

He burst out laughing. '*Mr Claremont?* Only my bank manager calls me that!'

He had absolutely no shame!

'How *dare* you assume that I want to sleep with you!'

His eyes glittered with amusement. He took a sip of his wine, watching her over the rim of his glass.

'That's a shame. I was going to suggest we find a quiet corner, there's a discreet area over there, behind those quilts on display.' He gestured through to the other room.

'Excuse me?' she spluttered, even more outraged at his complete lack of embarrassment. 'Maybe that's what you're used to, but you're not dealing with your usual London airheads anymore.'

He shrugged. 'What was I meant to think? You came up with a, quite frankly, a *feeble* ruse to get me to take my shirt off–'

'That was an accident!'

'And then you had the audacity to smile at me and engage in conversation–'

'I was trying to be nice!'

'And then you touched my chest–'

'I was removing the wine stain!' she blustered.

'So what else was I meant to think?' he continued, unfazed. 'I mean, in London, that's what we call foreplay. And the way you were looking at me? Well, that was just a brazen come-on.'

'I was only looking at you because you're, you're... aesthetically pleasing to the eye!' she spluttered.

'Why, thank you. You're highly attractive yourself. Especially when you're all agitated and outraged.' He folded his arms, struggling to temper the smile from spreading across his face. 'Anyway, I thought you said you were going to keep an open mind.'

'Obviously not as open as you're used to!' she said, brimming with indignation. Mallory didn't care if Johan thought the world of this debauched individual standing in front of her. She certainly didn't like him and couldn't imagine working with someone who had such little respect for women.

'I can't believe it normally takes twenty minutes for someone to do this,' she said, throwing her full glass of wine at his face. She watched in satisfaction as it ran down his chin in rivulets. A couple of onlookers gasped.

Without waiting for his reaction, she turned and stormed away, banging her empty glass down on a nearby table. In doing so she caught sight of Don's painting again.

Don's painting of her.

Which was so obviously of her and in which she was naked.

The painting Alex had been facing when they'd been talking.

Her knees went weak from the adrenaline draining from her body as a horrible little niggling doubt took hold. Had he been referring to the painting? Had she totally, *excruciatingly*, misread his comment?

She slowly turned to see Alex watching her, the half smile still playing on his lips as he wiped wine from the underside of his jaw.

Mallory looked at the painting, then back at Alex.

He nodded slowly.

'Oh, bloody hell,' she muttered as she hurried towards the nearest exit.

She knew running away was not the most derring-do of acts, but it was the easiest way to escape from the most humiliating situation she'd wound up in for a long time.

Sitting on a low wall outside, hiding behind an open fire exit, Mallory banged her head against the brickwork a couple of times in a vague attempt to induce coma but she remained disappointingly conscious.

How could she have thought he wanted to sleep with her from that innocuous comment? Why did she always have to jump in, feet first, without thinking… and as usual end up making an idiot of herself? Twenty-nine years of it and she'd still never learnt!

'Hello again!'

She cringed, recognising Alex's drawl, still unmistakably Scottish even after so many years in London.

'I've got some left.' Alex waggled his half-drunk glass of wine under her nose. 'In case you want to do it again. And if that's not enough I managed to retrieve an entire bottle, but,' he took a swig from the neck, 'it would be a shame to waste it as it's actually rather palatable for one of these events.'

He handed her the glass of wine.

'Thank you,' she mumbled, hoping he'd go away and leave her to wallow in embarrassment.

He sat beside her. 'It would seem my attempt at a breaking-the-ice joke fell a bit flat,' he said affably. 'I obviously need to try harder. I must be far too used to the London airheads who find everything I say hilariously funny.'

Mallory shuddered with embarrassment. 'I'm sorry. I had no idea you were referring to the painting.'

'As you pointed out, I do have that reputation. It was only natural that after a quick chat I'd be trying to jump into bed with you, especially as most women fall at my feet in awe as soon as I tell them who I am.'

She laughed despite herself. 'I'm so sorry. Oh God, this is horrendous. It's been a really strange night. I hadn't expected to see that painting by my... my... well, seeing it threw me off guard and I now think I should quietly leave while you forget the last ten minutes ever happened.'

He stretched out his legs in front of him, as if blocking her escape route. 'I don't think so. You've brightened up an otherwise tedious evening, although I still don't know your name.'

For that she could only be thankful.

'I think that's for the best.'

'You're not going to tell me?'

'Nope.' She really didn't want him to realise she was the one Johan had suggested he work with. She would just tell Johan to let Alex know she wasn't interested in any job and she could get on with her life and Alex would be none the wiser.

'Hmmm. Oh well, I'll just have to find it out for myself.' He smiled as he held up her bag.

In her haste to leave she'd forgotten to pick it up from the floor. She tried to snatch it back but he held it just out of her reach.

'Ah-ah *ahh*!' He unzipped her bag and took a look inside. 'Now, let's see if I can find out who you are.'

Mallory hated to think what relics he'd unearth; she regularly crammed the oversize tote bag full of junk and she hadn't cleared it out in weeks.

'An apple. Good that you look after your health. Oh, I think this used to be a banana,' he said, tentatively sniffing the almost entirely black piece of fruit. He laid them on the wall beside him. 'Another tissue. Does this wine and shirt accident happen to you often?' he enquired with a quizzically raised eyebrow.

'You're the first.'

'I feel honoured.' Resuming his search of her bag, his dark hair flopped over his forehead as he peered inside.

'Now then, *this* is starting to get more interesting.' He delved to the bottom of her bag and pulled out her Swiss Army knife. 'I do like a girl who's prepared for any eventuality.' He also removed a roll of duct tape, which she'd stuffed into her bag after wrapping up her last painting to take to Johan. 'Bit of kidnapping and torture on the side? I should be thankful I got away with just a wine-soaked shirt.'

Mallory couldn't help but laugh. 'That's honestly not as sinister as it looks.'

'No?' he asked, holding up her cordless hair straighteners. 'The law comes down fairly heavily on nipple clamping, you know. Aha!' he exclaimed, taking out her purse which bulged with old receipts and store cards.

He read the front of one of her cards. 'Ms M Caine. Now what does the 'M' stand for, I wonder.'

She groaned. 'Mortified.'

But instead of looking for further evidence of her identity he handed her purse back to her. 'Actually, I know you're Mallory. I recognised you from the photographs Johan showed me when I popped into his gallery earlier. I was on my way over to say hello.'

'So, all this was completely unnecessary?'

He smiled. 'Not completely.'

CHAPTER 5

Olly had been hiding behind a pillar in the gallery for so long people were starting to think he was part of the exhibition; a Gilbert & George-style human sculpture. Taking a deep breath, he slowly peered round the painted white column, scanning the crowd, then ducked back round as he saw the woman he was keen to avoid.

Making the mistake of talking to her at a previous gallery event, she'd clearly taken a shine to his shy and bumbling demeanour, gawkish nerdy looks and slight nervous stammer or *something* and had spent the next few weeks hounding him; waiting for him outside his studio, calling him, even sending him letters containing pieces of her hair, so many in fact, he wondered if she now had a bald patch.

Whenever Olly had told his friends about the situation, they'd laughed. 'You won't be laughing when you have to identify my body,' he'd said, more than a little piqued that they thought a woman lusting after him was hilariously funny.

He changed the times he came and went to the studio and avoided all his usual haunts in the hope she'd get the message and not think he was just playing hard to get. And now he really didn't want to bump into her again in case she saw fit to reignite her interest.

Olly checked his watch and wondered if it would be very rude to skulk off home to have a beer and watch the new Marvel series on Netflix.

Deciding he should stick it out for another half-hour he scanned the gallery and luckily couldn't see the stalker woman. He couldn't even remember her name, which was pretty poor really, considering the number of letters she'd written him (a couple of times in what looked, unnervingly, like blood). It wasn't as if he had women writing to him and following him home all the time; she was the only female who'd shown any interest in him in the last few months – just a shame she was a nutcase.

The gallery was full of people he could talk to, but he didn't have the energy; they'd only want to talk about their latest work, the latest work of so-and-so or, even worse, *his* latest work.

Scanning the crowd, he saw Mallory and was about to go over when he realised she was chatting animatedly to a guy wearing a badly stained shirt. Olly held back as he was pretty certain it was that celebrity guy, Alex Claremont, whom Caz had been getting into a tizz about earlier. He watched them for a couple of minutes, wondering if Mallory would look up and catch his eye.

But she remained oblivious to Olly.

Exactly how it had been for the past seven years, ten months and sixteen days; since he'd stood next to her in the student union bar.

The second she turned and smiled at him he swore he could feel the sharp point of an arrow penetrate his heart.

He even thought he could hear a celestial choir. In fact, he *could* hear a celestial choir, thanks to the special extended dance mix of a Faithless track someone had put on the jukebox.

The bar stool next to her was for the taking. But Mallory was not.

He knew he wasn't a fast mover. He wanted to be her friend

first. But as time went on, ice caps moved more speedily and Olly was just working up to telling Mallory how he felt when Mallory had met Don.

Don Marsden: artist and arsehole. Olly had to be content with worshipping her from afar. Then Mallory and Don split up, but by that point he and Mallory had become such firm friends that conversation never seemed to naturally lead to him declaring his love for her.

He'd rehearsed asking her out in front of the mirror many times and had the perfect seduction planned. He'd suavely sidle up to her in the studio, sit on the edge of her desk (and for some reason, in his daydream, he was wearing white linen trousers). They'd chat, (his fantasy self suddenly developing a deep, world service, well-modulated baritone instead of his usual south coast lilt) with him littering the conversation with well-timed and hilarious bon mots.

She'd be laughing. He'd be laughing. Then, suddenly, they'd look at each other intently, the laughter dying in their throats, Mallory would realise she'd been in love with him all along. He would lean in for a kiss, she'd be helpless to resist…

But he never quite managed to carry the daydream into reality. And he had to face facts – he wasn't a white linen trousers kind of guy.

Draining his glass of wine, he wandered over to one of the tables to get another. Beside it was a woman in a red suit, staring off into the distance, looking as bored as he felt.

'Having fun?' he said to be sociable.

She turned his way, her eyes slithering over him briefly before she turned back to staring straight in front of her. He had the distinct impression he'd been checked out and discarded.

He was about to slink away when she spoke, her accent threatening to cut the glass he was holding. 'Watching one's boyfriend flirting with another woman isn't my idea of fun,' she said, flicking her long blonde hair off her shoulder.

'No, nor mine,' he agreed, before realising the ambiguity in his statement. 'Um, not that I have a *boy*friend, you understand, but if it was my girlfriend, I wouldn't like it,' he elaborated as she turned to stare at him, her icy blue eyes penetrating his. 'Although I um, I don't… I mean, I've not actually got one of those at the moment either,' he trailed off under her unnerving scrutiny, 'a girlfriend, that is.'

'Really,' she said, elongating the vowels in a flat, bored voice.

They lapsed into silence again. Far from looking devastated at catching her bloke in a compromising position, the woman seemed completely poised, although there was a glint in her eye Olly didn't like the look of. He followed her line of vision which led to Mallory and Alex.

'Oh, that man over there? I think it's more business they're discussing,' Olly explained.

'Alex doesn't differentiate business and pleasure,' she said testily.

Despite the sour look on her face, she was very pretty in a posh, blonde, upper class English kind of way, Olly thought, but skinny, as he could see her collarbone protruding far too much to be healthy. He lifted up a tray of tiny pastry shells stuffed with a pinkish mousse and topped with prawns.

'Canapé?' he offered.

'I don't eat carbs.'

'You could always scoop out the middle,' he tried to cajole.

She gave him a look which made it clear she wasn't the sort who scooped out the middle of a canapé.

'What are you doing here?' she asked in her clipped, abrasive style.

'I was just getting another glass of wine.' He held up his full glass as vindication. 'But then I saw you and thought I'd make polite conversation because, quite frankly you look bloody miserable standing here. But, seeing as you really don't want to talk, I'll let you have your Greta Garbo moment and leave you alone, but only once I've filled myself up on some of these tasty treats, because I quite like carbohydrates, as they help soak up the alcohol of which I plan on consuming in vast quantities tonight.'

She looked at him for a moment, her face impassive. 'I meant, what are you doing here tonight at the gallery. Are you an artist?'

'Ah, right,' Olly said, a skewered king prawn halfway to his mouth. 'I see. Yes, I am an artist, well, I'm an illustrator, actually. Hold on…' He crammed the prawn into his mouth, chewing furiously as he rummaged through the pockets of his skinny jeans. 'I've got a business card somewhere,' he said, careful not to spray her with shellfish.

'I really don't think I'll need your services.'

'You never know.' He fished one out and handed it to her. She dropped it into her bag without looking at it.

She took a sip of her wine.

'You know there are carbohydrates in that too.' He gestured to her glass with another skewered prawn, dismally aware his small talk seemed more like a health awareness campaign.

'I don't eat *complex* carbohydrates.'

'Ah, you're more the simple type,' he joked.

She raised a pencil-thin eyebrow in disdain.

'Oh, ehm, I don't mean you're simple, as in stupid. I'm sure you're highly intelligent and…' He trailed off. Bollocks. He really didn't mean it to sound so bad.

'Excuse me, but I've got a boyfriend to go and keep in check.' She headed back into the crowd, high heels clacking short staccato bursts on the wooden floor.

He jumped when Caz tapped him on the shoulder.

'Why are you skulking over here? Oh, did you realise your crazy stalker's arrived?' she added gleefully.

CHAPTER 6

'$\mathcal{N}$ik is an amazing cook,' Alex explained to Mallory as they continued to amble through the gallery. She thought he might have left to change but he didn't seem at all phased by the state of his shirt, which was eliciting a few raised eyebrows. Alex was far too intent in telling her about his new venture – a restaurant he was opening up with his best friend, Nikolais Floros. 'We've been friends since we were both packed off to boarding school up north,' he continued, 'Nik's a journalist and has been a food critic for years, having his own place just seemed the logical progression.'

His enthusiasm was contagious as he told her more about the restaurant and Mallory was having a hard time keeping the bubble of excitement growing in her stomach at bay. The commission would be high profile, especially having Alex Claremont's name attached. She just had to make sure there were no more wine-throwing escapades or other mishaps which could jeopardise her chances.

'It's the big building on Blairgowan Street, set back from the road, do you know it?' he said.

She did. It was a beautiful building, but one that really needed a complete overhaul as the façade had chunks of plaster falling off it and the grounds it sat in were overgrown with weeds and acted as a graveyard for empty lager cans. But she didn't have time to answer as Alex was talking again.

'It's cavernous inside, well it will be once we knock down the partition walls. There's also a mezzanine level which is closed off at the moment but could look pretty spectacular. We're thinking of having it as a bar area.'

'Have you had any ideas about the design?'

'We've met with a couple of teams, but nothing's wowed us, nothing's been individual enough for us. But when I walked into the bar you designed I knew I had to see what you could come up with.' He stopped and gave her a sheepish smile. 'Sorry, I've just let my mouth run off at a tangent. Is this something you'd even be interested in doing? Do you even have time for it as it'll be a fairly big project?'

'Absolutely!' she said, jumping in before Alex went off again. 'I mean, with a bit of juggling it should be fine,' she added, not wanting to appear too desperate or for him to guess that her diary was as vast and empty as the Grand Canyon.

'Why don't you swing by tomorrow, I'll let our project manager, Paul, know you're coming. You can have a look around, think what you'd like to do and then we could meet up on-site, say Wednesday about eleven?'

'That sounds good.'

He smiled, then his attention was distracted by a tall slim woman coming towards them.

'Louisa! You made it.' He kissed her cheek as she flashed him a bright, if rather false, smile, her eyes lingering on his wine-stained shirt.

Pale blonde hair hung straight and gleaming halfway down her back and the hand she rested on Alex's arm was manicured to perfection, Mallory noted. The scarlet linen trouser suit looked a dead ringer for the one she'd seen in *Grazia* magazine – worn by

Zendaya and straight off the catwalk from the new Prada collection as Mallory recalled.

'What happened to your shirt?' Louisa asked.

'I was going for the abstract look.' Alex smiled, opening his arms wide and looking down at the mess.

'It's Gucci,' she said coldly.

'Oh, I thought it more Jackson Pollock,' he said, his face the picture of innocence. 'I'd like you to meet Mallory Caine, an exceptionally talented artist; Mallory, Louisa Chambers.'

'So pleased to meet you.' So obviously not by the look Louisa gave her.

Feeling as wanted as a bout of malaria, Mallory stood there with a polite smile as Louisa talked to Alex, frequently touching his arm to emphasise points in her conversation. Each time Alex tried to draw Mallory into the conversation, Louisa managed to manipulate it back to herself, trying to freeze Mallory out. Mallory was greatly relieved when, a few moments later, Johan joined them.

'Ah good, Alex. You've found Mallory.'

'Yes, we've just been talking about the restaurant.'

Johan smiled warmly at them. 'I cannot recommend her highly enough, although her painting skills are only the tip of the iceberg it would seem.' He chuckled. 'I had no idea what a phenomenally talented young woman she was until she handed in the most illuminating CV.'

'Johan!' Mallory rolled her eyes. He really was a sweet little man. Her old CV had been brief to say the least.

Alex smiled at Mallory. 'You must send me a copy.'

'I already have,' Johan said. 'I emailed it to you before I left this evening.'

Mallory wished Johan hadn't. She didn't think Alex would be impressed to know her greatest personal achievement was gaining her cycling proficiency badge and taking part in a sponsored cycle round the isle of Arran. Well, technically only half a sponsored cycle as she'd suffered a puncture and had to get a lift back to the ferry.

Louisa, obviously bored with hearing how wonderful Mallory was, made an excuse to get another glass of wine and sashayed away.

Johan, undeterred, beamed at Mallory. 'I felt quite inadequate after reading about Mallory's outdoor pursuits and musical talents.'

Mallory laughed in embarrassment. It was so typical of Johan to play up her attributes but she really thought he was being a little over-enthusiastic.

'And I had no idea you were fluent in Italian.'

CHAPTER 7

Mallory looked at Johan in horror. There was only one place she'd said she could speak Italian: her made-up CV. Somehow Johan had managed to get hold of it. And had then sent it on to Alex!

'Um, actually… there's an, um, I'm not…' she stammered.

Johan continued. 'She's an absolute wonder.'

'No! No, I'm not!' She tried to interrupt but Johan waved his hand in dismissal.

'But as always she's so infuriatingly modest,' he said, talking over her. 'I didn't know half of what she gets up to in her spare time. So typical of her to keep it to herself.'

Mallory tried to speak but her mouth had gone dry and nothing came out other than a strangled croak. She took a large gulp of wine but ended up half choking on it. Johan patted her on the back as she spluttered and hiccupped and tried to breathe normally again.

'Are you okay, my dear?' Johan asked as Alex brought her a glass of water.

She took a grateful sip and managed to stop choking. She was going to look a prize idiot telling them she thought her life was unadventurous and wanted to appear more interesting so made up a CV by following some advice from a self-help book her best friend had read. To be fair, Mallory pretty much already cornered the 'prize idiot' market but now she could definitely say goodbye to any aspirations of designing the décor for Alex's new restaurant.

And all the coverage it would bring.

And the doors such a prestigious job would open for her.

Unless… She took a shaky breath and looked up at the concerned faces of Johan and Alex. It wasn't as if she was lying about her professional career; all the factual information about her art was correct. Would there really be any reason why anything on her personal biography need ever come up again?

And as Caz had told her, she was going to start working towards becoming the person on paper. Why should she scupper her chances of such a big break when she could just play along for a few minutes?

She managed to stop coughing and composed herself. 'I'm fine, I'm fine!'

'You see, give her one compliment and she goes to pieces!' Johan laughed.

'It's nothing to get excited over, really,' Mallory said with a small laugh. 'I like having varied interests.'

'And they don't get more varied than abseiling and salsa dancing!'

'Abseiling?' Alex said. 'Bloody hell! You wouldn't catch me doing that. I can't stand heights.'

'It's not something I do regularly…' Mallory said, blushing slightly. Although she was going along with the fake CV, she knew she wasn't a very good liar.

'And she didn't even tell me she got engaged,' Johan said with a reproving look.

She'd forgotten Caz had typed she had a fiancé! Mallory was sure her face was turning puce.

'I know it's none of my business, I'm just surprised you never mentioned it to me,' Johan said, sounding a little hurt.

'It was all very sudden,' Mallory said, hating that Johan was offended at not being told about an engagement which had never even taken place!

Johan pressed her for details. 'When did you get engaged?'

'Now, when was it,' she repeated, stalling for time. 'Um, not that long ago. Quite recently,' she said, her face burning. 'I thought I told you.' Realising her ring finger was naked she quickly tucked her hand behind her back.

'So, who is the lucky man?'

Mallory's mind went blank. She swallowed nervously. 'You don't know him. It was all very whirlwind, and erm, he doesn't live here, in Scotland, um...' She needed to escape before she tripped herself up completely. And then, on the other side of the gallery, she spotted Olly by the buffet table flicking bits of pastry off his shirt.

'Oh, I'm so sorry, but you'll have to excuse me! I've just noticed someone I really need to talk to.' She started to back away. 'I'll see you Wednesday,' she added to Alex, and with a small wave to Johan, Mallory took her chance to escape before anyone could ask her any more about her amazing CV.

'You know, life's not that bad after all,' Caz remarked cheerily as she hurried over to Mallory.

Mallory took Caz's wine glass off her and drank most of it in one swallow, her hand shaking so much the glass nearly slipped from her grasp. 'You think?'

'Absolutely! I've just met Dag, a *gorgeous* Indiana Jones lookalike Norwegian photography student.' Caz gestured behind her.

Mallory looked towards a tall, intense young man fiddling with a lens cap, thinking him more Henry Ford than Harrison Ford. 'Lovely, I'm sure you'll have lots of fun while he raids your lost ark,' she said, dodging one of Caz's arm slaps.

'Where's Olly?' Mallory said, looking round for him. She'd had him in her sights but he seemed to have disappeared.

'Ah, yes! That crazy stalker woman is floating about so he's probably hit the deck and crawled commando-style towards the exit to go home. What's going on with you? You look a bit flustered.' Caz's eyes lit up with excitement. 'Oh my God! You've been talking to Alex Claremont!' she exclaimed with a hand clap, Dag momentarily forgotten.

'The one and only,' Mallory said tightly.

'I knew you couldn't remain immune to his charms!'

'What?'

'Look at you! Your face is flushed, you're sweating, you're jittery; all signs of being in the presence of a bona fide sex god, you lucky, lucky thing.'

'Lucky is the last word I'd use. I have a serious problem, Caz. He wants to take a look at the highly impressive CV Johan's been raving about. The CV which has my life jam-packed with excitement and daredevil stunts.'

Caz paled. 'But, I printed off your other one and put it in the envelope. Oh no! I must have posted the wrong one through Johan's letterbox.'

'I know!'

'Look, it'll be fine. Just say you made a mistake.'

Mallory took another swig of Caz's wine. 'The ship's sort of already sailed on that one. I was put on the spot and I didn't know what to do so I played along with it.'

'You didn't know what to do? Did you not think of just saying, *Oh! I'm sorry, there's been a bit of a mix-up, it's a funny story actually…* or something along those lines!'

When said like that it did seem quite simple.

'All the professional information about your career is true. He probably won't ever mention any of the other stuff,' Caz said with faux conviction. 'I mean, why would he bring up, up… what did we put?'

'That I salsa dance.'

'Take a couple of lessons. Hell, after a couple of voddies *everyone* can salsa dance. What else was there? Horse-riding, being outdoorsy...'

'Speaking Italian, rally driving. Oh, sweet Lord! I said I could play the guitar.'

'He's hardly likely to whip out his twelve-string and ask you for a rousing rendition of 'Stairway to Heaven', is he? Mallory, how likely is it he's going to bring any of these up again?'

'I don't know!'

'If he does I'm sure you'll be able to talk your way out of it and, anyway, people exaggerate on their CVs all the time.'

'There's a difference between embellishing school qualifications and making up a completely fictional life!' Mallory could feel herself starting to hyperventilate.

'If it's going to bother you that much tell him the truth.'

'If I *do* tell him the truth he's going to think I'm an idiot,' she said, practically hopping up and down on the spot in agitation. 'And he knows so many people in the art world, what if he spreads the word about me and my career is ruined.'

'Hmm!' Caz tapped her chin thoughtfully. 'Yes, I can see him being so *incensed* with anger he will spend the next thirty years plotting your demise. Starting with Britain, moving to Europe, through America and Africa, he'll run you out of every village, town, city and continent, all the time sitting in his Mr Evil headquarters laughing sinisterly as he lights up another section on his map of the world indicating all the places you can never return to. Until, one day, you finally find work as a sheep castrator in the Australian outback where you can never... paint... again!' She clutched Mallory's shoulders and shook her melodramatically.

'It's not funny!' Mallory said, batting Caz away. 'Johan also brought up my engagement.'

Caz looked momentarily stumped, then waved the problem

away. 'Just tell them you've split up in a wee while. Don't get so stressed about it, it'll be fine.' She leaned in closer. 'So tell me, is he as *totally* gorgeous in real life?' Caz's hands flew up to her heart, pretending to swoon.

It was typical that even in the middle of her current crisis Caz had a one-track mind.

'I suppose so, yes. If you like that sort of thing.'

'*If you like that sort of thing?*' Caz laughed. 'What? Devastatingly handsome with a roguish reputation and absolutely loaded? I can see how he'd appeal to such a small demographic.'

'Forgive me for being more concerned about my career than imagining him naked.'

'Ooh! So, you've imagined him naked.'

'Caz!' Mallory wailed. Sometimes Caz just refused to see the full seriousness of a situation.

Caz's eyes lit up. 'In fact, if he's still here, can you introduce me to him?' she said, making to return into the centre of the gallery.

Mallory hauled her back by her corset laces.

'I'm having an emotional meltdown here! Please think about something other than your rampant libido.'

'Spoilsport!' She pouted. 'Look, it'll be fine, you'll see. In fact, there *is* something slightly more pressing to worry about; if I don't get some food soon I'm going to faint.'

'It's gone,' Mallory informed her, nodding over at the empty silver platters piled up.

'What? All of it?' Caz looked stricken. 'But if I don't have crisps or *something* I'm going to die.'

Not feeling all that charitable towards her friend's plight, Mallory said, 'There's a corner shop on the next block. They'll sell snacks. And pick up another bottle of wine while you're there to take home, I think I need it.' She peered over Caz's shoulder. She couldn't see Alex. 'I'm going to take a leaf out of Olly's book of daring escapes and make a run for it. I'll see you back at the flat.'

'You know, if you end up working with Alex, you'll probably have to talk to him at some point.'

'I know, but I need time to think this all through, cover all bases in case I'm put on the spot.'

'Like coming up with a back story to continue your life of subterfuge?' Caz teased.

'I just don't want to risk bumping into him again tonight.'

Mallory could tell Caz was rolling her eyes as she hurried towards the exit.

CHAPTER 8

*S*lightly tipsy from the free wine on an empty stomach, Caz teetered along the road towards the corner shop in her knee-high leather stiletto boots.

Grabbing a couple of bottles of wine on special offer along with a loaf of white bread, some spreadable butter and a sharing bag of crisps, Caz joined the queue, thinking she'd have to swing by Olly's flat on the way home to retrieve the massive jar of mayonnaise she'd given him the week before when she'd removed everything with the slightest fat content.

'I've not tried that before, is it any good?' a voice from behind her asked.

She whirled round and found herself staring at a man. Her instant *mandar* did a once-over scan. About thirty, tall, well-built in a nice muscle-toned way but not so much that there wasn't a cuddly element (she would never want to snuggle up to the equivalent of a rock). Good-looking but not *too* good-looking to mean a horrendous ego or string of bunny boiler exes. Nice blue eyes. Bit tanned, but not enough to suggest sprays or sunbeds.

Caz re-evaluated his original 'good-looking' status. He was *very* good looking. Quite gorgeous in fact.

'The wine, is it any good?' he repeated, pointing to the bottles she clutched.

She looked up at him through her triple-coated mascaraed lashes. 'It all depends on what you're wanting it for. I mean, is it for a lovely romantic meal with your wife?' She quickly clocked his ring finger: bare. 'Or girlfriend?'

'Nope, I don't have either of those.'

Excellent! 'Good, because this wine wouldn't send out that signal. What signal do you want your wine to send?'

He smiled his lovely crinkly-eye smile. 'I'm looking for a wine that sends out the signal that I'm trying to chat someone up.'

Caz was delighted that it *had* been a chat-up line and he wasn't just some hopeless case in need of some wine advice. 'Ah, I see. Do you use this technique often, because sticking to wine is quite limiting. What if you want to chat someone up in B&Q?'

'I'm very location specific. I just trawl off-licences.'

'Much luck so far?'

'I have the numbers of a few sherry grannies and the local alcoholic's outreach programme.'

'Sounds like you need to be a bit more person specific.'

She smiled. He smiled. There was definitely a lot of smiling.

'I'll let you into a secret.' He leaned forward. 'I'm holding out for a Babycham Barbie.'

She looked down at the bottles of wine she clutched. 'These bottles, although not the cheapest in the shop, are on offer so you could probably categorise me as a Bargain Boozer, which is very different from a Babycham Barbie,' she said saucily.

His smile deepened and he sported an incredibly cute dimple.

'What category do you fall into?' she asked.

'That depends. There's a real chance I could end up a Whisky Whiner. I may have to resort to buying a bottle of malt and drink it while moaning that a Bargain Boozer walked out my life before I could get her phone number.'

'And why should I give you my phone number?'

'I'm hoping for the sympathy vote.'

'I don't think a Babycham Barbie fancier deserves any sympathy,' she said mock ruefully.

'I don't suppose you'd like to come for a drink with me sometime,' he blurted out. 'Sorry, crazy idea, we've only had a three minute and twenty second conversation.'

'Three minutes and twenty seconds? That's very precise.'

'I know, I've been watching the clock behind the counter. I don't believe in asking out a woman before the third minute.'

'That's a good philosophy.'

Caz reached the top of the queue and handed over the items and pressed her bank card to the machine.

'What do you say?' the man asked, smiling.

Caz looked him up and down, her *mandar* beeping frantically in approval. 'I say, why not.'

'What's your number?'

Smiling coquettishly, she dug into her ridiculously tight trousers, pulled out her business card and handed it to him before disappearing out the door, bottles clanking merrily.

Five minutes later, as she walked home in a completely smitten state, Caz was aware of a sharp piercing sensation at the top of her thigh. Stopping to pull out the offending item, she was perplexed to see her business card in her hand. She knew she'd only put one in her pocket that evening, so what had she given the delectable stranger in the off-licence?

A clammy sickly horror took hold as she realised the only other item in her pocket beside her bank card that night was the price ticket for her new trousers. After Feng Shuing her room she'd removed the bin, not wanting to suck good energy out.

Well, her present situation sucked, especially since he'd see she was a size sixteen.

CHAPTER 9

*M*allory shaded her eyes with her sketchbook and looked up at the building on Blairgowan Street. An impressive Grecian-style blonde sandstone building, it was set over two storeys with a sweeping staircase leading up to two imposing Doric columns flanking the entrance. Along the top of the entrance was a deep architrave engraved with an elaborate Egyptian keyhole pattern.

Her stomach flip-flopped with nerves. Since Paul, the project manager, had given her a tour a few days earlier, Mallory had worked solidly on design ideas and now had a bulging sketchbook full of them. She had everything crossed they'd be exactly what Alex was looking for. She reached into her pocket and rubbed the little garnet stone Caz had given her that morning, telling her it brought good luck in careers.

Taking a deep breath, Mallory started up the staircase as a man appeared from round the side of the building, carving a path through hip-height weeds with a giant pair of secateurs. He gave her a friendly wave.

'Mallory?'

She nodded.

'Hi, I'm Nik,' he said, loping up the steps towards her. 'Alex has told me all about you.'

Mallory shook his hand, hoping Alex had left out the more colourful parts of their first encounter otherwise Nik would probably think she was a bit of a psycho.

'So,' he said, looking up at the building, 'what do you think?'

'It's beautiful.'

'Isn't it,' he said with great pride. 'It's all a bit of a shambles inside as we're waiting on some guys to come and remove the old furnishings.' He stuck his sunglasses on the top of his head and opened the door for Mallory.

Inside, it looked as if a hurricane had hit. Since her first visit less than a week earlier, everything had been ripped out or pulled down and piled in the middle of the floor.

'I just keep focussing on the potential,' Nik said as he flipped the light switches, illuminating the burgundy-and-gold-flocked wallpaper and hallucination-inducing carpet.

'Did Paul show you the kitchen and the back rooms?'

Mallory shook her head. 'We just looked at the front space, the dining area, the bathrooms, that kind of thing.'

'Well then,' he said, opening the door at the back of the room and beckoning her to follow, 'come and have a look.'

The kitchen was in stark contrast to the other areas. It was all sleek lines and brushed-steel worktops as far as the eye could see and it looked about as cosy as an autopsy room.

'I wanted to get the kitchen fitted before anything else,' Nik said, running his hand across one of the many cooking ranges which had more dials and flashing lights than the Starship Enterprise. 'We've even got an indoor charcoal burner and pizza oven. And a brand-new coffee maker.' He indicated to what Mallory had mistakenly thought was a small spacecraft in the corner. 'What's your poison?'

Although she'd already drunk three large coffees that

morning the allure of freshly ground beans with a frothy milky top was just too tempting. 'I'd love a latte, thanks.'

As Nik was about to start making coffee, Alex sauntered in.

'Whose bright idea was it we meet at eleven?' he asked, yawning.

'Late night?' Nik asked.

Alex nodded, the back of his hand rasping against the stubble on his chin. Even though it looked as if he hadn't got a wink of sleep, the dark bruised circles under his eyes made him look quite sexy, which Mallory thought unfair because if she didn't get enough sleep she looked like an extra from *Night of the Living Dead*.

'How are you, Mallory?' Alex asked, turning his full-beam smile on her.

'Good, thanks.' Mallory swallowed down an anxious stomach lurch. Despite leaving him on good terms, their first meeting still caused Mallory hot flashes of embarrassment. She could be watching television or in the bath and she would recall the exquisite horror of just how she'd thrown the wine over his face or how prissy she'd sounded when she'd actually uttered the words *'aesthetically pleasing'*. My God, he must have thought she was straight out of a Jane Austen novel. And she didn't even want to *think* about the misunderstanding over the biography on her CV.

'Right, Alex!' Nik said with a grin as he stepped back from the coffee machine. 'Now you've deigned to join us why don't you make the coffee.'

'Bastard!' Alex retorted in good humour.

Nik folded his arms. 'Come on, I've shown you about thirty times already.'

'I know, I know.' Alex stepped up to the machine and tentatively pulled a lever. Nothing happened.

'First you have to switch it on.' Nik leaned over and flicked a switch. He turned back to Mallory. 'Alex, as you may have gathered, is rather hopeless in the kitchen.'

'It's my only failing,' Alex said with a helpless shrug.

Nik's blue eyes disappeared into tanned crinkles as he gave a bark of laughter. 'That you admit to!' He pulled up stools for Mallory and himself. 'I've told him that if he wants to be a partner in a restaurant he has to learn the basics. I've also challenged him to prepare me a meal worthy of a Michelin star.'

'And you'll get it, you'll get it!' Alex said, removing the bean-grinding container and looking inside. After giving it a shake, he fitted it back on the machine. 'I intend to dazzle you with my culinary skills.'

Nik leaned over to Mallory. 'He's already promised me a perfectly risen soufflé, I just can't wait to see what he has planned for the rest of the meal.'

'I'm keeping it a surprise,' Alex said, the tip of his tongue sticking out the side of his mouth in concentration as he pressed buttons on the machine.

As Mallory listened to Alex and Nik's good-natured bickering she started to relax. Alex had told her it would be nothing more than an informal chat and while she hadn't quite expected a 'light bulb in the face' style of interrogation, she never thought she'd be having fun!

Going by first impressions Nik seemed friendly and easy going; just the sort of person she liked working with and Mallory was also relieved that although being a full five minutes in his company she hadn't insulted him, thrown wine over him or accused him of wanting to sleep with her. Things were definitely looking up.

'Will you be doing all the cooking?' Mallory asked Nik as Alex continued to press buttons on the machine and swear under his breath.

Nik nodded. 'Although I'll be hiring other chefs and kitchen hands.'

Mallory was just about to ask what Alex's role in the business would be (clearly not the barista) when Nik volunteered the answer.

'I'm very lucky that Alex was looking for a business to invest in.'

'I thought it was about time I did something useful,' Alex said over his shoulder as he fiddled with the steam nozzle, accidentally letting it off. He then pressed another button and thick espresso streamed into the cup below. With a shout of triumph, he filled up a silver jug with milk.

Once they all had their coffees Mallory knew it was her moment. Giving the garnet stone one last rub for luck, she launched into the spiel she'd been practising.

She tried to stay professional and calm but before long the Javan blend kicked in along with her obvious enthusiasm for the project and she was jumping about from idea to idea like a grasshopper on speed, excitedly telling them her plans for the Greek style neoclassical building.

And the more she talked the more she desperately wanted the job; she wanted to see her designs breathe life into the beautiful old building. She showed them the sketches for the lighting effects, samples for the upholstery of the chairs, the colours she would use throughout and finally, the most ambitious part of the project, the frieze running around the tops of the walls.

'I thought it would be perfect for the frieze to follow a famous Greek legend, quite a long one considering the amount of wall involved. That's why I've chosen the twelve labours of Hercules. I think it's ideal, especially as Paul told me the name of your restaurant is Serendipity. The twelve labours of Hercules involves the Fates and the Gods and has adventure and love and bravery; everything you need when starting up this restaurant together.

'I think it would work brilliantly,' she added simply, hoping she hadn't gushed too much over her ideas. She pulled out the sketches and watercolours she'd done of

Hercules's fourth task, when he had to capture the Erymanthian boar while evading the Centaur's arrows. She held her breath as Alex and Nik looked through them all silently.

The longer they looked, the stronger her nagging doubts became. Had she gone on too much? Were the sketches as good as she thought? Johan was always telling her not to be so modest, but she hoped that in trying to be confident she hadn't come across as arrogant.

'And, um, although I want the Greek mythology theme running through everything I don't intend it to be like *Carry on Toga*.'

'Oh, I don't know, *Carry on Toga* does conjure up some rather interesting pictures,' Alex said.

Nik straightened up and exchanged a glance with Alex.

Mallory was figuring out whether it was a positive or negative glance when he turned to her. 'Time-wise, we need to be up and running as soon as possible. Luckily the survey was fine and the building is structurally sound and now that the kitchen has been installed it really is only the interior which needs the work. You'd be liaising with Paul and the electricians, plumbers, plasterers, etc.'

'I have to come clean, I've never dealt with anything on this scale before,' Mallory said, slightly overwhelmed by the amount of work to be done.

Nik guffawed loudly. 'Christ! I've never run a restaurant before.'

'And you expect me to bankroll you amateurs!' Alex exclaimed in mock horror before laughing and holding up his hands in surrender. 'The closest thing to work I've ever done was to traipse down a catwalk, trashed out of my mind.'

'Any questions you want to ask us?' Nik said.

She had about a million but she plumped for, 'Do you have many more people to see?'

'Ah yes, all the other candidates. How many were there at the last count, Alex?'

'I'd say about twenty, twenty-five.'

'It might take a while to get to the second round of interviews though, because of the trials we've got planned.'

'And of course, there's still the rigorous initiation for the lucky few who get through to the third stage,' Alex said with a twinkle in his eye. 'Walking over hot coals, wasn't it?'

'Hot pizza oven coals, to be precise.' Nik kept a serious face for a couple of seconds, before laughing. 'Look Mallory, as far as we're concerned we'd hired you the second we saw your work in the cocktail bar and they gave you glowing references.'

'I've got the job?' Mallory asked, wanting complete clarification. It all just seemed so easy.

'Yes, you have.' Alex held up his coffee mug and chinked it against hers.

Nik stood. 'Sorry to hire and run, but I've got a meeting with a prospective supplier. Alex will fill you in on any other details,' he said, heading for the door. 'I'm really glad you're on board, Mallory. And although it sounds a bit mercenary, having someone as dynamic as you will really enhance the PR aspect.' The door closed behind him.

She nearly laughed aloud; she'd never been called *dynamic* before! She sat for a moment letting the news sink in, by turns feeling giddy with excitement then sick with nerves. 'Wow! I have to say, I thought I'd completely ruined any chances of getting this job after our first meeting and... everything.'

'Ah yes, about that.' Alex set down his coffee and gave her a very serious look.

Mallory swallowed. Had he mulled it over and decided he was pissed off with her after all?

But his serious face gave way to a lopsided smile. 'I'm prepared to blank the entire shirt incident from my mind if you help me out with a favour.'

'Absolutely!' She'd even give the hot coals a try if it meant keeping the job.

'Do you have any plans for the weekend?'

'Nope, although I'll be working on ideas for this place.'

'Great! So, no plans for the Saturday night?'

She shook her head.

'Fantastic! I would like you to give me some advice on food.'

'What?' She laughed. Surely he'd be better off asking Nik.

He waggled his finger at her. 'Now, don't be putting your amateur gourmet cooking abilities down.'

'My amateur gourmet cooking abilities?' she repeated faintly, not liking where this was heading.

'Yes, Johan forwarded me a copy of your CV and there will be no hiding your talents. Johan warned me you're also infuriatingly modest,' he said firmly.

'Oh God!' she whispered, feeling the room starting to cave in towards her.

Not noticing her reaction Alex carried on. 'As he took such delight in telling you, Nik's challenged me to cook him a meal. I stupidly agreed, even offered to make him a bloody soufflé. The truth is, I can't cook my way out of a paper bag *and* he knows it. He's fully expecting a burnt spaghetti Bolognese but I hate to admit it, even *that* would be beyond me.

'I would love to see his face if I produced something absolutely knockout amazing. And that's where you come in. Could you show me how to make a soufflé and another couple of impressive dishes?'

She stared at him, speechless. Was part of the reason she got the job down to her biography? She couldn't risk telling him the CV was made up in case he withdrew the offer.

'I need something that will really impress him.' Alex carried on oblivious to her inner turmoil. 'Something he knows is difficult to do, which will wipe that smug look off his face.'

'Soufflé?' she repeated, feeling the milk from the latte churning to butter in her stomach.

'Yeah! We could have that as a starter and then anything you think would be good. I'm completely open to suggestions.'

She took a sip of her coffee, stalling for time in which to think up an excuse.

'I'll buy in all the ingredients. We can do it here.'

'But…' She gestured at her sketchbooks.

'There's nothing to do on-site for a couple of days before all furniture is cleared, so don't worry about the time.'

'Ah…'

'So, he's coming over on Saturday night.'

'*This* Saturday? As in three days from now?' Mallory tried not to sound too shrill.

'Yup, I can't believe my luck that you're free!'

'Well, when I said I was free…'

'Or we could do it Friday, or the Sunday. You name the day.'

What the hell was she going to do? Alex was looking at her expectantly. Then she remembered there were a couple of great delis close by and she was sure one of them did catering. It would be pricey, but she could pick up the food and pop round to the restaurant. She smiled, this time with more confidence. 'No, Saturday will be fine, just tell me when Nik will be arriving and I'll bring everything round.'

'No, no. I can't have you doing *all* the work, that would be incredibly unfair and, at the end of the day, I *would* like to try to pick up a few tricks from an expert. I was really hoping we could meet up early and you could show me the ropes. I'll be your sous chef. You can tell me what to whisk, when.'

Mallory felt the blood drain from her face. 'I, um, yup, that's fine. I'll be back in just a second.'

She stumbled off to the loos. Locking the door behind her she took a look in the mirror. Her cheeks were an unhealthy puce.

Oh God! She'd been in some tricky situations, but this was

beyond anything she'd ever done. How the hell was she going to fool Alex into thinking she could cook? Could she develop a rare flu virus in three days' time? Knowing her luck, Alex would just pole up with an anti-contamination suit. She took a deep breath.

'Right, Mallory, listen up,' she told her reflection sternly. 'You can do this. You are going to learn to cook. Three courses in three days.' That was all. She could do it.

In her favour, she was a great fan of cookery programmes. From the sexy, finger-licking approach of Nigella to the boiling temper of Gordon Ramsay to the cool, calm collectedness of Mary Berry, she watched them all. She'd just never lifted a pot or a chopping knife to recreate any of the dishes. Although it *was* something she'd always wanted to be able to learn... it would now be a little more hurried than she'd planned.

CHAPTER 10

'Con-grat-u-lations, and celebrations,' Caz sang cheerfully that night when Mallory returned home. 'I told you that lucky garnet would do the trick!'

'I think I'm going to have to hold on to it for a while,' Mallory said as she dumped bulging plastic bags on the kitchen table and unpacked three saucepans, a griddle and a blow-torch.

Caz looked on, inquisitively.

'I need to learn how to cook,' Mallory explained.

'In one night?' Caz queried, examining an egg separator.

'Pretty much.'

Mallory emptied another bag, piling Delia on top of *Larousse Gastronomique* on top of the Roux brothers and Marco Pierre White. She found the long till receipt and looked cheerlessly at the amount totalled at the bottom which she'd had to put on her credit card.

She unpacked four dozen eggs as Caz continued to look on.

'Alex wants to learn how to make a soufflé and wants me to show him the ropes and, if I don't, *I'll* be the one with the rope – noosed and wrapped tightly round my neck. But it doesn't stop at a soufflé – I also have to come up with more fantastic creations, but that's okay, because, after all, I'm an amateur gourmet cook, aren't I?' she said, aware her voice was verging on hysteria.

She picked up the first cookery book and flicked through it, stopping at the pages depicting how to debone a chicken. She turned it on its side, then upside down before shutting it over in despair.

Caz sat opposite her, cupping her chin in her hand. 'I think kitchens are sexy. Just *imagine* the sexual frisson! Your eyes meeting across a bowl of *whipped* cream, your hand *brushing* against his as you both reach for the olive oil, which you then *smear* over a slab of meat, your fingers *sliding* over the flesh. Bubbling pots causing the windows to *steam*, there's sweat on your brow, your clothes are sticking to you as the heat builds from the oven and the *loin* of beef *braising slo-o-o-wly* in...'

Mallory threw a dish-towel at her. 'It's not porn!'

'Spoilsport!' Caz pouted.

Ignoring Caz, Mallory picked up Delia Smith's *Complete Illustrated Cookery Course* book and opened it at page one. 'I love eating, so surely that's a good place to start, right?'

'That's the spirit. What can I do to help?' Caz picked up a wooden spoon and tried to balance it on the end of her nose.

'You can start by pouring me a very large gin and tonic.' She may never be able to emulate the scientific approach of Heston Blumenthal, but Mallory was quite happy to settle for doing it the Keith Floyd way.

At quarter to four in the morning Mallory stumbled into bed, wrist aching from all the whisking and feeling a bit queasy from eating underdone egg. Deciding she wasn't going to bed until she'd managed one perfect soufflé, she nearly wept with happiness when one finally came out the oven puffed up and golden and neither sunken in the middle nor blackened round the edges. She wondered if Jamie Oliver got as emotional over his Sunday lunch. Not even bothering to remove her apron she fell onto the top of her bed, exhausted.

Less than an hour later she was dreaming she was trying to turn the buzzer off on an oven the size of a semi-detached house when reality edged into her subconscious; her mobile phone was ringing. Still face down on the bed she wriggled to get her phone from her jeans pocket. She cast a bleary eye at the caller display: Don.

He'd gone through a phase of calling her late at night a few months earlier. She hadn't answered any of his calls and deleted the messages without listening first. She knew she should really have blocked his number from her phone but hadn't quite been able to, not that she'd admit that to Caz or Olly.

Mallory remembered one of their last night-time conversations, when she and Don still hadn't fully broken up. He'd phoned just after midnight, her time, and asked what she was wearing.

Her first assumption was that he was concerned for her welfare as she struggled through a Glasgow winter and she launched into a description of her bedsocks, fleecy pyjamas and the free Budweiser beanie hat she'd won at a pub quiz which she had to wear to bed to stop her ears from developing frostbite.

Disgruntled, he interrupted her and told her he was after phone sex and the woolly items weren't really doing it for him and she'd have to be a bit more inventive. So, she'd told him she was wearing a giant chicken suit and hung up.

With this episode still fresh in her mind she pressed the green button and steeled herself.

'Hello?' she said, pretending not to know who it was. It would do his ego good if he thought she'd deleted his number from her phone.

'Mal? Mal! Is that really you?' he slurred.

It was a shame he never seemed to call when he was sober.

'Yes, this is Mallory.'

''S'mee! 'S'mee, Mallory! 'S'Don! I can't believe you've answered. I thought I was going to have to continue our relationship with a machine.'

'We don't have a relationship anymore, Don.'

There was a pause. 'I know, and I'm so sorry. I really miss you. I can't live without you. I've tried, but I can't.'

Despite her best intentions, Mallory's resolve started to bend. Not break, but bend just a little.

There was a lot of background noise.

'Where are you?' Mallory asked.

'Some party in Manhattan. It's wild.'

'Yeah, I can hear that!' There was a sound like a giant wave crashing against the phone, then a whole load of people swearing and laughing. 'What's going on?'

'An arsehole just dive-bombed into the hot tub.'

Mallory kicked off her fluffy pink slippers. 'I can't for a moment believe you'd miss me while partying in a hot tub in Manhattan.'

'But I do. I miss you so much.'

Mallory hated herself for feeling a little jump of excitement.

'It's just meaningless empty sexual liaisons out here,' Don mumbled into the phone.

Mallory didn't feel quite so flattered anymore.

'It's sex, sex, sex everywhere. Everyone is shagging someone to get somewhere.'

'Most probably the SDT clinic if that's the way you all carry on,' Mallory retorted.

'I miss you because you're not like that. You're not some glamorous, big-titted blonde on the make.'

'Thanks,' she said, but sarcasm was lost on Don.

'Do you know something?'

She knew that she needed to get back to sleep so she could learn how to make pastry first thing in the morning.

'Last night I had sex with the most amazingly beautiful woman and it left me feeling empty,' he announced with such incredulity it was as if he'd just discovered a flaw with Newton's first law.

'My heart bleeds,' Mallory muttered, mightily pissed off he'd interrupted her sleep to tell her about his latest conquest.

'Because she's, like, the *most* sought-after woman here and everyone wants her, you know. And I got her and I'm… I'm really not that bothered. And I suddenly realised that if shagging her made me feel empty, I might as well be with you. It's like how sometimes you think you want steak, but really a burger is what you want deep down.'

Mallory was too enraged to even speak. As she sat there on the end of her bed, a dawn sun creeping into the room, she realised that Caz, Olly, Johan and everyone else in the universe who told her that Don wasn't worth a sleepless night was right.

Don was a complete dick.

How could she even have contemplated being with someone who thought it was flattering to woo her back by telling her he'd just shagged someone else? And then comparing her to a burger! She was seething so much she almost missed what he'd said next.

'Will you marry me?'

'What?'

'Will you marry me?'

Mallory sat for a moment contemplating what to say. She thought about launching forth a diatribe using all the swear words she knew to leave him in no doubt how she felt, but she didn't have the energy and she also didn't want to make the conversation last any longer.

She never, ever wanted to speak to him again, so she said the only thing guaranteed to have a weak-willed, commitment-phobe running for the hills, never to be heard from again.

'Yes. Yes, of course I will.'

She could hear him whoop down the phone and a champagne cork popping.

Her only concern was that he'd be too drunk to remember and would try to call her again.

'You really will marry me?'

'Of course I will,' she simpered down the phone. 'I'm going to buy the most extravagant Vera Wang dress I can find and hire Glasgow Cathedral, or hell, you're famous stateside now so why not hire the Empire State Building. We can fly everyone we know over and have the biggest, most spectacular bash in the history of weddings ever!'

'I can't believe you said yes.'

She bet he couldn't!

'Just let me know when you pick a date,' she said, hanging up and throwing her phone into the laundry basket.

CHAPTER 11

*A*s she suspected, Mallory didn't receive any more phone calls from Don – drunk or sober – over the next couple of days, leaving her able to carry on undisturbed in her quest to learn to cook. She definitely had new-found respect for Nik, the fact he wanted to spend most of his day and night in such a nerve-wracking way was beyond Mallory's comprehension.

In three days, she'd stressed over a lumpy sauce, fretted over scones and practically had a nervous breakdown attempting to make choux pastry. She'd been on a constant diet of Bach Flower Rescue Remedy to calm her down, gin to keep her sane, and even more coffee than usual to keep her awake enough hours of the day to be able to learn to grapple with the basics.

And now, Saturday afternoon had rolled round far too quickly as Mallory picked her way past all the skips and scaffolding to the kitchen door of Serendipity, quailing slightly at the task ahead.

She patted the back pocket of her jeans, comforted to feel the folded-up recipes of what she'd be cooking and told herself that everything was going to be okay, then tried very hard to believe it. She'd managed to cook nine perfect soufflés in a row that morning and Caz, who'd tasted them all, had loved them, before lambasting her for making her eat too many calories and raising her cholesterol levels.

Mallory knocked on the back fire exit and seconds later Alex opened the door.

'I feel we should have codenames and secret knocks, don't you?' He smiled, taking the bags from her and kicking the door shut with his foot.

He was wearing an old pair of faded jeans, flip-flops and a dark-blue T-shirt and although not stylish he still managed to look good. He'd not shaved and the dark shadow of his stubble accentuated his thick dark eyebrows, making his pale eyes even more startling.

His hair looked more raked through with fingers than combed and Mallory wondered if it really was him not bothering or if he'd spent hours perfecting the 'unkempt and natural' look.

She followed him past the larders and store rooms and into the kitchen which was slightly more welcoming than the last time she saw it on account of the strips of tea lights Alex had arranged over the counter tops.

'Hope you don't mind, I thought I'd try to cosy up the place a bit. Nik is in raptures about the kitchen but to me it looks bloody clinical. I've not dared venture into the cold room yet as I'm terrified I'll find a dead body hanging from a meat hook,' he said as he unpacked the bags.

'The candles do take away the mortuary vibe, I'll give you that. Although it still does look a little on the sinister side.'

Alex surveyed the room again. 'Yeah, all I've achieved is making it look as if a serial killer has made his pad romantic.'

'Just don't get any ideas.'

'Of being romantic or murderous?' he asked, picking up a chef's knife and laughing demonically. He put the knife back down. 'Okay chef, I'm all yours.' He gave her a rakish smile.

'Let's start with practising a soufflé so you know what you're doing later.' Hands shaking, she cracked an egg off the side of a bowl, and as she was about to separate it, Alex moved behind her. His close scrutiny unnerved her and she watched in dismay as the egg slithered down the side of the bowl, pooling on the work surface.

'Sorry chef, I didn't mean to crowd you.' He walked round the other side of the island as Mallory reached for another egg.

'Okay, we need to crack six yolks and, and...' Oh bugger, her mind went blank as to how many whites she needed.

'Fancy an aperitif?'

'Um, don't you want to practise this first? And we should start on the dessert as we need to let the pastry chill.'

'I'm sure we can manage to drink as we cook,' he said, going to the fridge and pulling out a bottle of champagne.

This wasn't how Mallory had imagined the afternoon panning out at all. She thought she'd be taking on a no-nonsense, Fanny Craddock approach, with Alex listening attentively and following out her every instruction. But instead, Alex was lounging around, offering her champagne, distracting her from the task at hand. In fact, Mallory was seriously starting to doubt his desire to learn to cook at all.

The next three hours were among the most stressful Mallory had ever struggled through. Every time Alex had his back turned she had to quickly shuffle through her notes to get a handle on the next stage of cooking and it all nearly went belly up when she left the instructions for the rack of lamb too near the gas and ended up singeing the edges.

By seven o'clock she'd started to enjoy herself and felt a little more relaxed – although she suspected it had far more to do with the amount of champagne she'd quaffed than her sudden ability to be a Cordon Bleu chef. She'd just noticed that the potato dauphinois had oozed its way over the top of the dish and welded itself onto the inside of the oven when Alex's mobile rang. As he answered, Mallory hastily chiselled off the molten gloop with a fish slice.

After a brief exchange he hung up. 'I'm afraid we're one less for dinner.'

'What?' Mallory said, drawing her head back from the furnace heat of the oven and surreptitiously throwing the burnt mess into the bin.

'Nik's sorry excuse for a car has broken down out at Loch Fyne, where he was seeing a man about some oysters. Anyway, breakdown rescue will be at least another hour, then he's still got the drive home,' Alex said, topping up her champagne. 'So, it's just you and me.'

Mallory looked at him aghast. 'Oh, no! I couldn't. I mean, Nik may still get a breakdown truck out in time and you two can still have a great evening…' Although without the presence of Nik at dinner, the pressure was off her slightly, she realised.

Alex topped up his own glass before sticking the bottle back into the ice bucket. 'Did you honestly think,' he said with a reproving look, 'that I'd get you round here to cook all this lovely food, then send you away when Nik arrived?'

That's exactly what she thought *would* happen.

'I'd wanted tonight to be a relaxed meeting between the three of us so we could discuss the plans for Serendipity.'

'But didn't you want Nik to think you'd cooked it all?' She started to mop up the puddles of spilt egg white on the counter.

Alex took the cloth from Mallory. 'I thought I'd hide you in the walk-in larder for a few minutes until I'd hoodwinked him into believing I'd done all this myself.' He smiled. 'I'm going to go and rummage in the store room for something drinkable as we seem to be on the last of the fizz. I'll not be long. If I'm not back in half an hour…' he paused, halfway out the door and clung to the door frame, 'be afraid, be very afraid.' He gave a mock scream and pretended to be yanked out the door.

Suddenly left alone in the kitchen Mallory felt a bit lonely with just the sound of the bubbling pots.

'Shit! The gravy!' she squealed as she frantically stirred the gravy which was turning to an unappetising sludge.

Alex returned a couple of minutes later, as Mallory had managed to get rid of the last gravy lump. 'I think this should be okay.' Alex opened the wine and took a tentative sip. 'Not a big selection, just a few contenders for our house wine. So, what's next, chef?'

'We, we…' Mallory dabbed her forehead with the back of her hand, feeling more than a little frazzled as she struggled to remember what she was supposed to be doing. 'We take out the potatoes to cool slightly then put in the soufflés to cook.'

'Sounds good to me. Now, I think it's high time you sat down and relaxed.' Reaching behind her he pulled loose the bow of her apron then led her towards a trestle table he'd set up in the corner. He held out a chair for her and as she sat he whisked out a red-and-white-gingham tablecloth. In the centre of the table, he placed an empty jam jar with a dandelion in it.

'Sorry, we don't seem to have any flowers out back, just this charming little delight growing between a couple of paving stones.'

'It's lovely,' she said.

And in its own way it was.

By the time they'd finished their meal, which Alex had announced a triumph, Mallory was feeling positively ebullient that she'd managed to get through the evening. Although fraught with moments of panic, at the end of the day, she had learned a new skill: the basics of cooking! So what if the potatoes were a bit well done on the top and the soufflés had collapsed a little on one side – it had all tasted magnificent and the lemon tart was absolutely delicious, so much so she'd just helped herself to seconds.

'This isn't too bad actually and it went well with the lamb,' Alex said as he topped up their wine glasses and set the bottle back on the table. 'I should have thought and asked your advice beforehand.'

Mallory chuckled. As if she'd know! She'd only ever watched the occasional *Saturday Kitchen* wine article, usually when she was recovering from a hangover and therefore not that enamoured to be hearing the merits of a cheeky little Beaujolais.

Then a horrifying, sobering clarity began to descend. She'd stated on her CV she was a wine connoisseur.

She crammed a huge spoonful of lemon tart into her mouth hoping to make further conversation impossible.

Alex twirled his glass between his index finger and thumb, the light from the candles glinting off the crystal.

'I should really have ransacked my father's cellar; he's got more than he could drink in a lifetime.'

Still chewing, Mallory tried to remember any wine information she knew. But the only thing that sprung to mind was throwing white wine over red wine to remove the stain. And that hadn't exactly worked when she'd put it into practice.

Alex carried on. 'We'll have to get you involved when we choose the wine list. The more input the better.'

She slumped, defeated, into her chair. She'd be spending the next day reading up about wine and enrolling in a couple of tutored courses. She crammed another spoonful of dessert into her mouth as she kissed goodbye to thoughts of a day lazing in the park with an iced coffee and a book.

'That um, that wasn't why I got the job was it? Knowing about wine?' she asked through a mouthful of pastry.

'You mean, were we hoping to kill two birds with one stone,

get an artist and sommelier?' He started to laugh then saw the expression on her face. 'Of course not, we hired you solely on your merit as an artist,' he paused, 'but I'm the first to admit that with all your other talents, it's pretty good from a PR aspect.'

Mallory swallowed, the pastry threatening to stick in her throat. 'Surely my hobbies have nothing to do with my work?' Mallory said, fearful of Alex's reply.

He rubbed his hand against his stubbly jaw. 'It doesn't to us, but...' he exhaled loudly, 'it all sounds so cynical but my involvement with the venture means it's a bit more newsworthy than your average restaurant opening.' He looked quite uncomfortable and it didn't look like false modesty to Mallory.

'It means there will be a lot more press focus. And probably a lot more people waiting in the wings with their knives out, and I don't mean alongside their forks to try our food.' He gave a rueful smile as he stabbed his own fork into the remains of his dessert. 'There's a big PR slant which will really help Nik get it off the ground. Luckily Nik knows how to work the press and is photogenic – don't tell him I said that, though.'

'Does there have to be so much PR attention?'

He rolled the base of his wine glass on the table and gave a small shrug. 'It's a necessary evil.'

Mallory was surprised at his negativity towards the press. 'I thought you loved all that though.'

He looked up at her, genuinely surprised.

'I mean, considering the number of photographs taken of you at parties and polo races and dinners...'

He sat back in his chair, eyes twinkling. 'Have you been checking up on me?'

'Not at all!' she exclaimed, feeling a bit foolish as it did sound as if she'd been playing Nancy Drew. 'My friend Caz is a magazine junkie and she told me.'

'Ahh.'

Emboldened by the wine, Mallory continued. 'She also

thought it was strange you decided to move all the way up to Scotland, because surely as the financial backer, you could perform that role from a couple of hundred miles away.'

He looked up at her briefly, a flicker of something in his eyes but before Mallory could read more into it, Alex's affable smile was back in place. 'True, but I've outgrown London. Constantly seeing the same faces in the same clubs was becoming dull. I wanted a break. I'd already spent March in Monaco, April in Barcelona and May in Rome. I hate LA because you have to get permission from the Fun Police to do anything. New York would have been too hot in the summer, and too many of my exes are currently holidaying in the Greek islands.'

He gave her another rueful smile. 'So, when I offered to back Nik's project I thought Glasgow was a good place to be. This way I can be more than a silent partner and be on hand to help.' He stretched, folding his arms behind his head. 'And I thought any altruistic inclination should be nurtured, wouldn't you agree?'

Mallory studied him over the rim of her glass wondering how much truth there was to his spiel about moving to Glasgow. For a split second, had it been wariness she'd seen in his eyes? Only for the briefest of moments before he'd returned to his usual glib self. She couldn't read him.

'You look thoughtful.'

'I'm still working you out,' she said.

He seemed to like her answer as he smiled. 'You'll find I'm not the person the press portray.'

'Next you'll be telling me you're quite shy…'

'Painfully so,' he agreed.

'And misunderstood…'

'Often.'

'And you've never really gone out with any models or actresses or…'

He laughed and held up his hands. 'Okay, so maybe I'm a little guilty as charged, but I like to have fun. I don't like taking anything too seriously.'

'Nothing?'

He shook his head. 'Not work, not relationships, not life.'

'Yet you just told me you got bored with parties in London.'

'Ah, but they weren't fun,' he said softly.

He was flirting. Mallory knew she'd been out of the loop a long time but had enough of a memory to know when she was being flirted with. He held her gaze, though technically she was still holding his too, as the room seemed to do a warpy in-and-out thing around her as all she could focus on was her breathing and how it was starting to get a bit faster.

A voice spoke from the other end of the room. 'This is very cosy.'

Mallory jumped and turned to see Louisa framed in the open fire exit.

'Louisa. This is a surprise,' Alex said easily.

'I'm sure,' Louisa said, not budging, her glossed lips compressed with displeasure.

Mallory looked from Louisa to Alex to Louisa again. Louisa looked livid.

'Come on in,' Alex said.

'I'd hate to think I was interrupting anything,' Louisa said tightly.

'You're here now, you may as well have some coffee.' Alex stood and headed over to the state-of-the-art coffee contraption in the corner. He didn't seem to notice the large dark cloud of pissed-offness which was hovering over Louisa's head. Or was it that he just wasn't bothered, leaving Mallory wondering exactly what their relationship was.

Were they together? From Louisa's reaction Mallory would guess very much a 'yes', but Alex hadn't mentioned Louisa once throughout their evening and he certainly hadn't acted like he had a girlfriend. Although that didn't necessarily mean they weren't involved. Just because Alex didn't take anything seriously didn't mean Louisa had the same outlook.

Even though nothing had happened, Mallory felt a lurch of guilt as she'd been more than happy to bask in the fuzzy glow of Alex's flirting.

'There's some amazing lemon tart in the fridge,' Alex said.

Louisa looked as if she'd been offered a portion of strychnine. 'Just coffee. No milk.'

'We've been discussing Serendipity,' Mallory piped up, keen to fill the gaping silence and to clear up any misunderstanding. 'Nik was meant to be joining us for a meeting to discuss the plans but his car broke down and we thought it would have been an awful shame to let all the food go to waste.'

Louisa sat at the table with a disdainful glance at the dandelion, which had started to wilt.

'So, what brings you out here?' Alex asked Louisa, pouring some thick black espresso into cups.

'I was passing and saw the lights on and wondered if it was you.'

Mallory very much doubted Louisa had been 'passing' as the building was at the top of a T-junction. Mallory would have bet money that Louisa had been trying to find Alex.

Mallory knew only too well what it was like going out with someone you didn't quite trust; she'd been sorely tempted to keep trails on Don a few times. Although she'd never caught him doing the dirty there was always a nagging doubt and she was pretty sure he'd been unfaithful. It seemed all men were the same.

'Were you working late?' Alex asked.

Louisa wrinkled her nose with displeasure. 'I had to go out to a stable and look at some horses. We've landed a new client and we're organising a race night for them.'

'Louisa works for her father's PR company,' Alex explained to Mallory as he opened a bottle of brandy and poured three generous measures.

Mallory nearly burst out laughing. Never had she met someone so ill-suited to working in public relations. All humour left her however as Alex added, 'They're also dealing with Serendipity's PR.'

Which meant Louisa would be hanging around a lot more and Mallory wasn't exactly keen on that scenario.

'I'm surprised you went near a horse,' Alex said to Louisa. 'I thought you came out in a rash just watching an animal documentary.'

Louisa bristled. 'I'm thinking of learning to ride.'

Alex leaned back against the worktop, warming his glass in his hands. 'Mallory could always give you some tips.'

Mallory, who'd taken a large swallow of brandy, choked, coughing as the spirit burned her throat and nose, making her eyes stream.

Horse-riding! This was too much!

Louisa didn't look in Mallory's direction despite the prompt. 'I thought *you* could teach me, Alex. You've always been a keen rider.'

'I don't have the time.'

'Oh, of course, I'm forgetting, your days are packed,' she snapped.

Unruffled by Louisa's mood, Alex ignored her jibe and gestured to Mallory with his brandy glass. 'I'm sure Mallory's a far more adept rider than I am.'

'Ayha...?' Mallory could only make a strangled noise.

'Do you own your own horse?'

Mallory gasped, trying to regain her composure. 'No.' At least that wasn't a lie.

'You'd be able to give Louisa some tips, wouldn't you?'

Louisa looked as if she'd rather gouge her eyes out with a rusty nail.

Mallory had to leave. If Alex knew about horses and started asking her equine-related questions he'd instantly realise she hadn't a clue. And she didn't want to get roped into a point-to-point or risk having anything else on her CV brought up. She cleared her throat. 'I think I'd better be off.'

'So soon?' Alex asked, surprised.

'It's getting late and I want to be up early to start on the design ideas. The ones we've been discussing,' she added for Louisa's benefit.

'At least finish your coffee. It's taken me ages to learn how the blasted thing works, you might as well reap the benefits.'

Mallory shook her head, rising to her feet. 'I really should go.'

'I'll call you a taxi.'

Louisa stared at Mallory, her eyes glittering and Mallory faltered slightly under their cold glare. 'Um, no, it's okay, I'll hail one on the main road.' She grabbed her bag and bolted out the back door, calling 'goodnight' over her shoulder.

Outside was dark and with no security lights on, Mallory stumbled along the path, cracking her shins on the boxes of junk waiting to get thrown into the skips.

Alex caught up with her as she reached the front of the building. He stepped in front of her, barring her exit. 'Hold on a second. Is everything okay?'

'Absolutely.'

He raised an eyebrow. 'You're practically running away. Do you turn into a pumpkin at midnight?'

'No, not a pumpkin, but possibly a gooseberry.'

Alex took a step back and looked at her quizzically.

'I think I've outstayed my welcome,' she mumbled, unable to make eye contact. 'You know, you really should get something to kill all the weeds,' she added, noticing the greenery poking up through the cracks on the path.

Alex gently tipped her chin back up with his index finger so he was looking her in the eye. 'Why would you think you've outstayed your welcome?'

His nearness and touch triggered a funny fizzing sensation in her stomach, one she'd not felt for a very long time. *Stop it!*

She took a small step back, breaking contact. She couldn't start thinking of Alex as being fanciable! Apart from the obvious reasons of him being her boss and that his very pissed-off girlfriend was sulking just a few feet away, Mallory categorically DID NOT GO FOR flighty, cheating playboys with no direction in life, who took nothing seriously.

No matter how good-looking and charming they were.

Or how buff they looked in a fitted T-shirt.

Mallory swallowed, dragging her eyes away from his well-toned chest. She looked over his shoulder, towards the road, willing a taxi to career round the corner.

'You think you were being a gooseberry? Between me and Louisa?'

'I wasn't referring to you and the dandelion.' Honestly! Mallory wondered if he was being deliberately obtuse. 'I just don't think your girlfriend was that happy to find us there. I realise how it must have looked to her, turning up and seeing us, over dinner, with wine... and how she could jump to the wrong idea.'

'I think *you've* got the wrong idea, Mallory.' He laughed, running his hand through his thick hair. 'Louisa and I aren't together. We had a very brief fling in London, but that was over a year ago and we've both moved on.'

'Both moved on... together to Glasgow?'

'Louisa got in touch not long after I moved up here. It turned out she'd been transferred up to the Glasgow office and heard on the grapevine that I was here too. She's going to be helping out the PR for Serendipity, but we're certainly not involved.'

Louisa had obviously missed out on that memo. Even if Louisa wasn't his girlfriend she clearly felt she had dibs on him.

Alex laughed gently. 'It's very sweet that you're so concerned to what she might think,' he teased, 'and that you've taken on the role of my moral guardian. Many would be daunted at such a task.'

'I just didn't want her to jump to the wrong conclusions because of how we looked.'

'And how *did* we look?' he asked quietly.

Mallory was glad it was dark as he wouldn't be able to see her face redden. 'Like a boss and his employee having a work dinner,' she said firmly. 'Because to think anything else would be *ludicrous*.' She gave a laugh of disbelief.

'Completely ridiculous,' he agreed. 'Although, it's a good thing I'm so thick-skinned, considering your complete disdain for me!'

'I didn't mean to insult you, I mean, I'm sure you're much sought after, and probably lots of people would be flattered to think you'd be interested in them...' She stopped herself, not quite believing what she was saying. Why did Alex have this effect on her? It wasn't that she was always the embodiment of sophistication and eloquence, but at least she could usually have a conversation without sounding like a tongue-tied idiot!

'Why thank you!' he said, his eyes twinkling with amusement in the moonlight. 'I guess this must be as much of a compliment as I'm ever going to get from you.'

'I didn't mean to insult you.'

'Thank goodness for that, I'd hate to think what you'd come out with if you did!' he said, unable to keep the smile from his face.

And now she feared she'd come across as protesting too much, because at that moment, with his eyes glittering in the moonlight and feeling the warmth of his body just inches away from hers and his delicious-smelling aftershave teasing her senses, she was in danger of losing the last vestiges of her dignity by throwing herself on him like some weak-willed, sex-starved, soppy heroine.

He laughed openly. 'I think I know what you're trying to say, and let's face it, I'd have to be a complete cad to move in on someone else's fiancé.'

'Um, yes,' Mallory agreed, feeling her face freeze into a smile at the mention of her fictitious fiancé. Had Alex memorised her entire CV?! She wished he wouldn't keep bringing things up from it. Contestants on *Mastermind* seemed to study their specialised subject with less vigour.

'Anyway,' she said, looking up at the stars, which seemed to be winking down at her conspiratorially. 'I really should be going. And it's such a lovely evening I'm going to walk home.'

'Are you sure?'

'Quite sure.'

And without further argument, he stood back to let her go.

CHAPTER 12

*C*az leaned over the back of the sofa, looking out the window onto the street below. She'd been sitting like that for the best part of an hour and had long ago lost the feeling in her right foot, but she didn't want to leave the window. She knew it was silly, farcical even, but she didn't want to leave in case she saw *him* again.

Him. The personification of the Love God, Eros himself.

AKA The One.

She closed her eyes, counted to ten, opened them and...

Nothing. The street below was still deserted, save for a stripy ginger cat slinking along the pavement.

Sighing, Caz lowered her chin onto her cupped hands and willed the stranger she'd met in the shop to walk round the corner.

She'd lit pink candles, burnt sandalwood and jasmine incense and had slipped on a rose quartz necklace she'd made, all in the hope that one of them would send a signal into the ether that she was ready, willing and able to welcome love into her heart. As long as love came in the guise of the man she'd just met, she added under her breath, to make sure the powers that be made no mistake.

She'd always believed that she would meet The One. What she hadn't accounted for though, was meeting him then letting him vanish from her life without even knowing his name. When she'd asked Aphrodite for help all those months earlier she hadn't realised she would need to be more specific. As well as asking to meet The One, she should have added that she wanted to *keep* The One. How could she have known the heavens would be so pedantic?

Mallory had been sceptical and reminded her that rarely did a week go by without Caz getting one of her tummy tingles – the fizzing sensation she got in her stomach whenever she met someone she fancied. This happened with such regularity that Olly had once given her a bumper packet of indigestion tablets and leaflets on irritable bowel syndrome.

But the other night had been different. What Caz felt went beyond a tummy tingle.

She'd felt it in her knees.

A definite solid ten on the Richter scale of knee tremors.

So, *why then*, had she played the coquette and not asked for his number? Why did she always see it as a man's prerogative to do the chasing? Why had she not even asked his bloody name – then at least she'd be able to refer to him as something other than Eros!

But surely Fate wouldn't just have given her the one chance of meeting him. As a firm advocate of the big F, she resolutely held on to the belief that one day in the (hopefully near) future, their paths would cross again.

She closed her eyes and this time counted to thirty before opening them. But instead of looking upon the embodiment of love, Olly stood on the pavement waving up at her.

A few moments later he was at her door with a chocolate cake.

'I didn't know if you're eating this kind of stuff at the moment but I thought I'd take the risk in the hope it would cheer you up.'

'Thank you.' They went into the kitchen and she popped the cake onto a plate and got out two forks, handing one to Olly. 'Hope you don't mind coming over on a Saturday night. I'm too skint to go out.'

'Course not,' Olly said as he wired into the cake.

'No hot date planned?' Caz fished.

'Nope, I'm here for you to vent your money and man woes to. I'll be your shoulder to cry on.'

'Do you think that sometimes you're a bit *too* sensitive and thoughtful?' Caz wondered aloud.

Olly paused, a forkful of cake half-way to his mouth. 'Um, no,' he said warily.

'It's just since I've known you, you always seem to fall into the no man's land, or more to the point, no woman's land category of friend.'

'And is that wrong?' he asked, blinking behind his glasses.

'I suppose it's a change from prowling Lothario types.'

For a long time, Caz had been confused by Olly. It just wasn't natural for a twenty-nine-year-old red-blooded male (even one who was a bit posh from the south coast, educated by priests, brought up with nothing but female siblings and cousins who was genuinely nice and sensitive and had a complete respect for women) not to be shagging about. Or at least shagging a bit.

Caz had deduced he held a candle for someone. One more robust than the Olympic torch, seeing as in all the years she'd known him he'd never given a hint as to who it was.

After studying his movements and habits around his friends of the opposite sex, and same sex (although her *gaydar* hadn't even given a slight beep – too many questionable prog-rock T-shirts and collections of Marvel and DC graphic novels), she narrowed his object of rather repressed affections to being either herself or Mallory, purely because they all spent so much time together.

After inviting him over once, when Mallory was away, getting him drunk and straddling him with wanton abandon and him thinking it was all hilarious and her taking the piss and being goofy and not for one moment taking it slightly seriously, she'd guessed it wasn't her.

Which left Mallory.

But if it *was* Mallory, he was careful not to give anything away. Very careful.

Like David Attenborough studying the natural habitats of a rare and skittish creature, she noted his every facial expression, body movement and voice modulation when Mallory was around. And the results weren't promising. There wasn't any difference in the way he acted. There was no reddening of the facial area and neck, no smoothing down his floppy hair, puffing out his chest when she appeared and his voice didn't change in register when he spoke to her.

It was all very disappointing.

Until the night of the gallery opening. The night when Mallory met Alex and Caz had observed Olly from the other end of the room. In total camouflage, hidden by other chattering artists and art devotees, he'd dropped his guard and was staring at Mallory across the (rather cheesy and stereotypical) crowded floor with such a look of melancholic longing that Caz thought she'd walked in on a Mills and Boon re-enactment.

As well as the longing, there was also a little undercurrent of jealousy as he watched her with Alex. Seconds later the looks were gone, but it was enough for Caz to know she'd been right. Olly fancied Mallory. In fact, Olly was *in love with* Mallory. And Mallory had no idea.

Would he ever let her know? Beating around the bush and procrastination were two of his favourite pastimes. Was Olly being in love with Mallory a good thing? It was great knowing

Olly wasn't a stoically repressed eunuch, but she didn't think Mallory's response would be the one he longed for. Caz knew Mallory loved Olly. But it wasn't a carry-each-other's-blood-around-in-a-vial love. It was a homely slippers-and-hot-chocolate kind of love, the type of love which meant Mallory felt comfortable enough to snuggle up beside him on the sofa and tell him all about her relationship problems; no doubt breaking his heart a little more each time.

'Caz?' Olly said, snapping her out of her reverie. 'Staring at me so intently is putting me off my cake!'

CHAPTER 13

Once all the furniture and fixtures had been removed from Serendipity and the area was no longer deemed to be hazardous, Mallory was able to get back on-site. Sitting at a table in the middle of what was going to be the main dining area, she rolled a stick of charcoal between her fingers, mentally mapping out the next series of sketches for the frieze; Hercules killing the Hydra of Lerna.

The monster, according to her various mythological sources, was half hound, half water-serpent and had many heads, but each time Hercules cut one of the heads off, two more sprouted in its place.

Mallory could relate to Hercules's plight. Just when she thought she'd succeeded with the cooking task from her CV, the wine connoisseur and horse-riding accomplishments had been brought to the fore.

Mallory had spent the previous few days trawling bookshops and the internet for wine guides. Precious hours when she should have been working had been spent reading about classic French grape varieties, and although she found it to be very interesting, she couldn't take her time to enjoy absorbing the information as it felt she was cramming for an exam.

There was one upside of being so busy; it had stopped her dwelling on that insane moment between her and Alex outside Serendipity when she'd felt that frisson of, of... lust? No, that was too strong. Attraction? No, it was surely just the combination of wine, flickering candlelight and the fact she hadn't even as much as looked at another man in months.

'Penny for them.'

Mallory jumped, banging her knee off the table leg. Alex stood leaning against some scaffolding a few feet away.

Rubbing her kneecap, Mallory laughed self-consciously. 'Just a penny? Surely they're worth more than that,' she said, unable to make eye contact with him for fear he had Derren Brown-like talents and could read her mind.

'But surely the value of them is in relation to what you were thinking.'

Mallory frantically tried to keep a blush at bay and ducked her head back down to her sketchpad.

Alex walked to the table and peeked over her shoulder. 'What you up to?'

'Sketching out the next of Hercules's twelve labours.'

'Going well I see,' he said, eyeing up the blank piece of paper.

She handed him a sketchbook. 'There's some more here.'

He was silent for a few minutes as he flicked through the pages and Mallory concentrated on not looking at his handsome profile.

'These are coming on really well. You must have been working flat out.'

'A bit.' Because of the guilt she felt devoting so much time to her enforced extracurricular activities, Mallory had balanced the time by working every other waking hour on the ideas for Serendipity. Absolutely exhausted, she was also single-handedly keeping the beauty counter of Boots in employment with the buckets of concealer she was getting through in a bid to hide the shadows under her eyes.

'How are things going with you?'

'Good, though I'm absolutely knackered,' he said.

He did look tired, Mallory thought, taking in his rather shambolic and unshaven appearance. Although what he was doing to be so tired she had no idea, as he only ever popped onto the site briefly. She wondered if he was partying every night until the wee small hours or maybe he'd just always led such a pampered existence that the slightest task made him reel from exhaustion.

'I've got some great news!' he said, opening his laptop. 'Louisa told me our website's up and running. It's still just a bit of a teaser, but we've got the before pictures of the site on it, a bit about our plans for the place and some information about us.' He clicked a few keys. 'Here we are!'

Alex turned the screen round to face Mallory and to her surprise her own face smiled back. It was one of the photographs Johan had taken of her at his summer party. That was bad enough, but what was below made her feel quite sick; her made-up biography.

She looked away. Seeing it in print made it all the more awful, as everyone could log on and read about her amazing accomplishments. There was no way she could back-track and confess now.

Oblivious to her misery, Alex pulled up a chair and plonked himself down beside her. 'Nik and I have sourced a fabulous place for the tables and chairs. Will you be free to drive out and have a look to see which ones you think will be best?'

'I don't...' she started then buttoned her lip. Alex looked at her questioningly, 'have a car,' she finished.

'Take mine.'

'I'm not insured,' she said, faintly hoping to dissuade him but he just laughed.

'That's okay, I trust you not to drive it into a ditch.'

As Alex clicked on other links on their website, Mallory sat glumly, wondering if her much-abused credit card could take the burden of a condensed weekend driving-school course, or if she'd be able to persuade Olly to give her a few refresher lessons.

'I don't suppose you're free the second weekend in September,' Alex said as he typed.

Mallory hesitated. If he wanted her to cook, ride, abseil or anything else, she planned on being busy every Saturday for the next decade. 'I don't know…'

'Relax! I'm not going to force you to cook another grand feast. I'm having some folk over. It's at my father's country house up north.'

'Oh…' She prayed it wouldn't be for a bunch of Italian friends who needed a translator.

'Despite your obvious enthusiasm, why don't you have a think about it,' he teased.

'Sorry.' Mallory realised she was possibly overreacting. 'That would be lovely.'

'Good. To be honest it started as a bit of a PR vehicle Louisa planned but I thought it could do with a bit of fun being injected into it.'

At the mention of Louisa and the words 'PR vehicle' Mallory suddenly wasn't so keen.

Alex closed his laptop. 'It's just an informal party, those of us directly involved with Serendipity and some old friends. Louisa was up for having a black-tie ball with a ton of people I'd never heard of being flown in but we've come to a bit of a compromise and there will be a journalist and photographer from a society magazine. Luckily, one of my good friends who's coming has a title so that's keeping her happy. And I thought that once the magazine folk leave the rest of us could just, you know, hang out and have some fun for the remainder of the weekend. You're welcome to bring a friend. Or your fiancé? I'm interested in meeting this mystery man.'

'He's very busy,' Mallory interjected. So far she'd managed to evade all questions about this non-existent man by explaining he very rarely had time in his busy schedule to come back and visit her. Also, by putting on an expression of utter dejection whenever the subject was brought up, people tended to move on as they thought she was too upset to talk about him. Eventually she planned on announcing they'd split up, citing their busy work schedules as the reason.

'Right then, I'll send you a link with map directions on how to get to mine. It's a couple of hours' drive from here.' Alex stopped at the door and turned. 'It's right out in the middle of the countryside and great for long walks, you'll love it.'

She heard him go and she sighed, giving her full attention to her work again. She tried to focus on the frieze and started on an outline of Hercules but she couldn't concentrate and gave up when she found herself sketching the hero in a backpack and pair of hiking boots.

It seemed it was time to embrace the great outdoors.

CHAPTER 14

*C*az sat on the sofa, cup of tea and plate of chocolate digestives within easy reach, and opened up her A4 book of accounts.

Half an hour later she shut it over with a sigh and reached for the last remaining biscuit on the plate. Her accounts were as red as her face would be if she had to go and ask her bank manager for yet another overdraft. By her calculations, even if she took another shift on at the pub, she would still only stay afloat for another six months and then Caz Lovatt, jewellery designer and businesswoman would be no more.

Feeling as if she were teetering on the edge of a cavernous black hole, Caz closed her eyes and placed her hands over her diaphragm. She took a deep breath; in through the nose... two... three... four... and out through the mouth... two... three... four... Better.

With the panic abating, Caz scuttled over to the magazine rack and picked up that month's number one best-selling self-help book. She thumbed to chapter eight, scanning down the page until she found what she was after – the subheading *Turning a Negative into a Positive.*

Having her career prospects turn to dust with no idea what to do with her life would probably be classified as negative, she figured. So how could she turn her situation into a positive? She read the instructions out loud.

"'Even though you live your life in a mentally nurturing and positive environment, you will, from time to time, be vulnerable to outside elements. At points during your life, you may find yourself in a situation you feel you have no control over. These situations are frustrating and can be spiritually stinting. You cannot be responsible for/ control others' actions and reactions. BUT YOU _CAN_ BE RESPONSIBLE FOR/ CONTROL _YOUR_ REACTION AND REACTIONS. You can influence your emotional outcome of the imposed negative situation.

There can always be a positive outcome to a situation. Make a list of these. Speak them out loud, remember, PROJECTION IS POWER. Do not allow negative thoughts to penetrate this meditative state. This is all about positive mind control. What you want to happen, make happen.

YOU are in control.

YOU can turn a negative into a positive".'

She shut the book and tried to think of a positive.

Maybe having to shut her little jewellery unit would give her a chance to explore new horizons and possibilities. Closing her shop would mean closure on that period of her life. She could move on, burst forth a butterfly (free and unshackled) from amidst the caterpillar larva (her stagnant career).

And would giving up her unit in the arcade really be that dreadful after all? At least she'd given it a go! And she couldn't say the entire _experience_ had been negative. By running her own business she had become more independent and far stronger.

A woman in charge of her own life, answerable only to herself.

Her own woman.

But had she really enjoyed being her own woman as much as she thought she would? She loved making jewellery, but she didn't love the hassle of filling in the tax returns for herself and the student she employed one day a week to cover when Caz was designing more jewellery or, more often than not lately, working a twelve-hour shift in the pub.

Looking at the clock, Caz realised with all her worrying about work, she was going to be late for it. Grabbing her bag and another biscuit, she flew out the door to catch her bus, mentally forming her own positive mantra to chant on the way.

Buzzing with healthy positive thought energy, Caz sat on the bus, not letting the ancient, ineffectual suspension mess with her auric shield. She even managed to rise above the body odour emanating from the man sitting in front of her.

As the bus stopped at traffic lights for what seemed like an eternity Caz whiled away the time chanting a self-motivation mantra, repeating, 'I am beautiful, intelligent and strong. I am beautiful, intelligent and strong...' as she idly looked out the window and into the car beside her, sitting in the filter lane waiting to turn onto the motorway. A fancy little convertible, the top was down to take advantage of the sunny day. Then Caz caught a glimpse of the man behind the wheel.

It couldn't be!

Could it?

She looked more closely at the man as he tapped his fingers on the steering wheel, banging his head in time to the music he was listening to. But she couldn't be mistaken as the man's face had been etched into her memory. She stared helplessly out the window, and then, as if sensing he was being watched, he turned round, his mouth opening in surprise when he saw her. She was right, it *was* the man she'd met briefly; the very same man that made her knees shake. Her very own Eros.

His features broke into a wide grin then he motioned using a phone and shaking his head.

'Sorry about the other night!' Caz mouthed.

'What?' he mouthed back and then the car behind him beeped its horn in impatience as the traffic light for his lane had turned green. He looked behind him and held his palm up as an apology as he turned onto the motorway.

She was torn between elation and despair. He *hadn't* just been a figment of her overactive imagination and he *was* as handsome as she remembered. But on the downside, still as unattainable as ever.

She frantically tried to turn this new negative into a positive. As a firm believer in fate, a second sighting was good, and obviously positive-thinking her own image had had a knock-on effect.

She began chanting, 'I am beautiful, intelligent and strong,' adding, 'and I *will* meet my Eros,' for good measure.

CHAPTER 15

*M*allory limped from Hall 1 to Hall 4 of her local sports centre, using her squash racket as a walking stick, trying to rise above the pain searing through her right arm and shoulder.

It was obvious she had a long way to go before reaching her physical peak, or even a physical hillock, as a lifetime eschewing exercise for the sofa caused her to sound like a geriatric with emphysema, and that was just during the brisk walk to the centre.

After her hour's squash lesson, Kevin, her instructor, told her that although she had no natural ability or grace she did have enthusiasm. More like desperation, she mused, but at least it was something to cling to.

She wasn't then able to indulge in a long soak in the bath, or even a quick shower as she still had so much to cram into her day. Considering her stress levels were at the max, she was in the perfect state of mind to benefit from her first yoga lesson, she figured, as she opened the door to Hall 4.

The weekly yoga class took place in a room resembling a mirrored cube and Mallory self-consciously made her way to the only mat not to have someone sitting cross-legged on it, hating the fact it was in the centre of the front row. Studiously avoiding her sweaty, red-faced reflection in the floor-to-ceiling mirrors, she sat on the mat. She planned on only needing a couple of visits, get a little know-how and she could wing it from there.

Bursting in on a cloud of patchouli incense, a wiry little man dressed in stripy purple trousers bounded into the room calling out greetings to the regulars. He stopped a couple of feet away from Mallory and unrolled a mat, then slowly curled down so that his forehead touched his knees then rested his palms on the floor a few inches behind his heels. Eventually he straightened up and eyeballed Mallory. 'Great! A new member. Welcome. My name is Zane and you are...?'

'Mallory,' she said quietly, feeling everyone's eyes on her, conscious of the sweat patches under her arms and down her back.

'Have you done yoga before, Mallory?'

She shook her head.

'Let me give you a little rundown on what to expect.' He spread his feet apart on the mat and breathed deeply before continuing. 'Yoga is about synchronising breath and postures to produce an internal heat which detoxifies, purifies and re-balances the body and mind. Sounds good, doesn't it?'

He slowly contorted into a shape Mallory didn't think possible – or legal – before gradually unfurling. 'And occasionally allows you to show off. But don't worry, I won't ask you to do that, just yet. It's taken me forty years to get to the stage I'm at.'

Mallory couldn't help but gawp. She'd put his age at late thirties, but if he'd been practising for forty years and hadn't started until he was...

'I'm fifty-four,' he said, helping with her calculations. 'Another good reason to practice yoga, I'm sure you'll agree.'

He moved over to a small stereo and a couple of seconds later the sound of rain, wind and animal calls filled the room. 'Right, come on, you sluggish bunch, let's get down to our first Asanas; salute to the sun.'

Half an hour later Mallory was once again sweating profusely, although she couldn't understand why, all she'd done was move into a series of positions, or Asanas, as Zane kept calling them.

'Now move into the second warrior position,' Zane called out and Mallory tried copying his graceful moves, but feeling more warthog than warrior.

'Keep the foot out, try not to turn it in. Shoulder higher, Mallory. And don't forget to breathe.'

Not relishing the thought of suffocating, Mallory took his advice and deepened her breathing as she turned her foot out.

'You're getting there, Mallory. Just straighten your back, keep the shoulders up, lengthen the right leg more, have the left leg at ninety degrees, and *breeeeeaaaaathe*. Remember that Ujjayi breathing is always through the nose. A circular breathing vessel, out and in, keep it a continuous rhythm.'

As Zane walked around, examining her posture, Mallory clamped her mouth shut and focussed on her nose, left leg, right leg, shoulders and their degree angles. All at the one time.

Unable to stop herself, she slowly keeled over onto the mat.

Zane crouched down beside her. 'Great stuff! You got into the position, just try to hold it for longer next time.'

She looked up at him and his exuberantly cheerful face, tempted to punch him on his Ujjayi breathing vessel.

'That was great, everyone!' he said, jumping up. 'Now lie down on your mats and practise breathing.'

Mallory had no idea that something she'd taken for granted could be so difficult. Lying on her mat, she breathed from her abdomen, her chest, her throat and her abdomen again. As she practised relaxing each muscle at a time, thoughts darted around her head. Elementary words from the 'Learn Italian' CD she'd listened to that morning blended with the list of equipment she'd need before she started horse-riding. She tried working out how much money she had in her bank account and how much of a balance she had on her credit card.

Then there was the salsa class she was going to go along to. The ever-lengthening 'to-do' list of jobs for Serendipity; Olly and the fact he'd been distant lately and she'd not had a chance to talk to him properly, and that she had her first driving lesson with him in just a couple of hours... and had she paid the electricity bill?... and she'd have to recharge her mobile phone... and there was no fresh milk in the house... and, and... and...

Gradually, as each muscle began to relax at Zane's modulated request, each worrying thought stretched into wings and circled higher, flapping their way out of her consciousness, leaving a vast cool expanse of relaxed space.

'Are you sure there was no one else you could have got to do this?' Olly asked Mallory forty minutes later.

Mallory nodded emphatically. 'I've been phoning round driving schools for the past couple of days, but they couldn't take me at short notice.' It wasn't a total lie. The first place she'd phoned had told her that all the instructors were booked up for the next week and no one had picked up from the second place she'd phoned. The third and final place she'd tried had quoted such an extortionate amount for the condensed weekend tuition, Mallory had to double-check she wasn't buying the car too.

And after discovering the price of horse-riding lessons she realised she would have to cut corners wherever possible.

'But what about organising lessons for next week?'

'Olly, I really need to learn as soon as possible, just in case.'

'In case of what?' he asked, baffled.

'Just, *in case*. Isn't the deserted car park a bit unnecessary?' she asked, changing the subject.

'Not until you're sure what you're doing.'

'I won't hurt your car, Olly. There's nothing I could possibly drive into, seeing as you removed that one lone trolley to beside the bottle bank.'

He gave her an uneasy smile and twisted round in his bucket seat to peer out the back and side windows. 'Okay!' he said, rubbing his palms on his thighs. 'Is your door closed?'

'What?' Mallory laughed.

'Is your door closed?' he repeated slowly, as if talking to a child.

'Of course it's closed,' she said in puzzlement. Olly knew very well that her door was closed because of the way he'd winced when she'd slammed it shut after getting in.

'Are your mirrors in place?'

'Yes, you just saw me positioning them.'

'Is your seatbelt on?'

'Olly!' Mallory pulled out the belt at her shoulder to show she was secure. 'I *have* driven a car before,' she said in exasperation. 'I had five lessons, so I know the basics.'

His tongue clicked against the roof of his mouth as he turned to look at her, appalled. 'You may have driven *a car* before, but you've never driven this. What do you see?' He waved his arm round the interior.

'A car. *Your* car. Red leather seats, a dashboard...' she guessed randomly, like a contestant on *Catchphrase*. 'A sporty black convertible car?' she added hopefully.

He shook his head pityingly at her. 'This isn't a car. This is a Maserati Spyder Cambiocorsa. It's not black – it's Nero Carbonio, with *Bordeaux* leather interiors.' He stroked his hand across the edge of his seat, as if titillating a lover. 'It has a 4200cc engine, electronic traction, heated seats, stability control, traction control, climate control. It is a magical, *heavenly*, feat of design and engineering mastery,' he said dreamily. 'When I turn on the engine I hear a symphony of music. Sirens calling out across the rocks couldn't make a sound sweeter than this car makes. Now, *please* Mallory, when you're driving it, think of all this. Respect it.'

Mallory scanned her eyes inside the interior trying to see what Olly could. To her it was a car, a method of getting a person from A to B, possibly more stylishly and speedier than in an ancient beat-up Ford Fiesta, but really, they were all the same to her.

She turned on the engine and tried to find the biting point, over-revving the engine so much that it seemed to snarl at her.

'Watch the clutch!' he warned in a strangled whisper, grasping the dashboard.

'It's fine,' she soothed, finding the point, releasing the handbrake... and immediately bunny-hopping forward.

'Check your gear!' he howled.

'Hang on, I thought I had,' she retaliated, thinking Olly maybe wasn't the best choice to go driving with after all. 'You're not doing much for my confidence.'

'You're not doing much for my nerves!' Olly gripped his seatbelt, eyes rolling fearfully.

'So, a few doughnuts would be out of the question?' Mallory joked, but seeing his face decided further attempts at humour would not make for a happy lesson.

Very slowly she applied some gas and eased off the clutch.

'What are you doing?' he asked in alarm as she headed towards the exit and indicated left.

'Going onto the main road.'

He looked at her as if she'd just announced her intention to remove his appendix with a rusty spoon.

He swallowed. 'First spend half an hour or so going through the basics, then we'll see.'

CHAPTER 16

*S*ettling down in front of the television with a big bowl of microwave popcorn for dinner, which was low in fat, had very few calories and would hopefully fill her up for hours, Caz flicked between channels for something to watch before she left for her shift in the pub.

Settling on an arts programme she munched away as she watched a review of a new French film. The critic raved about it but from the clips, it had far too many pauses in conversation which were filled with smouldering glances and meaningful shrugs to float Caz's boat. In her opinion there was no film that couldn't be improved by a few pyrotechnics and a car chase. The link went back to the studio and the presenter sat forward in her swivel chair to address the camera.

'And now we have a sense of our prodigal son returning. Last year, artist Don Marsden left Britain for the edgier fringe of the New York art scene where he was met with accolades and sell-out exhibitions. But Don has recently surprised the art world by his announcement that he is heading home with a new exhibition. Last week I went stateside to interview the *enfant terrible* of the art world.'

Caz's hand paused halfway to her mouth with some popcorn as the camera cut to another setting where Don lounged back in his chair grumpily.

Caz threw the popcorn at the screen. 'Arsehole!'

'Don, thank you for taking the time to talk to us about your forthcoming exhibition. So, the big question is, why do you want to return to Britain for your next exhibition?' the presenter asked.

'*Because everyone in America realised I was an arsehole and banished me*,' Caz said, mimicking his gruff drawl which already had traces of a pretentious American twang. She looked at the door, hand poised over the remote control, fearful Mallory would come back from her driving lesson earlier than planned. Caz knew Mallory was finally starting to get over Don, but she didn't want to risk her getting upset again by seeing him unexpectedly.

Caz turned back to the television where Don was talking.

'Drumming up some press attention for the exhibition. My agent and PR people thought it would be a good idea,' Don said tightly.

'*Oooh*, you have PR *people* now. Get you!' Caz said, eyes narrowing at the screen.

The interviewer gave a slight nod. 'But why come back to Britain at all? Your last two exhibitions in Britain, although commercially successful, weren't greeted as warmly by the critics. Why is it you feel the need to exhibit there again?'

Don looked as if he was about to chew up the presenter. He sat forward in his chair. 'First of all, I want to make it clear I'm not going back because I *have* to, but because I *choose* to. New York is an amazing city. For me, as an artist, there is an incredible buzz. I know I'm lucky to have been received so positively and I fully intend to stay here, in America.'

'Is it because you want the verification of the British critics then?'

'I don't paint for critics,' he snarled.

Caz stuck her tongue out at the television. What Mallory had seen as intense and deep about Don, Caz had always thought plain surly and rude.

'But won't this exhibition be quite a departure for you, they're all of the same subject matter, aren't they?' the presenter carried on gamely.

'They're all of the same subject, but not the same *matter*,' he said as the presenter flashed him a professional, if slightly strained smile and glanced down at her notes.

'It is a series of eight paintings depicting the beginning, middle and end of a relationship. The work stemmed from a one-off painting I completed entitled *Love Lost.*'

Caz stopped munching her popcorn. That was the painting of Mallory. Caz stopped making rude gestures at the screen and listened to what he was saying.

'And the subject matter is…' the presenter encouraged.

The camera focussed on his face.

'Someone very close to me,' he said, a nerve in his cheek flickering.

'Hah! Not anymore, mister!' Caz piped up, indignant on Mallory's behalf.

The presenter persevered. 'And this person… are you still close?'

Don hesitated. 'I see this exhibition as a cathartic expulsion of all my previous emotional baggage. You could say it's an apology. What I need to do to achieve forgiveness, mainly from myself.'

'You selfish, narcissistic ARSEHOLE!' Caz shouted.

'The last painting in the collection, *New Beginning*, is interesting. It's simply a flash of bright light, barely recognisable as the human form,' the presenter said.

'Yes. It represents purity and innocence and hope.'

'And are you hoping life will imitate art?'

Don gave the camera a chilly smile. 'I plan to start on one called *Reconciliation* very soon.'

'In your dreams!' Caz said in disbelief. Surely he couldn't be meaning Mallory. Why would he think Mallory would in any way want to even *speak* to him again, let alone forgive him or, heaven forbid, want to get back together with him!

'This series of paintings shows quite a markedly different style for you.'

'I don't believe there is any worth in an artist who doesn't evolve.'

The presenter gamely carried on. 'Yes, and I understand you'll be spending the next few weeks travelling?'

'Not so much travelling as immersing myself in another people's culture. I'll be living in Peru, studying the ancient art of the Incas.'

'We'll all look forward to seeing how that influences your work in the future.'

With obvious relief the interviewer turned back to the camera. 'You'll be able to catch Don Marsden's powerful new exhibition early next year.'

And as the presenter read out the dates of the exhibition the image of one of his paintings appeared on-screen. The subject; tall, slim, auburn-haired, was very obviously Mallory.

What an arsehole, Caz thought angrily. He and Mallory back together? As if! No doubt his 'people' had told him to say that to garner more publicity. Well, she wasn't about to tell Mallory about the interview. The last thing she wanted to do was upset her best friend for no good reason. Anyway, with any luck he'd get stranded at the top of Machu Picchu.

Forty minutes later Mallory had had enough of driving with Olly. It was akin to trawling through downtown Miami with a highly-strung maiden aunt in tow. After persuading him to let her leave the car park, each time she approached a junction or traffic lights,

Olly flapped beside her like an overwrought chicken having a panic attack, reminding her about her mirror, signal, manoeuvres.

Arriving back outside her flat (with Olly, not trusting her in busy traffic, having taken control of the driving once more) both Mallory's nerves and patience were shot.

Not even waiting until she was out of sight, Olly jumped out to inspect the undercarriage of the bodywork.

Wordlessly, she trudged back up the stairs to her flat.

Opening the door to the lounge Mallory was most puzzled to see a bowl of popcorn upturned over the top of the television.

She hoped this was a sign Caz's popcorn diet was over. She was fed up with the flat smelling like a cinema foyer.

CHAPTER 17

*T*he following Saturday, Mallory was awake and out way before the birds had even warmed up with some vocal exercises for their early morning chorus. Picking her way across a muddy field in the middle of nowhere she'd had to take a train, two buses and walk for half an hour to get to, she was ready for her first horse-riding lesson.

Having agreed to go to Alex's party and stay for the weekend, Mallory was more than a little apprehensive about what was on the agenda. She hoped there would be nothing more taxing than a little eating, drinking and possibly a low-impact ramble in the woods, but she couldn't risk it.

With Alex boasting about how much out in the country his house was and knowing he liked horse-riding, Mallory had to face up to the possibility of her encountering something equine during her time away. Seeing as the closest she'd come to a horse was playing the back end of one at a primary school play, she'd phoned round riding schools and managed to book herself a lesson at short notice.

Five girls, all looking under the age of twelve, were already sitting on their horses; backs straight, chests out, heads in the air, looking very much the future of showjumping. A bored-looking teenager, whom she presumed was the instructor, stood next to a huge auburn horse.

Mallory eyed up the horse suspiciously, hoping that it wasn't for her as she'd need scaffolding and a winch to get up onto it.

The girl handed her the reins. 'I'm Beth, this is Mars,' she said through a mouthful of bubblegum. Strawberry flavour, Mallory noted as Beth yawned widely.

'Hey Mars.' Mallory clapped his mane apprehensively, flinching slightly as he shook his great head. 'Is he named after the god of war?' she asked worriedly, not liking the connotations if he was.

'Nope.' Beth cracked her gum. 'He likes Mars bars.'

Mallory was almost knocked sideways as his nose nudged her shoulder as he snuffled against her jacket.

'Ignore him, he's just checking you over for food,' Beth said.

'Oh, I don't have anything.' But Mars had already deduced this and had returned to standing stoically, waiting to be mounted.

'Is he a liver chestnut?' Mallory asked, thinking back to the *Everything You Need To Know About Horses* book she'd borrowed from the library and skim-read in between sketching out Hercules's eighth labour – capturing the man-eating mares of Diomedes.

Beth nodded.

'He's very big,' Mallory added.

'Sixteen hands, but you'll need that for your height. I've just been telling the others we're going to start with a few easy things like walking and stopping and turning, okay?'

'Sure.' Mallory relaxed; that all sounded simple enough.

Beth turned to leave.

'Excuse me? Beth? How do I get on?' Mallory asked, ignoring the high-pitched giggles from the girls.

'You can use that mounting stool.'

Mallory eyed up the rickety wooden stool, half sunk into the mud. And just *how* did she use the mounting stool? But Beth had already gone to help one of the girls who'd started complaining loudly about the length of her stirrups.

Mars turned and appraised Mallory coolly from beneath his fabulously long eyelashes, his tail swishing lazily.

'Right then, Mars, we can do this,' Mallory whispered, holding onto the front of the saddle. She'd seen enough Western films to have gleaned a rough idea of how to get on. She secured her foot in the stirrup and heaved herself up.

As she was about to swing her right leg over, Mars took a step forward and Mallory slid off, rocking precariously on the stool before tipping forward, ending calf-deep in mud. With a great deal of effort and squelching noises, she managed to release her Wellington boot. Mars turned to look at her and Mallory could have sworn he rolled his eyes.

A haughty-looking child walked her horse over to them as Mallory dragged Mars back to the mounting stool.

'You need to be quicker, or you'll fall in the mud.'

Mallory gave her a strained smile and tried again. This time she overcompensated and practically fell headfirst over Mars's other side. With some wriggling and squirming she eventually sat upright in the saddle. She jammed her feet in the stirrups and clapped Mars's neck. He flicked his tail.

The girl looked at Mallory's legs. 'You should have worn jodhpurs, jeans chafe.' And with a toss of her head, she led the horse over towards the rest of the group.

Beth beckoned Mallory over.

Right! Now she just had to work out how to drive him. She bounced slightly on the saddle.

Mars snorted and they stayed rooted to the spot.

'Giddy-up,' she tried, to no avail.

By now the others were walking forward. Mallory very gently leaned close to his ears. 'Come on, Mars, how about following the others and not making me look like a complete prat, eh?'

With a swish of his tail, he walked forward and Mallory tried to relax into the saddle.

For the next hour they did nothing but start and stop, correct their posture and turn. As Mars followed her commands immediately and with no fuss, Mallory began to think she was a natural horse whisperer. Then, as they were walking around in a circle for the twentieth time, Mars's ears pricked up and he trotted towards the stables.

'Whoa, Mars,' Mallory said confidently as she gently kneed him in the belly, pulling the reins to the right. He ignored her. She tried again, but he carried on. 'Beth, I can't get him to turn,' Mallory called out over her shoulder.

'Do what we've been doing.'

'It's not working,' she said, pushing the riding hat out of her eyes as Mars jolted her about in the saddle.

With graceful ease Beth rode over to them, grabbed the reins from Mallory and pulled a stroppy Mars back to the group.

'What happened there?' Mallory asked a little shakily as Mars stood quietly, head slightly bowed.

'There's a new horse, Dorothy, that he's taken a shine to and he's always sneaking off to see her.'

Mars snorted in a most unattractive manner.

'But why did he ignore me? He's been following my commands up until now.'

'He's been here so long he knows the routine inside out. But we can't compete with Dorothy.' Beth chortled as Mars stomped up great clumps of earth.

'Right, we're nearly done, but before we go, we'll practice turning round in the saddle – it's called *going round the world*,' Beth called out.

'Going round the bend, more like,' Mallory muttered as she

returned to what she'd been doing at the start of the lesson – practising swinging her legs over the saddle.

And she'd come to learn if there was only one thing worse than giggling schoolgirls, it was giggling schoolgirls who had been proved right. She seethed as her jeans rasped and burned into her flesh where they'd made contact with the saddle. She was just thankful she'd brought clothes to change into before scooting off to her evening's wine-tasting group.

Heading back to the stables, walking like John Wayne with haemorrhoids, she couldn't help but laugh as little Miss Posh Jodhpurs tripped over an abandoned feed bucket and fell, face first, into the mud.

CHAPTER 18

On Saturday evening, Caz closed the door of her jewellery unit and locked it, wondering if she'd be unlocking it again on Monday morning.

Clearly she looked as miserable as she felt as Stuart and Gregor, the couple who owned the second-hand record shop, Disco Divas, next to Caz's jewellery unit, were hovering behind her, concerned looks on their faces.

'You got the letter then?' Stuart said.

Caz nodded. The letter from the arcade's landlord had been waiting for her when she'd opened up that morning to let her know the rent was being put up by a third. Caz struggled as it was and an increase was going to stretch her already taut budget even more. The irony was, she'd had the busiest Saturday for months and had sold loads of her jewellery. It had been so busy she'd not managed her usual Saturday fruit scone and cup of tea with Gregor.

'I barely manage as it is,' Caz said with a resigned shrug as she pocketed her keys. 'I'll have to take on so many extra bar shifts to make the rent I won't have time to make or even sell the jewellery. I just have to face it, I won't be here next month.'

Stuart enveloped her in a massive hug. 'It's so unfair.'

'Will you guys be okay?' Caz asked, but she knew they'd be fine as Gregor's main job was a music teacher and he only worked in his record shop on a Saturday and Stuart also worked part-time as a hairdresser and stylist.

Gregor confirmed it with a nod. 'Yeah, and we do a lot of business online so we may just focus on that if we feel it isn't worth it in the long term. Gregor gave Caz a sad smile then said, 'You never know, you might get a stand in one of the bigger shopping centres or why don't you look at getting your jewellery line into gift shops or even go online too?'

'I wouldn't bet on it, those stalls are very expensive.'

'But what will you *do*?' asked a panic-stricken Stuart, always the more dramatic of the couple.

'I don't actually know.' Caz looked up at their concerned faces. 'The thing is, this might not be all bad. You know I've been floundering with this place for a while. I wouldn't have lasted more than another few months anyway. This rent hike is the push I need to get out.' She paused before announcing the bombshell, 'I think it might be time to give up making jewellery completely.'

Saying it aloud seemed to remove the massive yoke of stress that had been sitting on Caz's shoulders.

'It's hardly been a money-spinner for me, has it?' she continued as Stuart and Gregor looked at her. 'I've being thinking for a while about a complete change of career. Possibly counselling. I mean, I read enough of the bloody books.'

Stuart gave her shoulder a squeeze. 'You know, I think that sounds a great idea.'

They all headed down the stairs and out into the early evening sunshine.

'Fancy a quick drink?' Stuart asked.

'Or coming back to ours for a takeaway?' Gregor added,

clearly both keen to raise her spirits but Caz didn't feel she needed cheering up anymore.

'Thank you but I'm going to head home.' Mallory had pinned a note to the fridge to say she'd be out until late at a wine-tasting group and Caz couldn't wait to take advantage of having the flat to herself and indulging in a long soak in the bath with a chilled glass of Sancerre to hand. Since Mallory had started on the wine courses the quality of the bottles they drank had definitely improved!

'You know to phone, anytime, if you change your mind,' Gregor said.

Promising she would, she waved them away.

Crossing the road, she decided to save the bus fare and walk home, and she paused to rummage around her bag for some chewing gum.

She didn't even notice the cyclist.

Speeding along the pavement silently, the first Caz realised he was upon her was when he yanked her bag and pulled it from her shoulder. Spinning round with the momentum, she landed on her bum on top of a pile of rubbish bags as she watched her knock-off Prada speed off into the distance.

'NO!' she wailed futilely.

She knew her purse only contained a ten-pound note and a few coins – she'd long ago learned to leave her cards at home for fear that she'd be unable to resist a spending spree, but she had a nearly full bottle of Miss Dior perfume rattling around inside. Thank goodness she'd left the cash from that day's takings in the safe at work.

Struggling to stand, she also realised she now had no keys, no perfume, no gum and had curry sauce plastered to her jeans.

Fighting back tears, she stood in the middle of the street for a couple of minutes at a loss as to what to do. Then with a cry of delight she realised she was wearing her jeans and had put her mobile in her pocket. She phoned Mallory but it went straight to voicemail.

'Mallory, if you get this in the next few minutes can you call me back, I've just had my bag stolen with my keys inside.' She ended the call and waited a few moments. Then she dialled Olly's number.

'Hey!'

'Are you home?'

'Um, sad as it is to admit on a Saturday night, yes I am.'

'Can I come over? I've just finished work and I was going to walk home and my bag was stolen and I don't have my keys and Mallory's not picking up and she's going out anyway and I don't have anywhere to go.'

'Oh, shit, Caz! Are you okay?'

'Mmhmm,' she mumbled, close to tears.

'Get a taxi, come straight round.'

'I have no money to pay for it.'

'I'll pay, my treat, just get round here.'

'If you're sure, okay, I'll see you in a few minutes. And... thanks, Olly.' Caz hung up.

As luck would have it she could see a taxi approaching with its 'For Hire' light on. She jostled her way through a large group of women celebrating a hen party, holding onto their pink Stetsons as they danced drunkenly along the street.

Caz reached her hand out to wave the taxi down, noticing too late there was someone in the back. Cursing the driver for raising her hopes, she cast a glance in the cab as it passed. Sitting beside the window nearest her, head bowed reading a paper, was *Him*, her Eros. She stood transfixed as he drove away from her. Again.

Then another cab pulled up beside her. She jumped in.

'Is that blood?' the driver asked in alarm. Caz looked down at her arm which was streaked in red.

'No, just ketchup.'

'That's a relief. Where you off to, love?'

All she needed to say was 'follow that cab', but when she looked along the road the taxi had already disappeared from sight. And she was very aware she smelled of bins.

She sat back against the seat and in a resigned voice gave the driver Olly's address.

CHAPTER 19

'Oi! Buxom barmaid, refresh my pint and give me a Diet Coke for my good friend,' Olly said to Caz as he and Mallory propped up the bar Caz worked in.

Caz gave Olly the finger and carried on emptying the glass washer. Only when she'd finished did she pour Olly and Mallory their drinks.

Since Caz's mugging a few days earlier, Olly had kept a close eye on his friend. Obviously Caz had been upset about having her bag stolen, and he knew that as well as her money worries she was also contemplating a career change. Although Caz appeared her usual bubbly self, Olly was concerned this was a façade and had been conducting some covert observation to assess her mental well-being.

Caz wiped the bottom of the glasses on the spill mats. 'Don't you two have homes to go to? I'm not in need of a babysitter, Olly. You've barely let me out of your sight since Saturday night!'

Maybe not as covert as Olly thought.

'He's worried about you, as am I,' Mallory said, sliding off her bar stool. 'I'm going to the loo, back in a minute.'

Caz came over and patted Olly's hand. 'You are incredibly

sweet to worry about me, but I assure you, I'm fine. I'm even excited at the thought of a new career. And I promise you, if I start having a breakdown, you'll be the first person I call to talk me off a window ledge. Deal?'

'Deal.'

'Can I give you some advice?' Without waiting for Olly to answer, Caz carried on. 'I think you should come right out and tell Mallory how you feel.'

Olly froze, his pint halfway to his mouth as he stared at Caz. *How did she know?* He could just deny it.

'There's no point in denying it,' Caz said, wiping down the bar top. 'I know. Have done for a while.'

Damn. 'Does…' Olly whipped round, looking out for Mallory.

'Hasn't a clue.'

Olly put his pint on the bar, feeling slightly shaky. He was so sure he'd kept his feelings hidden. 'I really don't want to lose her friendship as well by scaring her off.'

'But you're looking at the worst-case scenario. Life's too short to waste daydreaming.'

'I'm fine the way things are.' Olly shrugged, sawing a beer mat against the edge of the bar.

'I just think you should maybe hint…'

'Don't you think I haven't already? I thought maybe after Don was out the picture something would happen but I don't have his looks or his confidence. When I chat up a woman, I don't tend to get a phone number, all I get is embarrassed silence. It's the way things are.'

Caz shook her head. 'Don't, whatever you do, compare yourself to Don bloody Marsden. Yes, he has looks and confidence, but he has an ego the size of a continent and he's an utter twat. *Quick*! Here's your chance!' Caz raised her eyebrows.

'Your chance for what?' Mallory asked as she plonked herself back onto the bar stool beside him.

Olly turned, getting a subtle waft of her perfume; a combination of flowers and vanilla and general loveliness.

'Um... my chance to turn into a karaoke legend, it's the entertainment for tonight,' he improvised, noticing a poster on the door.

Mallory turned to read it, her long hair flicking round so he got a mouthful of auburn curls that tasted faintly of coconut. He loved coconut.

She turned back and gave him a heart-stopping smile. 'Great, so what'll you do? A classic like Sinatra, or a bit of glam rock?'

'Probably more like Noël *Coward*,' Caz intoned from the left.

Olly gave her a dagger of a look which she ignored.

As Caz bustled off to get another customer a drink, Mallory turned to Olly, her green eyes very close to his. They reminded him of mint juleps, not that he'd ever actually had one, or even seen one but he remembered reading a novel where the heroine's eyes were described as being as green as a mint julep and it had stuck with him.

He suddenly realised he wasn't actually listening to what she was saying.

'Sorry?'

'See? My point exactly! You're so distracted lately. How are you? I feel I haven't seen you for ages, not properly. We keep missing each other at the studio.'

'Yeah, I know, but I'm fine. Grand in fact.' He puffed out his cheeks. 'Work's not been so hectic lately so I've had a bit more free time.' He didn't bother to tell her he'd started working on a graphic novel, only realising the heroine had an uncanny similarity to Mallory and he was slightly embarrassed for her to see it, so he'd been working at home in the spare room he'd set up a drawing board in.

Mallory took a large gulp of her drink and the movement caused him to catch another whiff of her perfume.

'Want another?' Olly asked as she almost finished her Diet Coke.

'No thanks, I need to head soon and get an early night as I've got a horse-riding lesson first thing. And I've got a salsa class lined up. I'm so grateful that the yoga's helping me relax.'

'You're nuts,' Olly said. 'I don't understand why you feel you have to race through everything on your made-up CV. Why not come clean? Honesty is the best policy.' He felt a complete hypocrite giving her that advice when he was exhibit number one of the 'do as I say, not as I do' brigade.

'I know it seems a bit much, but I really do *want* to do all this and I'm having fun learning new things. Oh, I don't suppose you're free a week on Saturday?'

'As a bird.' He didn't need to check his diary, not that he owned one, but he knew there was nothing on, and even if there was he would always reschedule if it meant the possibility of spending time with Mallory.

'Fancy coming away with me for a dirty weekend?'

He practically stopped breathing.

'Don't look so panicked!' She laughed. 'I mean in the muddy sense. Alex has invited me to his country estate and he's told me it's great for walks and outdoorsy things. I could use some moral support. I thought you, me and Caz could all go, but Caz is having to work. It should be fun.'

Olly got his wits together, hoping he hadn't flushed scarlet or had given anything away when he thought, for one moment, she was propositioning him.

'Um, sure.' He nodded and took a deep swallow of his pint. He was seriously starting to wonder if he had a masochistic disorder, a secret liking for being tortured by spending as much time as possible being alone with the woman he loved who thought of him as nothing more than 'good old dependable Olly'. He really was such an idiot.

'Oh, they're starting already,' she said, looking over his shoulder.

Olly turned to see a karaoke performer taking the microphone – a woman, adorned in enough gold to clear a small nation's debt and sporting a wet-look gelled perm. She belted out Gloria Gaynor's 'I Will Survive' in a strong Glaswegian accent.

Maybe that should be his theme song. If he could survive a weekend away with Mallory and summon up enough courage to tell her how he felt, Olly was sure he could survive anything.

CHAPTER 20

*I*t was all very well writing on her CV that she loved hillwalking, horse-riding and other pastimes which embraced the great outdoors, but there was one glaringly obvious drawback Mallory hadn't quite thought out properly; they all involved her actually *being* outdoors.

While, in theory, she loved the idea of marching amidst the heather-clad hills, fleece tied round her waist, compass in hand, the reality wasn't quite as romantically winsome. Brisk walking was knackering, clouds of midgies waited to attack, and the weather was usually such that when you did manage to huff and puff it up to a vantage spot you couldn't see anything for cloud and drizzle.

And yes, there would definitely be drizzle.

She'd checked the weather forecast and it seemed the glorious summer was about to end as there was low cloud, rain and even a thunderstorm predicted for that weekend.

And she had to dress accordingly.

Mallory sighed at her reflection in the full-length mirror as she pulled up the hood on her waterproof jacket, tugging at the side cords so it tightened across her forehead. She'd spent an absolute fortune on her latest incarnation, money she could ill afford, and all it did was make her look shapeless and feel as if she was inside a mobile steam room, despite the ventilation air holes in the armpits of her jacket. In fact, she couldn't think of anything she wanted to wear *less* than something which required ventilation air holes in the armpits.

Caz whistled at her from the doorway.

Mallory struck a pose. 'Think I'll cut a swathe?'

Caz stroked her chin and circled her. 'You need some accessories.'

'As luck would have it, there's a matching rucksack.' She pointed to it lying on her bed.

'Oh, you're so on trend, dahling!' Caz belly flopped onto Mallory's bed and rummaged through Mallory's haul from the local Trespass shop. 'Glow sticks?' she queried, pulling them out and waving them above her head. 'For those impromptu raves on the moors?'

'Hardly,' Mallory said, pushing the hood back, her forehead already getting clammy underneath the nylon. 'They're to summon help if I need it.' She wondered if 'help' consisted of standby hairdressers as her hair would soon turn into a mass of frizzy curls if she was out in a drizzle for more than a minute.

'Mallory, you're going to a posh country house to drink gazillion-year-old malt whisky in front of roaring log fires,' Caz said, dropping the sticks back into the rucksack. 'I doubt very much you're going to be stranded up a mountain.'

'Munro, actually,' Mallory said, unzipping her jacket and sitting on the edge of the bed. 'I've been reading up about them.'

'Scintillating, I'm sure,' Caz said, feigning a yawn.

Mallory didn't admit to not getting beyond the introduction. 'I'm going to make the most of this weekend. I think it'll be fun,' she added, trying to convince herself as much as Caz. The truth was she was terrified about the numerous potential areas for disaster the weekend could bring by spending so much time with Alex and Nik, not to mention Louisa and her 'PR vehicle' party.

Mallory untied her hiking boots, dismayed to already feel the skin on her heels beginning to tingle at the contact against the rigid material. She'd need to get some heavy-duty blister plasters on the way.

'A thermal blanket?' Caz said, returning to the contents of the rucksack. She rubbed it against her cheek. 'Aw! I can just see you and Alex, snuggled under this, gazing up at the stars and nibbling on a Kendal mint cake.'

'There will be no nibbling of anything!' Mallory said firmly, snatching the blanket off her and cramming it back in the rucksack. 'Are you sure you can't come?' It would be so much fun if Caz could join her and Olly but although she'd been attempting to wear Caz down for days, Caz was adamant she couldn't join them.

'You know I'd love to,' Caz said dejectedly, 'but I need to work in the pub to save money.'

'I can lend you some.'

'No, you can't,' Caz said firmly. 'This is my responsibility. And you need all your money, I saw the price of all this gear, remember. Anyway, you'll have Olly to play with.'

As if on cue Mallory's mobile pinged.

She read the text then looked at her watch. 'Olly's just leaving. Shit! I've not packed yet!' She threw her phone on the bed. 'I've no idea what to wear!' she said, opening her wardrobe wide and surveying it, but all the clothes swam in front of her as she had a full-on fashion panic attack, unable to think what would be suitable.

There was only one thing for it; scooping most of her clothes out, she threw them, hangers and all, into her case. Then she picked up her travel kettle and wedged it down the side along with a jar of coffee and a few tea bags.

'Seriously?' Caz said.

Mallory threw in some toiletries on top. 'You know I need my regular caffeine fix.'

Caz helped by squashing everything down as Mallory zipped it up.

§♣

Olly's tuneless whistling woke Mallory. Sitting up and hastily wiping off a bit of drool from the car door interior, she rubbed her eyes and looked to where Olly was peering out of the windscreen: an open gate leading onto a long drive.

'Are we here?'

'According to the satnav we are.'

Olly drove slowly over the cattle grid and made his way along the tree-lined drive.

'This looks really pretty.'

'Yeah,' Olly agreed, wincing as the car drove into a pothole.

Mallory had a quick check in the sun visor's mirror and fluffed up her hair on the side she'd been sleeping on.

'Bloody hell!' Olly said as they turned a corner. 'You didn't mention we'd be staying at a stately home!'

From the angle they approached it, it looked like one of the houses filmed at the start of the *Antiques Roadshow*. Nestled in a large clearing and flanked by Scots pines, Mallory could see round the side of the house where an army of workers were busy; some carrying flowers, others outside heaters and a few vans were loaded up with cases of wine and beer. 'Seems to be a lot of trouble for a small gathering,' Olly said as he rolled the car forward and up the impressive sun-dappled drive.

'Alex said there was going to be press, Louisa the PR person arranged it,' Mallory said, stifling a yawn and rolling her neck. For all Olly's 'respect the car' antics and 'design classic' enthusiasm, it hadn't been that comfortable to sleep in. 'Alex also said we should park round the back.'

As Olly followed the drive along the side of the house, more vans came into view.

'How many are expected?'

'I've no idea,' Mallory said. 'I know Alex had thought it would just be his good friends and some locals, but Louisa took matters into her own hands and rounded up a few more. It was one of the reasons he wanted the weekend house guests to come earlier; so we wouldn't get caught up in the chaos.

'Oh, I think that's Nik there.' Mallory pointed over to a crowd of folk carrying cases of wine towards a marquee.

'Why don't you go and say hello and I'll bring the bags in.'

'Thanks, Olly!' Mallory said as she got out of the car and stretched. Walking towards the house she couldn't help but feel a little flutter of excitement at what the weekend might bring.

CHAPTER 21

*A*s Mallory disappeared off towards the group, Olly parked the car and retrieved the luggage from the boot, doing a double-take when he saw just how much Mallory had brought. He took great pride in the fact that no matter where he was going or how long for, he always managed to squeeze everything into his rucksack – even if he did spend half an hour squashing everything down to make it fit.

It took him a few minutes to wrestle with Mallory's luggage, loading everything up so he didn't need a second trip. He couldn't understand what she'd packed as he staggered towards the entrance; it was a long weekend they were away for, not an eight-week cruise!

He got to the steps leading up to some decking as a young woman strode towards him from the other direction carrying two dead plucked chickens by the feet, blood splattered all down the front of the apron she was wearing.

Olly stopped a moment, taking in the sight.

She smiled at him. 'Hi.' Then her face fell. 'Oh bum, you're not press are you?'

'No, I'm not press, I'm a guest, Mallory's friend.'

The woman's smile returned. 'Oh, she's the designer of the restaurant, yes, I've heard all about her. I'm Irini.'

He went to shake her hand but couldn't loosen a hold of the luggage for fear the lot would topple over. At the same time Irini seemed to realise her yellow Marigolds were also splattered with blood and she quickly withdrew her hand.

'It's nice to meet you.' She smiled, pushing her brown tousled pixie-cut hair from her eyes with her forearm. 'I'm afraid we're a wee bit behind. The security firm wanted to do a recce first thing this morning and banned us from the house for hours. You shouldn't be seeing this.' She laughed and brandished the chickens. 'It's part of tomorrow's dinner.'

'That's a relief, I was worried there was going to be some ritual sacrifice.'

'Hardly! The magazine would pull out, screaming. It wouldn't fit with the usual coverage of afternoon teas and posh soirées. Let me dump these and I can help you with the bags.'

'No, no, they may look heavy but they're deceptively light,' he said, attempting to straighten up under their weight.

She raised an eyebrow but said nothing.

'This is some place. Do you work here?'

'More of a case of getting roped in. The usual housekeeper had a fit of the vapours when she heard about the upheaval, so Alex gave her the week off and it's a case of all hands on deck.'

'You're a friend of Alex's?'

'Yeah, my brother Nik and he went to school together so I've known him forever.'

'Nik, as in Alex's business partner?'

'The very one.'

They stood for a moment and watched as a photographer unloaded light-diffusers and a ton of equipment.

'You know, Alex wasn't expecting it to be like this,' Irini said. 'He thought it was going to be a photographer with a digital camera and a few selected guests.'

'How could he not know what his own party was going to be like?'

'He didn't organise it. The magazine supply all this. As a result, Alex has gone to ground with a bottle of malt.'

Olly, trying not to look too pained as he struggled for breath under the weight of the bags, was mightily glad when Irini said, 'Come on in and I'll show you where you're staying.' She walked into a lovely farmhouse-style kitchen where she put down the chickens and removed her gloves then led the way through the house, nodding at the doors on the way past, pointing out the boot room, dining room, lounge and study. There were other doors but Olly guessed they were on a need-to-know basis only.

Eventually they came out into a large reception hall, which he realised would be at the front of the house. It was very formal with a dark oak staircase lined with red carpet and brass runners leading to the upstairs. A large chandelier hung imposingly from the ceiling. It was very grand, if a little austere.

The staircase was wide with a stained-glass window at the half landing where the stairs branched off symmetrically into two other staircases which led to the floor above.

Olly knew very little about Alex Claremont, but he was surprised this was the kind of house he'd choose.

As if reading his mind, Irini said, 'It's really Alex's dad's house, Louisa insisted the backdrop to the article had to be somewhere grand. Nik and Alex would have preferred to have had it at the restaurant site but evidently that wasn't good enough. Anyway, you're staying in the yellow room. Take the right-hand stairs, follow the corridor round and you're about halfway along on the left. You'll know it's the right room because, well, it's yellow. You're opposite Mallory, she's in the floral room.'

'Cheers.' He started up the stairs, his knees nearly buckling under the weight of Mallory's bags.

'Are you sure I can't help you with those?' she called up to him.

'Positive, I've got it covered – you go wrestle with your chickens.'

'Okay then. I'll see you later.'

'Sure.' He attempted to give her a nonchalant thumbs up but only succeeded in dropping his rucksack. They both watched it bounce down the stairs, the zip bursting open and a pair of particularly lurid Green Goblin-patterned boxers landing on Irini's feet.

CHAPTER 22

*M*allory's room was well named; never in her life had she been surrounded by so many floral patterns. From the wallpaper to the curtains to the duvet cover, every metre of fabric had either roses or daisies or dahlias printed on it. Even the paintings on her wall were of flowers. On checking out the en suite, she found it also had wallpaper adorned with a pattern of large poppies, and the soap was scented with quite an overwhelming rose fragrance.

From first impressions, Mallory thought it was all very grand and she could relate to how Elizabeth Bennet felt on seeing Pemberley for the first time.

Being in such sumptuous surroundings only made it even harder to decide what to wear. All her clothes were strewn across her bed – and she tried to survey them without being distracted by the busy cottage garden pattern on the duvet beneath them all. But despite having brought most of her wardrobe she was having a fashion-freeze moment. And time was marching on!

It hadn't helped that she'd lost a couple of hours soaking in the sumptuously deep bath as she listened to Learn Italian on her iPod. She'd lost track of time and only when her skin had started to prune had she jumped out, wrapped herself in a towel (with a rose motif border) and sifted through her clothes. Usually, she could swoop in and select the perfect outfit in seconds but not tonight; as she tried on and ruled out more and more, she was seriously starting to consider wearing only the towel.

She'd already discarded half her clothes for being too formal, too casual or just plain wrong – like the brushed cotton lilac pyjamas emblazoned with kittens her grandmother had given her for her Christmas which she'd thrown into her wardrobe hoping never to see again but had scooped up into her case without realising.

Not knowing whether to go for funky, sexy, sophisticated or trendy, she ended up plumping for what she hoped was classically understated and picked out a black, silky, slash-neck dress which she'd forgotten she owned as it had been jammed at the back of the wardrobe.

With no time to do her hair, she let it hang loose down her back in voluminous auburn curls. Slipping her feet into her ancient and well-worn cowboy boots and accessorising with a chunky belt and some of Caz's jewellery, she finally left her room, realising she'd missed the window of fashionably late and had lapsed into rudely tardy. Olly, bored waiting for her, had knocked on her door half an hour earlier to tell her he was in need of a drink and would see her at the party.

Traipsing downstairs, Mallory remembered why the dress had been jammed at the back of her wardrobe; the neckline was so wide and the material so slinky, it kept slipping off her shoulders, threatening to become a belt if she wasn't careful. And walking was a problem too, as the bottom of the dress kept gathering too much static and inched up her thighs and she kept having to haul it back down. Her boots, although looking very cool, were already starting to rub away at the soles of her bare feet and by the time she arrived downstairs she felt completely flustered. She contemplated going back to her room and changing but knew another root about her clothes wouldn't unearth a fabulous designer outfit she'd overlooked the first time.

Knowing that Alex had demanded all non-staying guests were to keep to the grounds, Mallory headed along the corridors to the back of the house, forcing herself not to get distracted by all the beautiful rooms on the way; she had all weekend to explore. Squeezing past the burly security policing the doors, Mallory took a couple of steps into the gardens before stopping abruptly.

There must have been almost two hundred people milling about. Alex had told her there would be food and, used to her friends' outdoor parties where everyone chipped in and brought some beers and a couple of sausages for the barbeque, she was a little taken aback to see an entire catering team poled up on the expanse of lawn with a champagne tent alongside.

The word 'party' conjured up good friends chatting over wine and beer and a bit of cheesy music on the stereo. Even knowing that the press were covering it, she still hadn't realised it would be quite as, as... well, *footballers' wives!*

She did a double-take when she saw an ice sculpture in the middle of the lawn. Bizarrely it looked like a rake, a sail and a lollipop propped against a boat. It took her a minute to realise it was a knife, fork, plate and spoon against a bowl obviously in honour of the restaurant. Mallory was lucky if she even remembered a bag of ice for the gin and tonics when she was having a party.

Feeling well and truly out of her depth she stood for a moment, socially paralysed, as she scanned the crowd for Olly, Alex or Nik.

They weren't to be seen, so taking a deep breath, she migrated towards the champagne tent. Helping herself to a glass and anchoring down the hem of her dress with her other hand, Mallory had another glance around the garden but still didn't see anyone she knew, although some of the guests did seem vaguely familiar, no doubt the 'faces' Louisa had organised.

'Oi love!'

Mallory turned as a guy thrust a bottle of champagne at her.

'Stop gawping and top up the glasses.'

Too stunned to say anything, she mutely took the bottle and as she did, another woman dressed in a classically understated silky black dress walked up to her with a tray of empty bottles.

'This is a right thirsty lot,' she said, grabbing another two bottles, 'especially the premier league footballers,' she added, sashaying back over to a group of guys Mallory couldn't have picked out in a line-up. Mallory looked about her, at the other folk topping up glasses of champagne. She was dressed the same as the waiting staff.

Clutching the champagne to her chest, Mallory had a horrible flashback to the days of the school discos when she'd also hovered on the periphery, too tall and gawky to fit in, always looking for someone she knew to talk to. She never seemed to be wearing the right clothes then either.

With the passing years though, the refreshments had improved, chilled champagne was far more palatable than warm flat cola. She sipped from her glass of champagne and shivered slightly as the September sun slipped away. Taking the bottle as well as her glass with her, she headed towards the much warmer-looking marquee.

CHAPTER 23

$\mathcal{M}$allory heard Louisa's clipped tones before she saw her; ordering a very pissed-off-looking Nik to go back to the kitchen in the main house to get his picture taken.

Mallory was about to double back to the champagne tent figuring waitressing was preferable to suffering the wrath of Louisa but Nik had already spied Mallory and was heading her way.

'This is a fucking nightmare, please don't make me go through this alone,' he said, taking her hand and pulling her after him. 'Louisa has completely railroaded the party and we now have a full-on PR exercise on our hands.'

'Where's Alex?'

'That's what I'd like to know. At this moment I could quite cheerfully string him up. He's not answering his mobile. Come on.'

Nik turned and stomped towards the house.

'I didn't think we were allowed inside,' Mallory said, hurrying after him into the kitchen.

'Louisa beat him down to letting the magazine folk access to this room.'

Luckily, on a similar scale to the rest of the house, the kitchen was large enough to contain a photography crew plus hangers on. Behind all the cables and lighting equipment Mallory could see it was a beautiful room, very much a country kitchen, with a flagstone floor, big Aga and an old sagging sofa next to it which was covered in cushions all with crocheted covers. A large oak table took prominence in the middle of the floor.

'What a lovely room,' Mallory said, gazing up at a shelf full of antique-looking teapots.

'It's great, isn't it?' Nik agreed, his face momentarily softening. 'Mrs Young, the housekeeper, insisted on a homely feel and threatened to walk out if Alex's father made it too like the rest of the house. It's just as well she's not here this weekend as she'd definitely be locking horns with *him*.' He nodded over to the photographer who was barking instructions at his young nervy-looking assistant.

As if sensing an audience, he looked up from repositioning the light-diffusers.

'Who's this?' he asked, eyebrows raised as he gave Mallory a once-over.

'Hi, I'm Mallory.'

'She's the artistic director of Serendipity. She should be in the shots too,' Nik said as he was manhandled back into place. 'Sorry,' he whispered to her, 'but I don't want to suffer alone anymore.'

'She won't do,' the photographer said after taking a couple of sample shots of her. 'She's wearing a white bra and the flash will pick it up and it'll look like she has glowing orbs under the black dress in the photographs.'

Everyone, including Louisa, turned to look at Mallory's chest.

'I, um, didn't have a black strapless bra,' she said, crossing her arms in front of her. Despite throwing most of her wardrobe in the cases, she'd managed to completely bypass her underwear drawer.

As the photographer and Louisa discussed the situation, Nik grabbed a moment to speak to Mallory. 'Can you go up and see if Alex is hiding out in his room? If he is, drag him back down while I finish up with David flamin' Bailey over there.'

Glad to escape Louisa and the photographer, Mallory slipped out of the kitchen and made her way to the great hall and started up the stairs only then realising she had no idea where Alex's room was. At the point the stairs branched out, she picked the left side and headed up, tentatively knocking on the first door and opening it a crack.

It had clothes strewn across the bed and unless Alex was a closet cross-dresser with a penchant for shift dresses and lacy black underwear, it belonged to one of the other weekend guests. The next had more masculine clothes and toiletries but was also empty. The third room was full of storage boxes and canvases propped against the walls. She was about to leave again when curiosity got the better of her and she had a closer look at the artwork.

Nearly all the paintings were unframed. She picked up the first one, a fabulous oil painting of a horse, as finely executed as any Delacroix. Her fingers traced over the shiny coat of the beast, rippling with life and practically rearing out of the canvas. She was impressed. There were a dozen or so other equine paintings, all equally beautiful. Intrigued, she went over to the other wall where there were even more canvases.

She became engrossed as she looked through them; each was exquisite. There were rich-toned life studies, of which the chiaroscuro was stunning and obviously had more than a little nod towards Caravaggio. There were elegant portraits, which really made Mallory gasp as the skin tones rivalled the luminosity of Ingres' work.

She tried to make out the signature on the bottom right of them all but it was too much of a squiggle.

It was only on hearing a floorboard creak in the room next door that she remembered she was meant to be finding Alex. Reluctantly she put down the paintings and closed the door behind her. At the next room she knocked quietly before poking her head round the door.

Alex stood at the far end of the room, his back to her, looking out onto the garden below. A case lay open on the bed, clothes strewn over the entire room and a towel lay crumpled on the floor.

Mallory stood in the doorway, not sure what to say, not even sure she'd be a welcome interruption as his stance seemed tense and unfriendly.

'You know, I don't even know a tenth of the people down there,' he said, not bothering to turn round. 'Bunch of free-loading sycophants,' he whispered.

Mallory wondered if he actually realised there was someone else in the room with him as he could easily have been talking to himself, or maybe he thought she was Nik.

'Um, I'm not Nik,' she said, instantly realising how ridiculous she sounded.

'I'm bloody glad,' Alex replied and she could hear the smile in his voice. 'I'd really wonder what had got into him if he'd started to wear jasmine perfume, not to mention the off-the-shoulder look.'

Mallory hoisted the dress's neckline back into place, realising that he could see her reflection in the glass as the sky outside had darkened considerably.

'The rain's not far away,' she observed. 'Looks like it's going to bucket down. The whole weekend is meant to be stormy, with thunder and lightning predicted too.'

Alex turned to look at her and took a swig from his glass, of what looked like a very generous measure of whisky. 'Did you come up here to deliver the weather forecast?'

'I actually came to see if you're coming downstairs for the photographer.'

'He can fuck off.' Alex turned back to the window.

Nik had warned her Alex was in a mood. Regardless, she walked into the bedroom and over to the window where she stood beside him, looking down at the guests.

'You must know *some* people here,' she said, watching as a few umbrellas went up and people headed for the marquee.

'Hardly anyone. They're all here for the free booze. And the publicity. That lot down there can smell a journalist and a photographer at a hundred paces. It's all part of Louisa's *momentum gathering* PR campaign.' He said it with such disdain, Mallory wondered if he'd missed the irony, considering he was usually photographed at functions exactly like this one.

He took another swig of his drink.

'Louisa sent out the invitations,' Alex added, cradling the glass to his chest, 'but it looks like a lot on my list got a bit waylaid in the post. Luckily though, all the movers and shakers and well-known faces got included.'

He swallowed down his sarcasm with another swig. 'I managed to phone the neighbours and a few of my local friends at the last minute. I know they're probably far too rough and ready for Louisa, being ordinary everyday folk, but they should be here. If not, I could imagine them thinking I've got airs and graces above myself.'

Nik was right, Alex was in a foul mood.

'Is Johan here?'

'Another one Louisa *forgot* to contact.' Alex rested his glass on the windowsill. 'I called him this morning but he already had plans. No doubt if I hadn't told you and Nik in person you wouldn't be here either, but thank God you are as I don't want to be going through this alone.' He turned and gave her a look of such intensity he seemed to bore into her retinas.

Mallory tried to ignore the fizzing sensation which had started up in her stomach again. 'Nik's going through it alone.'

Alex bowed his head. 'Did he send you off on a search and find mission?'

'Yup, so do I have to go back down there and tell him that the target is hostile and unwilling to cooperate?'

He sighed and closed his eyes, leaning his head against the windowpane.

'Alex, if you hate it so much, why go along with it?' She really couldn't work Alex out. He seemed to have spent a large part of his life in magazines, as far as she could tell.

He turned and looked at her as if he was about to speak then stopped when he glanced down at the bottle of champagne she still clutched.

'You bring gifts!'

'I nabbed it from the champagne tent.'

He checked the label. 'Could you not have nabbed something vintage?' He gave her a ghost of a wink. 'Oh well, needs must.' He took a swig and handed her the bottle. 'Sorry, but apart from a toothbrush holder I don't have any other glasses up here.'

She took a swig, imagining the looks of horror on the faces of her wine appreciation group. They would certainly not approve of drinking from the bottle as her first meeting had all been about studying the colour and clarity of wine in the glass. It had seemed an eternity before she even got to sniff the damn stuff.

The sky had turned a dusky grey and the last of the natural light made Alex's pale-grey eyes glow ethereally as he turned to her.

'I wasn't sure you were going to make an appearance. I thought you maybe saw who was here and decided to stay in your room.'

She felt a tingle of pleasure that he'd noticed she was late. 'Time ran away with me a bit.' She took another swig and managed to spill champagne down herself.

'But it does mean you're now part of this pantomime.'

She wiped her chin with the back of her hand. 'Isn't there another way you can get publicity without having to sell–'

'Our souls?' he finished for her, cocking his head and looking at her through his dark lashes.

She had been about to say 'sell out' but realised it could possibly have come across as rude. 'I sincerely hope *I've* not made a pact with the devil,' she said with a small laugh.

He smiled faintly. 'I suppose I should view it as a necessary evil. I'm focussing on when everyone gets taxied out of here later tonight.' His eyes found hers again. 'Then we can start to enjoy ourselves a whole lot more.'

A little shiver of anticipation ran up her spine.

Then Louisa's voice wafted up the stairs, calling for Alex and giving Mallory a shiver of an entirely different kind.

'Bugger!' Alex groaned.

'Game's over.'

He winked. 'Not necessarily.'

'But…' Mallory glanced back at the door. Louisa didn't strike Mallory as the type of person who'd take 'no' for an answer.

'Do you really want to go back down there?' he whispered.

She couldn't think of anything worse.

'Shhh!' he said with a grin and, grabbing hold of her hand, he pulled Mallory across to the other side of the room and through a door which turned out to be a massive cupboard, but with all his clothes hanging up and rucksacks and shoes and boxes littering the floor it was more squash-in than walk-in.

'Where are you taking me, Narnia?' Mallory said and gave a laugh as she followed him in.

Alex hushed her again and grabbed the key then shut the door, plunging them into darkness. Reaching behind her he quietly put in the key and turned it, locking them in.

Pressed up with her back against the door there was only a

whisker's breadth between her and Alex and she could feel the belt buckle on his jeans, pressing against her.

'Alex?' Louisa's voice became louder.

Mallory jumped when, a few seconds later, the cupboard door handle rattled brusquely. It jabbed painfully into her behind and she jettisoned forward, straight into Alex. Pinning her against him, he briefly pressed his index finger against her lips, bidding her to keep quiet.

CHAPTER 24

*C*rushed up against Alex's chest, Mallory was very aware of the heat emanating from his body through the cotton of his shirt and the only way to keep her balance was to snake the hand not holding the champagne round his back. In that position she couldn't help but notice how toned and muscular he felt and it took incredible willpower not to run her hands up his back.

And he also smelled delicious! With her face mere millimetres from his chest, she caught the subtle cedarwood and musk scent of his aftershave mingling with the whisky on his breath. The entire situation was proving to be quite distracting.

She tried to push herself away from him slightly but he continued to pin her to him and she was certain she could feel his thumb idly stroking the ends of her hair against her back, sending little pinpricks of electricity through her body.

Through the heady closeness of Alex, Mallory could hear Louisa talking on her mobile phone from the other side of the door.

'I've no bloody idea where he's gone... yes... disappeared.'

Mallory became aware of Alex shaking, not just a slight tremor, it seemed his entire body was shuddering uncontrollably.

She hoped he wasn't having some sort of fit brought on by claustrophobia but, as his head landed on her shoulder, she realised he was trying to keep in laughter.

And the situation *was* bloody funny! Two grown adults hiding in a cupboard from an overzealous PR woman.

Mallory felt a giggle bubbling up inside her, which only seemed to make Alex worse as he jammed his mouth against her shoulder.

'I'm going to check the pub in the village about half a mile away as there's a strong possibility he's slipped out. He was working his way down a bottle of malt when I last saw him... bloody typical.' Louisa's voice was getting fainter as she left the room.

Still terrified to make too much noise, Mallory and Alex stayed in the same position for a couple of minutes, wheezing with laughter.

'Do you think she's gone?' Alex whispered; his lips close to her ear.

'Yeah, I think the coast's clear,' she whispered back, her body tingling from the sensation of his breath on her skin.

'I'm sorry, I nearly gave the game away.' He laughed into her shoulder, his hands slipping down to rest on her hips. 'I realised how ridiculous we must look.'

Mallory swallowed. The dark was making her super aware of all her other senses; touch being the most prevalent, as his hands burned hot as branding irons through her dress.

'We must look pretty funny.' Mallory's voice felt unnaturally tight in her throat.

'Do you think we could get away with hiding here all night?'

Mallory had a sudden flash of spending the night stuck in the cupboard with Alex and what they could do to pass the time. Even though it was dark, she closed her eyes. Oh God! Had she completely taken leave of her senses? She didn't go for men like Alex, but here she was having hot lusty thoughts about him!

'It's your party. You can't abscond,' she said, hoping she sounded like she meant it.

'Surely,' he said in barely more than a whisper, 'if it's my party I can do whatever I like.'

Dearly wanting to know what it was he'd like to do she managed to stay cool. 'And that involves standing in a small dark room which is running low on oxygen?'

'We could always sit.'

She laughed. 'There are people waiting for you downstairs.'

'I would tell them you held me prisoner.'

'You dragged me here!'

'You willingly followed.' Alex carried on blithely. 'You even brought your own refreshment. Well, I'm presuming it's the bottle of champagne which is the long hard thing pressed against my thigh, unless there's something you've not told me?'

'You were the one who locked us in.'

'You're nearest the key.'

'Ah, but you're restraining me.' She tapped his hand which still rested on her hips.

'You're barring my exit.'

'You... you're infuriating!'

'And yet, you still aren't leaving,' he whispered, his breath tickling her collarbone.

Oh bugger, he was right. She was far too keen on the delicious sensations at being so close to him.

Just then Alex's phone rang.

And rang.

'Shouldn't you get that?' Mallory asked.

'Should I? I've managed to avoid answering it all evening.'

'It could be important.'

There was a pause. Then he reached into his pocket. As he answered the phone Mallory quickly unlocked the door behind her.

'Yes, Nik,' Alex said tetchily, 'she found me. We're coming down. No, it's fine. Yes, I know.'

Back out into the light of the bedroom Mallory smoothed down her dress and took another large swig of champagne as Alex collected his whisky glass from the windowsill.

Without checking to see if Alex was following, Mallory bolted from the room and down the stairs to the great hall where she almost collided with Louisa and a tall, thin, dark-haired woman carrying a small dictaphone.

'Oh! Hi Louisa,' Mallory said, trying to sound as casual as possible, even though her stomach lurched guiltily, which was ridiculous as nothing had gone on between her and Alex. Well, nothing outside her furtive imagination.

But Louisa wasn't looking at her, she was looking over her shoulder, eyes glittering angrily.

Mallory turned to see Alex ambling down the stairs. He stopped beside her, drained his whisky and handed the empty glass to Louisa.

'Fiona wants to do the interview now,' Louisa said testily.

'Once I get another drink,' Alex said as he walked past her, towards the kitchen.

'You've had enough,' Louisa snapped, close on his heels. Mallory saw Fiona scribble down shorthand in her notepad as they followed.

In the kitchen Nik stormed over to them, seething. 'About bloody time! I swear I'm going to ram a blasted spatula up that photographer's arse in a minute! I need some of that,' he said, spying the champagne Mallory still clutched to her chest. 'He wants to see you next,' Nik added, turning to Alex.

'Fine, I'm ready for my close-up, Mr DeMille.'

'What about the interview?' Louisa snapped.

'Oh, don't worry about that, I can wait,' Fiona said calmly, settling into a chair.

'And you might want to remove the make-up from your shirt

first,' Nik added to Alex in a low voice, with an ever so slightly raised eyebrow.

Mallory was mortified to see her shade of lipstick smeared just below Alex's collar.

Alex merely peered down at it and laughed. 'That'll get them talking.' Taking the bottle from Mallory, he poured himself, Mallory and Nik a glass each, not even attempting to remove the make-up.

Louisa practically incinerated Mallory with the hatred in her eyes. Mallory turned away and swallowed yet another large glug of champagne, welcoming the slightly numbing effects of the alcohol.

'I now know how Kate Moss feels on a *Vogue* fashion shoot,' Nik said with a long-suffering sigh.

'Nik,' Mallory whispered, grabbing his arm, as the photographer commandeered Alex. 'I know it looks bad with my lipstick on his shirt, but nothing happened between me and Alex.'

Nik didn't look convinced.

'Really! It must have rubbed off onto him while we were hiding in the cupboard.' She could feel her face begin to flush as she realised how ridiculous her excuse sounded.

Nik paused; glass raised halfway to his lips.

'It was a very *small* cupboard. It was to get away from Louisa.'

He threw his head back and laughed. 'That has to be the lamest excuse I've ever heard! It's priceless!'

'It's what happened! It was totally innocent,' Mallory added as indignantly as possible, trying to block out the memory of what Alex's body felt like rammed up against hers.

'You know, I do actually believe you. You've got far more sense than to fall for him. But I don't think it's me you need to convince,' he added with a knowing look towards Louisa.

CHAPTER 25

*M*allory took another large swig of champagne. 'I'm so confused.'

'So you keep saying.' Olly nodded. 'And now I am too because you won't tell me what you're confused about.'

'You're not Caz. I need Caz.' Mallory looked at her phone hopefully, but there were no bars of signal. She blinked as her wallpaper photo of a soufflé started to blur out of focus.

'There'll be a landline phone somewhere here.'

'Would it be secure?'

'Well, I'd put money on MI5 having better things to do than listen in.'

'But what if the calls go through a switchboard or are recorded?' Mallory couldn't risk Alex playing back her call seeing it was Alex she needed to talk to Caz about!

'We're not in a spy novel!'

Mallory shook her head. 'Can't risk it.'

'If you need to talk just pretend I'm Caz,' Olly said helpfully. 'I can bang on about weird shit and psychobabble if it makes you feel better.'

Mallory swiped Olly's arm.

'Ow! That hurt!'

'Good! Don't be so mean! Apart from being able to help me with the confusion thing, I really need Caz for her underwear.' She checked to make sure no one else was in earshot before explaining. 'I completely forgot to bring any and I've only got the bits I arrived in. Not even a black bra!' She peered down her top at the white bra which had offended the photographer so much. 'I'll have to go commando unless...' she sat forward, with a sudden great idea, 'I borrow yours!'

'But I didn't bring my black bras either.'

'NO! I mean pants. Oh, it's not Y-fronts you have is it? Commando would be preferable to Y-fronts.'

Olly looked very uncomfortable and Mallory felt a fit of the giggles bubbling up to the surface. He could get so embarrassed about the silliest of things!

'Why don't you ask Louisa or one of the other women who're staying the weekend. There's Nik's sister Irini,' Olly suggested.

'I bet it *is* Y-fronts! Go on, let me have a look.' She snapped at the waistband of his skinny jeans and he backed away from her.

'For all you know I may go commando too,' he joked, trying to act cool even though he was blushing to the roots of his sandy blond hair.

'That would be very risqué! Okay, I'll bet you another driving lesson in your car, if you do.'

Her bluff worked as he looked aghast and quickly backed down. 'Eh, no, you're all right. I wear boxers and I've only brought enough for my own needs. I'll away and find Irini as I'm sure she can help.' With that he bolted off outside again.

With the ghastly magazine people gone, and therefore the majority of the guests, and the rain starting up, Alex had relaxed the 'no house' rule and now the kitchen was a hive of activity. Squeezing past a group of Alex's neighbours, Mallory made a beeline for the wine and poured herself some more, realising she'd probably had enough when she overshot the glass and splattered Pinotage over the kitchen counter.

Grabbing the dishcloth beside her she mopped it up, realising too late she was using a scarf; her heart sank as she realised it was silk and Hermès.

'Shitshitshitshitshit!' Darting over to the massive Belfast sink, she shook the scarf out, watching red wine drops land on the white ceramic before rinsing it under the tap and wringing it out.

'Hi Mallory, can I possibly do a quick interview?'

Mallory whipped round to find Fiona, the journalist, a couple of feet away.

She quickly hid the scarf behind her back. 'Um, right now?'

Fiona nodded.

'Ooooooooooookay! What would you like to know?'

'Well…' Fiona looked round as another gaggle of half-cut guests staggered in from the garden. 'Do you mind if we sit down, I've been on my feet all evening.'

'Sure!' Behind her back, Mallory managed to wring out some more of the water from the scarf and hooked it over the back of her belt. 'I'll just get my wine.' Still facing Fiona, she sidestepped back over to where she retrieved her wine glass, topping it up carefully. 'Bit of a drinking problem.' She laughed, pointing to the puddle of wine, then checked herself at who she was talking to. 'Not that I'm an alcoholic, I was making a joke.'

'Relax.' Fiona laughed. 'You don't have to watch everything you say, I'm really only after a bit of padding. Alex wasn't exactly forthcoming so we'll need to include some information about you and Nik. Maybe make it a more general lifestyle piece than solely focussed on him.'

Seeing how cantankerous Alex had been with the journalist earlier, Mallory felt quite sorry for her, she was only trying to do her job after all. Mallory held up the bottle of wine. 'Can I pour you a glass?'

'I've got the car, but I suppose I could have a small one. I wouldn't normally but it's been a bloody long day, not made any easier by having such a reluctant subject.'

Fiona watched as Mallory fetched another glass from the cupboard.

'Sorry to ask, but I don't suppose I could have something to eat? I missed dinner and the catering lot have cleared up and are away now.'

'Of course.' Sure Alex wouldn't mind her trying to keep the journalist sweet, she grabbed a terrine of pâté from the fridge and half a baguette from the bread bin. Mallory now knew her way around the kitchen due to hiding out in it for the entire evening.

Having felt a little out of her depth with all the famous faces, and keen to avoid Louisa, Mallory had taken sanctuary in the cosy room. She'd even helped out the catering staff, figuring that she already looked like one she might as well act as one. For good measure she retrieved a half-eaten tube of Pringles she'd been nibbling on all evening and shook it. 'Salt and vinegar okay?'

'Perfect.'

They headed over to the squashy sofa next to the Aga and Mallory flopped back onto the bouncy springs with Fiona perching on the edge.

She pressed the record button on her machine. 'So, for a bit of background, how did you and Alex first meet?'

Mallory took another swig of wine. 'That's a really funny story, actually.'

'What a bastard,' Fiona said after Mallory had told all.

'I know!' Mallory exclaimed.

Fiona shook her head sympathetically and leaned over to top up Mallory's wine. Mallory made a mental note to tell Alex how nice Fiona was, nothing like the stereotypical journalist at all! She was so understanding and interested. Mallory hadn't meant to talk about Don, but their relationship had sort of slipped out. In fact, she couldn't even remember how she got onto the subject. It had seemed they'd been talking for hours about everything!

'What's the time?' Mallory asked, unable to make out the digital clock on the cooker from the other side of the kitchen.

Fiona glanced at her watch. 'Almost one.'

'And time you were going,' interjected a rather pissed-off-sounding voice.

Mallory threw her head back over the arm of the sofa and saw an upside-down Alex in the doorway, arms folded, looking far from pleased.

Fiona stood. 'I've got everything I need now anyway.' She turned back to Mallory as she slung her bag over her shoulder. 'You don't mind if I corroborate a few things?'

'Corror... Corbor... Go ahead,' Mallory said, struggling to get up from the comfortable confines of the sofa; her legs didn't seem to be working all that well.

'Bye,' she called out to the departing Fiona, wondering what needed to be corroborated.

'You okay?' Alex asked as he crouched beside her.

She looked at him for a moment, studying his grey-blue eyes, his strong jaw and firm sculpted lips, wondering what they'd be like to kiss. She swallowed down her lustful notions with the last of her wine. He really was an incredibly handsome man.

He smiled at her. 'Why thank you.'

'What?' she said, startled.

He looked at her in bemusement. 'You just told me I was an incredibly handsome man.'

Shit! She hadn't meant to say that out loud! She rolled her head back against the sofa in despair. 'Don't let it go to your head.'

'You're pretty stunning yourself.'

She struggled to sit back up and squinted at him. 'Liar! I've got red-wine-stained lips and a white bra on under my black top. I'm not a very coordinated woman.'

'Come on, time you went to bed. Can you coordinate your way up the stairs?'

Alex gave her a hand up and she half stumbled against him.

'I think my boots are broken,' she said, wobbling slightly.

He laughed, linking her arm in his as they walked through the house together.

'Where's everyone gone?' she asked, for the first time noticing how quiet it was.

'Home.'

'Everyone?'

'Yup. It's now just those of us who are staying for the weekend who are left.'

'Nik?'

'He's still here.'

'Even Louisa?'

'Even Louisa.'

'I don't think she likes me,' Mallory said as she started up the stairs.

'Sometimes I don't think Louisa likes anyone,' he said, walking with her.

'What are you doing?' she asked.

'Making sure you get to bed safely.'

'Are you suggesting I'm too drunk to get there by myself?' she said, blinking a few times to focus on the task in hand. She was about to tell him she was absolutely fine and could manage herself, but decided it was quite helpful having him to lean on.

Suddenly they were outside her bedroom door. Alex pushed it open.

She reeled back round. 'Thank you for escompanying me...' She shook her head, that didn't sound right. 'I mean escorting and accompanying me to my room.'

'My pleasure.' He smiled. 'Will you be okay?'

She grinned up at him then clamped her mouth shut, sure her teeth would be stained from all the red wine. 'My mouth feels dry. Must be from the tannin. Do you know about tannins? They're...' she was about to launch into a long explanation but realised she didn't have the energy, 'important. Would you like to come in for a coffee?' she asked instead, teetering slightly in the doorway.

'Coffee? In your bedroom?' he asked in amusement, reaching out to steady her.

'Yes, I have a travel kettle and coffee with me. As an ex-Girl Guide I'm always prepared. Dib dib dib,' she said, liking the warmth of his hands on her shoulders.

'Isn't "dib dib dib" the Scouts?'

'I was so good the Scouts headhunted me.'

He smiled. Dropping his hands, he jammed them into the pockets of his jeans. 'I can't believe you bring coffee when you stay with other people. You know I can make you some whenever you want.'

'Ah, but it's best I have it to hand as I'm a complete grump if I don't have my caffeine first thing. It's not pretty.'

He laughed softly, scuffing his boot against the skirting board. He looked at her through the longish bit of hair which fell in front of his forehead. 'Thank you, but it's late.'

'That's okay,' she whispered, leaning forward and almost falling into him. 'Coffee can't tell the time.'

He helped steady her once again. 'I think you should get to bed,' he said quietly, gently pushing the hair from her face.

Mallory swallowed. She didn't want him to leave, she was enjoying the closeness of him too much and all evening she'd been thinking to when they'd been stuck in the cupboard together. 'I also have tea...'

He laughed again, breaking contact with her and taking a step away. 'It's got nothing to do with the quality of beverage. It's late and I think you should start sleeping off your hangover. I left some water in your room. Go in, drink it and get to bed.'

And suddenly that did seem like a very good idea. She slumped against the door frame. Feeling a lump at her back she reached round and pulled the still-damp scarf from her belt.

'Oh!' She squinted to focus on it. 'One of your guests may be looking for this. There was a bit of an accident, some wine got spilled and I think someone tried to clean it up with this.'

Alex took it from her, trying not to laugh. 'I'll ask around.'

She started to close the door, wondering if Alex thought she'd been coming on to him by inviting him in for coffee. She had been but hoped it hadn't been obvious and he hadn't twigged. She'd have to clear up any misunderstanding.

Opening the door wide she called out after him, 'It would only have been instant.'

Halfway along the corridor he stopped and turned. 'Sorry?'

'If you had come in, it would only have been instant.'

He looked at her, mouth open in confusion.

'I wouldn't have wasted filter stuff on you, you know. You're not that special.'

He looked at her for a moment then burst out laughing. 'Right! Instant *coffee*! Goodnight, Mallory.' As he carried on to his room she could still hear him laughing to himself.

Closing the door and ricocheting off the wall on the way to her bed she couldn't think what he'd found so funny.

CHAPTER 26

*M*allory lay on the bed wondering if her head would completely roll off her shoulders if she dared attempt to sit up. She was still contemplating such an audacious move when her mobile rang. Delighted she had even just a half bar of coverage she answered it with a 'Hello.' That came out as a croak and she realised her voice sounded as pathetic as her body felt. Even her mobile felt like a ton weight as she tried to hold it against her ear.

'You sound like you're just up?' Alex's voice drawled lazily down the phone at her.

'I've yet to progress to "up".'

'Ouch! Did you have a good night?'

'I think so, but the morning is proving to be a bit of a killjoy.' She peeked out of the top of her duvet to check the time. It was almost eleven.

'Breakfast kind of passed everyone by, so we're doing brunch in half an hour then heading outdoors to have some fun. I hope you're drinking your water?'

She was on her second bottle of Evian.

'So, how do you think it went as a momentum-gathering

exercise?' she asked, rolling onto her side. She felt momentarily queasy then the feeling passed. She stayed on her side.

'Who knows? The journalist was pretty pissed off with me as I was giving nothing away.'

Mallory had a vague notion she'd talked to the woman. 'Did I speak to her?'

'Yup, you ended up very friendly.'

'Did we?'

'You were talking to her for hours.'

Mallory started to get a horrible nagging feeling of anxiety in her chest. She had a recollection of talking to her about Don. In fact, she suspected she went into all the sordid stories of their relationship. The queasiness returned.

She rolled onto her back and emitted a groan.

'You okay?'

'Yeah, I just remembered some of the things I was talking to her about.'

'I hope you weren't saying how much you hate your new boss,' he teased.

'No, nothing like that.' She didn't even think she mentioned Alex once.

'I wouldn't worry about it. You were saying how well you both got on when I walked you to your room.'

He'd walked her to her room?

The nagging feeling in her chest strengthened to a panicked palpitation as memories flooded back. She'd been standing in the doorway inviting him in for coffee. Oh God! She told him about her travel kettle and coffee jar secret, he'd now think she was weird. She also remembered having the most inappropriate thoughts about him.

Shit! Had she begged him to come in to her room? Her forehead started to get hot and clammy as she tried to remember more clearly what had happened. *Horror upon horrors,* had she made a pass at him?

'This is really awful to admit, but I have rather a few blanks about last night. I didn't do anything, you know, inappropriate, did I?' She screwed up her face and held her breath.

He gave a laugh. 'Define inappropriate.'

What the hell had she done!

'Something I wouldn't want my mum to witness me saying or doing.'

He laughed again. 'You were fine, although there was something…'

She tightened her grip on her phone.

'But the owner hasn't come forward yet to claim it.'

Mallory had a sudden flash of that beautiful silk Hermès scarf. 'The scarf! Oh bugger, is it ruined?'

'The pattern is so busy you can't even see the stain. Don't worry about it!'

'I'm never drinking again,' she moaned.

'Until tonight. Or, in fact, this morning. Nik's making up a batch of Bloody Marys. That'll do the trick.'

'Oh don't!' She laughed, despite the pain it caused her. 'So, there was nothing else truly awful I did?'

'Nope, well, not that I saw anyway. If you did any table dancing, I'm afraid I missed it.'

'Probably for the best.'

'So, you're going to survive?'

'Is that why you phoned? To make sure I was still alive? I must say, your staff welfare policy is very good.'

'I'm that kind of a boss,' he said warmly. 'Anyway, I'd best go and help with the food. See you in thirty.'

'Sure.' She hung up, grinning, until she caught sight of her reflection, to discover her hair defied all laws of gravity. Momentarily forgetting her hangover, she ran straight for the shower.

When she got to the kitchen, Alex, Olly, Nik and four others she hadn't met before were already there, sitting round the gigantic table. The room was spotless, as if the previous night's party had never happened. She plonked herself next to Olly.

'Hiya! How are you?' she asked.

'Much better after one of these.' He held up a Bloody Mary. 'Did you get your underwear dilemma sorted out?'

So, it had been Olly she'd told about forgetting her underwear – she knew she'd told someone! It also explained why there was a brand-new pack of M&S pants sitting on her dressing table when she came out of her shower.

The woman on the other side of Olly leaned forward and held out her hand.

'Hi, I'm Irini, Nik's sister and underwear fairy. Olly told me of your plight and I brought a new pack over from my house.'

'Thank you so much!'

'I'm Connor,' said a big burly man. Lantern-jawed and with a weather-beaten face, he was wearing a kilt, hiking boots and a massive chunky knitted jumper and looked the epitome of 'big rugged Scotsman'.

'I'm Gordy,' said a rotund and rosy-cheeked man at the end of the table, helping himself from a massive plate of sausages.

'Sash,' said a dark-haired woman with a grey pallor sitting at the table. Gordy sat next to her and, as he dug into his sausages, Sash turned slightly more ashen.

Not normally one for the hair of the dog, Mallory nevertheless took the glass Nik held out for her, welcoming anything which would possibly make her feel better. She figured she would also need a little Dutch courage to face whatever 'outdoors fun' Alex had in mind. In her current delicate state, she hoped there would be nothing more taxing than a stroll around the gardens and then maybe a gentle game of charades. She took a sip of her Bloody Mary and the Tabasco numbed her lips.

Taking a big gulp, she welcomed the sensation of her body blocking out the pain.

'That hits the spot,' Olly said.

'So does this!' Connor said, cramming a forkful of bacon and black pudding into his mouth.

'Coffee?' Alex asked Mallory, a small smile playing on his lips. 'It's filter. For my special guests,' he added with a barely perceptible wink.

Mallory knew she was reddening as she had a sudden flashback to their final conversation of the night. Her whole body went clammy with embarrassment.

'Oh God, give me a cup would you, darling,' Louisa demanded, flouncing into the kitchen like a cover girl from *Clay Pigeon Shoot Weekly*, complete with Hunter boots, satin padded jacket and Hermès silk scarf tied round her perfectly coiffed head. Mallory wondered miserably if the other scarf had been hers too. Louisa looked the type of woman to own more than one.

'Christ! She thinks she's the queen,' Sash muttered before resting her head on her folded arms on the table.

'I can imagine there are a few hangovers this morning,' Louisa said breezily, checking out her perfectly made-up face in the blade of a knife.

'Louisa, this is Connor,' Alex said. Connor raised a hand in greeting. 'You've met everyone else, I think, oh this is Olly.'

Olly had just taken a huge mouthful of breakfast and waggled his knife at her in greeting too. 'We've already met. The exhibition, remember?'

'Mmm,' Louisa said vaguely.

'Yeah, you weren't that enamoured with my small talk. It was more miniscule talk, to be fair,' he added with a good-natured laugh.

Louisa gave him a tight-lipped smile in response.

Olly, obviously mistaking her unresponsiveness for amnesia,

persevered. 'You told me you were really pissed off because you thought Alex was flirting with Mallory.'

Irini stifled a laugh by taking a sip of coffee, while Alex burst out laughing.

Louisa smiled faintly and ripped off a piece of croissant and rammed it into her mouth.

'Ah, so you're back on the carbs now, I see,' Olly said.

CHAPTER 27

As a Scout leader, Duke of Edinburgh Gold medal winner and all-round nature zealot, Connor was keen to spend as much time outdoors as possible. He was the only one who showed any interest when Alex mentioned he had something planned to get them all out in the fresh air while the marquees were taken down and all evidence of the previous night's party was removed. In fact, before Mallory could say 'I hate fresh air, get me out of here', Connor had hot-footed it up to his room and returned to the group with his rucksack and waterproof jacket slung over his arm.

Half an hour later they were all trampling over fields and Mallory knew she would have to avoid Connor for the rest of the weekend. It wasn't that he was horrible, far from it, he was lovely, not to mention very fit and good-looking, he was just a little too 'gung-ho' for Mallory's liking.

Obviously Alex had mentioned her alleged love of outdoor pursuits to him so he'd taken every opportunity to engage with her and she'd had to take every opportunity to wriggle out of any conversation which was in danger of veering towards hillwalking, orienteering or bivouacking.

Hoping not to appear completely unfit and out of breath, she let him do all the talking, with only the occasional gasp from her which he took to be noises of agreement. Eventually, after a steep incline where Mallory thought she was going to black out from trying to match Connor's pace, they came to a halt at the top of a hill and Mallory's stomach dipped with terror, her Bloody Mary almost making an unscheduled reappearance as she realised where they'd been heading towards: a paddock, complete with horses.

'I thought it would be fun to organise some riding,' Alex said, coming to stand next to Mallory. 'My neighbour runs a riding school and I arranged to book out the horses for all of us.'

She turned to him, completely speechless, which Alex mistook for unbridled joy.

'I thought I would surprise you.'

He'd certainly done that.

Alex addressed the group. 'I know we don't all ride, but I thought we could go for a bit of a trek. It'll blow the cobwebs away.'

'So would a twelve-bore shotgun and probably wouldn't be nearly as painful,' Mallory whispered to Olly as she clambered over the fence, almost falling flat on her face, her legs were shaking so much.

'The non-riders can take their pick of those over there.' Alex pointed to some lovely old docile and overweight nags before turning back to Mallory. 'These are ours. I've got Samson the chestnut, Connor you've got Ricky in the middle, and Mallory, you've got Diavolo. The big black one.'

Mallory had thought Mars had been big, but the horse which Alex pointed out to her was absolutely gigantic. And powerful; she could see his muscles rippling beneath the glossy black coat.

'Diavolo, eh? You can talk Italian to him,' Olly said with a surreptitious wink as he headed over to the other side of the field.

With a deep breath Mallory tentatively walked over to Diavolo. At least Alex had said 'trek'. She thought she'd be able to cope with a nice slow trek. She'd done plenty of ambling along on Mars.

'I'm not used to riding one quite this size,' she said, hoping to excuse herself if she ended up face down in the mud while attempting to mount the horse but as she looked around there didn't seem to be anything to use to mount, not even a rickety old stool. Alarmingly though, her eyes did alight upon an awful lot of fences and jumps.

'Alex, are we using those?' she asked, hoping her voice didn't betray the blind terror she felt.

Alex looked up from tightening his horse's stirrups. 'No...'

Mallory nearly sank to the ground in relief.

'I thought we could just go for a gallop...' *GALLOP*? He'd said trek! 'while the others have a trek, but feel free if you want to give them a go, Diavolo's a natural jumper.'

'Haha, no, it's okay. After last night, I'll just stick to a trek too. Don't want to be jostling around in my saddle too much,' she said as jollily as possible, hoping Alex didn't see her hands shaking as she held on to the reins.

She put her foot in the stirrup, held on to the pommel and bounced a couple of times on the ball of her other foot and with momentous effort she pulled herself up, swinging her leg as high as she could. Almost dislocating her hip in the process, she swung (in what she hoped was an elegant arc) before landing squarely in the saddle.

Perilously close to throwing up, she fixed the strap of her riding hat.

Mallory's consolation was that she wasn't the only one looking scared; Louisa had paled significantly under her St Tropez tan and bronzer. Sash hadn't even bothered to try to join them, far preferring to return to her room for a lie down and some aspirin. Mallory wished she'd done the same.

Diavolo circled on the spot and Mallory clamped her jaw shut to stop her teeth chattering with fear. With Connor in the lead, the others slowly headed, single file, out of the field and down the country lane.

'Come on then, we'll bring up the rear,' Alex said, swatting the air. 'Bloody horseflies! They're out in force today.'

Mallory looked on as an ugly insect dive-bombed Diavolo's flank. The horse reared slightly, shaking his head. She cried out as her horse kicked his back legs out behind him and bared his teeth.

'It's okay, just hold on to the reins firmly, he must have been bitten,' Alex said, leaning over in his saddle to help, but before he could reach her Mallory was bucked back in her seat as Diavolo started to canter.

A scream caught in her throat as fear rendered her mute – she'd never gone faster than a trot before. To her horror, Diavolo continued to speed up and each thud of his hooves reverberated through her entire body as she desperately tried to regain control of him.

He was having none of it and continued to run wild until he changed direction and with a sense of new-found purpose, headed straight for the first jump.

CHAPTER 28

Unable to do anything other than shut her eyes and hope for the best, Mallory, white-knuckling the reins, braced herself for impact followed by inevitable pain. Clamping her legs hard against the horse's flanks she felt a soaring sensation as her stomach flipped over... followed a couple of seconds later by a jolting thud as they landed, causing the reins to slip from her fingers. Throwing herself forward she blindly grabbed hold of the saddle with one hand and a clump of mane with the other, thankful to still be alive.

She opened an eye...

...just in time to see him curving for the next jump.

This is it, she thought. *This is the end.* And again, she braced herself, feeling the ground fall away beneath his hooves.

This time on landing she lost her stirrups and her hat came down over her eyes, which was actually a blessing as she really didn't want to see where they were heading next. Throwing herself onto his neck she clung on with every ounce of strength, his mane filling up her mouth and rubbing roughly against her cheek as he tossed his powerful head about.

Alex hollered instructions to her in the distance but seeing as she was hanging on for dear life and in no position to 'reach for the reins' she chose to block him out.

As Diavolo continued to snort and career around the field Mallory completely bounced out of the saddle, sliding further up his neck, ending just inches from his ears. Sick with terror and heart hammering wildly, she steeled herself for another jump but it seemed the horse didn't think it was much fun jumping with a novice on his back who pulled at his hair; instead, he sailed past it.

When his pace had slowed to little more than a walk Mallory tentatively let one hand go of his mane to push her hat back out of her eyes.

With the blood still whooshing in her ears and Alex still shouting out for her to reach the reins, Diavolo turned and ambled over to the water jump. He stopped at the edge and slowly lowered his head.

With nothing left to hold on to, Mallory slid down the remaining length of his neck, headfirst, dropping into the icy stagnant water.

She jumped up, coughing as she hit the air. With water cascading into her boots, she waded as quickly as possible to the edge but the sides were too slippery to gain purchase on and she stood thigh-deep in water, miserably watching as Alex jumped off his horse. She could see Connor in the distance trying to calm down the other horses which had got spooked at Diavolo's sudden adventure.

'Are you okay?' Alex shouted, running over to her.

Her teeth began an involuntary castanet chatter in response.

'If you wanted to do the jumps first you should have just said,' he deadpanned, crouching at the water's edge as Diavolo looked on with haughty curiosity. 'Are you sure you're not hurt?'

She nodded.

'Give me your hand.'

'I can manage.'

He sat back on his heels slightly, his elbows resting on his knees. 'I'm sure you can, but why not humour me for a moment and let me act the hero. It does wonders for my ego,' he mocked gently.

He reached out his hands and Mallory reluctantly gave him hers. He pulled and she felt herself leave the water. Too fast, as she ended up bowling into Alex and they both lay sprawled in the mud, with her on top of him.

He laughed and Mallory tried to roll off him but she was so wet and muddy she just resembled a fish flailing about on land. Alex, still laughing, was no help, but eventually, using her elbows to grip, Mallory managed to break free and roll onto her back, where she lay, exhausted and wet.

Alex rolled onto his side. 'Really, Mallory! People will talk!' He laughed as she struggled to her feet.

'Sorry,' she said, completely flustered.

'Don't be,' Alex said. 'That was the most fun I've had all weekend. I mean that last bit, not your near-death experience.' He jumped to his feet. 'Are you sure you're okay?'

She nodded, which made her shoulders shake uncontrollably with the cold.

'Come on, you need a hot bath and a hot drink.' He removed his jacket and made to place it over her shoulders.

'I'll get it all wet,' Mallory protested.

'Which is far preferable to you coming down with double pneumonia,' he argued, throwing it over her shoulders and pulling it tight at her neck.

Mortified and freezing, Mallory took a step, feeling the trapped water gush out the top of her boot and she squelched all the way across the field.

'She's okay!' Alex shouted out to the others. 'I'm just going to walk her back to the house.'

'I can manage,' Mallory said, still mortified. 'I don't want to spoil your fun.'

'And I don't want to risk you passing out from hypothermia, pneumonia, or anything else ending in *ia*.'

'Hernia?' Mallory joked weakly, still squelching water from her boots. 'Chlamydia?'

He smiled. 'You'll actually be doing me a favour as I need to sort out a few things anyway.'

'Ah good, glad to have fulfilled my role as diversion.'

'Don't mention it.'

She stumbled over a rock.

'And no broken bones, okay?' Alex grabbed hold of her hand. Even through wet woolly gloves it felt nice.

'Okay,' she agreed.

ॐ

Only when her skin was a happy medium between prune and Californian raisin did Mallory get out of her bath and wrap herself up in a big fluffy towel.

On getting back to the house she'd been so desperate for her bath she'd just peeled off all her clothes and dumped them on the bathroom floor before submerging herself in hot fragrant bubbles, but as she stood towel-drying her hair she realised Alex's jacket was at the bottom of the pile of discarded sodden clothes. Rescuing it and giving it a tentative sniff, she was relieved it didn't smell as strongly of stagnant pond as did all the other clothes she'd been wearing.

She should return it to him in case he needed to have it dry cleaned. She quickly threw on her jeans and a shirt, a deep gold colour she knew brought out the rich dark auburn of her hair. She gave her lashes a quick coat of mascara, her lips a slick of gloss then ran her fingers through her hair. Without bothering to style it, her hair bounced naturally into loose ringlets. She would never pass for a sleekly groomed sophisticate but tonight she was more than happy to settle for fresh-faced and freckly. With a final spritz of perfume she scuttled along the hall to Alex's room. As she was about to knock, her stomach gave a little flip-flop of anticipation. Excuses of having his jacket dry cleaned aside, Mallory knew she really just wanted to see Alex.

Despite knowing that he was her boss and had the rakish reputation, she knew she was starting to like him. Slightly. Only an itty-bitty crush. And it had only been an itty-bitty crush since the start of the weekend and it could easily be explained by the mix of fresh air and too much wine. And near-death experiences.

And probably, in fact, *most certainly*, when they got back to the normal routine in Glasgow she'd not find him nearly as attractive as she did at that moment. She could almost envisage Caz on her shoulder whispering that this was healthy, that she'd been single and celibate for way too long and that she should *go for it*, although, as she raised her hand to knock on the door, Mallory had no actual idea what it would be she'd be going *for*.

Then the door opened and Alex practically jumped out of the very small towel he had wrapped round his hips.

'Jesus!'

'Sorry, I was about to knock.' She lowered her hand as it looked as if she was about to clock him one on his forehead.

Obviously just out the shower, he was slick with water, skin gleaming with the remnants of a late-summer tan. Only on Michelangelo's 'David' had Mallory seen such exquisite musculature before. Her gaze lingered on a drop of water, rolling from his chest down his defined abdomen. Aware she was staring, she snapped her gaze back to his face.

'Here you go,' she said, brandishing the jacket.

He looked at it then down at his naked torso. 'Are you the modesty police?'

'No, no! I don't mean for you to wear it now. I had no idea you were… I mean, I wasn't hanging around outside your room waiting for a chance to see you naked and give you this!' Mallory laughed, struggling to maintain eye contact as she was sorely tempted to drop her gaze to below his jawline for another peek.

'Shame,' he said, giving her a very sexy look.

Her stomach gave another little flip-flop flutter. Yup, definitely an itty-bitty crush.

'Sorry to disappoint but I'm not an Alex groupie hanging around on the off-chance I get to see you naked.' Although, having now seen him almost in the altogether, she could be persuaded.

'Whyever not? Are you made of stone?' he joked.

She sighed, feigning boredom. 'You've seen one naked man in a towel, you've seen them all. Anyway, what were you doing, about to have a streak round the house?'

'I was actually going to find a bigger towel.'

'Is that meant to impress me?'

'I wouldn't attempt to try to impress you with anything.' He laughed as he turned and walked back towards the bathroom. 'Come on in. Mrs Young, the housekeeper, obviously gave away all the good towels to the guest rooms and I got two hand towels and a flannel. Oh well, I suppose I can make do. Hang on a sec, I'll throw on some clothes.' He walked back into the bathroom.

Tempted to shout out not to bother on her account she nevertheless held her tongue. For all their flirty banter she had no idea what was going on in Alex's mind. He probably acted the same way with everyone and he *was* still her boss and there was a line to be drawn. It was enough to allow herself to frolic in the fizzing thrill of the crush in a 'look, don't touch' way. It was also nice to know her libido hadn't completely left her. Maybe she *was* ready to move on.

She wandered into Alex's room, noticing how much messier it had become from the previous evening.

'I'm intrigued to hear what you think an "Alex groupie" is like,' he called through from the bathroom.

She didn't miss a beat. 'Blonde, tanned, good-looking in a stereotypical model kind of way.'

He poked his head round the door. 'I do believe you've just described Nik. And Louisa. Shall I tell them you think they're my groupies?'

'I'm basing my answer on the photos of you and various *female* company in *Hello!* and *OK!* You obviously attract a certain type,' she rallied back.

'I love your incredibly low opinion of me.' He laughed, ducking back into the bathroom.

Among the mess, Mallory saw half a dozen packing boxes already filled and parcelled up. They hadn't been there the previous night. She could also see that his cupboard had been emptied, the contents most probably what was packed away in the boxes. There was an open suitcase beside the bed which was also packed with clothes. He hadn't mentioned he was moving. She wondered if he'd gotten bored with life in Glasgow already and planned on moving back to London. Her stomach gave a little lurch at the thought of him not being around anymore, but then she reminded herself that once they were back in Glasgow, his allure would wear off. Probably.

She sat on the unmade bed, and immediately jumped back up as something jabbed into her. A quick rummage under the rumpled duvet unearthed a book. She opened it at the first page where there was a very rough sketch of the view from Alex's window. Fascinated, she turned the pages to find more; sketches of the house, the grounds, birds. Many were rough, nothing more than a few lines scratched onto the paper, but others had such incredible attention to detail they were breathtaking.

Feeling as though she'd stumbled onto something personal and private, she re-hid the book and stood as Alex appeared from the bathroom in jeans and a shirt, smelling subtly of the delicious aftershave he wore.

He ran his hand through his still-damp hair, the ends of which were curled into black question marks against his head. 'I don't know about you, but I'm starving!'

CHAPTER 29

When Mallory and Alex got to the kitchen, Irini and Nik were already there, aprons on and bickering contentedly as they prepared dinner. Mallory and Alex were directed to sit down and told not to interfere as plates were plonked down before them.

Although brunch had been pretty hearty Mallory felt as if she hadn't eaten for a week and gratefully pounced on a chunk of baguette Alex ripped off and handed her.

'Fresh air makes me hungry too.'

Gordy wandered in carrying a dog-eared Robert Ludlum novel and a bottle of Tanqueray gin. He waggled the bottle. 'I'll get some preprandial aperitifs sorted, shall I?'

Without waiting for anyone's answer he sloshed most of the bottle into a pitcher, added some lime wedges, ice and very little tonic, and plonked it in the middle of the table.

'Pour me one of those bad boys, lover!' Sash said, walking in. 'I can just about face the hard stuff again. Heard you had a bit of a tumble. You okay now?' she asked Mallory, sitting down and tearing off some bread.

Mallory nodded.

'She was a magnificent vision!' Gordy said as he poured the gin into glasses. 'Like Boudicca hanging on for dear life in battle!' Gordy handed a glass to Sash, giving her a little kiss on the lips.

'Hardly,' Mallory said, feeling uncomfortable at the comparison.

'Thank God you survived it!' Sash said.

'Hear, hear,' Alex agreed. 'I'd hate to have to find another artist at such short notice.' He took a large swig of his drink and dodged out of the way as Sash threw the end bit of her bread at him.

'I'm off to get wine,' he said, throwing the bread back at Sash, hitting her on the head with it then escaping out of the kitchen before she could retaliate.

Sash brushed breadcrumbs out of her hair. 'If you couldn't stay and play anymore you'd be leaving Irini and I to fend off the evil Louisa on our own.'

'Sash!' Nik warned, turning round and pointing a wooden spoon at her.

'What?' she said, mock innocently. 'You know it's true. She sees any female as direct competition. Which just shows how deeply insecure she is. Not a woman's woman at all.'

Sash leaned forward, out of Nik's earshot as he turned back and attended to a tray of little roast potatoes. 'And she absolutely hates when you're with Alex.'

'But nothing's going on between me and Alex!' Mallory quickly interjected but Sash dismissed her with a wave of her hand.

'She was *spitting* when the two of you emerged all rumpled and flushed from his room at the party last night.'

'But we were hiding! From *her*! It was Alex's idea!'

But Sash merely smiled in an 'I know best' way. 'When Alex had his flingette with her we all hoped it would run its course quickly, which it did, thank goodness. But she just won't let go. Short of hanging onto his bumper and towing a Pickfords van all the way up to Glasgow, Louisa couldn't have made her intentions any more obvious.'

Mallory glanced over her shoulder; Nik was still concentrating on his potatoes. 'So, it wasn't just a coincidence that she moved to the Glasgow office?' Mallory whispered.

Sash gave a snort of derision. 'Louisa can't abide Nik because he and Alex are so close and Nik really doesn't have any time for her. Irini doesn't even register on Louisa's radar, watch how she talks to her, she addresses her as if she's the hired help. She puts up with me and Gordy because he's got a title and we know too many of the people she tries to ingratiate herself with to be openly hostile. She won't give Olly the time of day but she likes Connor because he's a strapping lad and might be a bit of a distraction, and at best make Alex jealous. *You*, she wants out the way. It wouldn't surprise me if she spooked your horse.'

Mallory took a gulp of her gin. The only thing that had spooked Diavolo was her ineptitude.

'I'm only telling you this because I'm very fond of Alex.' Sash smiled. 'Not in *that* way.' She patted Gordy's knee. 'Been there, done that. Both sixteen, drunk and neither of us has any inclination to revisit that particular fumble again.'

She laughed and sat back. 'Thing is, he's been bloody miserable for so long. No focus, just drifting from one party to the next. It was fun when we were twenty-one, but while the rest of us joined the real world and got jobs Alex kept on at it. Finally, at thirty, he's growing up. This restaurant is the best thing that could have happened. London was no good for him but he's content up here and he now has something to get out of bed for. And you're good for him too. You're nothing like the usual half-wits he gets involved with.'

'But there's nothing going...'

'Immaterial. You don't fawn over him, you're not false.'

Mallory looked away, unable to meet Sash's eye.

She was relieved to see Olly amble in.

He sniffed the air. 'Wow, something smells good.'

'Plonk yourself down and pour yourself a drink,' Irini ordered. 'You too, Louisa,' she said a little louder, with a warning look to Sash as Louisa appeared in the doorway.

Instead, Louisa went over to the range to inspect what was cooking.

'Would you mind rustling up a little salad, I really don't think I'd be able to cope with such a rich meal,' Louisa said plaintively. 'And I don't eat meat.'

'You didn't mention you were vegetarian,' Irini said.

'Oh, I'm not! I eat chicken and fish, but no one really eats red meat anymore, do they? Especially not with pastry *and* potatoes.'

'It's beef stifado with rosemary roasted potatoes and there's some spanakopita bites to start,' Irini said in disbelief.

Mallory's stomach gave a growl of anticipation. She could think of nothing she'd rather eat.

'Just scrape out the spinach from the middle of the pastry, Louisa,' Sash said irritably, as Alex returned with bottles wedged under his arms.

Alex plonked down a couple of bottles of red and got to work on them with an opener. 'Might have to let this breathe for a bit.'

'Chance will be a fine thing in this atmosphere,' Sash whispered, making a face, as Louisa walked past Mallory in a pyroclastic cloud of Coco Chanel.

Eyes smarting from the intense perfume, Mallory noted that Louisa had really gone to town with her clothes; while everyone else sat around in jeans, Louisa had gone for the LBD paired with vertiginous heels.

Mallory wondered if her dress was too tight from the way Louisa hovered around, not sitting down, until it dawned on her she was waiting to see where Alex was going to sit first. There were five chairs to choose from and she obviously didn't want to pick the wrong one. Then all of a sudden, Alex sat next to Gordy.

Louisa scooted over as fast as she could but her heels, lovely as they were, proved her undoing as she couldn't get to where Alex was in time as Connor walked in and immediately sat next to Alex. Which meant Louisa was between Connor and Olly.

Connor rubbed his hands in eagerness as Nik brought over the stifado. 'Wow, Nik, this looks amazing!'

'This has nothing to do with me,' he said. 'This is all Irini's work; I'm allowed to help.'

'As long as he doesn't get under my feet,' Irini added as she brought over the potatoes and a platter of vegetables.

'I wish you'd reconsider my offer,' Nik said.

All eyes went to Irini who ducked her head in embarrassment.

'What offer's this?' Sash said, loading her plate. She handed the serving spoon to Mallory who was practically salivating by this point.

'I've suggested she come on board with Serendipity. I still need to hire more staff and it would be great working together.'

Irini laughed. 'We'd kill each other!'

'We would, but it would also be fun.'

She shook her head. 'I love cooking but I don't think I'd like it under pressure.'

Mallory took a spoonful of the stifado and nearly wept with happiness; it was so mouth-meltingly delicious!

'We'll see,' Nik said despite the look Irini gave him.

As everyone tucked into their food Mallory saw Louisa picking at her pile of salad leaves although she did look at everyone else's plates quite enviously, no doubt regretting her outburst.

Dessert was something sublimely creamy and boozy with fruit in it, and when the last spoon hit the bowl everyone complained cheerfully that their trousers were all too tight round the waistband. Despite the guests being a little on the pale side earlier in the day the fresh air had seemingly caused a mass recovery and very soon the wine from dinner had disappeared.

'Right!' Alex said, tipping the last dregs of the bottle into Olly's glass. 'It's time to pay a visit to the cellar again.' He stood.

'Quick, guys, let's ransack the house of all the art and antiques while he's not looking,' Gordy stage-whispered.

Alex laughed. 'Feel free, it's got nothing to do with me anymore.'

'Eh?' Gordy asked.

But Alex just shrugged enigmatically and as he walked past Mallory he grabbed hold of her hand, hauling her out of her seat.

'I'm just going to take my wine guru with me to make sure I pick my father's most expensive bottles.'

'Wha... Alex!' Mallory managed to free herself from the table legs as he dragged her off into the utility room. 'I'm sure you don't need me to help,' Mallory said, quaking at the thought of deciphering the contents of an entire cellar, but Alex stubbornly held on to her hand.

CHAPTER 30

'You're not afraid of the dark, are you?' Alex asked Mallory before unlocking a door and leading her down some steps.

She gingerly followed, unable to see in front of her. Once at the bottom he let go of her hand and a moment later a bare bulb flickered on. It hung from the ceiling with a table directly under it. He nudged the bulb and they watched it swing, creating wide arcs of light against the walls.

'Is this where you conduct all your interrogations?' Mallory said.

'Nervous? Scared I'll find out your darkest deepest secrets?'

She didn't tell him how close to the bone he was but instead she had a look around the cellar. As well as there being hundreds of bottles in the open racks, there were crates of wine, stacked up against the walls. There were another couple of storage areas beyond the first room with the same number of bottles in each one. She didn't bother taking a look as it was quite creepy, not to mention cold.

'You know, most people's "cellars" are just cardboard boxes in an airing cupboard.'

'My father converted it when he bought the place back in the eighties.' Alex's voice echoed in the room as he brought over a selection of bottles and set them on the table.

'So, what are you picking?' Mallory asked, hoping she'd know a little about the wines he'd selected.

Alex shrugged and blew his hair out of his eyes. 'Haven't a clue. Whatever it is it will be highly collectable and horrendously expensive.'

'Won't he mind?'

Alex rubbed some dust away from the label with his thumb. 'He has no idea what he has down here. He hires someone from an auction house to bid on his behalf so it looks impressive. He hardly ever stays here now, so I'm the only one drinking it. Start piling them up.'

Mallory pulled another couple of bottles out of the racks and set them beside the others. They were Côtes du Rhône and she knew she liked that style of wine. She also spied a couple of them were 2015 and knew they were great vintages.

'When was the last time he was here, at the house?'

'He stopped living here permanently about fifteen years ago. He occasionally comes for Christmas and New Year but he prefers the climate of the Caribbean these days.'

Mallory thought of the paintings upstairs.

She looked over at Alex who was brushing cobwebs away from the wine racks. She'd wondered if it had been Alex's father, James Claremont, who was the artist responsible for the paintings she'd stumbled upon. If it was, he could seriously think of changing his career. But then, why would Alex have a sketchbook in his bedroom? From the brief glance she had it could easily have been the same artist. But if Alex was the artist, why go to the bother of hiring Mallory to design Serendipity when he could easily do it himself?

Alex turned around and caught her staring at him. 'You okay?'

'Yeah, just thinking.'

'Thought you looked pained.'

'Cheek!' she exclaimed in mock offence.

'Let me know if you find any spiders.'

She dusted her hands against the back pockets of her jeans. 'Why, plan on coming to my rescue?'

He raised an eyebrow. 'Heavens no! It'll give me time to run.'

'Who said chivalry was dead,' she grumbled, lining up the bottles on the table.

He walked over to her to check out her selection. 'I already came to your rescue today and once every twenty-four hours is my limit. And, as I recall, you were a slightly reluctant rescuee.'

'Would you prefer if I threw myself at your feet, weeping with gratitude?'

'That would be a start.'

Mallory looked down at the table, making circles in the dust with her index finger. 'Well, thanks.' She hated to think how ridiculously amateurish she must have looked. She wondered if Alex, who knew about horses, had realised just how inexperienced she was.

He laughed. 'I certainly won't get a swollen ego from the adulations.'

She looked up at him. 'I think your ego does okay.'

He leaned back against the table. 'I'm just glad you weren't hurt.'

'Yeah, as you said, it would be far too much bother to find yourself another artist.'

He looked at her seriously, his eyes burning into hers with an intensity that caused her breath to catch. 'That's not why I was concerned. And I think you know that,' he said quietly.

Mallory realised she didn't know anything anymore as she looked at him.

'Cooooooo-eeeeeeeeeeeee!'

Both Mallory and Alex jumped as Louisa's voice called down

to them. Standing on the top step, she was bent over, trying to see them without having to descend the stairs.

'I thought I'd come and chase you. We're all getting rather thirsty up here!'

'We'll be right up,' Alex called out, not breaking eye contact with Mallory. He leaned forward slightly. 'People will definitely talk now,' he whispered so only she'd hear. 'That's twice we've hidden in a cupboard together.'

As they traipsed upstairs, Mallory clutching half the bottles of wine to her chest, she couldn't help but hope there would be a third time.

CHAPTER 31

$\mathcal{A}$fter dinner, when everyone had flopped onto the sofas in the lounge, Olly let himself out onto the terrace to get some fresh air and have a sneaky cigarette. Despite having officially 'stopped' a couple of years earlier he still occasionally indulged, usually when he had some thinking to do. And that night, he had quite a lot to mull over; by all accounts it was turning into a rather strange weekend.

First, there was the surreal party with celebrity wannabes and rather obnoxious people all vying to be photographed. Luckily they'd all departed, leaving some genuinely nice people and he felt he could start to chill out. But then there was the weird horse-riding experience which reminded him of being five and being led about Newquay beach on a donkey.

And also that although he was a guest of Mallory's, he'd not seen her for practically the entire time they'd been here. Which was odd, but even *more* odd was the fact that it didn't really bother him. And it was *that* which had come as a bit of a shock.

For as long as he could remember, Mallory was all he ever thought about. His day was made if she even just popped into their studio for five minutes to grab a coffee and a chat. But today, after the horse-riding, he'd been more intent on having a hot bath to soothe his muscles than seeking out Mallory.

And then, after his bath, he'd gone for a walk in the gardens, loving the fresh air, with all the greenery and birdsong reminding him of the lush and verdant countryside of where he'd grown up.

Lighting his cigarette, he wandered down the steps and followed the path around the house trying to work out exactly what kind of seismic change of heart had occurred. Completely lost in thought, he started, when a couple of feet before him the kitchen door opened and he just managed to sidestep away from a handful of bacon rinds landing on his head.

Irini, the cause of the projectiles, poked her head round the door. 'Sorry! I saw the security light come on and assumed it was the cat who wanders about.'

'It's okay, you didn't hit me!'

'If you fancy a walk, there's a lovely route down to the water feature.'

'Yeah, I went there this afternoon. I'm not really out walking anywhere in particular.'

'Ah, just following your feet and your thoughts, were you?'

'Something like that.'

She looked up at the sky. 'It's probably too dark to see anything anyway. Too cloudy for stars and moonlight.' She stood and looked out at the grass, frowning slightly. 'I hope that cat comes before Connor sees it.'

'Oh, are only polecats and wildcats welcome, to add to the rugged Scottish realism?'

She laughed, wiping her hands on a dishcloth. 'Nope, he's absolutely terrified of them!'

'What! A big tough man like Connor?'

'Screams like a girl,' she whispered conspiratorially.

'It shouldn't, but hearing that makes me feel so much better about myself. Dinner was great, by the way.'

'Thanks.' She bustled back into the kitchen, wedging the door open so she could still talk to Olly while he finished his cigarette.

'You're an amazing cook as well as chicken murderer. Although come to think of it, there was a noticeable lack of chicken tonight.'

'They're roasting in the oven at the moment for lunch tomorrow and the stock will be for soup.'

Olly, leaning against the door jamb, caught a whiff of rich roasting meat and herbs, and although still full from dinner, looked forward to the next day's food. 'Don't you ever stop? Everyone else is in the lounge, in front of the fire.'

'Which means no one noticed me slip away to get everything ready for tomorrow.' She pressed the button on the industrial-sized dishwasher and it came to life with a deep gurgle. 'And, if I'm organised now, it means I'll be free to join in with the fun tomorrow!'

'Sounds ominous!'

'Yeah, I heard Alex and Connor discussing some good walks.' She untied her apron and slung it over the back of a chair. 'Are you an outwards bound kind of guy?'

'I can't believe you have to ask!' He took a step back, opening his arms wide. 'Is it not obvious by my physique that I spend hours in the wilderness being at one with nature? Me,' he thumped his chest with his fist, 'and the rugged terrain! I'm like Sir Ranulph Fiennes!'

Irini tried to keep a straight face. 'I'm sorry I doubted you.'

He winked. 'I don't like to brag.'

There was a clattering in the kitchen as Connor entered, noisily banging the door shut behind him. 'I'm heading out for a walk. That bloody woman is doing my head in! She's been twittering on about the house being too cold, her bed being too firm and there not being any mobile phone coverage. She certainly won't get any coverage if I shove it up her– Oh! Sorry, mate.' He stopped his rant as he noticed Olly.

'Don't mind me.' Olly raised his hand in greeting.

'Ah, right, well… I'll see you later.' Connor turned and gave Irini a kiss on the cheek then headed out the door.

'I think Louisa is winding up a few folk,' Irini said with a sigh once he'd gone. 'Which was another reason I fancied popping down here. I can hide.'

'Hmm,' Olly agreed, watching Connor stride out, over the grass, until the security light clicked off again.

'So, you and Connor…' He left the sentence open.

'Me and Connor?'

'Are you, you know, an item?' He inwardly cringed at such an old-fashioned term.

Irini laughed. 'God no!' she exclaimed, then looked sheepish. 'Sorry, I didn't mean to sound so horrified. He's a great guy, he really is, but all that fresh air and exercise? It can't be good for you.' She smiled.

And for some reason this new information pleased Olly no end.

CHAPTER 32

*W*aking up and feeling quite a bit brighter than she had the previous morning, Mallory stretched, luxuriating in the comfiness of the bed and lay for a few minutes listening to the birds singing outside. Although she wasn't quite at the stage of throwing off the covers, jumping out of bed and singing alongside as if she were in a Disney film, she was definitely in a buoyant mood.

And it wasn't just down to the country air and good food. She ran over the conversation she and Alex had in the cellar for the zillionth time, mentally pausing on the '*And I think you know that*' comment. Also, for the zillionth time, she cursed Louisa's untimely interruption and wondered what would have happened if she hadn't followed them.

As it turned out, they didn't have a chance to continue with the conversation as Louisa monopolised Alex for the rest of the evening. And after Sash's comments Mallory had become uncomfortably aware of just how often she'd found Louisa's cold blue eyes narrowed her way. Mallory was so freaked out that on going to bed she'd even resorted to pushing the armchair over to the door and barricading herself in just in case she was offed in the night by having a stiletto heel embedded in her head courtesy of a psychotic Louisa.

She sat up, hugging her knees to her chest.

'And I think you know that.'

So, did Alex think she knew that he knew there was a bit of chemistry between them? She'd been so sure her itty-bitty crush had only been in her head that she hadn't thought that it would be a two-way thing. And that, she mused, leaning over to flick on her little travel kettle, put an entirely different slant on things!

A shower, two coffees and a quick change later she was ready. She checked her phone, more out of habit because the signal was still patchy, and saw she had a missed call from Caz. Caz would no doubt be ready to burst for gossip, wanting to know who'd been at the party, how things were going with Alex, what the house was like and at least another dozen questions.

With momentous effort Mallory managed to pull the chair away from the door without slipping a disc. Opening it, she nearly careered into Alex.

'Hi, I thought I'd repay the favour and hover about your room to scare the wits out of you.' He handed her a croissant, strawberry jam oozing out the sides. 'And I wanted to give breakfast in the hall a go, breakfast in bed's such a cliché, don't you think?'

Mallory was rather tempted to explore the possibilities of breakfast in bed with Alex but hastily covered up her lascivious thoughts by taking a bite out of the croissant, flakes of pastry instantly sticking to her artfully applied lipstick.

Alex tried to peer into her room over her shoulder. 'Is everything okay? I thought I heard a lot of thuds and scrapes.'

'Oh that! Um… just rearranging some of the furniture.'

He looked at her quizzically.

'Feng Shui. In a bid to keep bad spirits out.' She carefully popped another bit of croissant into her mouth, trying not to ruin any more of her 'natural' look make-up.

'I thought we could go walking, make a day of it. Just us. If you like?'

Mallory did like. Very much.

'There's a great walk Connor was telling me about. It's about a half-hour drive away to get to the start of it.'

'Sounds good!'

'Best wrap up warm as the temperature's really dropped overnight.'

She darted back inside her room to change, delighted she'd get to make use of her new walking gear. She pulled on an extra-thick pair of socks before her hiking boots as she'd not managed to break them in. She was just checking her rucksack for blister plasters when her mobile beeped at her.

It was another missed call from Caz. Mallory thought Caz *must* be desperate for gossip. She tried accessing her answer machine once again but with no luck as there still wasn't enough of a prolonged signal. Mallory pulled on her bulky jacket, woolly hat with its gigantic pompom and her gloves, finishing off with her waterproof outer layer.

She bounded down the stairs to where Alex was waiting for her.

She never thought she'd be so happy to don a cagoule.

'We're lost.'

Alex stood on a raised stone, surveying the area, before looking back down at his compass again.

'What are our coordinates?' Mallory asked.

'Absolutely no idea.' He held up the compass. 'I only brought this thing along for show.'

She took the compass off him and double-checked the map she'd dug out from the bottom of her rucksack. She stared at it for a moment or two, trying to work out what she was actually meant to be looking at but thought she'd have better luck deciphering the Rosetta Stone.

He jumped down beside her, pulling on her woolly hat. 'I blame you. If you hadn't been distracting me I could have paid attention far better. I never thought anyone could look cute in waterproofs and a pompom.'

Before she could reply he turned and looked out behind them. 'This part doesn't look that familiar, does it?'

She looked out at the scenery, confused. Not from trying to work out where they were (she'd long ago given up on that) but by Alex. One minute they'd be talking about a film or a book then he'd throw in a comment about her looking cute, but then immediately start talking about the restaurant. Or the scenery. Or anything that changed the subject.

Through their lunch he'd been attentive and the perfect host, having brought along a half bottle of champagne in a chiller sleeve to keep it cold, strawberries as well as lovely delicious hams and cheeses for them to eat as they perched on some rocks Alex had thrown a tartan picnic rug over.

At first Mallory had thought, because he wanted to be alone with her, that something was going to lead on from the previous night and when she saw the lunch she thought she was on the right track as strawberries and champagne were definitely a step up from a squashed ham salad roll and a warm Capri Sun, but although there was the odd occasional compliment there were no lingering looks or smouldering glances; just two friends out for a walk and joking around.

Now she was starting to think that any flirting or chemistry she thought there had been was all in her imagination! And maybe Alex always ate that kind of lunch and if it had been Olly or Nik in her place he'd have brought along the same things.

'I really don't like the look of that sky.' Alex frowned. 'Forecast is for strong winds and rain and it looks like it'll be on us in about ten minutes or so. I think if we head back down here we should eventually follow the path round in a curve which will lead us to the car. Does that sound like a plan?'

Mallory wasn't about to argue. She was wearing enough fleece and waterproof layers to be warm and dry but she was far from comfortable. And she hated the rasping chaffing noise her gear made every time she took a step.

He started off down the hill and Mallory followed, carefully picking her way back down the path, taking care to move sideways as the smaller stones acted like ball bearings under her feet.

'It's still amazing though, don't you agree, despite the wind and rain and heavy cloud? It's one of the main reasons I wanted to move back up to Scotland; for the sheer rugged beauty of this.' He stopped a little in front of Mallory and held his face up to the slight drizzle of rain.

Mallory was focussed on not slipping. She came to a stop beside him and pulled her hood back so she could see the view. It was, indeed, pretty spectacular with the blanket of rain sweeping in, and the last rays of the watery sun rolling over the glen below them.

'Hmm. Makes you want to paint,' she said lightly, watching Alex for a reaction.

He threw her a glance then turned back to the view. 'You're the artist, you must get inspiration from scenes like this.'

'But I'm guessing I'm not the only one.'

He turned to her again, this time with a guarded look in his eyes.

'I found some paintings in the room next to yours.'

'Oh?'

'They're very like the style I found in a sketchbook in your room.'

'Regular Nancy Drew, aren't you?' He laughed, but there was a look in his eye which said she'd hit a nerve.

'They're really good.'

'That so?'

'Yes! Are they yours?'

'We'd better head back.'

'Have you ever approached a gallery? Spoken to Johan?'

'It's going to pour any minute.' Alex turned and started marching back down the path.

'Alex–'

'I'm not talking about this anymore, Mallory.'

And he didn't, because as he turned to look back round at her his foot slipped and he tumbled over the edge of the verge.

CHAPTER 33

*J*rini sniffed the air appreciatively. 'I love it when you can smell the rain coming.'

Olly gave a tentative sniff but could only smell the cow dung he'd stood in earlier.

Irini delved into her rucksack and pulled out a flask. 'Fancy some soup?'

'Absolutely!' He patted his stomach.

'It's tomato with a bit of a kick; I added some chillies.'

'Great! I do like it nice and hot,' he said heartily, then saw Irini's eyebrow shoot up. 'I mean, I like chillies nice and hot, that's all,' he said, back-tracking from his unintentional innuendo. He took some of the soup and wondered dismally why his conversation skills had dried up.

'I like really hot baths,' Irini added in an obvious attempt to make him feel more at ease.

'Oh yeah, baths are good being hot, although my Aunt Susan ended up fainting in hers once because it was too hot. Luckily Uncle Mike was on hand to pull her out. Did you know that most of the emergency admissions are a result of mishaps in the home?'

Irini was blowing on her soup, trying not to laugh. 'No, I did not.'

'I, um, so there you go. It's nice soup.'

'Just watch you don't scald yourself,' she said, offering him an oatcake. 'I don't want to have to take you to Accident and Emergency.'

'Aye, no, that wouldn't be a very good idea.' Well, he certainly needn't worry about cutting himself on his sharp wit! 'Last night, Nik said he'd like you to join him in Serendipity. Are you tempted?'

Irini sighed. 'A bit. I'm in a rut with my job. I'm the general manager for a nearby hotel. I've been there so long and there's nothing really left for me to bring to the job. I had been toying with the idea of a change. But working with Nik? I don't know.'

'He seems a very affable guy.'

'Yeah, but not if you're his little sister. Our dad moved around a lot with his job which is why Nik and I went to boarding school. Our schools were only a few miles apart and he took the role of older brother and protector very seriously. I worry if I end up working with him and living in the same city he'll fit me with a tracker device and I'd be under a curfew!'

She gave a laugh. 'Okay, so he's maybe not that bad, but, do I take the risk? We're also both stubborn and think we know best which could end up being quite a fiery combination in a kitchen!' She dunked an oatcake into the soup and munched on it thoughtfully for a moment. 'I'm sure if he had a girlfriend to keep him busy he'd forget to be my constant chaperone. I had high hopes he'd be bringing someone this weekend.'

'Yeah?'

'Yeah. He went on at great length about meeting someone but so far, there have been no introductions, which is very frustrating. And I tried asking about her but he clammed up and changed the subject. I even wondered if she was a figment of his imagination!'

'You think?'

'Something odd's going on. He's gone from saying he's met the woman he's going to spend the rest of his life with to becoming very cagey about her. He's got such romantic notions. Always has. I mean, calling his restaurant Serendipity is case in point!'

'My friend Caz is a bit like that. Totally believes in fate and how things are meant to be.'

'Is she annoyingly positive, like Nik?'

'Yeah, quite a lot of the time, actually.'

'Ah, sounds like they could both do with a healthy shot of cynicism!' Irini said, jokily.

They finished their soup in companionable silence then Irini stood.

'We'd best get going. The rain's getting closer, we'll be in for a right deluge.'

'Here, let me carry your rucksack.'

'It's not heavy…' She started to protest but he'd already swung it over his shoulder.

They smiled at one another.

It was hardly a scintillating one-liner but, as his granny had always taught him, good manners maketh the man.

CHAPTER 34

'Alex? Alex? ALEX!'

Mallory peered down the side of the verge, leaning out as far as she dared. It wasn't a sheer drop, but it was pretty steep, with lots of trees to bounce off. About halfway down she could see his rucksack dangling off a branch. She heard a groan.

'Hang on, I'm coming to get you.'

Stepping over the edge, she half walked, half slithered on her hands, feet and bum to where his rucksack was. When she was almost at it, she could see Alex just below, head down, his foot entangled in a tree root.

'Are you okay?' Mallory gasped as she scrambled over to him.

He was ashen. 'My leg.'

She looked down at it and felt a little queasy. There was a gash in the side of his leg about five inches long which was slicked with blood.

If he had broken his leg she probably shouldn't move him, or was that just in case the person had broken their neck? Crap! She had no idea. A couple of large drops of rain splashing on her head decided it for her.

'Hang on a minute,' she told him as she emptied out the contents of her rucksack and first aid kit.

'Damn! I was hoping to hot-foot it out of here and head to a party.'

'I see you didn't bruise your sarcasm on the way down.' She grasped hold of the small foldable spade in her emergency kit. 'Right, I'm going to have to free your foot. Do you think it's broken?'

'Don't think so.'

She started to dig up the tree root, careful not to jostle Alex's foot. When it was free she untied his boot slightly then flicked open her army knife.

'If you're about to amputate, I'd rather we wait for a second opinion.'

'I'll let you keep all your limbs for now. I am, however, going to have to operate on your jeans.'

He gave a slight laugh. 'That's all right, I don't think I'll be wearing them again, the ripped look is so last season.'

Mallory tore the fabric along the seam to get a good look at the wound. Close up it looked worse. She checked over the array of first aid accoutrements lying on the bracken and laid aside the ones which looked most promising, or the ones she at least knew what they were.

She grabbed her water bottle, sluicing water over the wound. From what she could see there didn't look as if he had anything stuck in his leg. The best thing she could do would be to bandage it up and take him to someone who had an actual clue as to what to do. She handed him the end of the water and two Nurofen, figuring anything was better than nothing.

'Don't suppose you've got a hip flask on you?' she asked.

'Ahh.' He reached into his inside pocket and produced a slim silver one. 'Good thinking.'

But she snatched it off him before he could raise it to his lips.

'This may hurt,' she warned, ignoring his protests. 'In fact, it will.'

'Thanks for your words of comfort.'

She drizzled some spirit over his wound and Alex gritted his teeth at the pain.

The wound was still bleeding freely so she shrugged off her jacket, removed her top jumper then peeled off the Thinsulate layer below, still leaving a T-shirt and vest top.

'Do you really think this is the time or place?' Alex joked feebly.

'Don't get too excited, I need to secure a bandage. I figure I can tie round something with sleeves but my jumper's too thick.'

She rolled up the body of her top and pressed it to the wound. She could see Alex struggling not to wince.

'You're being very brave, have a sweetie.' She crammed a piece of Kendal mint cake in his mouth.

'Ugh, that's vile.'

'Eat it! I don't want to risk your blood sugar dropping from shock at the blood loss.'

'Where did you learn to do all this? Was this down to your Girl Guide training too? Before the Scouts got you?'

She scrambled into her clothes again. 'Nope, this comes straight from an episode of *Casualty*, when half the cast ended up on an outward-bound course.'

'Did it end well?'

'As long as we don't meet a logging truck and a minibus full of OAPs on the way to a war memorial we'll be fine.'

He lay back on his elbows and looked up at the trees as she bandaged his leg as best she could. She didn't have many big bits of wadding so she put her woolly hat on top of the other fabric before wrapping the arms of her discarded top round his leg, tying the bandage tightly. It maybe wasn't the most hygienic thing to do but she hoped it would stop him bleeding to death.

'Okay, you're going to have to stand up now.' She handed him her walking poles and together they managed to get him upright.

'How does that feel?'

'Will you think I'm less manly if I shriek like a girl?'

'Shriek away.'

They started their very tentative descent as there was a deep roll of thunder above them.

'Excellent,' Alex said. 'I was thinking we could do with a bit more drama.'

'We need to get down to the flat before the ground gets slippery with mud. Use one pole and lean on me.'

'I'm too heavy.'

'Doesn't matter.'

He stopped. 'Why don't you leave me here and get back to the house and bring help. I promise not to run off anywhere.'

'We're going together. I don't leave a man behind.'

Alex laughed. 'How very Sylvester Stallone of you.'

It took them almost an hour to get to the bottom of the verge, but luckily, on the descent, they saw Alex's car through a gap in the trees and Mallory was cheered to know at least they'd headed the right way.

By the time they got to the car the rain was hitting the ground full pelt with some pretty spectacular special effects courtesy of thunder and forked lightning. Alex, although trying not to, was leaning heavily on her, his face shiny with sweat at the effort of walking. Mallory's back and shoulders burned with pain.

It was only when Alex threw Mallory the keys that she realised she was going to have to drive.

'Just don't be doing any of your rally driving stunts on the way. Probably best if we head for the doctor's surgery in the village, we'll pass it on the way to the house.'

Alex eased himself into the passenger side, hauling his injured leg in last. Blood had soaked through the bandages as Mallory could see her woollen hat had a scarlet patch. Alex's face was so white and for a chilling moment Mallory feared he'd lost too much blood.

'You okay?' she asked as she got behind the wheel.

'Yup, those painkillers really hit the mark.' He tried to laugh, but gave up and threw his head against the seat and closed his eyes.

Mallory turned to the dashboard and all the instruments in front of her.

'Select first gear,' she mumbled, doing just that. She checked the mirrors, not really expecting to see anyone as they were in the middle of nowhere. She mentally went through her checklist. *Find the biting point, give it some gas, release the handbrake and lift off on the clutch.* To her delight they moved forward along the rocky muddy lane.

After a couple of miles, she got the car to the main road and it shuddered before she remembered to go up into second gear. Her hands were clammy on the steering wheel, and she hoped she wasn't going to get stopped by overzealous traffic police.

On driving along the main road she realised she couldn't see too well, owing to the rain bouncing off the car. Locating the wipers took a moment and she also managed to turn on the lights, which was a great improvement, owing to the darkening sky.

She glanced round at Alex who was watching her with a bemused expression on his face.

'You know, you can go a little faster, possibly even go up another gear if you like, I'm not going to scream out in pain every time you hit a pothole.'

'Uh, sure.' She put her foot on the gas slightly and dared go up into third.

He was watching her rather too closely for her liking. Time to take his attention away from her driving. 'I have to say, you do go to some lengths.'

'What do you mean?'

'To evade my question about your artwork.'

He turned and looked out the window.

'Why don't you want to talk about it?'

He said nothing.

'But...'

He turned to her abruptly. 'Mallory, will you please leave off the subject, it's not up for discussion.' He gave her a look which told her not to keep pushing for answers, which made her even more curious.

They drove the rest of the way to the village in silence.

They got to the surgery just before it was due to close and Alex, too busy wincing in pain from the wound in his leg, didn't mention her appallingly bad parking.

By the time they made it into the reception Alex looked slightly green from the effort of walking.

'Is Geoff about?' he asked the receptionist.

'He's got a patient–' the receptionist started to say as the door next to them opened and an elderly lady walked out clutching a prescription.

'Dr Carmichael? There's someone here to see you.'

A grey-haired man stuck his head round the door.

'Alex!' he said jovially, then looked down at the bloody woolly hat attached to his leg. 'What the hell happened!'

'Had an argument with a tree. I think it won.'

'Come in, come in.'

Still helping to prop Alex up, Mallory went with him.

Geoff dragged a seat over for Alex to sit on. 'I didn't realise you were back.'

'I'm not really, I'm just up for the weekend.'

Mallory wondered if Alex was delusional from the injury as she was sure he'd said he'd been staying at the house since the work had started on Serendipity.

'Right, let's take a look at this.' Geoff gently untied Mallory's makeshift bandage.

'Luckily Mallory's a bit of a hillwalker so she had a bag of tricks with he– YEAOOOW!' Alex almost leapt up from the chair as Geoff peeled away the woolly hat.

'Sorry, ooh yes, that's nasty. Looks clean though.'

'I had a quick look in the wound,' Mallory said. 'I couldn't see anything so I just squirted it with water…'

'And my cask-strength Talisker,' Alex grumbled.

'Smart,' Geoff said. 'That'll kill off a few nasties.' He stood. 'Tetanus for you, young man, then a couple of stitches. Mallory my dear, would you care for a cup of tea, Wendy can see to you, unless you'd like to stay and watch?'

Alex cut in. 'No, she wouldn't. And seeing as I won't be in a fit state to drive home, I think I'd like my hip flask back, thank you!'

CHAPTER 35

'Geoff said you were very brave.'

'Stoic,' Alex agreed as Mallory drove them back to the house from the surgery. 'He told me the best route to recovery was lots of whisky and fawning over.'

Mallory smiled, not daring to take her eyes off the road. 'He told me elevation and painkillers every four hours.'

'You must have misheard. This is us here.'

With great relief Mallory signalled and turned into Alex's drive. They'd been a couple of hours in the surgery and by the time they'd left the weather had taken a turn for the worse and as well as driving in the dark, Mallory had to contend with howling wind, torrential rain and forked lightning being the only illumination along the country roads.

'That's funny.' Alex leaned forward in the passenger seat and peered out the windscreen as she parked around the back of the house. 'The lights aren't on, and Connor's car's gone. I bet we've had a power cut and they're off seeking solace in the pub,' Alex said, leading the way, hobbling on two crutches. He hadn't really needed them but he'd wheedled them out of Geoff so he could glean extra sympathy from the others on the strict proviso he'd return them in a couple of days.

Mallory locked the car and followed.

Inside, Alex flicked the light switch by the kitchen door but nothing happened. Mallory tried a couple too, but they remained in darkness.

Alex hopped over to the cupboard under the sink and produced a couple of stumpy candles and bag of tea lights.

'We're used to temperamental electrics around here,' he said, lighting a few.

As they sputtered to life Mallory noticed a note on the table addressed to the two of them. She read it aloud.

Dear Alex and Mallory,

It's dark and cold and scary so we've gone to the pub to get something meaty with chips. Presume you're out gallivanting and haven't been taken by wolves in the middle of the night.

Nik.

'Looks like it's just the two of us.'

'Looks like,' Mallory agreed.

They fell into silence, the only sound being the wind and rain battering against the window as they looked at one another. The candles flickered, the soft light glancing off the planes of Alex's face, accentuating the angles of his cheekbones, the darkness of his brows, while his eyes glittered brightly.

They were alone in the house, with the weather creating wild merry hell outside.

She could feel her breath quickening and saw the rise and fall of his chest matched hers. He moved closer, not taking his eyes from hers. He rested his hand on the table behind her, his face just inches away.

Mallory shivered slightly.

'Cold?' he asked.

But before Mallory could answer the door flew open and Nik, half laughing, half yelling, bowled into the kitchen.

'I beat the Land Rover! We raced the last five hundred yards and I beat him.' He gasped as Connor's car headlights swept into the kitchen. 'School sprinting champion! I've still got it! Oh God, I feel sick,' he added, leaning against the table. Mallory and Alex took a step back from each other as the others streamed in.

The only one not laughing was Louisa; she looked as if she'd spent the entire evening sucking lemons.

The others were full of bonhomie as they quickly lit more candles.

'Had a good evening?' Alex asked.

'Absolute top!' Gordy said. 'Where the hell did you two get to?'

Sash shrieked when she noticed the crutches. 'Yikes! What happened?'

'Managed to rip my leg open on a tree stump,' Alex said glibly. 'Just got back from the doc's, he stitched me up and sent us on our way.'

'Ooh, is it all mangled and bloody? Does it hurt?' Sash asked.

'I'm working on the pain relief, in fact I'm due my next dose of medication right now.' Alex grabbed hold of his crutches and started to head out of the kitchen. 'Single Islay malt. Now can one of you buggers come and help me get the fire going in the lounge?'

'Count me out,' Louisa said, grabbing a handful of tea lights. 'I'm off to have a bath.'

'The empathy just oozes out of that one,' Olly said, once she'd gone.

The others trooped out, taking the lit candles with them, wailing like drunken, giggly ghosts.

Mallory stood in the dark kitchen, wondering what had

happened. Or almost happened. Had Alex been about to make a move on her? If he had, wouldn't he have been keen to have gotten rid of the others so they could be alone again? She was so confused. And tired. And not really wanting to get involved in any game playing.

'Hey, are you coming through?' Olly asked, poking his head back into the kitchen. 'Are you all right?'

'I'm fine. I... um... Do you ever get the feeling you have no idea what's going on?'

He gave a small chuckle. 'Frequently. What's happened?'

She knew she was being cryptic and although she would dearly have loved to have sat with him and told him all that was on her mind, something held her back. For a start she didn't want to risk someone, especially Louisa, overhearing. And, she didn't really think Olly was the best person to speak to. He'd been different with her lately, especially this weekend and she felt a little awkward at even the thought of talking to him about Alex.

'Och nothing. It's just been a long day. Would you mind going back to the lounge and passing on my apologies. I'm knackered and off to bed.'

Olly handed her his candle. 'Take this. And don't stray onto the moors,' he joked before going to join the others in the lounge.

Once in her room Mallory peeled off her hiking boots and all her layers of clothes. It was probably just as well she and Alex hadn't ripped each other's clothes off in a fit of passion, the urge would have probably gone off them long before they'd gotten to the thermal underwear.

She changed into her kitten-emblazoned pyjamas, glad she'd brought them considering the sudden drop in temperature. She dithered over shoving the chair in front of the door to Louisa-proof her room again, then had a brief, hopeful thought that Alex may possibly try to sneak in later, so wondered about changing out of her kitten-emblazoned pyjamas into something slinkier before realising she didn't have anything slinky to change into. She tried to put all thoughts out of her mind as she snuggled down under the duvet.

CHAPTER 36

*a*fter saying goodnight to Mallory, Olly went back to the lounge, where Irini was sitting. They were slightly separate from the others, who were playing a noisy and competitive game of charades. Multiple candles flickered on all the surfaces and the large fire illuminated the room with a warm orange glow.

'Red suit you, madam?' he asked, producing a bottle of wine.

'Lovely, thank you.'

'I've got some nuts too, if you fancy something to nibble.'

Irini burst out laughing. She had *such* a dirty laugh.

'I meant these.' He held up a bag. 'KP Dry Roasted. I got them in the pub earlier.'

'So, tell me some more about the illustrations you're working on at the moment,' Irini said, settling back into the sofa and patting the space beside her.

He handed her a glass of wine, sitting down. He wondered if she was just being polite because he'd been talking about his art that afternoon or if she did genuinely want to know. She seemed interested but he didn't want to send her to sleep. 'It's just a couple of things, nothing too exciting.'

She swivelled on the sofa so her body faced him, her arm brushing against his. 'You don't get excited by your job?'

'I do. I mean I enjoy it. I've been illustrating a series of children's books from the start of the series, which is a sweet story about a little boy who's actually a space alien. And I'm doing a classical poetry book too.'

She took a sip of her wine. 'But it's the graphic novel you're loving most?'

He hadn't realised she'd been listening in to that part of the conversation when he'd been chatting to Gordy. 'Yes.'

'Are you going to focus on that?'

'It's not a commission, just my own little project. A hobby, you could say.'

'Why keep it as a hobby?'

He toyed with his wine glass. 'I don't think I could make any money from it. I suppose I could publish it myself and hope it would find an audience.'

'Money isn't everything,' Irini pointed out as she shook some nuts onto the palm of her hand. 'Money aside. What makes you most happy?'

'I like all the work I do.'

'There must be something you want more than anything else though.'

'I suppose, if pushed I'd say, be Batman.'

'Seriously!' She threw a nut at him.

'Seriously? To be honest I'm happy to go with the flow for now.'

She looked at him as she licked the salt off her finger, which he found rather sexy as her lips were full and quite pouty. 'Do you have the same amount of passion for all your work?'

'I do.'

'Then you are truly living the dream.' As Irini gave him an alluring smile, Olly realised it wasn't just the passion for his illustrations he felt.

CHAPTER 37

Feeling very much like a heroine in a Gothic novel, Mallory lay in bed by the light of the candle and listened to the rain lashing against the windows and the wind howling around the house like an over-enthusiastic banshee. She was starting to give up on the notion of falling asleep as every time she started to drift off, Alex would pop into her mind. She'd run through their conversations during the weekend, analysing his every comment and interpreting his body language so many times she felt as if she'd competed the mental equivalent of The Marathon des Sables.

One by one she heard the others head off to their bedrooms until, gradually, the house settled back down and the floorboards stopped creaking as everyone obviously drifted off to sleep. Everyone apart from her. She reached over to her phone and saw that it was only just after midnight, although it felt as if it was about three in the morning. She got up, deciding some hot chocolate would probably help.

She padded down the stairs, lighting her way with her torch – another handy inclusion in her rucksack. It was only when she got to the kitchen she realised that with the power still not being on she wasn't able to switch on the kettle. Luckily the cooker was gas.

She upended the torch on the table and it threw off enough light for her to be able to see her way around, but a quick search of the cupboards didn't unearth any hot chocolate. There was, however, a bottle of whisky on the kitchen table. Figuring enough of it would also have the desired soporific effect, with the bonus of not having to wash out a milky saucepan afterwards, she fetched a glass and poured herself a hearty measure.

'Pour one for me, will you?'

Mallory let out a small shriek and nearly dropped her glass.

She turned to see Alex leaning against the door frame, empty glass dangling from his fingertips. His shirt was half unbuttoned and she caught a glimpse of his toned chest beneath it. He stood staring at her through his hair which had flopped over his forehead. With his heavy eyebrows and pale eyes he looked every bit as dark and brooding as Heathcliff, Darcy and pretty much every other fictional romantic hero rolled into a sexy, tousled, fit body.

The effect was like Mike Tyson hitting her solar plexus.

Still leaning on his crutches, he hobbled into the room.

'I, erm, I thought everyone had gone to bed,' Mallory said, trying not to look at him, but the combination of his half-bare torso and smouldering eyes proved too tempting. She raised her eyes to his. And she knew then she was lost. She'd never understood when people talked about 'eyes meeting across a crowded room' but right at that moment a brass band could have marched past them and Mallory wouldn't have noticed.

'I couldn't sleep. You?'

Not trusting her voice to come out as anything other than a squeak she shook her head. He took the bottle of whisky from her, his fingers lightly brushing against hers, setting an electric charge crackling up her arm and straight to her stomach.

He poured himself a drink and took a sip of the whisky,

watching her over the rim of his glass. The static between them was palpable and Mallory's hands shook as she clutched her glass. The way he looked at her… it wasn't flirty, jokey Alex, it was intense, serious Alex.

She'd only caught glimpses of this side to him, but now the full-on effect of this Alex thrilled and terrified her in equal measure. She felt as if she were at the point on a rollercoaster, after chugging to the top of the first slope, she'd paused for a moment, heart in mouth, waiting for the carriage to dip over the top and plummet down to start the chest-thumping, blood-pumping, biggest rush of her life.

He put his glass down on the table and took a step nearer and Mallory's heart was thudding so hard she was sure he would be able to hear it in the stillness of the room.

He then took her glass from her and placed it on the table. Without breaking eye contact he took her hand in his and gently circled his thumb over the inside of her wrist.

'Your pulse is racing.'

'I'm scared of storms,' she said, her voice barely above a whisper, her skin singing under his touch.

He took her hand and placed it on his chest. It was also beating wildly.

'Are you scared of storms too?' she asked, light-headed with desire.

'Nope.'

'Scared of me?'

'Should I be?' His mouth twitched into a half smile.

'Maybe.'

'Why, do you bite?' he said hoarsely before lightly brushing his mouth against hers, a whisper of a touch and for once Mallory was one hundred per cent certain she wasn't misreading his signals. Her hands slid up over his chest, feeling the taut muscles through the cotton of his shirt as Alex pulled her to him, his lips searching out hers, savouring her, like she was the finest

Burgundy wine. His lips travelled lazily down to her throat, exploring her neck and Mallory felt as if she'd been plugged into the mains as every nerve ending leapt.

Light-headed with longing, she threw her head back, at the exquisite sensations taking over her body as his mouth travelled south, light as air, on her tingling skin as heat pulsed between her legs.

They stumbled, banging against the edge of the table, laughing as they clumsily pulled off each other's clothes, their fingers struggling to undo buttons in their haste... until a movement outside the window caught Mallory's eye.

It took her a moment to register that she was looking at someone watching them.

She gave a little scream.

Alex's head snapped up. 'What's wrong?'

Mallory stared speechlessly beyond Alex, at the voyeur.

Alex turned to see what had startled her. 'Jesus Christ!' He ran for the back door, forgetting his wounded leg, and stumbled, swearing in pain.

The voyeur drew back from the window but not before Mallory recognised the slightly gaunt face and intense brooding eyes.

The power chose that moment to come back on, illuminating the kitchen and triggering the security lights outside, along with the burglar alarm, where a very pissed-off Don stood waiting to be let in.

CHAPTER 38

 allory could only look on in stunned disbelief as she hastily rebuttoned her pyjama top as Alex limped over to the door and yanked it open. 'Who the hell are you and what the *fuck* are you doing?' he shouted over the insistent '*whoop whoop whoop*' of the alarm.

A very wet and bedraggled Don squared up to Alex. 'And who the hell are *you*?'

'The owner of this property. You're trespassing!'

'Technically, so are you!' Fury flashed in Don's eyes and Mallory started to get a very bad feeling.

'What!' Alex half laughed at the absurdity.

Mallory ran over. 'Alex, wait!'

As Alex turned to Mallory, Don seized his chance and shouldered his way into the house but Alex swung round, grabbing him and propelling him back outside. Don roared with rage and tried to rugby tackle Alex, but even injured, Alex was too quick and tripped him up, sending him sprawling at Mallory's feet.

Grabbing his crutch, Alex thrust it into the base of Don's back, pinning him to the floor. Nik, Connor and Olly all ran into the kitchen, closely followed by Louisa, cream silk negligée and matching peignoir billowing out behind her.

Everyone looked at Don in shock, all except Olly who was looking at Mallory, eyebrows raised questioningly.

Nik hurried over to the control panel and punched in a code which mercifully stopped the alarm.

'Once again, who the hell are you and what are you doing at my house?' Alex asked, his voice unnervingly calm but his eyes flashing angrily.

Don looked up at Mallory.

'Now might be a good time to speak up,' he said, his face taut.

Mallory felt everyone's eyes on her.

'You know him?' Alex said, turning to her.

'Um, kind of.'

'Kind of!' Don spluttered.

'This is Don. Don Marsden.'

Don glowered at everyone. 'Her fiancé.'

Everyone looked back at Mallory, obviously waiting for her to either confirm or deny her betrothed status. Even Don was watching her expectantly.

'He's your fiancé?' Alex said, incredulously.

'I um…'

'Yes,' Don said. 'I proposed, she said yes, ergo, engaged.' With a thunderous look to Alex, Don knocked the crutch away and stood, leaving a puddle of rainwater on the floor where he'd lain. He was soaked through.

Despite his unkempt appearance and the fact his wool coat smelled like wet dog, Don still cut an imposing figure, with his tall sinewy frame filling the room. He ran a calloused hand through his buzz cut and down over his face to get rid of some of the rain.

He turned to Mallory. 'I got a call from a journalist who wanted me to confirm a few facts from a story you told her. It didn't exactly put me in a very good light. Luckily, I was in

London, so I got the first flight I could up here and took every form of bloody transportation to get here so we could talk.'

That familiar feeling of queasy anxiety tweaked at Mallory's insides. She inwardly cursed herself for getting so drunk and speaking to that bloody journalist! She couldn't even completely remember what she'd said.

'I ended up walking the last few miles,' Don added as he turned to Alex and gave him a haughty look. 'As for your ludicrous accusation of trespassing, your gate was wide open and as nobody heard me knocking at the front door I came round the back, where I saw you.' He turned to Mallory.

Mallory squirmed with embarrassment at being spied on in such an intimate moment.

Alex, though, still looked furious and took a step towards Don again but Nik stepped between them, placing a restraining hand against his chest.

'So, *you're* the fiancé?' Louisa piped up. 'I was starting to think you didn't exist.'

'You weren't the only one,' Alex added, turning his attention to Mallory.

Mallory didn't know what was worse, Alex's cold stare or Olly's expression of disappointment. She had no idea how to begin to explain the situation she found herself in. She would have to go back to the beginning and start with the fictitious CV, which was something she wanted to speak to Alex alone about. Although she supposed she should really set Don right first and explain the misunderstanding.

'You did tell people we're engaged, didn't you?' Don said, looking pointedly at Alex.

'Not exactly,' Olly said, frowning at Mallory.

Don glanced over at Olly. 'You're still hanging around I see.'

'I'm her friend. I look out for her,' Olly said coldly.

Don gave Olly a brief chilly smile. 'How very gallant of you.'

Nik watched Alex warily in case he was about to take another lunge at Don. Don was looking imperiously at Olly. Connor appeared confused and slightly uncomfortable, and Mallory stood tugging on the hem of her pyjama top knowing she'd reached an entire new level of ineptitude because she hadn't the faintest idea what to say, or who to say it to. The only person who looked at all happy was Louisa.

Connor was the first to move. 'Uh, well, good to meet you, I'm Connor.' He shook Don's hand. 'I think it best we all get some sleep now and have a catch-up tomorrow. I'll leave some clothes out for you for the morning in case those haven't dried out by then.' At that he quickly left the room.

'Mallory, we need to talk,' Don said.

Mallory nodded. She turned to Alex. 'Alex…' She desperately needed to speak to him and explain it all but she knew she had to tell Don first. She owed him that much. She gave a helpless shrug and pointed to Don. 'I have to… you understand?'

'Perfectly,' Alex replied, although his face looked thunderous.

'And is there somewhere I can have a shower?' Don asked.

Mallory nodded. 'Uh, sure, use the one in my room.'

With a final glower at Alex, Don followed her out and up the stairs. Inside her room she turned to face him, stomach churning.

He held up a hand to stop her from speaking. 'First thing I need is a shower,' he said and stomped into the en suite and closed the door. Seconds later the shower started up.

Mallory sat on the bed, feeling slightly sick.

There was a knock on the door. *Alex!* He'd come to talk to her and she'd be able to tell him everything and they'd clear up the misunderstanding!

She bounded over to the door.

'It's not what it…'

Instead of Alex, Olly stood there, arms folded. 'What the hell's going on?'

She glanced at the bathroom door but it was firmly shut. She took a step into the hall, pulling the door closed slightly behind her.

'It's not what it looks like.'

'I'm so glad, because it looks really like you and that waste of emotional space are engaged.'

'We're not!'

'So why does he think you are?'

'Okay, I didn't say anything to you and Caz because I know how you feel about him,' Mallory blurted, desperate to get all the words out so he would stop looking so disappointed in her. 'A few months ago, he started phoning me again... but I didn't answer,' she hastily added, seeing Olly's face contort in disbelief, 'but he kept leaving me messages telling me he loved me, he missed me, that sort of thing. He phoned one night, really late. It woke me up, and I decided to answer and tell him in no uncertain terms never to contact me again.'

He gave a small snort. 'I'm guessing something must have backfired!'

Annoyed at Olly's self-righteous manner she snapped back, 'That's bloody obvious, isn't it!' As quickly as her anger flared up it dissipated. She was tired and wanted to tell Don to leave then find Alex and tell him the entire story. She rubbed her brow wearily where a headache was starting. 'Don was drunk,' she explained in a calmer voice, 'and wasn't in any mood to listen to reason. He asked me to marry him and, and... I said yes because I wanted to get him off the phone.'

Olly stood looking at her for a moment and sighed. 'That was a bit stupid wasn't it?'

'I didn't think he was serious!'

'Well, I think we've ascertained he was.'

'I honestly thought if I said "yes" he'd run a mile. You know what a commitment-phobe he is.'

'It seems he's over that particular personality defect.'

'Because I didn't hear from him again I thought my plan had

worked and didn't really think any more of it,' she added, close to tears.

'Looks like your reverse psychology backfired.'

'Looks like.'

From inside the en suite the noise of the shower stopped.

'I'd better let you go and break the news. You know where I am if you need a shoulder to cry on. Or a burly man to help kick him out. Actually, for that you're probably best to knock on Connor's door. He's in the room next to me.'

Mallory went back into the bedroom and paced the floor, waiting for Don to come out. The sooner she got it over with the better.

She walked to the window and looked out. The torrential rain had stopped and the clouds had lifted slightly allowing a few stars to twinkle down. She scanned the skies in the hope of seeing a shooting one she could make a wish on, but the heavens were obviously closed to granting wishes. She was on her own.

She looked down at the terrace below. She could make out a figure leaning against the balustrade.

Then the figure turned his face to the side and she saw it was Alex.

Don's appearance had instantly dampened her desire, but watching Alex looking out, surveying the land beyond, she felt a powerful throb of lust. Heat ran through her body at the thought of continuing where they'd left off. She needed to sort Don out then go and see Alex immediately.

She willed Don to hurry up as she gazed down at Alex's strong profile. If only he'd look up and see her so she could give him a wave of reassurance, or a sign or *something* to let him know it would all be okay. She knocked on the glass but she couldn't be heard above the wind. She tried fiddling with the latch but couldn't get it to yield. As she was struggling she saw Louisa glide out, still in her negligée, to join him.

From the angle she was at Mallory could see Louisa had an

eye mask perched on the top of her head. She was even wearing a pair of those silly boudoir-type slippers, the ones adorned with Marabou. Mallory had always wondered who bought those kinds of things. She watched as Louisa sidled up to Alex. At first he ignored her but then she snuggled closer to him, rubbing the tops of her arms, feigning cold.

No one falls for that! Mallory thought, bemused at Louisa's pathetic attempts to get Alex's attention. Then she watched as Alex draped his arms around her shoulders, pulling her close to him.

She hated when women played the helpless creature role to ensnare a man. Luckily most men weren't that gullible! Louisa should go back inside if she was that cold! Then she watched in horror as Louisa snaked her body around Alex's so she was in front of him, her perfectly manicured hands encircling his neck as she drew him down towards her.

Jealousy ripped through Mallory's chest.

Don't do it, Alex, don't do it! Don't kiss her back!

But Alex bent down towards Louisa, crushing his mouth against hers.

Mallory raised her hand to bang on the window but stopped, frozen as she watched him run his hands up her thighs, lifting the delicate fabric of her negligée. Lips still locked together, Louisa unbuttoned Alex's shirt as he lifted her up so she could circle her legs around his waist.

Unable to take any more, Mallory fell back from the window. Her insides physically ached, as though Alex had reached inside her chest and lacerated her heart. Legs weak, she stumbled to the bed and sat down.

She thought there had been something between her and Alex, something incredible. She'd felt it surge through her body when they'd touched and she thought he'd felt the same. All he had to do was wait a few minutes until she went back to explain the misunderstanding. But if he could so easily go from her to *Louisa* of all people within half an hour, it obviously hadn't meant anything to him. But why would he, he'd assumed she was engaged because of that stupid made-up CV!

Mallory had believed what she wanted to believe; that he'd fallen for her. But of course, he hadn't! All he ever wanted to do in life was to have fun – his words echoed hollowly as she remembered he'd told her that himself! If she'd thought the future was mapped out with romantic dinners and bunches of flowers she was nothing more than a gullible fool! Richard Curtis movies had a hell of a lot to answer for.

CHAPTER 39

*M*allory was dimly aware of Don coming out of the bathroom. He was wearing her dressing gown. He sat beside her on the bed.

'You look as if you're in shock.'

She just stared at him.

'Please, before you say anything, can you hear me out first?' He gave her an imploring look.

Mallory really didn't feel up to speaking and he took her silence as consent for him to carry on.

'Right.' He ran his hand over his head again and exhaled noisily. 'I know I didn't speak to you again after that call.' He looked at her, making sure she knew which 'call' he referred to.

She nodded numbly.

'And I feel dreadful about it. I really do. I don't know how to even begin to justify not calling you the next day, but you have to know I had every intention of coming to see you direct. First thing the next morning, I booked my flights back to the UK. I got it into my head that the next time I spoke to you it needed to be in person.

'So, I touched down in London and that's when my agent

called, he'd been trying to set up some meetings. I went to those and it was all good and then, well, I basically felt so overwhelmed. I couldn't make that final journey up to see you. I didn't know what was stopping me. If you knew all the times I nearly jumped onto a flight to Glasgow... but I didn't know what to say to you when I saw you. And the longer I left it the harder it became. Can you understand that?'

She nodded. She wondered where Alex and Louisa were, if they were in the lounge or if they'd made it up to the bedrooms. Would they be in Alex's room, with all the mess and half-packed suitcases lying about, or Louisa's, which she no doubt had ready with strewn rose petals and scented candles. She struck Mallory as the sort of woman who would always be prepared for seduction. Unlike her, who had thought she could tempt Alex with a pair of too-small pyjamas with a kitten motif and a pair of bright canary-yellow fluffy bedsocks. Despite her misery she felt like laughing; had she seriously thought she could compete in Alex's world of designer daywear, country estates and sophistication?

Her attention was brought back to Don as he stroked her arm.

'I can understand that with not hearing from me you must have thought I'd gotten cold feet. Or worse, that I hadn't meant it in the first place. But even fearing all this I was still paralysed into inaction. I only, *finally*, got my act together when that journalist called to tell my side of the story.

'I couldn't get my head round some of the things you'd said, but I had to admit to myself they were all true. And that's when I realised I couldn't keep playing around with your feelings, or mine. It dawned on me that when I asked you to marry me, you'd said yes and I figured that if you trusted me enough to say yes after everything I'd put you through, you were the girl for me.'

'But–'

He took her hand in his. 'No, please let me speak. It's taken me a long time to get to this. That's when I knew I had to see you as soon as possible. I'd had the jolt to spur me on. And when I saw you through the window...' He trailed off slightly, shaking his head. 'I was so angry, Mallory, you have no idea.'

He took a deep breath, massaging the backs of her hands with his rough calloused thumbs. 'Tell me one thing, who is that guy? Is it serious?'

'Alex?' she said faintly, hurting from even just saying his name out loud. She shook her head. 'It's not serious. Just a bit of fun.' She spoke with as much conviction as she could muster, hoping her heart would hear and believe it.

Don stood and started pacing, his hands thrust deep into the pockets of her dressing gown. She hoped he wouldn't stretch it.

'Mallory, can we scrub everything that's happened before; before this time. Right now. I want you to know I'm here in mind, body and spirit and I have total faith in us. As a couple.'

Numbly, Mallory looked up at Don, finally registering what he was saying. He really hadn't a clue. As usual he had no idea how she felt. It didn't even cross his mind that she only agreed to marry him to get him off the phone. It was all about *him* deciding they were engaged, *him* deciding he was ready.

But then to Alex, it was all just about having fun. He hadn't thought of her emotional involvement or that she may have misread the signals and thought it could lead to something more.

She'd gone straight from one arrogant male to another.

She cleared her throat. 'I only agreed to marry you because I thought it would be the quickest way you'd get off the phone and for you to stop calling me.'

Don stopped his pacing. 'Wow,' he said after a moment, looking as if he'd had all the air sucked out of him. 'Shit, I suppose I deserved that.'

He sat beside her on the bed and stared off into space for a couple of minutes. Eventually he looked round at her. 'It's funny, but I always thought it would be you and me against the world, forever.'

'I used to think that too.' And she *had* felt like that, until his mood swings and selfishness got in the way and gradually eroded their relationship.

'We used to love each other so much.'

Mallory nodded, feeling close to tears. The previous twenty-four hours had been so emotional she felt she'd welcome the release that tears would give her. And she *had* loved Don. *So much.* But he'd broken her heart and it had taken her so long to get over him, and when she thought she had she went and made the mistake of nearly falling into bed with Alex.

Don put his arms around her and drew her to his chest.

'I love you, Mallory,' he said, talking into her hair. 'I always have. I know I made a complete botch-up of it before, but you have to know I've changed. I've even had counselling and it's shown me where I went so wrong. My counsellor said I have always sought out public adoration.'

Mallory snuffled into his chest. 'I could have told you that for free.'

'But see, I wouldn't have listened to you. Well, clearly I *didn't* listen to you. I was willing to throw away what we had for a fleeting moment of fame in the US.'

'But it was worth it, they love you over there.'

He sighed. 'Not really.'

She pulled back slightly and looked up at him.

'They're all talk, enthusing over everything, and I believed it all. But the reality is, I was a one-hit wonder. I was new and different, but after that first exhibition, no one wanted to know.'

'You never said.'

'How could I? I traded the one good thing in my life for what turned out to be a pipe dream. But even if it had worked out, it still wouldn't have been worth it, if it meant losing you. I want to come home: to Scotland and to you.'

He got off the bed and went down on one knee.

'I want to do this properly, without being drunk or an ass.

Mallory, it worked so well between us for so long I believe we can get that back. And I want to prove to you I'm completely, totally, unflinchingly behind us. Will you do me the honour of becoming my wife?'

She stared at him. Her night was becoming more bizarre at each turn. Now was when she had to tell him to go, once and for all. But looking down at him, at his face looking up at her so sincerely, worry etched across his eyes, she remembered how much she'd loved him and how much she'd wished for this very moment.

She'd loved Don once. When he'd left her she'd been a wreck. She'd missed him like hell and that was despite his faults. But if Don was being true to his word and had new self-awareness and had ironed out those faults, all the bits she hadn't liked before, maybe it *could* work.

And what was the alternative? Risk the hurt and humiliation of falling for someone else only for it to explode back in her face? She wasn't a risk taker, never was. She looked at Don, his handsome hawk-like features, his close-cut hair, slightly greying at the temples. She'd loved him once. You couldn't just permanently turn off feelings that strong, surely.

'Okay,' she said.

As Don picked her up and spun her round in delight, her only thought was that she wished he was wearing something different as he looked quite ridiculous in her pink terry towelling bathrobe.

CHAPTER 40

*N*ext morning, Mallory slipped out of bed, straight for the bathroom, careful not to wake Don. She let the hot water of the shower pummel into her back, between her shoulders as she squeezed some shampoo into the palm of her hand, wondering how she was going to break the news of their engagement. Her mum and dad wouldn't be that over the moon as they'd never been keen on Don. She found herself wondering what they'd have thought of Alex.

Mallory threw the shampoo bottle onto the floor of the shower. She was *not* going to think of him now! Alex had no place in her life anymore. Well, apart from the fact he was still her boss, but she could easily manage that. In fact, keeping him at arm's length was far better considering her fake CV. It was crucial he didn't find out about that or how hurt she'd felt when she'd seen him with Louisa – she couldn't bear the humiliation. Which was all immaterial now anyway, she reminded herself, as she was engaged to Don and was deliriously happy!

Or she would be as soon as the news sunk in because all she really felt was numb. But that had to be expected she reminded herself; it had all happened so quickly!

Her mum and dad would come round eventually to the idea of her and Don. The prospect of a big do, a fancy hat for the mother of the bride and an excuse to show off to the neighbours would hopefully placate them. Mallory was more concerned about how she was going to break it to Olly and Caz. Olly's disapproval was bad enough, and that was when he thought it had been a misunderstanding.

Now she had no excuse. Although technically she didn't *need* any excuses. It was up to her whom she married. Olly was just going to have to accept she'd got back with Don permanently. It wasn't as if she was asking *Olly* to marry him, or even spend any time with him, she reasoned as she vigorously shampooed her hair. It wasn't as if she was going to change. Just because she was with Don didn't mean she couldn't be friends with anyone else. She would still be the same person. Yes, Olly would be angry with her for a while but, ultimately, he'd respect her decision. She hoped Caz would have the same outlook.

She was just running over possible ways of breaking the news to them when the shower door opened and Don appeared, eager to join her. In more ways than one.

Mallory tried to cover herself as best she could with a travel-sized shower gel and loofah mitt, averting her eyes away from his very alert nether regions.

It hadn't been that long ago when she'd have loved nothing more than to screw him senseless in a shower and, although she was trying not to look, she could tell he was still fit and had obviously continued working out while stateside. But the idea of being with him made her feel weird.

The previous night had been so wrought with emotion they'd stumbled into bed, cross-eyed with tiredness. She'd fallen asleep in the crook of his arm which had felt more safe than sexy.

Her lack of responsiveness obviously had an effect and Don reached for a towel to cover himself with.

'I'm sorry,' she said, hating the fact she was apologising. 'It's just a bit soon. I'm not ready. Yet. I need to get my head round all of this… us.'

'Sure. However long you need.'

That was different for a start. The old Don would have taken 'no' as a slight to his ego and would have stomped off in a mood.

He closed the door, not before he ran his eyes over her body again, leaving her alone.

She turned her face to the spray and wondered briefly if she'd ever be ready.

She managed to get dressed by using the same under-the-towel technique she used when changing her bikini on a beach on holiday. But Don had his back to her as he changed into the clothes Connor had left for him outside their door. There was an awkward moment when they both tried to go through the door together then both stepped back, wanting the other one to go first. Mallory ended up taking the lead and they headed down for breakfast.

Irini and Nik were there already, squabbling over how to do the eggs. Obviously Nik had filled Irini in on the previous night's events as she turned round, completely unfazed by the new arrival, and introduced herself.

'Nice to be met by someone who doesn't think I'm a burglar,' Don said, sitting down at the table.

'I could hit you over the head with my rolling pin if you'd prefer,' she said and gave a laugh as Don helped himself to some orange juice.

Mallory could see Olly outside, sipping from an espresso cup and having a cigarette. She knew she'd have to go and tell him what had happened before he came in and wondered at the cosy scene of domesticity and why Don wasn't on the first mode of transport back to America.

Then Louisa swept in, full of the joy. Still wearing her seduction get-up, the heels of her fluffy slippers clacked against the flagstone floor like pistol shots. Her hair looked tousled but her make-up had been applied perfectly and Mallory guessed she must have been up an hour before trying to achieve the natural look. That morning Mallory's look was *natural* natural, complete with puffy eyes and a crater-like spot making an appearance on her chin. The fact she ever thought she could compete with someone like Louisa was farcical. Louisa was just so *polished*.

'Isn't it a glorious morning!' Louisa trilled, grabbing the cafetière of coffee Irini was about to place on the table.

Everyone looked outside at the weather. The best that could be said was the heavy rain had ceased, otherwise it was a rather nondescript grey day.

Louisa sailed over to the sink and pointedly grabbed two mugs from the draining board and swept out of the kitchen again.

'Someone got theirs last night!' Irini laughed. 'She must have worn down Connor!'

Mallory hid her hot face in the fridge as she rummaged around for the milk.

But Irini's idea was shot down instantly as Connor ambled into the kitchen.

'What's that about me?' he asked.

Irini looked at Nik, who cast a sideways glance at Mallory.

'Well, it wouldn't be Gordy,' Nik said, looking faintly surprised.

Mallory could feel her face flushing and chose that moment to go and speak to Olly.

She caught up with him at the steps leading down to a series of borders edged with box hedge and interspersed with massive stone urns filled with the last of the bright bursts of asters and chrysanthemums.

'Morning,' Mallory said tentatively.

'Has Don left yet?'

'Um, not quite.'

'Can't imagine anyone wanting him to hang around. It's probably best that I stay out here until he slinks off.'

Mallory said nothing.

Olly idly kicked at the loose stone chippings on the path as he took a draw on his cigarette. 'I hope he took the news suitably badly.'

'He's still here,' Mallory blurted out before Olly said anything he'd later regret considering Don was going to be around a fair bit more from now on. 'We're officially engaged.'

Olly turned; mouth open in disbelief.

'We spent all night talking,' Mallory gabbled on, as if hoping the quicker she spoke, the sooner Olly would understand. She gave him the edited highlights of their conversation, taking time to explain Don's new-found self-awareness courtesy of counselling and his realisation that he'd been chasing after fame and it wasn't what he really wanted.

'Are you sure he's not just saying that because he's maybe not as big a name as he'd like?' Olly said when she'd finished.

Mallory had briefly wondered the same thing but after listening to him bare his soul to her into the wee small hours of the morning, she truly believed Don was a changed man and that fame or no fame, he'd realised America wasn't his destiny.

'He's changed, Olly. I really do believe he's changed.'

The muscle in Olly's jaw pulsed a few times. 'He'd better had. Well, it's your decision,' he said, finally. He shrugged. 'As long as you're happy.'

Mallory squeezed his shoulder as she walked past him into the house again. Happiness was something she could work on.

She'd spent so long outside talking to Olly that when she got back to the kitchen everyone had already eaten and gone, leaving behind a ransacked table.

She boiled up the kettle for a coffee and made herself useful by loading the dishwasher. She hoped Don wouldn't want to hang around; she could be packed in no time and they could be away before she'd have to look at Louisa's cat-who-got-the-cream expression again. At least Louisa seemed happier; now she'd got her man she didn't act like she wanted to turn psycho crazy on Mallory.

Although not seeing Louisa was a bonus, it was really Alex that Mallory had no desire to bump into. She had no idea how she'd react when she saw him. Should she act blasé, as if her fiancé turned up and interrupted her sleeping with another man all the time, or maybe she should be aloof and ignore him?

She scraped some remnants of porridge into the waste disposal unit and decided that ignoring Alex may alert him to the fact he'd hurt her and then she'd risk him pitying her or being embarrassed on her behalf and she couldn't bear that, especially if she still had to work with him for a few weeks.

Her best tactic was to make it look like everything had worked out for the best. She slammed the dishwasher door shut and reminded herself that everything *had* worked out for the best!

She'd just turned to put the butter back into the fridge when Alex appeared in the doorway.

All thoughts of ignoring him or acting blasé went out the window as awkward embarrassment edged into first place.

There were a couple of beats before either of them spoke.

'Morning,' Mallory said first, attempting to put on a cheery face. Unable to make eye contact she studied the butter wrapper.

'Morning.' Alex hesitated a moment before walking past her and retrieving a clean mug from the cupboard. 'You, um... is everything okay with you and your fiancé?'

'Don?'

Alex turned towards her. 'You have *another* one?'

Mallory felt her cheeks flame. 'I, uh, no... we're fine.'

He scratched his head and stared at the kettle as it came up to the boil. 'I didn't realise he was still on the scene. You always seemed cagey about him, and you didn't have a ring... I just assumed you weren't together anymore.'

'It was a funny sort of engagement,' Mallory said, watching Alex's back. *That* was an understatement. 'We'd had a misunderstanding. Things hadn't been going well.' Alex nodded as he spooned instant coffee into a mug; his broad shoulders seemed tense as he moved stiffly.

Neither of them spoke as he poured on the water and splashed in some milk. He added sugar and stirred.

'Last night...' he said, staring into the swirling depths of his coffee.

Damn! Mallory had hoped they'd never need mention it again.

Alex turned round. It was the first time Mallory had properly looked at him since he came into the kitchen and he looked rough. Really rough. Still sexy, with his stubble making him look dishevelled, but his red eyes and wan complexion pushed him over the edge. Oh well, that's what he got for being up all night shagging Louisa, she thought uncharitably.

Mallory swallowed, pushing the thought of Alex and Louisa together out of her mind.

'I, um... I think we both got a bit carried away.' She wanted Alex to know that she could be just as flippant about him as he was about her. 'And let's face it,' she forced a laugh, 'it would have been a big mistake. For one, you're my boss.'

He took a sip of coffee.

'Shall we just agree to forget it?' she said, trying to sound breezy and nonchalant even though she felt like hell.

He flashed her a smile. 'My thoughts exactly. I blame too much whisky and painkillers on an empty stomach. I was so out of it; chances are I'd have made a pass at Nik if he'd appeared at that time.'

'*Or Louisa*' was on the tip of her tongue but she held back; appearing bitter would blow any attempt at acting poised and unbothered. Watching him calmly blow on his coffee Mallory knew that although she felt like hell now she'd have felt a hundred times worse if she had slept with him only to have him act this indifferently to her. She'd had a lucky escape. It didn't matter how many sparks of chemistry she'd felt when they'd touched, it amounted to nothing if it was all one-sided. It was obvious she hadn't meant anything to him at all.

Well, she wasn't going to waste another minute mooning over Alex Claremont or ponder *what could have been's*. She had a real live proper fiancé waiting on her upstairs and she was determined to make it work with him.

She looked down at the butter to find she'd been squeezing it so tightly it had half melted and a big blob had oozed out the end and landed on the flagstones.

'As long as there's not any awkwardness or anything like that between us,' she said, grabbing some kitchen roll and cleaning up the greasy mess.

He looked at her, his eyes impenetrable. 'Should there be?'

'Of course not! I mean, it's quite funny actually… you and me.'

'Yeah,' he agreed. He picked up his coffee and left the kitchen.

But not one part of Mallory wanted to laugh.

CHAPTER 41

*O*lly was sitting on the kitchen step, empty espresso cup hanging from his fingers when Irini poked her head round the door.

'I wondered where you'd got to! What you doing?'

'Just been mulling over how I don't understand women. It's like they're a completely strange species.'

'Oh-kay. I choose *not* to be insulted by that remark.' Irini sat beside him on the step, hugging her knees to her chest.

'I don't mean you. I mean, not that I don't think you're a woman, but…' He shook his head. 'Maybe you can tell me why an intelligent beautiful woman could fall for a complete tool time and time again.'

Irini sucked on her teeth for a moment pondering this. 'No idea, but I too have known quite a few intelligent beautiful women to fall for complete tools. It's something we're quite skilled at. As a completely strange species, that is.' She rested her head on her knees and smiled impishly at him.

'It's Mallory and Don. She's been here before with him. He's treated her like a doormat and I had to pick up the pieces. And now it seems she's conveniently forgotten what he was like.'

Irini tugged at the tendrils of hair of her pixie cut. 'Maybe she loves him.'

Olly snorted.

Irini continued. 'On first impression he cuts quite a dash. He's handsome and seems–'

Olly held up his hand to silence her. 'Why are women shallow enough to fall for the good looks and austere attitude? Why is it always the handsome bastards that get the girl and the nice, kind, funny, slightly quirky guys get trodden on and forgotten about? I just don't understand women.'

'So you say, but sometimes there's a really nice, intelligent, fairly good-looking woman who likes nice, kind, funny, slightly quirky guys.'

He shook his head. 'Such a thing doesn't exist.'

Irini gave him a look and stood abruptly. 'Maybe if these so-called nice, kind, funny, slightly quirky guys managed to shrug off the chips on their shoulder and opened their eyes, they'd realise that we do.' She stalked back into the kitchen slamming the door behind her.

Olly was even more confused than ever. He *really* didn't understand women.

CHAPTER 42

'Blasted bloody Nytol! I took it so the storm didn't keep me awake and I ended up missing all the fun!' Sash moaned as she came across Mallory in the lounge. Mallory had slunk in there in the hope she could avoid speaking to anyone else until it was time to leave.

'I hear there was high drama last night when we got an unannounced visitor!'

'Just a bit.'

Sash flopped down on the sofa beside her looking troubled. 'Is it true, is he your fiancé?'

'Yup.'

'Oh.' Sash looked taken aback. 'I just presumed it wasn't on the cards anymore.'

'It wasn't really that serious before, but we got talking last night after he arrived and we decided to make a proper go of it.' Mallory rattled off this already well-worn account. She felt like taking out a page in *The Herald* to print the explanation.

'But I thought things with you and Alex… Oh dear, I don't normally misread situations so badly,' she said, looking vexed.

At that moment Louisa poked her head round the door. 'Here

246

she is.' She beamed at Mallory and entered the room dragging Don with her and shouting for Alex and Nik.

So much for Mallory's bid to stay under the radar. Once everyone had been corralled into the lounge Louisa sidled up to Alex, linking her arm through his. Mallory tried to ignore the jealousy that ripped through her.

'I've just had the most marvellous idea!' Louisa gushed, giving Alex's arm a covetous squeeze. 'I've been having the most *wonderful* chat with Don here and it turns out these two haven't even discussed an engagement party.'

'There's no rush,' Mallory said.

'But you don't want to waste any time! And I hope you're not going to have a long engagement! They're so outdated now! You need to move on to the main event as soon as!'

'I'm... I'm sure we'll discuss it.' Mallory felt a bit dizzy at the mention of *marriage*. She was still getting her head round being engaged to Don.

'You need to discuss an engagement party immediately!' Louisa said, rather forcefully.

'We're both a bit busy at the moment. And these things take such a huge amount of organisa–'

Louisa clapped her hands together. 'Not if you know someone who arranges events for a living!'

'What are you suggesting?' Mallory wanted clarification as it sounded alarmingly like Louisa was offering her services to help take charge of their engagement party.

'Why don't we combine the opening of Serendipity with Don and Mallory's engagement party!' Louisa cried out, almost bursting with happiness. 'Serendipity. Love. It all works so well. And just think – even more press attention. It will be amazing!'

Don looked at Mallory. 'Why not.'

'Do we need an engagement party?'

'Of *course* you need a party!' Louisa said, horrified that Mallory could even conceive of not having one.

'I suppose this would show everyone how serious I am about us,' Don said, and Mallory noticed he gave Alex the briefest look of smug satisfaction.

Alex looked entirely unruffled and any last vestige of hope was extinguished in Mallory's heart.

'But it's only a few weeks away,' Mallory said, attempting one last time to dissuade Louisa. 'And I don't want to draw any attention from the restaurant.'

'You won't, in fact it'll *add* attention to the restaurant. Restaurant openings are ten-a-penny at the moment but this is an opening which is also its first high-profile function – a world-famous artist's engagement to a local woman.'

Mallory tried not to feel too snubbed.

'And because I'll be organising it all you can still devote all your time to your job and leave the rest to me.'

Mallory could feel her breath quickening as her chest constricted. This was all happening so fast and Louisa clearly wasn't taking 'no' for an answer. In fact, she was already running away with ideas.

'We'll have to have live music!' She turned to Nik with a defiant stare. 'That won't be a problem will it?'

'Uh, no. I'll look into the licence.'

'Live music, love songs, how wonderful!' Louisa enthused.

'Why not make it even more special,' Alex suggested. 'Why not get Mallory to do a number, she's a singer after all.'

Mallory swallowed nervously, trying to read Alex. Was he having a dig? Had he discovered her lies and was about to disclose her fake CV to the gathered group like the denouement in the final scenes of an Agatha Christie whodunnit? But Alex didn't say anything else; his face betrayed no emotion.

'I didn't know you sang,' Don said.

'She's full of surprises,' Alex said and sauntered off in the direction of the kitchen.

'Maybe just the one song,' Louisa said sniffily. 'You don't want to hog the entire evening.'

❧

'Are you sure you want to go ahead with the party?' Mallory asked Don a few minutes later, in her room as she packed.

He lounged on the bed watching her. 'Why not! The sooner the better.' He sat up and grabbed her, encircling her waist with his arms. 'Now it's official I want everyone to know. And I want you to realise I'm committing to us one hundred per cent. One hundred and twenty per cent. A thousand per cent!'

She wriggled out of his embrace. 'I need to pack all this stuff. Olly's leaving in ten minutes.' She didn't want to hold him up in case he reneged on his offer of a lift. She really didn't want to push Olly's good nature, especially if it meant she'd have to stay a moment longer in the house. 'It's just a two-seater, I'm afraid.'

Don stood. 'No problem, I'll see if someone else can drop me off at the airport.'

Mallory paused, mid-pack. 'Airport?'

'I know, it's awful timing, but I need to get to London to attend a meeting for this exhibition I'm doing. I thought my agent was going to kill me when I said I was coming up, but he managed to reschedule.'

Mallory resumed packing, a little voice nagging at her that it couldn't have been *that* last minute and 'whim-like' coming up, if he'd had time to talk to his agent to rearrange a meeting. Would he have still have come up if he couldn't have rescheduled? She pushed the thought from her mind as all that mattered was he *had* come up to see her and propose.

'I doubt I'll be able to come back up to Glasgow to see you before I head back to the States. My flight is in two days, and I'll have to spend some time tying things up.'

'How long do you think you'll be?'

249

'Probably a couple of weeks, I should think.'

'Oh, okay.'

'Please don't be sad.'

She wasn't. Maybe she should be. Of *course* she should be; her fiancé was about to jet off to another continent for a fortnight. But she didn't feel anything. She just stood there looking at him.

He jumped off the bed and engulfed her in a hug.

'Can't breathe,' she gasped.

'Look, I'm as disappointed as you, but the sooner I clear everything up, the sooner I can be back home, with you.' He ran his finger down her cheek and with no other seductive preamble, kissed her. Don's mouth was hard and insistent, his tongue lashing against hers as he grabbed hold of her hips and pulled her to him so she could feel his erection through his jeans. Never one for a lingering slow-burn arousal, Don was all about the fire and passion.

Then Don abruptly broke away and gave Mallory a wolfish look. A horrible thought crept into her mind that he hadn't been acting out of helpless desire, but control, as if to claim her.

'That's a little something to remember me by until I get back from the States. I'll go see who can help me out with a lift.'

Alone in the room, Mallory sat on the bed.

Her mouth felt numb and bruised from his kiss. Don had an insatiable sex-drive and sex with him was always explosive, but could often make her feel like she'd been put through a military training obstacle course.

She quite liked the notion of an entire evening of tenderness. A log fire, some champagne, protracted kissing sessions which didn't make her fear she'd lose a filling. Despite herself Mallory couldn't help but compare Don's roughness with the luxuriating slowness that Alex had taken, the way his lips held the promise of amazing delights as he explored her body, so unhurried as if they had all the time in the world... Mallory felt desire heat her body at the memory.

She jumped up, snapping out of her daydream. Angry at her emotions for betraying her she threw her remaining belongings into her case and squashed it down to zip it up. Alex was the last person she wanted to think about.

She and Don were meant to be, they'd be able to fall back into their relationship. But as she hauled her bag along the carpet ready to bump it down the stairs Mallory had a momentary doubt that she wanted her love life to be full of carpet burns and bruised knees again, as a comfy mattress and fluffy pillow could be just as alluring.

CHAPTER 43

Olly was in no mood to chat and the journey back to Glasgow was a subdued affair. He drove as fast as he dared without risking skidding off the road and plunging straight down the Rest and Be Thankful or risking getting caught by a speed camera. Putting on his favourite Spotify playlist, he cranked up the volume vetoing any conversation, not that Mallory looked in any mood to chat either; she just stared out the window, lost in thought.

As Kasabian's jangling guitars filled the car Olly finally felt able to breathe and allow himself the headspace to think about Irini.

Of all the drama that had unfolded in the past twelve hours it wasn't Mallory getting back together with Don which upset him the most. As the scenery flitted past him along the A83 he realised it was Irini's reaction to him when he'd been sitting outside on the step which had him flummoxed. He replayed the scene over and over and the only thing he came up with, was that she very possibly liked him and had been trying to get it across to him but he'd been too bloody preoccupied thinking about Mallory to have properly picked up on it.

Olly desperately wanted to smack his head off the steering wheel in frustration at not noticing the signs with Irini but the risk of concussion or being arrested for dangerous driving were not ways he wanted to spend the rest of an otherwise lovely weekend. And the reason the weekend had been lovely was pretty much down to Irini.

Why hadn't he picked up on her attempted pick-up?

He sighed.

Now he'd dissected it all in his head and concluded he was an idiot, he didn't want to think about it anymore.

Stopping at Mallory's flat, he helped her upstairs with her bags, and said goodbye in a very awkward and stilted fashion. Back in his car he pulled out his phone and selected Caz's number. She'd be at work and hoped she wouldn't be too busy and could take his call. She did.

'Yo bro! How's it going, you ho?' Caz said down the phone in a dreadful fake rapper voice.

'We have a bit of a problem,' he said and launched into the story of Mallory's engagement to Don.

'That explains why Don called me and asked me where they were,' Caz said once he'd finished. 'But it wasn't me who told him!' she added hastily.

'I didn't think you did. He probably got it from the journalist, or a quick Google would turn up the address, I'm sure.'

'I tried calling Mallory to warn her Don was looking for her but I think she had her phone turned off.'

'The reception wasn't good.'

'What do we do? Is it time for some bang and burn?'

'What?'

'Is it time for bang and burn?'

'What and what?'

'Bang and burn,' Caz repeated slowly. There was a moment's silence from the other end of the line before she sighed and explained, 'Sabotage, Olly. Is it time for a bit of demolition and sabotage?'

'Sabotaging what?'

'Mallory's so-called engagement to tosshead Don, you dunce! That is why you phoned, isn't it?'

He'd really just called to have a moan.

'What do you suggest?' he asked hesitatingly. He didn't like Don but it was Mallory's decision and for reasons only she knew, she had got back together with him.

'Not sure, but whatever it is it will have to be black ops!'

'Have you been watching your box sets of *Spooks* again?'

'We may have to send in a nugget.'

'We're not in the Stasi! Please can we stop the lingo and just talk normally. Do you really think it wise to try to split her and Don up?' Olly wasn't terribly keen on meddling in other people's relationships, it never ended well.

'Oh no, we're not going to try to split them up!'

'Oh good! For all I dislike Don I'd feel odd about doing something like that. So, what's all this burning nugget nonsense about then?'

'Splitting them up is for amateurs! We have to be way cleverer than that! We're going to have to make her realise she's in love with Alex!' As soon as she said it Caz gasped and swore under her breath. There was a moment's silence before Olly heard her say, in a very small voice. 'I'm sorry.'

Olly felt his face flush slightly. 'What have you got to be sorry about?' he bluffed.

'Because you've found out that Mallory is in love with someone. And it isn't you.'

He forced a laugh. 'Judging by what you say, it isn't her fiancé either.' Olly watched as a woman walked by with a dog, pausing to let it sniff a puddle. 'You know, I kind of always knew it wasn't going to happen. And I'm okay with it.'

'Are you? I thought you wanted courage to seize the day.'

He thought briefly about Irini and smiled. 'You know, I think I do, Caz. But it may not be Mallory that I want to seize the day with anymore.'

'Good. Want to talk about it?'

'Not at the moment, I have some thinking to do first.'

'So, a slow seize then.'

'Kind of. But, you really think Mallory's in love with Alex?' He was always astounded at how Caz just seemed to *know* things like that.

'I'd been *sure* of it. The way she talked about him. The way she always denied liking him in a *lady doth protest too much* way. But it's really weird you say she's engaged to Don. Four days ago she was glad to have seen the back of him. Now she's engaged to him. What happened while you were away?'

'Um, nothing I can think of.'

'God, you're useless. *Some*thing must have happened.'

'She *did* fall off a horse.'

'Oh my God! Maybe she banged her head and got a strange amnesia where she's forgotten the last year of her life and she thinks she's still going out with him!'

'I don't think so, Caz. I spoke to her the night he turned up and she told me it had all been a big misunderstanding and she was going to tell him to leave. Next morning, she was engaged to him.'

'Blackmail! It has to be.'

'There is another option.'

'He hypnotised her!'

'No Caz, what if…' He hated even saying it out loud, as he couldn't stand the vain, obnoxious man. 'She does genuinely love him and misses him and wants to be with him. She told me he'd changed.'

But Caz was not for accepting it. 'It's time I got the big guns out.'

In her current mood Olly feared she did actually possess a Kalashnikov and was not afraid to use it.

Luckily, it wasn't what she meant. 'I'll stop off on the way home to buy some tequila.'

CHAPTER 44

*A*fter unpacking, Mallory spent the rest of the day sitting on the sofa, watching forgettable daytime television programmes.

She knew she was really just biding her time as she waited for Caz to get in from her shift at the pub. Telling Olly about her engagement to Don was one thing, but Mallory knew it would be awful trying to convince her best friend she was doing the right thing, especially as Caz could see through her in a nanosecond if she thought Mallory wasn't fully behind her decision.

Since morning she'd had a knot of anxiety in her stomach. She thought it was because she wanted to get away from Alex and Louisa but with each mile she and Olly travelled away from Claremont House, Mallory became more and more uneasy. The events at the house had been so bizarre it had almost acted like a safe haven from reality, but as they got nearer to Glasgow, Mallory realised she was returning with an almighty bump, which wasn't just due to the potholes and Olly's rather erratic driving.

She'd called Don in the early afternoon to tell him it was a big mistake but after a very brief hello he said, 'They're calling my flight.'

'Don...' she'd said, about to launch forth into a split-up speech.

But he'd misread her tone. His voice softened. 'Leaving is tough for me too. I love you. You've made me so happy. And I promise I'll make you happy too!' he said as she heard a tannoy in the background announcing the flight to London was boarding.

She couldn't go through with it. She couldn't split up with him, not twelve hours after accepting his proposal. And not over the phone. She mumbled something about him having a safe flight and they'd talk soon and she hung up.

By the time *A Place in the Sun* had started she'd convinced herself that it *was* a good idea to be back with Don.

Most engaged couples had doubts, it was a healthy reaction, she decided.

But now as she heard Caz opening the front door she wasn't so sure.

Caz was all smiles when she popped her head around the lounge door. Mallory would have bet her last pound on Olly having phoned Caz the second he'd dropped her off and she'd fully expected Caz to greet her with a frown, demanding an explanation.

'Hey you!' Caz said.

'Um, hi.'

She beamed. 'Olly called me and told me your good news.'

This was getting very weird. Mallory had expected Caz to go on the rampage and that she'd end up spending the next hour justifying her decision to get back with Don; she'd even rehearsed the reasons in her head. Instead, Caz flopped down beside her on the sofa. Unnerved didn't begin to describe how Mallory felt.

'You think it's good news?'

'If you're happy then I'm happy. Who am I to say who you should or shouldn't be with?'

Mallory had a quick scan around to see what Zen life-enhancing self-help book she was reading but there was nothing apart from the latest *OK!* magazine and a dog-eared Mills and Boon.

Caz jumped up from the sofa. 'Come on through to the kitchen, I've got us a treat.'

Feeling the whole scenario was like an episode of a surreal sitcom, Mallory dutifully complied and once in the kitchen Caz set about making Margarita cocktails.

'Let's celebrate!' Caz said as she poured the contents of the cocktail shaker into the glasses. 'To your engagement.'

Mallory nervously licked a bit of salt off the rim of the glass and took a sip, the lime and tequila zinging onto her taste-buds.

'So, tell me all about it, was it heavenly and romantic?' Caz clutched her hands to her heart.

Mallory took a large gulp of her drink. 'Mmm-hmm.'

'Did he go down on one knee?'

'Yes.'

'And...?' Caz's eyes sparkled.

'And...' To her embarrassment Mallory found her eyes filling with tears as she couldn't get the image of Alex out of her mind. Now, *that* had been a romantic encounter, knee-tremblingly erotic and with more charge than the Pamplona bull run. But it was Don she was engaged to.

She blinked furiously as Caz narrowed her eyes at her in suspicion.

'Wow, that's a strong Margarita, my eyes are watering,' Mallory said to cover herself.

'And?' Caz prompted her again. 'Tell me all about it!'

'You know, it's been such a hectic weekend I'm going to go and have a long bath and a really early night.' With great willpower Mallory forced herself to leave the cocktail on the table. Tequila always acted like a truth serum and she feared if she drank any more she'd end up blurting the entire story out to Caz and she had too much going on in her mind to have another person's viewpoint in there too.

For the moment she was just relieved that Caz seemed pleased for her. She was under no illusion that Caz disliked Don, but she didn't want someone else telling her she was making a mistake when she had even a slight niggle of doubt herself.

She needed a proper sleep; one she could wake from with the total clarity that getting married to Don was the right thing to do. She hoped the longer the sleep, the better chance she was giving herself.

CHAPTER 45

$\mathcal{M}$allory had rather naively believed Louisa when she'd said that Mallory wouldn't have to do anything towards the organisation of her engagement party. Fair enough, she didn't have to sort out any food, as that was Nik's domain, but Louisa did want her to get back with ideas of bands and started pestering Mallory daily about the list of who she wanted to invite, along with the design of the invitations, the wording and of course, the dreaded song she had been roped in to perform.

Among all the things Mallory had put on her CV, being a singer had to be one of the most ridiculous. She'd prefer to cook a meal or discuss the minefield that made up the Burgundy wine region any day. She'd even happily converse in Italian or get on a blasted horse again *and* abseil (for charity or not) as long as she didn't have to stand up in front of a roomful of people and sing!

What had possessed her to put that down as something she'd like to do? At least with all her other 'hobbies' she did want to do them. She was thoroughly enjoying most of them (though the squash thing she'd let slide slightly, mostly through lack of finding a partner willing to get bruised beyond belief from her rather erratic aiming) but even contemplating singing gave her The Fear. As well as anyone else who had the misfortune to hear her.

Time spent in the shower now resembled an *X Factor* audition. She couldn't believe the police hadn't been round and arrested her for serious crimes against music as she'd murdered Celine Dion, abused Florence and the Machine and seriously assaulted Kate Bush as she sang into her loofah mitt in the vain hope she'd stumbled across an artist or song she could have a decent stab at.

'What about some Streisand?' Caz suggested as they ploughed through a collection of easy listening classics on Spotify one morning, a few days later, at Serendipity. "Woman in Love' would be apt. Very romantic – you could even dedicate it to Don.'

'I couldn't possibly sing Streisand, Caz,' Mallory said, trying to concentrate on the finishing touches of the frieze, as she carefully painted Hercules stealing the golden apples of the Hesperides.

"Fly Me to the Moon!"

'Is that a suggestion or a request?' Mallory said miserably.

'Don't you worry, we'll find something. Maybe ask Don. What's his favourite song?'

Mallory thought for a moment. 'I don't know.' She guessed it was something jazz-based, but she'd already tried out some of the big band jazz numbers by the likes of Dean Martin, Nina Simone and Sinatra, figuring if she chose one everyone knew, people could sing along and hopefully drown her out. But her 'Feeling Good' would make people feel anything but, her Sinatra cover of 'I've Got You Under My Skin' really *would* get under people's skin... and make them crawl, and her rendition of 'Moon River' sounded more like a foghorn going off at full tide.

Caz pressed the issue. 'He must have a favourite song.'

'Probably,' Mallory mumbled. Whenever he'd taken her to a concert she'd usually zoned out and luckily could recall very little of the evening once she'd gotten home.

'Give him a phone!'

'Maybe later. He's really busy at the moment, tying everything up, you know.'

To Mallory's surprise Caz's support of the engagement had carried on. In fact, she was a little *too* behind the engagement for Mallory's liking. If it wasn't Louisa pestering her for decisions it was Caz asking her questions. She'd even started talking about the wedding, dropping big hints about looking good in taffeta.

Mallory felt as though she'd been caught up in the engagement planning slipstream; she was hurtling along at speed but had absolutely no control of anything. And it was no good talking to Don as he was happy to leave everything up to her.

She'd not even managed to have a proper conversation with him in the intervening days since they'd seen each other. It was partly down to the time difference as he'd had to fly out to New York again, and partly down to the fact they were both working flat out; Don tying up the loose ends in the States and Mallory finishing off the frieze before the end of the week so she could get back to her studio and continue work on the three long panel paintings of the Fates and finish the design of the ceiling.

The only time she and Don conversed was when he tweeted her, but Mallory felt strange having their relationship played out among strangers. It was all far too impersonal, especially as Don had a lot of followers who also liked to throw their tuppence worth in on their relationship, especially one guy called Mike from Tallahassee who'd started to get a little *too* involved.

Her mobile rang and she answered it, only to have Louisa ask if she could email her the invitation list for the engagement party.

'She won't leave me alone!' Mallory wailed as she hung up after promising to get her the names for the next day. 'And I really need to be left alone,' she added, hoping Caz would take the hint. As well as needing to get back to the studio, Mallory wanted to finish off at the restaurant site as soon as possible to reduce the risk of running into Alex. She'd avoided him all week but mainly because he was away, doing something 'personal' Nik had said, although he was also in the dark as to what the 'personal' business was, as Alex had been very vague. Mallory presumed he and Louisa were loved up together, the only time Louisa coming up for air seemingly was to pester her.

At the top of the ladder, Mallory reached over to rub some gold leaf onto the bottom of the frieze to give it more of a rich antique look.

'Have you even started on the list yet?' Caz asked.

'No, Caz, I haven't.'

'Luckily I've got a pen and some paper. You carry on with the frieze and we can go through the list of names together. Obviously there's your mum and dad...'

'Um, I'm not sure they can make it.'

'Why?'

'They've got Dad's golf club's annual dinner dance that weekend.'

'I'm sure they won't mind changing their plans! It's their daughter's engagement party after all! Are they excited about the wedding?'

Mallory focussed on laying on some more gold leaf; her hands were shaking and she couldn't seem to lay it straight. 'Mmmm.'

'You have told them, haven't you?'

'Not really. I did phone them, but it wasn't the best time.'

She'd fully intended to tell them, but when she'd called, her mother was far too interested in gossiping about their next-door neighbours' new gazebo and hot tub.

'We'll put them down as a possibility for now. Don's parents?'

'I suppose so.'

'Other relatives?'

'Don't know.'

'Ok-ay! Let's leave his side for now, shall we. I'm guessing Olly and I are invited.'

'Obviously.'

'Stuart asked me if he and Gregor could come.'

'Of course..'

'The usual suspects?' Caz reeled off names of their crowd of friends.

'Yeah, that'll be good.'

'Ooh, what about Johan?'

Mallory's heart sank. Johan had already been in touch – word got out fast – to ask if it was true she was engaged to Don.

He'd not said anything negative but Mallory could tell by his tone he didn't approve. He'd had dealings with Don in the past and he wasn't that enamoured with him.

'Yes, invite him too.'

'That's a bit of a start at least. Now all you need to do is give Don a call and get him to tell you his names. Think you can manage that tonight?'

'Yes,' Mallory said obediently, hoping that would be an end to it.

'Have you thought about what you're going to wear?'

'No. Well, sort of. I'd already bought a dress for the opening. I'll wear that.' She'd spent a fortune in a vintage shop on a white silk halter-neck dress which was full-length and cut on the bias. As soon as she'd tried it on she felt she was channelling forties' movie stars like Rita Hayworth and Katharine Hepburn.

'Ooh! Have you got Don a ring?'

'A ring?'

'Yeah.' Caz looked at her as if she was stupid. 'An engagement ring?'

'Do I need to?'

'You don't *have* to get one for the man, but it's a nice touch and becoming more popular. You should at least ask him if he wants one. Have you chosen yours yet or is he going to surprise you with one?'

For some reason the thought of the engagement ring made Mallory feel rather dizzy and she struggled to breathe. She felt the room spin slightly and she dropped the gold leaf to cling onto the ladder.

Caz shrieked. 'Mallory! Are you okay?'

Mallory closed her eyes but could do nothing other than hold on to the ladder, comforted by the feel of the cool metal against her cheek.

'I'm fine,' she whispered.

'Can you get down?' Caz asked from the bottom of the ladder.

'Sure, but I'll just stay here for the moment, if you don't mind.'

Mallory couldn't believe it, she was only five feet up on a secure ladder on a flat surface, yet she felt as if she was fifty feet up and balanced on a see-saw.

Eventually, she managed to loosen her grip and start her descent, albeit it shakily and still with her eyes shut.

She half slid, half fell in an ungainly heap on the floor when she got to the bottom.

'What happened?' Caz asked, crouching beside her.

'Don't know.'

Caz put her hand on Mallory's forehead. 'You don't have a temperature. It's probably just a panic attack. Or...' she paused dramatically and Mallory looked up at her, 'you're pregnant.'

Mallory laughed. 'Most definitely not!'

Caz raised an eyebrow. 'I know it's been just over a week since you last saw Don, but you could already be having symptoms. I've heard of women who are practically throwing up the second they conceive, mind you, that could just be down to bad sex.'

Mallory looked up at Caz. 'It would have to be the immaculate conception. I've not had sex with Don!'

'Really?'

'Really.' She saw Caz's surprise. 'I didn't want to rush into anything.'

'Right, so getting engaged and having the party within weeks is taking it slowly?'

It was the first time Caz had said anything slightly negative about the engagement and she quickly checked herself. 'But obviously you know your own mind and are happy about it.' She paused for a moment then said, 'What about Alex? Did you sleep with him?'

Mallory felt her face grow hot. 'NO!'

'Right,' Caz said lightly. 'I just thought something might have happened with him while you were away.'

'Whyever would you think that?' Mallory bluffed.

'Because before you went away you talked about Alex pretty much all the time…'

'I didn't!'

'You did. Then you go away for a weekend with him, come back engaged to someone else, don't mention Alex at all and you've been pretty much avoiding me for the past week.'

'I've been busy.'

Caz gave Mallory a sly look. 'And Olly told me *everything!*'

'How did he find out? He couldn't have! He wasn't there! Did he see us?'

'Haha!' Caz shouted gleefully and Mallory realised she'd been had.

'Olly only said you'd been together a lot and then suddenly you were cooler than an iced frappé in the Antarctic.'

Mallory felt her face flush. 'Alex and I… we may have had a snog.' She underplayed the X-rated steaminess of it. 'But it didn't progress to anything else and unless biology has changed a hell of a lot in the time I've been single, I am definitely *not pregnant!*'

But Caz had stopped listening at the word 'snog'.

'Oh my God, I knew there was something brewing between you two! So, tell me all about it!' She acted even more excited than she had at the news of Mallory's engagement.

'There's nothing to tell. We kissed and it didn't lead to anything.'

'That I find very hard to imagine. So how the hell did you go from snogging that desirable hunk of sexy manhood to getting engaged to that tosshead. I mean Don.' Caz gave her an apologetic look. 'Sorry. Old habits.'

'Ahh! So, you're *not* that happy about the engagement after all!'

Caz threw up her hands in resignation. 'Not one bit, it's been killing me having to be nice and supportive and pleased for you.'

'Why even try?'

'Because you're so bloody stubborn. I knew if I was against it you'd dig your heels in even more. I thought if I acted gung-ho and positive you'd eventually tell me why you had a sudden moment of madness and got back with that tosser.'

'Tell me how you really feel, why don't you?'

Caz sat beside her on the floor.

Despite her best attempts to fight them, Mallory could feel tears welling up. 'Oh Caz, I feel like such an idiot. I really thought Alex liked me.'

'He obviously *did* enough to kiss you.'

'I thought so too. I couldn't work out if he was flirting with me or was just being his usual self but then, during the power cut, we bumped into each other in the kitchen and something happened.'

'You created your own electricity?'

'Yes. Well, I thought we did.'

'What happened?'

'Don turned up.'

Caz clasped her hands together. 'Was there a fight?'

'Not a proper fight, just a lot of awkwardness. Don said he was my fiancé. Which… he thought he was…'

'Olly explained all that mix-up. He said you were all ready to tell him the truth but next morning you were properly engaged. What happened to make you change your mind?'

'I fully intended to tell Don, but while I was waiting to speak to him I spied Alex getting it on with Louisa.'

Not even Caz had an answer to that.

'And then when Don started talking to me he opened his heart and we covered old ground and he apologised for the way he treated me in the past. He wanted us to make a fresh start of it. Obviously I'd been completely wrong about Alex. He told me he doesn't 'do' relationships. The ironic thing is it seems he's still with Louisa so he can't be that against them.'

'You can be with someone for a while and not define it as a relationship,' Caz pointed out. 'And is it possible that Alex ended up with Louisa because he thought you were engaged to Don and he was hurt?'

Mallory shook her head. 'I told him I was going to clear it all up. He said he understood but obviously he didn't care. He hardly had a moment to pine for me, did he?'

'But that's still no reason to get engaged to Don!'

'Don and I worked together once. Now he's ironed out all his faults he's perfect.'

Caz's eyebrows had shot up towards her hairline.

'Okay, maybe not *perfect* but remember all those months ago when we did that stupid goddess worshipping thing? I had, in the back of my mind, a picture of Don but with all the negative bits removed. It would seem that he's now that person.'

'If you're all that happy why is it when we talk about the engagement you go as white as a goth at a Fields of the Nephilim concert?'

'It's a little overwhelming, that's all. I think it will be better when Don's back here. But aside from that, I really need to get on with this place as I've still got so much to do before the opening. It's not fair of me to question anything about Don when I've so much on my mind I can't think straight.'

Finally, Caz took the hint and to Mallory's great relief left her to work on the frieze.

CHAPTER 46

$\mathcal{T}$hat night Mallory managed to evade Caz's clutches and the threat of being asked more questions when the bar called and asked if Caz could cover a couple of hours at short notice. Mallory knew she should really call Don and ask him about the invitation list but every time she went to call him she came over a bit odd.

Determined not to read anything into it and keep herself busy, Mallory decided to go back to the restaurant and finish off the frieze.

First, she sent Louisa a text (she wasn't quite brave enough to call her in person) telling her not to worry about invitations, gave her a rough number and added that she'd let her know the names nearer the time. She told her she'd organised the band (a lie, but she figured she'd call round a few the next day and pick one).

At the restaurant Mallory unlocked the fire door and went through the inner door, into the kitchen, and was surprised when the alarm pad didn't beep at her. Having no idea where the light switches were, she felt along the wall, hoping she'd stumble across them but with no luck.

As her eyes became accustomed to the dark she made her way

over to the swing doors which led into the restaurant as she knew where the lights were through there. She'd just got to the door when she heard the floor creak from the other side. But it wasn't the creak of someone walking about, it was the slow creak of someone creeping about. Mallory froze. A couple of seconds later she heard the noise again. And she saw a quick flash of torchlight under the door.

The entire building was in darkness. Anyone with a legitimate reason to be there would have put on the lights.

It dawned on her that she must have stumbled across a burglar!

She stood for a moment with no clue what to do. Then she heard another creak from the other side of the door. They were getting nearer, possibly only a couple of feet away from her. She looked behind her, to the back door. She'd never make it without being seen. And as she couldn't run for toffee the perpetrator would catch up with her before she could make it to the main road.

The only thing to do was hide.

To her left, just a couple of feet away, was the walk-in larder.

She quickly removed her shoes and, cradling them to her chest, tiptoed as quickly and quietly as she could across the tiled floor and into the larder, pulling the door over but not fully shut so she could sneak a peek.

She held her breath as she heard the swing door slowly open and through the tiny gap in the larder door she could see the sweeping light of a torch.

Maybe whoever it was, was on their way out. She listened for the back door opening and shutting. It didn't.

Bugger! What if she'd made a noise and the burglar had heard and was checking it out? She mentally crossed her fingers that he'd have a quick scan round the room, see that no one was there and go back into the main area to carry on with his looting or whatever, giving her a chance to slip back out and run round the front and away and call the police.

Thankfully she hadn't locked the gate behind her so wouldn't have to worry about fumbling for the key. Yes, she would run out the larder, through the back door, through the fire door into the little fenced-in courtyard, run through the gate, along the side of the building where, luckily, all the rubbish had been removed which would mean she wouldn't trip over anything, out past the front and onto the road where she could call the police.

She was just imagining the scene where the police congratulated her for her bravery and level-headedness under pressure when Mallory realised that the swing doors hadn't swung again. The burglar was still in the kitchen. *Why wasn't he leaving?* She could still hear his footsteps as he walked around.

Then she momentarily stopped breathing as she heard the seal on the walk-in freezer open, then close. Oh shit! Mallory felt the adrenaline pump. He'd definitely heard her and was checking everywhere to find her.

It would only be a few more seconds until he opened up the larder.

She needed a weapon. The shoes, still clutched to her chest, would cause a nasty bruise if the heavy sole made contact with his skull, but she doubted it would be enough to stop him.

Aided only by the glow of the green exit sign, she checked along the shelf, hoping for something heavy and brick-like, but there was nothing apart from some small freeze-dried herb jars. She crouched down and this time what she found was a lot more promising, well, at least a lot heavier. She quietly put her shoes on the floor and picked up a heavy sack. Standing behind the door, she held her breath as it opened slowly.

With a cry like a tortured banshee, Mallory jumped out in front of the burglar, swinging the heavy sack round to hit him dead in the midriff.

CHAPTER 47

here was a satisfying 'oof' as the wind got knocked out of the burglar and he stumbled back against the door, falling to the floor on all fours. Mallory raised the sack again and this time dropped it on his back, sending him sprawling.

The force of the blow caused the sack to split and a couple of kilos of flour puffed up into the atmosphere. The man managed to sit up on his haunches but was coughing so much from inhaling the flour he dropped the torch and it rolled the length of the larder.

He was still bent over, blocking the doorway and Mallory knew she'd have to move him before she could get out. She quickly retrieved the torch and pointed it directly at him while picking up one of her shoes, ready to smack it down on his head if he gave her any trouble.

She could hardly see anything for flour. 'I've already called the police, so there's no point in fighting back as they're waiting outside.'

'Are you...' the burglar started to say in between coughs, 'making... a... a... citi... zen's arrest, Mallory?' he wheezed.

How did he know her name?

Then, through the settling flour, she looked more closely at the slightly-too-long hair, now white instead of black. He raised his head up, familiar dark brows pulled together over eyes squinting up at her through the bright light.

'Alex?' she said faintly, as she tried to air-sweep the flour away but only managed to disturb more into the atmosphere. She'd spent the past week avoiding him and now she had bumped into him she couldn't have planned a more awkward moment if she'd tried.

He coughed. 'Would you mind not pointing that in my face,' he said, holding his hand up against the light.

She lowered the torch. 'Sorry. I thought you were a burglar.'

'I'm relieved to hear this isn't your usual greeting.'

'Can I help?' Mallory took a step forward but stopped when he raised his hands to block any assistance.

'I think you've done enough,' Alex said, getting up and switching on the light in the larder, which was reminiscent of a club which had overdone the dry ice machine. He looked down at himself and the pile of flour on the floor, nudging the split bag with his foot and another cloud puffed out. 'You thought I was a burglar? Is crime-fighting another of your talents? Are you our new security guard or were you just passing and your spider senses tingled,' he said, shaking some flour from his T-shirt.

'You should be glad I bothered to investigate!' she argued back. 'Would you have been happy for me to let someone just go ahead and loot everything!'

With a sigh he gave up trying to get rid of any more flour and he hooked his thumbs in his belt. 'But it wasn't anyone looting anything, *it was me!*'

'How was *I* meant to know that! There were no lights on, the alarm pad wasn't set and then I saw torchlight under the door and heard someone creeping about.'

'I was hardly creeping about.'

'You didn't exactly holler a big welcome.'

He stared at her for a moment, the muscle in his cheek pulsing. 'If you thought I was a burglar why didn't you run? You could have been hurt.'

'Like you care,' she snapped, pushing past him.

He grabbed her arm and pulled her back round so she faced him.

'Of course I bloody care!'

His eyes raked over her face and Mallory started to feel light-headed. But unlike the light-headedness and heart-racing of earlier, this time there was no doom-laden sensation of panic. This dizzy, chest-constricting sensation was because she was inches away from Alex and she could feel the heat from his body, the scent of his skin and she knew if she reached forward just a little more her lips would be on his and she'd be able to taste him.

Suddenly, he let go of her arm and took a step back as if she'd burned him. The movement made him wince and he bent a little and tentatively touched his ribs.

'Did I hurt you?'

He looked up at her. 'I'll live,' he muttered. 'So... so, why are you here?'

'Um...' Mallory tried to think why she had wanted to come, but she couldn't get past the shock of the chemistry she still felt with Alex. She'd thought she was over him. In fact, she'd spent the previous week telling herself there was nothing *to* get over, that anything she thought she'd felt was in her imagination.

But now she was appalled at how her skin thrummed at his nearness. She didn't want to feel anything for Alex. She didn't want to be reminded how his body felt against hers and how her skin had felt electric when they'd kissed. She needed to think of Don. And their engagement.

'I was here to finish off the frieze.' She stumbled through the kitchen trying to put as much distance between her and Alex as she could.

'At this time? Why not leave them until tomorrow?'

'I want to do some work.'

'It's late.'

'I know.' She was about to add that she wasn't sleeping well, but didn't want to risk him asking why.

He moved round her and stood blocking her way into the restaurant.

'It's not that safe at the moment, there's some scaffolding in the middle of the floor.'

'That's okay, I'll work around it.'

'But it's a mess, I… I've moved things around.' He tried barricading the door with his body but started another coughing fit and Mallory sidestepped him and went through the doors, hitting the overhead lights switch as she went.

And stopped.

There was a made-up camp bed in the middle of the floor.

Mallory stared at it. Alex, still coughing, came up behind her.

At first Mallory thought it was some strange love-nest hideaway Alex had arranged for him and Louisa but as she looked around Mallory realised Louisa wasn't there and there was nothing remotely cosy or romantic about it.

The bed was only big enough for one, and even then she doubted that that one would be very comfortable. On the floor beside it was a half-eaten takeaway and a couple of beers and his laptop open to BBC iPlayer.

'Are you staying here?'

He sighed, running his hand through his hair and dislodging some more flour. 'Just temporarily.'

'How long have you been here?'

'Pretty much since the inside was gutted.'

'But that's been weeks!'

He shrugged.

'Does Nik know you're here?'

'No.' Alex went over to the bed and sat on it, the middle sagging dangerously close to the ground as the springs protested.

He rested his elbow on his knees for a moment before reaching down for his open bottle of beer.

Mallory stood awkwardly in the doorway. There had been no sign that anyone had stayed, although she'd been certain she could smell pepperoni pizza the other morning despite no one else being at the site with her.

'How have you managed?'

He threw his hands up in exasperation. 'Does it matter?'

'I'm curious how you've managed to keep up a double life for so long?' she said lightly.

He sighed. 'If I tell you will you leave?'

She nodded.

'I pack everything up really early and stow it in my car. I've been able to shower at Nik's; I've a spare key and go when I know he's out.'

'But why?'

Alex gave a slight laugh. 'I don't have anywhere else to go.'

'But you've got that beautiful house... I know it would be a bit of a trek to do it every day but you don't have to come to Glasgow that often...'

'I can't stay there.'

'I didn't think your father minded.'

It took about a minute before Alex replied. 'He doesn't. But I do.'

She took a couple of steps closer, tentatively in case, like a wild animal, Alex would bolt. 'I'm all for independence but normally when people leave home, it's to go to another one, not the floor of a half-finished restaurant. Couldn't you have at least stayed at the house until you'd found somewhere else?' Mallory wondered if Alex and his father had had an argument.

He shook his head.

'What about staying with Nik?'

'Not enough room.'

'Louisa?'

He looked up sharply and gave her an odd look. 'No.'

'Why not just book into a hotel? Anything has got to be better than this.'

'Mallory, look, no offence, but you wanted to finish off the frieze. Now you've seen this you may as well go ahead.'

She looked at him as he sat there on his camp bed, swigging his beer. She had so many conflicting thoughts going through her head about him but one thing she was sure of, he looked utterly miserable and as if he needed a friend.

'Bugger that! You're right, it's too late to be working. But I could really do with a beer.'

Alex sighed but she could see a small smile twitch at the corner of his mouth. He stood. 'I guess I'll go get one then,' he said and walked through to the kitchen.

Mallory followed him. 'So, why aren't you living it up in some boutique hotel somewhere, throwing televisions out the room and ordering ridiculously overpriced bottles of Krug?'

Alex opened the fridge and pulled out another two bottles of beer. He opened them and turned round. 'Because I can't afford as much as a Travelodge or bed and breakfast let alone buy or rent somewhere.' He handed her a bottle and leaned back against the kitchen worktop. 'I have no money.'

'But your father…'

'Oh yes, he's like King Solomon, but that's him. Not me.'

Mallory looked at him, not sure what to say. 'What about savings?'

He put his head to one side and for the first time that evening, properly smiled. 'Do I look like the type of person to have savings?'

'Well…'

He held his beer bottle up in the air. 'Here's to impoverished and idealistic artists.' He reached over and chinked his bottle against hers.

She paused, the bottle halfway to her lips. 'So, the paintings I found *are* yours?'

He nodded and took a long swallow of beer.

'What have you done with them? Are they still at the house?'

'Some are in storage along with most of my belongings. Some are with Johan, in his gallery store room along with my paints and brushes. It's where I spend most of my day, and evening, and occasionally the wee small hours; painting.'

Mallory thought back to those times Alex appeared, unshaven and exhausted. She'd assumed he'd been out partying.

'Why don't you stay with Johan?'

'I do from time to time. When I've been up late, painting, I manage to sneak in my washing but I've not told Johan the extent of it. He still has a soft spot for my father and I don't want to upset him.'

'Did your father throw you out?'

Alex rubbed his hand over his face. 'It's not that I can't stay there, it's that I won't. Turns out I've become a bit principled, I kind of threw the trust-fund money back at him in a moment of idealistic pride, and told him I wanted to make my own way in life.' He gave a laugh, but it quickly died in his throat. He picked at the label of his beer. 'Remember that day when we went for a walk and I ended up taking a nosedive down the hill?' he said, after a moment.

'Yeah.' She gave a small laugh. 'It kind of sticks out in my memory.'

'Mine too.' He looked up at her, through his dark curtain of hair and Mallory felt her insides start the familiar fluttery dance as she remembered the rest of that day and what else had happened, or rather nearly happened, that night. She cleared her throat. 'What about it?'

'You told me you thought the paintings were good.'

'Yup. And you didn't want to hear it.'

'I know. It's not that I didn't want to. I didn't dare believe.'

'But they are. In fact, they're not just good, they're amazing!'

He smiled. 'I've only just started to think that myself.'

'You should show them to your father.'

Alex carried on chipping his nail at the beer label. 'Oh, I have.'

Judging by his tone Mallory didn't think the story was going to end with James Claremont offering his undying support towards his son's first exhibition.

'Evidently I don't have the right perspective. I have no appreciation of the human form.' Alex raised an eyebrow. He carried on picking the points off on his fingers. 'My technique is clumsy, I don't have the patience, I don't have the natural talent.'

'But the ones I saw were...'

'Those were the ones I've honed my technique on, while I tried to find my style. They've been there for a few years, gathering dust. I have others, ones I've been working on for the past eighteen months...' He trailed off for a moment, staring at the bottle of beer. 'He laughed, called me ridiculous. Even if they're not amazing, I just know they're not as bad as he made out.

'That was when I realised he's nothing more than an old man who's scared of not being the star anymore. I took them to Johan. I completely trust his opinion and I knew he'd tell me straight. If he thought I was wasting my time I would have moved on. But he loved them. He also showed them to another critic – anonymously. He also thought they were good and wanted to see more. For years I've been perceived as this waster who has no direction in life, but the truth is I did have a direction, I just never thought I was good enough to follow it.'

Mallory would never have thought Alex as someone who'd battle with insecurity.

'Anyway,' Alex continued matter-of-factly, 'the upshot is Johan offered me an exhibition and I told my father. It sounds so silly now, but I honestly thought that with Johan and the other critic on board, Dad would change his opinion. But he told me that if I went ahead with the exhibition I'd be embarrassing him. He told me to go on holiday and carry on drinking through my trust fund.' He looked up at her and gave her a grin.

'That was the point I told him to go screw his trust fund. And then, with the worst possible timing, Nik came to me with the idea for Serendipity. He'd already found the site, was working out the figures. He was so excited about it and I knew the only thing in his way was money. He didn't ask me for it, didn't even consider asking, but before I could think it through properly I offered to put up the money. Luckily I did have some in the bank, and it all went towards this place. There was enough to cover the initial set-up and for me to get by, but not in fancy hotels or rented accommodation. I know, as a stakeholder, I'll get it back as I have total faith that Nik will make it a success.'

Alex rubbed his hand over his face again. 'I'm glad we've managed to pay you!'

So was Mallory, considering how much extra she'd had to put on her credit card lately. Her new hobbies didn't come cheap.

'It's why I'm putting up with the publicity deals. The money will definitely help Serendipity, and give me a little breathing space.' He gave a rueful laugh. 'For years I've never thought twice about posing for photographs. But it's so bloody typical that as soon as I get fed up with that world, turns out I need it. But they're definitely getting their pound of flesh.'

'So, the weekend away…?'

'I needed to finish clearing out my things and I decided one last party was fine, if a little hypocritical. I just couldn't say no to the money they offered, and I don't think the magazine would have been quite so keen photographing me in a half-finished room with a camp bed and old takeaway cartons littering the floor.'

'But it *does* have an amazing frieze.'

He looked up at her, his face softening. 'That it does.' Mallory took a swig of beer.

'You know,' Alex said, his eyes earnestly searching out hers. 'I wasn't lying when I said I was bored of London. I realised all the people I went around with weren't my friends. I told a couple of them about my paintings and they thought it was funny that I was bothered to do something with my life. It was the reality check I needed. That's why I decided to come up here permanently to work with Nik. Despite only having this place to sleep in. I needed a clean break.'

'What about Gordy and Sash, and Connor?' Mallory asked. 'They seemed genuine.' She missed out Louisa's name from the list but Alex didn't pick up on it.

'Oh, they are. Along with Nik and Irini, they're the only ones worth knowing. They've stuck by me all this time, ignored me when I acted like a spoilt idiot. I suppose they were waiting for me to grow up and come good. Although I'm worried that when Nik finds out about all this he may not want to be part of that elite number anymore.'

'I doubt it.'

'I could have risked everything.'

'But you didn't. You found a way out. Do you think you'll get back in touch with your father?'

Alex sighed. 'I don't know. He's a bit of a bastard. Always has been and he's not mellowed with age. The irascible persona he honed for the press carried on at home. Years ago, I suggested he let me be part of his business but he didn't like that idea either. Said I wasn't cut out for it. Gave me more money and told me to go have fun. And for years I was happy to play up to that.'

Mallory didn't call her parents nearly as often as she should but knew they were there for her and would always support her. Not having that comfort was beyond her fathoming, which made her feel even more guilty about not telling them Don was back in her life, let alone the fact they were having an engagement party.

But Don was the last thing she wanted to think about. She wanted to forget all about invitation lists and working out the time differences so she'd be able to snatch a brief moment's chat with Don in between him running late for meetings. She just wanted to be close to Alex, drinking beer and talking about art.

She cleared her throat. 'You should tell Nik.'

'I know.'

Mallory handed him her phone.

Alex turned it over in the palm of his hand. 'He's going to be majorly pissed off I kept this from him.'

'He's going to be more pissed off if you're trying to bed down for the night in the middle of service.'

He laughed. 'True.' He pushed himself off the counter and they made their way back into the main restaurant. The little camp bed looked pathetically small in the middle of such a cavernous room.

Just then the fire door slammed shut and a second later Nik shouted an enquiring 'hello' from the kitchen.

'You see, that's what most people do,' Alex said in mock exasperation.

'That was quick,' she said.

'And psychic. I hadn't texted him,' Alex said with the ghost of a wink as Nik poked his head round the door.

'Hi guys, working late?' His eyes then rested on the camp bed. He looked over at them in puzzlement.

'You'd better come in,' Alex said.

'Is everything okay?' Nik asked.

'I think it's time we talked,' Alex said to Nik as Mallory subtly slipped through the kitchen, ready to go home to give them privacy.

Alex caught up with her as she was leaving the back door. He stood looking at her as if he was unsure what to say. He ran his hand through his hair.

'I uh… thanks for listening.'

'You're welcome. Anytime.'

There was a moment's pause and then Alex leaned forward

slightly and kissed Mallory on the cheek. She automatically closed her eyes and breathed in the scent of his skin, feeling his rough stubble graze her cheek. She fought the urge to burrow her face in the space where his jaw met his neck, just below his ear, and inhale. It was intoxicating and she had to pull herself away.

If it had any effect on Alex he didn't show it and she watched as he turned and walked back into Serendipity.

CHAPTER 48

Olly was sitting with his feet up on the table in his studio finishing a cup of tea and engrossed in the latest DC comic where Batman's death-defying heroism saved Gotham from the clutches of organised crime when there was a knock.

He looked up at the heavy door, propped slightly open by a fire extinguisher. Nobody ever knocked; visitors always just walked straight in. He stared at the doorway suspiciously, but apart from a slight shadow he couldn't see who it was. Someone to read the electricity meter? Some local politician canvassing for votes? He quite fancied airing a few choice comments about the state of the roads – he feared the potholes would permanently damage the undercarriage of his car.

As he was gearing up for a political spat he saw a slim arm reach up and tentatively knock again, this time accompanied by a familiar face peering round the doorway.

'Hi,' Irini said with a shy smile when she saw him.

Olly nearly fell off his chair in shock. 'Hi!'

'I… um… are you going to invite me in?'

'Ah, well, that depends,' he said, trying to hide his surprise at seeing her. 'Are you here to read the meter?'

'Nope.'

'Sell me something or are canvassing for a political party?'

She shook her head.

'Are you a vampire, poised on the threshold, waiting to be invited in?'

She took a step over the doorway and held out her arms. 'No bursting into flames, see?'

'Technically you wouldn't burst into flames, you just wouldn't be able to penetrate the forcefield of protection surrounding the building.'

'I see. Technically this is a public building, isn't it, a studio you share, so I would be able to walk right on in anytime I liked.' She smiled.

'Oh well, that's me done for.' He liked that she knew vampire folklore.

Her smile widened. 'I promise not to bite.'

Olly laughed along but found himself a little flustered. He'd been thinking of Irini a lot since he'd been back in Glasgow. He'd been on the verge of asking Mallory to get her number from Nik a hundred times but always chickened out at the last minute. But now she was standing just a few feet away and he no doubt had a soppy look on his face.

'Can I get you a cup of tea?' he said, hoping to divert attention from him acting weird.

'No, I don't really have any time. I only dropped in to say hello. And to apologise.'

'Apologise?' That was surely his role for being a lunkhead and not noticing when a really cute woman was coming on to him. Or *possibly* coming on to him – he'd wavered back and forth on that one for a while.

'Yeah, for the last time I saw you.' She jammed her hands into the pockets of her jeans and gave him a sheepish look. 'I was a bit hard on you.'

'Oh, right.'

'So, I'd like to make it up to you by taking you for a drink.'

'You really don't have to.'

'I want to.'

'Honestly, I'm over it…'

'Okay, that's great, but I'm sort of asking you out here and it would be nice if you didn't bat my attentions away, unless you really don't want to go out with me. In that case, bat away and I'll make a hasty retreat.' She made a motion to turn and leave.

He held his hands up. 'No batting!' Now he really was grinning like an idiot but he didn't care. She was asking him out!

'So, you came to Glasgow to ask me out?' he joked, trying to cover his delight slightly.

'Don't flatter yourself too much,' she said, her eyes glittering mischievously. 'I came down to visit Nik and thought I'd pop in to see you and make amends. Mallory gave me the address.' She slid a bit of paper over to him. 'Here's my number. If you fancy getting together give me a call.'

Olly picked up the piece of paper as she turned and walked away.

He looked at the numbers in front of him; it was a genuine number! It wasn't '5318008' which spelt 'Boobies' upside down or some other joke or trick; Irini wanted to go out with him! He quickly punched the numbers into his mobile and her phone rang as she got to the door.

She turned, pulling her phone out of her pocket. 'Hello?' She smiled at Olly.

'Hi, it's Olly here, just wondered if you fancied going out sometime?'

'That would be lovely. What did you have in mind?'

'Drink?' he said without thinking it through, then wondered if he should aim higher. 'Dinner?'

'Two of my favourite things. Know anywhere nice, I'm not from these parts.'

'The Keg,' he said, naming the first one that came to mind. The one he spent most time in. The one which Caz worked at. He was about to back-pedal and suggest somewhere else but it was too late.

'Sounds ideal. When?'

'How about tomorrow, 7.30?' He had no idea if Caz would be working or not, but what the hell, he hoped he'd end up introducing them at some point, he figured he might as well get it out the way.

'Great, text me the address.' And with that she turned off her phone, winked at him and left.

CHAPTER 49

*W*ith a triumphant flourish of her squirrel-haired brush, Mallory stood back and admired the finished frieze. With the ladders and scaffolding down she could finally get the full effect and it was pretty stunning, even by her own admission.

The gold leaf glinted opulently as the evening sun hit the wall through the newly cleaned windows. She did a little self-congratulatory dance on the spot for a moment before turning to the sections of MDF the joiner had left out for her, which were going to make up the section of lowered ceiling. She had three days to create something magical and mythological before the electrician came with the lighting and the workmen returned to fit the ceiling pieces together.

Luckily it wasn't the entire ceiling she had to work on, but it was still close to about half the surface area, the very central section.

She opened up the tin of paint, for once not using acrylic or watercolour but good old emulsion with a sheen finish. She slapped on the darkest of the shades with the widest paintbrush B&Q had to sell.

After the cross-eye-inducing detail of the frieze, it felt liberating for Mallory to cover so much space in so short a time with broad strokes and also made the tight timescale feel more achievable, especially as she still had to finish the canvases of the three Fates.

While painting she put on her playlist. She was still agonising over which song to sing. Thumb poised over the random play button she decided that whatever song played first, that would be the one she'd go with. No matter what.

She closed her eyes and tapped the button. A moment later a song came on; the track she was going to sing. At least she knew it! As she sang along (not too horrendously out of tune she thought) she cringed at how cheesy the loved-up lyrics were. Were they really that apt? Well, with time marching on and no other song picked, she knew she'd have to go for it. Listening to the song again, Mallory continued her painting.

She didn't wait for the coats of paint to dry completely before adding each additional colour, a few minutes was enough as she wanted to be able to blend the colours together. In between the downtime she read the next chapter of her Italian book, on past subjunctive verbs. She was rather pleased with her progress especially as she'd watched *Cinema Paradiso* and managed to follow chunks of it without resorting to the subtitles.

Once all the paint was applied, Mallory got out the piece of paper she'd printed off the internet and, after studying it for a few minutes, lifted up her Black and Decker drill and started work.

When she finished she glanced up at the clock, it was half past nine. She'd wondered if Alex would turn up to make up his bed while she'd be there but he knew she'd be working late and was probably staying out of her way. She tried to ignore the pang of disappointment she felt.

Standing up and brushing down her jeans from all the

powdery shavings of MDF, she grabbed her jacket and bag and headed home.

With no painting or singing or Italian to distract her she had only one thought floating around her head, and it wasn't really floating, far more like ricocheting around her brain.

Alex.

Since discovering him camping out in Serendipity, he was all she'd been able to think about. With him out of sight she'd managed to convince herself that he meant nothing to her and that she was happy being with Don. But then she saw him and experienced that raw gut-twist of attraction. Each time Alex popped into her head, which happened with more regularity than a Jack-in-the-box with a faulty lever, she tried to counter-think him away by imagining Don. But Don just didn't seem to have the same effect on her as Alex did.

She'd been going crazy trying to figure out what she felt.

By the time she got home she was a mess of indecision. She went into the kitchen for a drink, opening the fridge and pulling out the already open bottle of Coke and poured herself a glass.

She was pretty sure it all came down to physical attraction. Alex was all about the fireworks and the fizzing head-rush sensations. So what if there was no 'fizz' with Don. She could hardly expect the same giddy level of attraction on getting together with him a second time. They'd had that and they'd moved on and what they'd end up with would be far deeper and more meaningful. Just less fizzy.

A bit like the Coke she was drinking which had been opened a bit too long, she thought as she took a sip. It still tasted of Coke, it still refreshed as much as it did before, but it was a little different and there weren't any bubbles to go up your nose. Simply because the Coke was a bit flat was no reason to open up a new bottle.

In another few weeks' time she'd never see Alex again and

then she could restore sanity to her life and focus on her future with Don. And she welcomed that.

She heard the front door open and a couple of seconds later Caz bowled into the kitchen, out of breath.

'I think I've got a blister,' she moaned through trying to catch her breath.

'Caz, what *are* you wearing?'

Caz looked down and plucked at the baggy knees of her leggings. 'I know they're ancient but I'm just running in them.'

'I meant the balaclava.'

Caz touched her woolly face. 'Oh this! Well, I won't be wearing it again, it's rubbing too much. Can you get the equivalent of jogger's nipple but on your nose? She peeled it up over her head and examined her face in the back of a spoon.

Mallory knew she'd probably regret asking such a silly question but she had to know. 'Caz, why are you wearing a balaclava to go running? Is it some kind of detoxification thing?'

'No, I didn't want anyone recognising me!'

'But did you not think you may look a tad suspicious wearing a balaclava, at night, and running?'

'Oh, I never thought of that. Wearing it was justified. I stopped at a lamp-post to take it off for a moment to let my face breathe and a car peeped its horn and flashed its lights at me.'

'Probably just someone you knew.'

'Well, it put me off. And I'd also forgotten how much I hate jogging. Everything wobbles so much!' She spied Mallory's glass of Coke. 'Ooh, can I have some?' she asked, picking it up and taking a swig. She made a face. 'Ugh, it's flat.'

'It's fine. I like it flat.'

Caz gave her an odd look, filled a glass with water and downed it in one.

'I think I'll buy one of those fitness DVDs, like Davina or someone like that.'

'You bought one of those last year.'

'I did!' Caz raced through to the lounge again and searched through their piles of films. Mallory followed, nursing her glass of Coke.

'Want to join me firming up bum and tum?'

'That would be a no!' She went into her room and returned with an Italian vocabulary book.

'I admire your dedication,' Caz said. 'I thought you were just going to brush up on the basics. You'll have to visit soon, so as you can put all your hard work to good use.'

'Mmm, that would be lovely.' Mallory would love nothing better than a holiday to Italy after she'd finished up at Serendipity. Hours spent trawling round Roman ruins followed by bowls of pasta washed down with wine.

'You and Don could go there on honeymoon,' Caz said pointedly.

Honeymoon!

Mallory's mouth went dry at the thought.

She took a large gulp of Coke.

'That's if you haven't told him it's off.'

'Caz, I told you, I'm sticking to my decision. It's going to work out with Don.'

Caz shrugged then a moment later shrieked with delight as she pounced on a DVD and once again Mallory tried to concentrate on her Italian as Caz huffed and puffed her way through a series of knee lifts and scissor jumps as a ridiculously perky woman barked out orders, accompanied by a mariachi band covering Phil Collins' greatest hits.

CHAPTER 50

*N*ext day, a very stiff and sore Caz stood at the checkout in Boots, looking into her basket and wondering how she'd managed to add two eyeshadows, a reduced-calorie chocolate bar, seaweed body mask, shower mitt and ylang-ylang essential oil to the tube of deep heat muscle rub she'd popped in for. Such was the mystery of Boots the chemist.

She shifted her weight, trying not to wince as her *gluteus maximus* seized up once again. She should have stopped at the recommended twenty repetitions of the leg lifts instead of trying to get to 200. Turning the other cheek to Mallory's goading encouragement would have been far simpler and wouldn't have ended with her *pulling* the other cheek.

The checkout assistant scanned her items and announced a ridiculously high total for such a small amount of toiletries. Handing over her much-abused credit card, Caz happened to look up at the door and her heart jumped into her throat. Ducking to see past the gaggle of beauty therapists congregating around the Lancôme stand, Caz tried to get a better look at the man walking past in case she'd been mistaken, but her sudden rubber-kneed reaction told her it was Him. Eros.

Grabbing her receipt, Caz hurried towards the exit as fast as her seized-up buttock would allow. By the time she'd got to the door, she could still see his head mingling in the crowd. This was it!

Crossing the threshold of the shop, an alarm sounded in her ear and a burly security guard with a heavy aftershave habit stopped her. She flapped her receipt at him.

'Look! I've just paid for them.'

'You'll need to get the magnetic strip removed.'

'But…' Realising she'd look far more suspicious if she argued any more, she handed over her bag to the sales assistant who took the offending metal strip off the essential oil. By the time Caz reached the door again she couldn't see any handsome blond hunks. Undeterred, she hurried off in the direction he had been walking, wading her way against the sea of oncoming pushchairs. Scouring the interior of each shop she passed, she worked her way around the mall until she found herself at the exit, with Buchanan Street and Sauchiehall Street sprawling in front of her, her Love God nowhere to be seen.

CHAPTER 51

Olly looked up at the door then checked his watch. 7.32pm. She was only two minutes late. A mere one hundred and twenty seconds. And it could be that his watch was two minutes fast, or even three or four minutes. A couple of his friends always berated him to get a better watch ('better' equating to expensive) but Olly was loyal to his little Swatch, with the black plastic strap and the glow in the dark hands. Despite it being fast. Or not. He glanced over to the bar where Caz was watching him, a mischievous smile on her lips.

Olly sighed into his pint. There was only one thing more anxiety-inducing than a first date, and that was a first date with an audience. He was only grateful that Mallory wasn't there. Or even worse, his mother. The indomitable Mrs Walsh would have been on the first train up had she known her only son was going on a date. In fact, he still half expected her to barge through the doors, order a gin and tonic and settle down to give Irini the once-over, such was her sixth sense on these things.

Despite already being a grandmother courtesy of his sisters, she would only rest easy once Olly, too, had settled down with a 'nice' girl and carried on the Walsh progeny. It maddened her that she couldn't keep a closer eye on her boy and she was convinced he was meeting the wrong sort of girl and getting mixed up in Glasgow gangs.

He'd explained many times that he wasn't meeting *any* girls and the only gang he was involved with was the comic club he met up with once a month. And although they liked to think of themselves as a 'gang' they were really just a bunch of nerds who debated the merits of invisibility over superstrength and argued over who was sexier; Wonder Woman or Catwoman; an argument Olly thought completely redundant as it was obviously Wonder Woman. And they were far more interested in saving the world than destroying it. But for Mrs Walsh, Glasgow was a metropolis of evil.

He was so lost in thought that he didn't notice Irini sneak in and tap him on the shoulder.

'Hi!' she said a little breathlessly, sitting on the chair opposite. 'You looked miles away, what were you thinking about?'

'Oh, just my mother.'

Irini raised an eyebrow.

'Ah, shit, that probably wasn't the most romantic thing you could have heard. I mean, not that I'm trying to be romantic... although I'm not *not* trying to be romantic. Let me get you a drink,' he said, aware his cheeks were blazing. He was encouraged to see she looked a little nervous too.

'Vodka-tonic, thanks. If it makes you feel any better I could think about my father until you get back?' She laughed.

'And then we could invite Freud over to analyse us to really get the party swinging!' Olly gave a laugh before sloping over to the bar where an eagerly waiting Caz pounced on him.

'She's pretty!'

Olly was rather irked to hear her sound quite so surprised.

'Good legs,' Caz added. 'Not what I thought you'd go for at all. Small. Petite. Short hair, but it really suits her, shows off her bone structure.'

'Look, when you've finished dissecting her, can I have a vodka-tonic and put another one in there.' He handed Caz his pint glass.

'Ice and a slice?'

'It tends to spoil the beer, but you can stick them in the vodka.'

'Will do.' Caz didn't make a move to get the drinks.

'Tonight would be nice.'

'I'll bring them over.'

Olly narrowed his eyes at her. Caz never did table service. She hated the very thought of it and often said that if a customer wanted that much personal attention he should go to a lap-dancing club.

'No,' he said firmly. 'I'm not having you coming over and acting like the grand inquisitor!'

Caz harrumphed and flounced over to the optics. 'I'll pour you a double, give you a little extra help.'

He eventually got back to the table.

Irini raised her glass. 'A toast.' She waited until Olly raised his pint. 'Here's to more time spent in Glasgow!'

'You're staying?'

She took a sip of her drink and smiled one which showed off a very slight gap between her front teeth, which Olly thought rather sexy.

'Yup, Nik finally wore me down. I'll be helping him in the kitchen at Serendipity, just at the start. We're both probably barking mad as we'll be at each other with the frying pans within hours no doubt, but it might be good fun too. And I like the *big city*!' She laughed and her eyes twinkled at Olly.

He had to admit that he now liked the city a lot more because she was in it.

He should have realised that Caz wouldn't let it be. As the evening wore on she looked over at him so often Olly felt a bit like a Care in the Community patient being reintroduced into society again under supervision.

'Is everything okay?' Irini asked, turning round to look at whatever it was Olly kept glancing over at.

'I'm really sorry, when I invited you here I hadn't realised my friend would be working and she's rather interested in meeting you.'

Irini turned round and gave Caz a wave. It was all the encouragement Caz needed and she almost vaulted over the bar in her eagerness to get to them.

'Hi, I'm Caz.' She thrust a menu at them both. 'Pretend you're reading that in case my boss sees me.'

'Caz, this is Irini, Irini, this is Caz,' Olly said wearily.

'Hello.' Irini smiled and took a sip of her drink.

'This isn't at all awkward,' Olly said faux-cheerfully.

Caz gave the table a perfunctory wipe. 'I gave you a double in case you needed beer goggles with this one.'

'Oh, I don't think I'll need it,' Irini said.

Olly felt his face flush slightly and Caz gave him a surreptitious wink of approval.

Caz stood. 'Right. Can't stand around talking all night, I don't want to lose this job!' Then she mercifully left them alone.

❧

A little later when Olly had visited the gents Caz was waiting for him outside the door.

'She's into you! Her body language says it all.'

'Caz! Can you get out my way!' he said in annoyance, but couldn't help feeling ludicrously pleased. 'I really like her, she's so easy to talk to, just like it was when we met up at Alex's house. We like the same films and bands and she even likes comics.'

Caz looked slightly appalled at that confession.

'She prefers Marvel to DC but I'm sure we can work around it.'

'That's weird but good.'

'Caz, can you maybe get out my way so I can get back to her and she doesn't think I've got stomach issues?'

Caz stood back and let Olly return to his table.

'Caz seems nice, and very keen to keep an eye on us,' Irini said as Caz went behind the bar again and waved over.

'I won't go suggesting she join MI5 anytime soon, she's hardly surreptitious.'

'She'll just be concerned that I'm an evil harridan about to lead you astray.'

'Talking of leading astray, fancy getting some dinner?'

'That would be lovely.'

Hours later, after a fabulous meal at a sushi restaurant where the time seemed to fly by, Olly reluctantly realised that the waiting staff were clearly hovering around, waiting for them to pay up and go.

Leaving the restaurant together, it felt the most natural thing for Olly to take hold of Irini's hand.

They ambled along in companionable silence for a couple of blocks.

'I've had a really nice time tonight,' Olly said.

'Me too.'

'Fancy doing it again?'

'That would be good.'

'Umm…' This was the awkward bit. It was half past eleven, which Olly considered fairly early-ish. He didn't know whether to suggest another pub, which would likely be closing as soon as they got there; a club, which he would hate; or to ask her back to his, which could be construed as rather presumptuous.

She read his indecision. 'I'm going to have to get back. I'm staying with Nik at the moment and he'll send out a search party if I'm not home soon. I think he thinks I'm twelve, not twenty-eight. Greek older brothers are the worst!' She rolled her eyes.

Olly hoped he'd been gentlemanly enough as he didn't fancy having an irate protective Nik land on his doorstep. 'I'll flag down a cab for you.'

Olly hid his disappointment that he managed to wave down a cab within a couple of minutes. He was pleased to see Irini looked disappointed too.

She hesitated, hand on door. 'Shall I call you?'

'That would be good. Unless I call you first.' He winced at how cheesy he sounded, but Irini just smiled and stood on her tiptoes to kiss him.

It took him by surprise, but he soon remembered the protocol and kissed her back. Her lips were soft and warm on his and although the kiss was rather brief, there was a lot of promise.

'I'm looking forward to the next time,' she said huskily, breaking away. He couldn't help but get excited at the naughty twinkle in her eye as she got into the taxi.

He waved at the departing taxi, tentatively touching his bottom lip, still feeling it tingle.

Jamming his hands in his pockets, he headed home, feeling happier and more positive than he'd felt in a very long time.

CHAPTER 52

*C*az spent the day lolling about the flat eating Ben and Jerry's ice cream from the tub as she scoured through the list of resources she'd need for her counselling course, which was due to start in mid-October. She knew it was a massive change of direction, but everything about it seemed a natural progression for her and she felt genuinely excited about studying again.

By mid-afternoon she'd finished off the ice cream and had waded into a family-sized bag of Cadbury's Buttons when revved up with sugar, positivity and do-gooding vibes she decided to have another stab at getting Mallory together with Alex.

She just couldn't accept that it was all over between them before it had even begun. She knew Mallory well enough to know that she was valiantly trying to convince herself she was doing the right thing by being engaged to Don.

Caz thought that if she managed to get Mallory and Alex together they would see the chemistry was still there.

The issue of Louisa and Alex was a little thornier and the only point where Caz had any doubts, mainly because she had no idea how serious Alex felt about the PR harridan, but to Caz's amateur, but hopefully soon to be professional, opinion it definitely sounded as if he'd only gotten together with Louisa when he thought Mallory was with Don.

Caz had met Alex a couple of times when she'd been at the site with Mallory, so she didn't think it would be out of character for her to appear at Serendipity unannounced. As Caz walked there, she felt her work as grand relationship fixer was well underway. She opened the door to the restaurant and asked the nearest man in a high-vis vest where Alex was.

He looks very lovelorn, Caz thought to herself as she saw him standing by the window staring out, lost in thought. She paused a moment, drinking in the sight of him; God, he was delicious! Even a canary-yellow hardhat couldn't diminish his strong profile and good looks. His chest was well-toned and his bum looked good enough to squeeze encased in his old jeans. If Mallory hadn't liked him and she didn't have her own elusive Eros to chase, Caz knew she'd be swooning at his feet too.

'Hi Alex!'

He turned round. 'Oh, hi Caz.'

Caz was delighted to see he looked dark-eyed and hollow-cheeked, hopefully from sleepless nights pining for Mallory.

'Is Mallory about?'

Alex walked over to her. 'No, she's not here. She's pretty much finished here now and is working at her studio.'

Caz rolled her eyes. 'Doh! Stupid me! I totally forgot she told me that!' She found the daft bimbo routine alarmingly easy to pull off. 'Oh bugger! Now, I don't know what to do.'

'Is something wrong?'

'Possibly. Tonight is our salsa class but I need to let her know my dance partner, Stuart, can't make it, he's not well. Which means I'll have to pull out on her, but I'm not going to have time to swing by the studio as I've got an appointment to get to.'

'Can you phone her?'

'I can't, she left her phone at home and there isn't a landline to the studio.' She held her breath in the hope that Mallory hadn't called Alex for any reason that day as he'd know Caz was lying.

But Alex didn't question her – the risk had paid off.

'I don't suppose you can magic up another partner for me, can you?' Caz laughed ruefully. 'Oh, but wait! What about you? Are you free tonight?'

Alex's eyes widened. 'Yes, but I've never salsa danced before.'

'Don't worry about that, I'm hopeless too. I really just go for Mallory's sake. She loves it you see, but she can get a bit shy and if I wasn't there she might not want to take part and that would be letting Gregor down too. You'd get me out of such a bind if you came along!'

'Well...'

'And isn't it rude for a man to turn down a dance invitation?'

'I, uh...'

She widened her eyes and tilted her head towards her shoulder, not enough for overkill but just enough to win him over.

It worked.

'Okay then, I'll come. I couldn't have you not having a partner.'

'Fantastic! You are such a lifesaver.' She scribbled down the name of the bar on a piece of paper and handed it to him. 'We meet about seven so we can have a couple of drinks first to get the rhythm flowing better. See you then!' she trilled and hurried out.

She congratulated herself on a job well done. If things *were* serious with Louisa surely he wouldn't have wanted to spend the evening dancing with another woman.

CHAPTER 53

*O*lly stood on the pavement for a good couple of minutes before the truth finally sank in; Graphics had closed. His favourite graphic novel shop was no more. Olly couldn't understand why; it was always so busy, a safe haven where like-minded folk could meet up.

He hadn't cared it was dingy (all the windows had been covered in original tour posters) or that it smelled odd (a peculiar combination of digestive biscuits and smoked haddock) and he even hadn't minded the strange owner (who had a squint and cleaned between his teeth with his nails). It was the place Olly spent hours happily trawling through boxes of new releases, rarities and second-hand superhero comics. It was where he had picked up an original mint-condition copy of a classic early Green Lantern release. And now, in place of the cave of wondrous superheroes, manga and detective classics was a To Let sign.

He was still standing there, looking at the window and mourning, when the door opened and a man in his late thirties with a dark suit and garish yellow-and-purple tie stepped out.

'Come on in! Don't stand about on the pavement!' He reached

out and shook his hand, pumping Olly's arm up and down energetically.

'I'm Dave.'

'Hi,' Olly said. Too surprised to offer up any resistance, Olly allowed himself to be dragged inside where he was practically pushed into a seat.

Dave, rather portly with a ruddy face and very short hair which accentuated the roundness, sat on the table in front of Olly in a faux-relaxed pose.

'Now, tea or coffee?'

'I really…' Olly attempted to rise up out of his chair but the man put a hand on his shoulder in a friendly restraint.

'Come on, be decisive, tea or coffee?'

'Uh, coffee. Thank you,' Olly said, sinking back into the chair, giving in to the bully-boy tactics of the squashy springs and wondering what the hell was going on. He looked around nervously in case there were hidden cameras.

'What did you think of the schedules Margaret gave you on Thursday?'

Olly turned back to Dave as the penny dropped; he'd not been kidnapped by an overeager salesman, there was obviously just a case of mistaken identity. He guessed there would probably be a lot of skinny, bespectacled sandy-haired folk wearing a vintage Batman T-shirt that would be interested in leasing the comic store.

Olly made a conciliatory gesture and once again made to stand up. 'There's clearly been a bit of a misunderstanding, I'm not wanting to lease this place.'

Dave let out a wail of animalistic fury and Olly quickly parked his bum back in the chair.

'I knew it!' Dave said, stomping over to the coffee pot sitting on a hotplate. 'What made you change your mind?'

'Well, you see…'

'If you're interested in all the stock, we can throw that in to sweeten the deal too. Although why anyone would be interested in those cartoons is anyone's guess.'

'Did the previous owner not want them? What happened?'

'Lottery win. Decided to up sticks and move to California of all places! Bought a place pretty much the same as this but in the sunshine.'

Olly was impressed. There were some amazing graphic novel stores in LA. He felt a little stab of envy.

Dave was staring at him intently and Olly found himself saying, 'Tell me the details of the lease again?'

'Great!' Dave sprang into action, jumping over to his desk and handed him a folio before returning to the coffee. 'Now then; milk and, let me guess, one sugar?'

'Ah, yes, thanks.'

Dave looked absurdly pleased with himself. 'I'm a great reader of people.'

Just a bad memory for faces, Olly thought as he took the proffered cup, but it seemed to be working to his advantage.

'You not having one?'

Dave shook his head. 'I've had plenty today, too many and it sends me a bit crazy!' He did a rather manic *jazz hands* motion.

'Ah right, yes.' Olly looked down at the schedule he'd been given as he slowly lowered his mug onto the table and with hands shaking from excitement turned over the page and began reading through the entire schedule.

It really wasn't much money at all. He could definitely afford it. He had a brief daydream about what he'd do with the shop. There was also a good chance it would be quiet for a large chunk of the day which would allow him to do his usual illustrations and give up the spot in the studio, which would free up some money. And working in the store would no doubt help his creativity when it came to the graphic novel he was producing.

He'd obviously redecorate. From the brochure he could see there was a spacious area in the back, next to a small kitchen and bathroom; the perfect place to hold tabletop role-playing game nights.

He took a large gulp of coffee, starting to feel very excited indeed.

Dave leaned forward. 'You'd be perfect for this place. Why don't you seize the day!'

CHAPTER 54

'So, what's it to be?' Mallory asked Caz who had been sitting for the past ten minutes hogging the cocktail menu, not letting her have a look-in. It was taking so long for their first order to get to them Caz had decided they'd be best to order the next couple in advance.

'Right!' Caz said with a decisive nod. 'I *think* I've decided. I'll have a Gin Sling, then a... Brandy Alexander, the-en a... ooh, a Margarita... then... a...'

'Gastric pump?' Mallory suggested.

'What's in that?' Caz asked, scrutinising the salsa club's cocktail menu. Realising she was being teased, she gave Mallory a withering look then glanced over at the bar, craning her neck to see along its length.

Sitting at the edge of the table, with her back towards the rest of the bar, Mallory twisted round to see what Caz was looking at. Since they'd sat, Caz had been checking out the bar every couple of minutes and acting rather edgily. In fact, Caz had been acting most peculiar for the entire day.

Mallory had been working in the studio when Caz called round and told her to get to the bar a bit earlier than usual, claiming she wanted to get a good seat. She'd also brought some clothes for her to change into.

Normally Mallory just went in whatever she was wearing but Caz had raided Mallory's wardrobe and brought a new, rather low-cut, strappy turquoise-and-yellow flower print summer dress with an intricate chain belt she'd bought in the end-of-season sale, on a whim. It was far more suited to Cuba than Glasgow, which had already started to embrace autumn as it marched through September.

Nevertheless, Mallory changed into it and by the time she and Caz turned up Gregor and Stuart were already there and Mallory didn't know if she was just being overly paranoid but as soon as they saw her there was a lot of nudging and 'hushing'.

'Why don't we just stick to ordering one at a time,' Gregor suggested. 'Look, they've a non-alcoholic cocktail menu at the back, we could always do one for one.'

'Hark! I hear the enemy of fun,' Stuart said with an exaggerated eye-roll. Turning his back on him, Stuart, wearing a red sequined top, slid along the red leather seats of their waltzer-like booth to cosy up to Caz. 'Let's get absol*utely* stocious!' he said, *sotto voce*.

Caz giggled mischievously in reply as they huddled over the menu.

A waiter arrived with the first round of drinks they'd ordered; four vodka martinis with the mixed canapé plate.

Stuart clapped his hands. 'Ooh, look! Caviar! I *love* caviar!' he announced, pouncing on a blini.

'When have you ever had caviar?' Gregor asked, distributing the martinis. 'Fish sometimes gives you a funny tummy.'

'Well, I know that when I try it I'll love it. And I'll be fine!' Stuart sniped back, popping one in his mouth. He closed his eyes with a little shudder of joy.

Then Caz's face split into a wide grin as she looked towards the bar.

'Guess who's just strolled in?' she whispered gleefully to Mallory across the table.

Mallory turned, immediately honing in to whom Caz referred. Letting out a beacon pulse of white-hot energy, Alex stood at the bar.

Mallory whipped round, slamming back against the seat while Stuart sat up like a meerkat to get a better look.

Mallory pressed herself further into the booth, hoping to melt completely into the leather. 'Sit down!' she hissed. The last thing she wanted was for Alex to see them and come over.

But instead of sitting, Caz stood and waved.

'What are you doing?' Mallory tugged on Caz's sleeve to get her to sit down again.

'Grabbing his attention.'

'I don't want his attention grabbed!'

'But I invited him.'

'You WHAT?'

'I popped round to see you at the restaurant, totally forgetting you were at the studio.' She gave her a goofy look and slapped her forehead. 'I mentioned we were going salsa dancing and sort of invited him.'

'But Caz…'

'Great, he's seen us!' Caz announced, eyes sparkling.

To try to look as calm as possible, Mallory reached out for an olive, nonchalantly throwing it into her mouth. It missed, bounced off the bridge of her nose, landed in her lap and proceeded to roll down her leg, leaving a trail of oil. She lunged to retrieve it, watching helplessly as it came to a stop by a pair of brown leather shoes. Her gaze slowly travelled up long muscular legs clad in faded jeans, over a battered old leather belt, up towards a lean, taut stomach with a T-shirt stretched tantalisingly across it.

'Oh! Hi!' Mallory said.

'Hi,' Alex replied and they smiled awkwardly at each other.

'I'm so glad you made it. Come on, scoot up, Mallory, let him sit down!'

With a glower at Caz, which Caz ignored, Mallory slid along the booth to give him as much space as possible, practically landing in Gregor's lap and causing him to spill some of his martini.

Alex sat, but it was at the exact time that Mallory leaned over to pick up her bag from the floor, and for one excruciatingly embarrassing moment, her face almost collided with his crotch.

Caz stifled a giggle. Mallory straightened up sharply, her shoulder nudging her martini.

With lightning-quick reflexes, Alex caught the toppling glass. Settling it back on the table, he licked the spirit off his hand.

'Martini,' he acknowledged. 'Shaken or stirred?'

Definitely shaken, Mallory thought, taking her glass from him. She took a large gulp, eyes watering at the strength of the spirit searing a path down her windpipe.

'I'm so glad you could make it!' Caz said for the second time, face beaming.

Alex glanced round the table. 'I seem to be a fifth wheel though.'

'Oh, I'm only here for the drinks,' Stuart said quickly with a pathetic attempt at a cough. 'I'm too ill to dance.'

It was the first Mallory had heard that Stuart was ill. She wondered when he'd suddenly been struck down with a malady and took a wild stab at guessing it was about the time Caz invited Alex to the salsa evening.

'I almost didn't ask you as I just assumed you'd be out on a date,' Caz piped up.

Mallory cleared her throat to try to catch Caz's attention to stop her talking but Caz carried on regardless. 'So, *are* you seeing someone at the moment, Alex?'

Mallory kicked her under the table.

Stuart yelped in pain.

'Sorry,' Mallory mumbled, but Stuart, too agog at the drama unfolding in front of him, dismissed it with a breezy wave of his skewered olive.

'I, um, no, I'm not,' Alex said.

Caz looked at Mallory, eyebrow raised.

Mallory glowered back at her, wondering what the hell her friend was up to.

'I'd heard there was something between you and your PR person, Louisa, isn't it?'

'You heard wrong.'

'Oh, I thought you and she…'

'We went out briefly a long time ago, ancient history. I'm just going to get myself a drink,' Alex said, looking uncomfortable. 'Same again for everyone?'

The second he'd got to the bar, Mallory exploded. 'What are you doing, Caz!'

Caz, the picture of innocence, shrugged. 'I invited him because we were going to be a man down.'

Stuart nodded. 'I felt dreadful this morning, and I called Caz to cry off.'

'You seem in rude health now.'

'Was one of those six-hour bug things,' Stuart said airily, diving into the canapés.

'That's a load of bull, Caz. I know fine well you'd use the excuse of being partnerless to go and chum up to the dance instructor you find so attractive.'

'Ricardo *is* rather sexy, with those lovely bulging thigh muscles in those tight stretchy trousers…'

'Caz! Focus!'

'Okay,' Caz said with a sigh. 'I thought it would be nice to invite Alex.'

'But surely you've realised if I wanted to invite him I would have!'

'Sorry, I think it's such a shame you two aren't as close as you used to be.'

'I'm fine with it so why couldn't you leave well alone!'

Caz ignored this. She leaned forward over the table, almost dipping her cleavage in a tomato and basil bruschetta. 'At least we know he's not seeing Louisa!'

'Caz, he can still be shagging her, just not in a relationship with her. Remember, he told me he doesn't "do" relationships.'

Caz sat back, eyes twinkling as she played her trump card. 'All that aside, at least this way he can see you salsa dancing. I know you were worried about your CV, because of the horse fiasco and having to drive in front of him.' She turned to Stuart. 'Forgot to get out of second gear,' she said as an aside. 'And let's face it, the more you can prove you can do now the better, as it still might go pear-shaped when you do your rock star bit and sing at the engagement party.'

'You're singing?!' Stuart, who'd been at a memorable karaoke session where Mallory had performed Meat Loaf's 'Bat out of Hell', looked horrified at the notion of her repeating it.

'I'm meant to be but I haven't rehearsed it yet.'

Stuart patted her hand. 'You know what they say, rehearse, rehearse, rehearse. Or mime.'

Caz slapped the table. 'Right! I've changed my mind, I don't want another martini, I want a Singapore Sling. Mallory, would you mind telling Alex I've changed my mind.'

'Why me?'

'You're closer and I'm bursting for a pee!'

'I'm too ill to get up,' Stuart added.

'And Gregor will only order a round of Virgin Marys,' Caz added.

Gregor looked put out. 'Make mine a Singapore Sling too,' he said out of pique.

'And me,' Stuart piped in.

'Fine!' Mallory stomped her way to the bar.

'Change of order I'm afraid,' she said, sidling up to Alex. 'Singapore Slings all round.' She might as well have one too, she figured. 'So, how are your sleeping arrangements?' Mallory asked, conversationally.

He turned and raised a quizzical eyebrow.

Realising her question could be misconstrued she reddened slightly. 'I mean, are you still camping out at the restaurant or have you found somewhere else?'

'I'm staying at the site for another couple of days then moving in to Nik's for a while. Irini's staying with him on the sofa bed but she's found somewhere to rent.'

'That's good.'

'Yeah, it is. It's worked out well. In fact, he took pity on me and bought me a deluxe inflatable bed to use until I get to his.'

The barman came over to take their order and Alex turned back round to Mallory. 'I must say, I'm intrigued at seeing your salsa.'

'You are?' Mallory dreaded to think what Caz had led him to believe.

'Absolutely! You'll have to teach me everything you know.'

Mallory stared fixedly ahead. He had the slight teasing flirty tone to his voice and she battled against the desire to sneak a look at him as he was as disarmingly handsome as always; the strong profile, the thick dark hair, the way his lip twitched at the corner, as if he was always about to smile, but she knew she had to stop thinking about him like that. Tonight she had to keep conversation between them to a minimum and it would probably be best to stick to work topics.

The drinks were taking so long Mallory wondered if the barman was off to the Raffles Hotel in Singapore to get them. She willed him to hurry up as the already gaping silence between her and Alex widened further. Finally, the barman returned with a tray of delicious-looking red cocktails with frothy tops and placed them on the bar with a flourish.

Clutching the drinks, they weaved their way back to the table as the bar had suddenly become packed due to the imminent start of the salsa class. They were almost at the table when Stuart fled past them. Gregor wasn't far behind, carrying their jackets, an apologetic look on his face.

'While Stuart is willing to love caviar, it seems caviar isn't prepared to return the favour. We're getting a taxi home. Enjoy yourselves,' he said, kissing Mallory goodbye. 'Oh, and I think you may have lost Caz too.' He nodded towards the corner, where she was pressed up against Ricardo, the instructor, as they went through some of the moves they'd learned at the previous session.

Alex and Mallory slid into their booth as more couples took to the dance floor to warm up, writhing against each other's bodies as they practised their moves. Caz, too, was practising her shoulder rolls, her impressive cleavage jiggling about enthusiastically.

Mallory took long sips of her cocktail to keep herself busy and unable to talk. She finished hers in no time and moved on to one of the ones for Gregor and Stuart.

A couple of minutes later Caz swanned over to them, saving them from the conversation graveyard.

'Change of plan this evening, Ricardo needs a partner to show off the next move with, so I selflessly volunteered which means you two are going to have to dance together.'

'But...' Mallory tried to interject a protest but Caz talked over her.

'Which makes far more sense because height-wise, you're both better matched.' Then she leaned across the table and grabbed Mallory and Alex by the hand each and hauled them up onto the dance floor as some pounding salsa music started up.

CHAPTER 55

*M*allory and Alex took their places on the dance floor.

Ricardo weaved his way through the couples. 'We're going to have a recap tonight before I start on some more advanced moves, so get in position, people!' the instructor shouted.

'You're going to have to show me what to do,' Alex said.

'We don't have to do this; we could leave if you're uncomfortable. I'm sure you've got far better things to do,' Mallory said quickly, hoping he'd take her up on it as she suddenly didn't entirely trust herself to be so close to him without doing something stupid like looking up into his eyes and getting lost for a while, or even worse, being tempted to kiss him.

But Alex just smiled. 'I can't think of anything else I'd rather be doing. Anyway, I don't think Caz would let us leave, she's a bit of a force of nature, isn't she.'

That was one way of putting it, Mallory thought as she got into a hold with Alex. Too late she realised that the Singapore Sling must have been stronger than she thought as everything was starting to get a bit fuzzy round the edges and she knew she was in serious danger of falling under his spell again. She forced herself to think of Don and took a step back to keep Alex at arm's length, hoping she didn't get a whiff of the delicious combination of his skin and aftershave and whatever pheromones he'd doused himself in before coming out.

For the next few minutes, they practised the same moves and Alex picked it up instantly, his body moving in sync with Mallory's as the music pounded, vibrating up from the floor and into their bodies. Mallory concentrated on a spot just over his left shoulder and tried not to get distracted by his well-toned torso. Gregor was lovely and Mallory was very fond of him but he had a dreadful habit of looking at his feet and counting out loud when going through the moves.

'You know, you're a very good dancer,' Alex said, half shouting to be heard over the music as they incorporated a spin into their moves.

Mallory dared a look at him to see if he was being sarcastic, but he was smiling down at her. 'Thank you. You're not so bad either.'

'To be honest I'm having a hard time keeping up and not collapsing in an exhausted heap!' He laughed.

'You feel ve– I mean you *seem* very fit to me.' Oh dear, she hoped he didn't think she was flirting with him. She waited a beat. 'I mean, it would appear from your general appearance that you exercised a lot, um…' She trailed off, letting her words get swallowed by the music and she hoped he'd not managed to hear her.

She could feel him watching her and she knew without looking he'd have that sexy half smile playing about his lips. Yup, he'd heard her.

'My general appearance thank you for noticing,' he said over the music.

'What's your regime?' she asked, hoping to come across as being interested in his health and welfare rather than have been eyeing up his body.

'My regime?' He laughed, a great big belly laugh, throwing his head back. 'You mean, do I get up at five for an ice bath then breakfast of three raw eggs in a protein shake followed by a twenty-mile run, then forty lengths of a pool?'

His eyes twinkled down at her. 'I'm afraid I could never be that disciplined. I very occasionally jog, usually just when I want to clear my head. I have a couple of kettle bells I work out with most days and I do push-ups and stomach crunches when I remember or can be bothered.'

Judging from his physique, it was obvious he *could* be bothered.

'And what about you. What's your secret regime?'

She was about to say she didn't have one when she realised she did. 'I do this at least once a week. I do a lot of yoga, which also involves a bit of meditation each day which is fantastic.' And it was, in fact, Mallory often wondered how she had managed for so long without it in her life. 'My yoga instructor thinks I may be able to make it up to the advanced class soon.' She'd been over the moon when Zane had taken her aside after class one day to tell her that. Her practising every day had really paid off.

'You must be very flexible,' he said as he flung Mallory out to the side for a spin.

She was so surprised at what he'd said she dropped a step and nearly collided with the couple next to them. Alex pulled her back into a hold again.

She wondered if she'd misheard him as his face was completely neutral. The complicated steps went out of her head and Mallory tripped up on the dance floor.

'Maybe scrub what I just said about you being a good dancer!' He laughed as Ricardo swooped in.

'No, no, no, no, NO! You could drive a bus between the two of you! Closer together please, you must touch each other, hip to hip. It's not that much of a chore, surely!' he said with a wink and Mallory had no idea if he was addressing her or Alex.

Then with his hands on the small of both their backs, Ricardo thrust them together. 'Much better!' he said and turned to the couple beside them to chastise them on their flat-footedness.

Flustered by the enforced body contact, Mallory was acutely aware of Alex's hands seductively warm on her hips as they moved to the beat of the music and she had to clench her fists to stop them sliding round the back of his neck. His head was so close to hers she could feel his breath on her cheek.

As the music intensified and the tempo speeded up slightly, it seemed to Mallory that no one else existed in the room, it was just her and Alex in a little salsa bubble, their bodies moving in perfect time, pelvis to pelvis. Even in just her light dress, Mallory felt the heat soar with the close proximity of so many other bodies, her skin on fire with the passion of the dance and the music and having Alex hold her.

From somewhere behind them Ricardo shouted out for everyone to incorporate the backward dip. Pressing her to him, Alex dipped Mallory backwards and she could feel the ends of her hair sweep the floor, he then pulled her up so fast she slammed against his body, her hair flying everywhere. He pushed it away from her face in a move so gentle and intimate Mallory's chest ached. He briefly cupped her face in his hand, his thumb gently brushing her cheekbone.

Mallory's body pulsed with longing in time with the music. Why didn't the salsa class come with an X-rated warning! She glanced around at the other couples to see if they were emitting the same wanton lust she felt was emanating from her and Alex but they all seemed to be going through the moves with perfunctory precision.

She reluctantly unlocked her fingers which had become entwined around Alex's neck, as his hands slid down to her hips. They looked at each other, the half smile gone from Alex's expression.

'You know, I think I should maybe sit this one out,' he said.

Heart beating wildly, Mallory nodded.

'Yeah, uh, I'm thinking that this maybe wasn't the best thing to do. My, uh, my leg still isn't quite healed yet.'

She looked at him dumbly. She'd completely forgotten about his injury. The lust she thought she saw in his eyes was most probably pain at her galumphing about.

The glow from the Singapore Sling had well and truly slung its hook.

'You should sit down,' she said, her voice barely above a whisper.

'Probably for the best,' he agreed, dropping his hands from her hips as he ran his fingers through his hair distractedly.

She turned to leave, but found she couldn't walk away.

Quite literally.

She and Alex were stuck together, the intricate loops and chains of the belt on her dress having managed to catch on Alex's jeans buckle.

'Um, we're caught,' she said, giving her belt a tug as a couple narrowly avoided colliding with them.

He looked down and tried to free them but to no avail. 'It's too dark to see properly.'

Another couple banged into them.

'We need to get off the dance floor,' Mallory said, tugging more frantically at her belt.

'Come on, left foot reverse,' he said, grabbing her round the waist and pinning her to him. With Mallory in reverse, they strode off the dance floor to a quieter spot at the side where they both fumbled with their belts for a few seconds with no success.

They looked up at each other and burst out laughing.

'How did we manage to do that?'

'Must have been when you dipped, I told you you were flexible,' he said with a flirtatious look.

After another few moments of pulling and pushing at their belts, Alex shook his head ruefully.

'It looks like you're stuck with me, kiddo.'

'Great!' she said in mock exasperation then they burst out laughing again.

'We'll be like Siamese twins.'

'Yeah, I can just imagine trying to explain that to Don!' She giggled.

'Great, because I'd love to hear what you've got to say,' Mallory heard Don say from behind her.

CHAPTER 56

Oh God, now she was hallucinating, Mallory thought in despair! It was true, she *was* going mad; completely doolally, round-the-bend bonkers as she was conjuring up Don's voice. It must be her guilty conscience struggling from all the lust-fuelled fantasies she'd been having about Alex.

She chose to ignore it but Alex was staring at something behind her, his face an impassive mask. Mallory whirled round to see a very corporeal Don leaning against the bar a couple of feet away.

Mallory's stomach lurched guiltily. 'Don!' she said, her voice unnaturally high-pitched.

'You know, I'm getting tired of turning up and finding the two of you joined at the groin.'

Mallory could feel herself flush scarlet.

'This is really not what it looks like, mate,' Alex said.

'I am not your mate,' Don said coolly, pushing himself off the bar and sauntering over to them.

'Look, our belts are caught!' Mallory said, wondering what Don was doing back in Glasgow.

Don looked at the tangled belts she held up, his lips a thin line.

'But what the hell were you doing to get so up close and physical to get them caught?'

'We were just dancing together. Caz invited him because Stuart wasn't well.'

'Why isn't it Caz standing here with her belt caught?'

'She was doing a demonstration with the instructor...'

'And I stepped in so Mallory wouldn't be partnerless,' Alex finished.

'Aren't you the hero,' Don said with a chilly smile.

'You can believe what you want as it makes no difference to me but Mallory and I were only dancing together,' Alex said smoothly, completely unruffled by Don's appearance.

Mallory didn't feel so composed; her mouth was dry and her heart was jumping about nervily. She wondered just how long Don had been there. Had he seen them dancing, and if so, had it been obvious from her demeanour that lascivious thoughts had been running through her head with such unfaithful abandon?

But Don wasn't looking at her; he and Alex hadn't broken eye contact. Don glowered at Alex for a moment longer before marching over to a table and picking up a knife.

Mallory gasped. 'Don't hurt him!'

Don turned to frown at her. 'Hardly,' he said wearily and picking up the tangled belts he sawed through Alex's, finally freeing them.

Mallory jumped back from Alex.

'Thanks for standing in at such short notice,' Mallory said to Alex stiffly, aware of Don watching her. 'I hope you've not done any serious damage to your leg.'

'I'll be fine.'

'So, Don, what are you doing here?' Mallory said with an over-exaggerated excitement she didn't entirely feel. 'You're not supposed to be in Glasgow until next Friday.'

'I thought I'd surprise you. I changed my flights from LAX so I could have tonight in Glasgow. With you. I'm on the first flight to London tomorrow.'

'But how did you know I'd be here?'

'You mentioned in your last text you had your salsa class tonight and I've already been to another five Latin evenings before coming here. Shall we continue marvelling at my tracking skills back at yours?' he said, jaw pulsing in anger.

'You be okay?' Alex said, looking at Mallory, inclining his head slightly towards Don who was still staring menacingly at Alex.

'She will be once we get out of here,' Don said.

Mallory looked at Don. 'I wasn't aware we were leaving,' she said, unable to hide the edge to her voice. She'd forgotten just how often Don decided what they were doing without bothering to check with her first.

'Go get your coat,' he commanded.

'What? I've pulled?' Mallory said sarcastically, not budging an inch.

'It looked like you had a couple of minutes before I interrupted you.'

Mallory's face flushed again but before she could retort Alex had taken a step towards Don.

'You need to apologise to Mallory for that.'

'I don't *need* to do anything!'

Although he kept his voice low, Alex's voice was clear and not open to misinterpretation.

'Why don't you show her a little respect and believe her when she tells you nothing's going on.'

'Or what?' Don sneered. 'Are you going to make me?'

Alex said nothing, but held his ground, eyeballing Don.

'Or are you going to go and get Daddy to help you out, because from what I've heard, you'd be nothing without him,' Don sneered. 'Let's face it, you're actually nothing *with* him either.'

Mallory looked at Don in horror. His words were cruel, but

Don had no idea just how terrible they were, given the relationship between Alex and his father. Alex turned to look at Mallory and for a second she saw such hurt in his eyes she instinctively reached out a hand to him, but he took a step back from them both, his expression guarded.

'You know nothing about me,' Alex said to Don, his voice unnervingly calm.

'I know enough…'

'Right! Home time, I think!' Mallory said, breaking in front of them. 'All this cavorting about has me bushed and I'm up early in the morning. Right, Don, would you mind going out to flag down a taxi while I go get my bag?'

He looked unhappy to leave Mallory and Alex together.

'The sooner we get home the more time we can salvage to be together,' she soothed, rubbing the top of his arm and gently pushing him in the direction of the door.

With a shake of his head Alex turned and walked away, back through the dance floor, narrowly missing collisions with the dancers, all dipping and spinning at great speed.

'Good riddance,' Don said under his breath.

'Taxi!' Mallory ordered and Don stomped off, slightly happier because he'd got his way.

Mallory knew it was weak giving in to him but she really didn't fancy another hour in the salsa club with Don glowering at Alex. She knew that Alex would stay to wind Don up which would lead to Don monopolising Mallory and dancing with her all evening just to make a point, the only snag being Don couldn't dance and he would get annoyed and descend into an even fowler mood which would mean Mallory would resort to drinking cocktail after cocktail in a bid to tune him out, resulting in a stinking hangover tomorrow, rendering her unable to work properly. Going home was definitely the better option.

Alex was back sitting at their table when she got there.

'I'm so sorry about what Don said.' She reached for her bag and slung it over her shoulder.

'You shouldn't have to apologise on his behalf.'

'I know, but you're going to have a very long wait to hear it from him.'

Alex turned to her, his clouded eyes raking over her face.

Mallory suddenly felt tongue-tied under his intense gaze. 'I want you to know I didn't say anything to Don about you and your father,' she said. 'I've not told anyone. And I won't.'

Alex said nothing.

'I'd better go find him.' She backed away, leaving Alex with the remains of the Singapore Slings.

Outside, Don was already sitting in a taxi waiting for her.

She got in and Don ignored her, choosing to stare sulkily out the window.

'That was nasty and unnecessary.'

He turned to her. 'What?'

'What you said to Alex was nasty and unnecessary.'

'You're taking *his* side?'

'It's not about sides! It's about trying to act like an adult and not a contestant in a mud-slinging competition.'

'Did you hear how he talked to me?'

'You should have the good grace to rise above it.'

'I can't believe you're defending him,' Don exploded with fury. 'What the hell is it between you two?'

'What do you mean?' Mallory stalled. 'There isn't anything between us.'

'I don't believe that.'

Mallory said nothing because she wasn't sure she believed it either, which added to her guilt and confusion.

'I don't like him.'

'If it's any consolation I don't think he's your biggest fan either,' Mallory retorted.

'You know, the reason I decided to stop over to see you was

because you sounded so glum on the phone. I thought it was because you missed me.' He sounded like a petulant child.

He continued to stare out the window as they flashed through the west end, towards Mallory's flat. She *did* miss Don. Or, she missed something, she thought, as all week she'd been walking around with a massive empty feeling in her chest, which she assumed was Don-shaped. His being away was probably why she was still having inappropriate thoughts about Alex.

'You can't be missing me that much if you're off having a whale of a time at a salsa club.'

Mallory was about to say she was trying to keep busy so she didn't miss him too much, but stopped herself. That's exactly what the old, appeasing Mallory would have said to Don, anything to soothe the ruffled feathers and get back on an even keel. But she was a different Mallory now, one that didn't swallow Don's acting-up for an easy life.

'Sorry to disappoint, but I'm not about to put my life on hold for you. Not anymore.'

He'd turned away from the window to look at her, his jaw slack with surprise at her confession.

'Yes, I do miss you. I miss you because, having decided to give it another go, you immediately jumped on a plane and flew back to the States. And yes, it's a crap situation, but I don't sit and pine for you every minute of the day because I've got my own life to be getting on with and a lot of that involves me getting out and doing fun stuff I love.' She sat back feeling quite emboldened by her little outburst.

'And are you sure you want to?' Don said quietly.

'What? Do fun stuff?'

'No, give it another go? Because it seems you're so different I feel I don't know you.' He turned round to face her on the back seat of the taxi, taking her hand in his. 'I need to know for sure, Mallory, are you with me one hundred per cent?'

She looked at him. Was she one hundred per cent sure? No,

but was anybody? Alex muddled with her head but she knew she was chasing rainbows with him. 'Thing is, Don, I've changed. I've always been this person but I wasn't always honest enough to show you the real me.'

For the first time that evening Don smiled at her. 'I like this new Mallory.'

'Good, because she's staying.'

'You know, you look really sexy tonight.'

'Thanks.'

He traced his thumb in circles on her palm. He looked at her with meaning and Mallory knew she was going home to sleep with Don. Her stomach gave a little flip-flop of… was it lust, trepidation? Possibly a mixture of the two because in some ways it seemed too soon, they'd only just got reacquainted.

Mallory knew she needed to sleep with Don to finally quash any doubts that being with him was the right thing to do. And to also get any messed-up feelings for Alex out of her system once and for all.

She squeezed his hand back.

As soon as they were inside her flat, Don pounced on Mallory, kissing her hard on the lips as he kicked the door shut behind them. Just when she thought she was running out of air, he pulled away but before she could do anything he'd turned her round, pressing her against the wall. Breath coming in ragged bursts he pushed up against her as he kissed her neck, sliding the spaghetti straps of her dress off her shoulders.

With her breasts flattened and her right cheek pressed uncomfortably against the plasterwork, Mallory tried to push back against him to get a little breathing space, but Don took this as more of a come-on and slammed into her and pulled her dress up against her waist, his fingers stroking the inside of her thighs.

Feeling more frisked than frisky, Mallory tried to turn round but only succeeded in bumping into the packed coat stand which fell into Don, knocking him to the floor.

He lay back on the hall rug, looking momentarily dazed. Undeterred, Mallory threw herself enthusiastically on top, straddling him as she undid the buttons of his shirt. She teasingly kissed his neck and chest with light fluttering touches, noticing that he smelled of the chemical lemony-scented wet wipes flight attendants gave out. He must have used dozens of them as the scent was so strong she could feel her eyes smarting.

'Oh God, you're so hot!' Don whispered into her ear. Mallory had to stifle a giggle. With his slight American twang, Don sounded straight off a really bad porn film.

There was more fumbling below as he tried to slide his fingers inside her underwear, but as it was her hold-everything-in-so-nothing-jiggles-about-while-dancing big pants were suctioned onto her body.

'Shit, Mallory, is this a fucking chastity belt you're wearing?' he grumbled as he gave up, his hands flopping by his side.

Mallory made no attempt to hide her laughter and collapsed onto his chest.

'I'm sorry,' she said, wiping away tears of laughter when she finally sat up and saw the far-from-amused expression on his face. 'It's just really funny.'

She slid off him as he sat up.

'I'm starting to think coming to Glasgow was a bad idea,' Don said wearily, stifling a yawn.

'No, it wasn't, it was very sweet.' She patted his hand in a comforting motherly way. 'Look, it's late, you're tired and jet-lagged and will be up again in about four hours. Why don't I make you some hot chocolate?'

'I wanted tonight to be amazing.'

'Hold that thought until Friday when you come home properly, okay?'

That night they slept in Mallory's bed. She tried snuggling up to him but the chemical wet wipes scent caused her nose to itch.

After half an hour of sneezing onto him she rolled over with her back towards him.

When she woke the next morning he'd gone.

CHAPTER 57

*B*efore heading to her studio, Mallory had a fortifying breakfast of two double espressos and a pain au chocolat from the café at the end of her street. She tried phoning Don but it went straight to voicemail. She left a rather garbled rushed message due to the nerve-jangling amount of caffeine and sugar which had just bombarded her system then another message apologising for the first one. Then she texted him to say she was looking forward to seeing him on the Friday night.

Without knowing the times of his flight or anything about his schedule she had no idea if he was mid-flight or back in meetings again, and being perfectly honest she found it odd he needed to have so many meetings at all. Whenever she was exhibiting at Johan's gallery they would have a 'meeting' which consisted of Mallory bringing along a couple of Danish pastries and Johan sticking on the kettle until he decreed the sun was over the yardarm (which it invariably wasn't, unless he was going by local Abu Dhabi time) and opening up a bottle of wine.

And at Serendipity, they didn't have meetings so much as gossipy teasing sessions where they talked about the next stage of development and how on target they were all doing. But Mallory supposed with Don having made a break to work in the US he probably had visa technicalities to deal with over there and possibly, because he had an agent, he needed to plan his next move back on British soil.

Despite him being so much more of a household name than her, Mallory wouldn't have liked the extra stress that went with it. She far preferred jogging along, well, probably more ambling along, at her own pace completing commissions, planning new pieces and interspersing those with projects like Serendipity. She wasn't likely to be asked to feature in the culture pages of the *Sunday Times*, but she was happy and, for the most part, nicely solvent. Although she'd have to pull her finger out and step it up a gear if she wanted to finish off the panel paintings of the three Fates for Serendipity's opening in a fortnight's time. Leaving a tip on the counter of the café, she gathered her things together and headed to the studio.

Despite her pressing timescale, the first thing she did when she got in was to look in all the cupboards for her missing Italian book. Its disappearance was starting to annoy her. She was convinced she'd left it at Serendipity but when she'd gone back it wasn't there and none of the guys on-site had seen it.

She'd then turned the flat upside down looking for it with no luck and deduced that the only other place it could be was the studio. But a thorough search didn't unearth it there either although she did find some unused tubes of acrylic paint, the Fleet Foxes CD she thought she'd lost, and Olly's secret cigarette stash.

Making another coffee she popped outside and had a quick pre-work caffeine fix and fired off a text to Olly asking if he'd seen the Italian book anywhere and letting him know she'd found his hidden cigarettes.

She'd just pressed 'send' when a very flashy scarlet BMW pulled up and Louisa got out wearing a well-tailored blue silk suit that was so tight-fitting it looked as if she'd been poured into it.

Since the weekend away there had been a definite thaw in Louisa's attitude to Mallory, and Mallory gave her a friendly wave but Louisa's face, or what Mallory could see of it under her huge sunglasses, looked fierce as she picked her way across the uneven pavement towards her, tripping and nearly going over on her ankle.

'I decided that if you're ignoring my calls the only thing I can do is hunt you down!' Louisa snapped, teetering up to her and brandishing her phone at her. It immediately buzzed with an incoming text, but Louisa ignored it, instead rounding on Mallory. 'I'm starting to think you're being purposefully evasive about the invitation list! I've had to put the magazine on hold until I find out who's coming and unless they know by end of play today they're threatening to pull four pages.'

Mallory had no idea what 'pulling four pages' meant but she guessed by Louisa's agitated demeanour it wasn't good. 'I sent you the number.'

'But I need to know *names*!' Louisa came up close to Mallory, supposedly to appear more threatening but all Mallory could see was her own reflection in Louisa's dark glasses. The glasses along with the blue suit made Louisa resemble a big bluebottle, especially as her phone started up its annoying buzzing again as someone else tried to get in touch.

'See! They're hounding me!'

Mallory doubted an editor would be desperately pulling his hair out just because he didn't have a final decision on whether her Aunt Denise's dodgy hip would be okay for the following Thursday, but Louisa was obviously in dire need of a Valium and a lie down in a darkened room so Mallory took pity on her and reeled off the names of those she knew would definitely be there.

'There's me and Don, obviously, Caz, Olly, Gregor and

Stuart...' She counted them off on her fingers but Louisa held up her hand to hush her.

'I need to know *names*!'

Mallory looked at her blankly. Wasn't that what she was doing?

'*Famous* people!' Louisa said in exasperation.

'Oh!' Mallory wracked her brain. 'I don't think there is anyone famous coming. Apart from Don, that is. And Johan. A lot of people know Johan.'

'The little foreign man?' Louisa said sceptically.

'He's German.'

She gave a *whatever* wave of her hand. 'And that's it?'

Mallory thought for a moment then nodded.

'I thought we'd be able to get some famous people.'

'But aren't you doing that for the opening?' Mallory didn't want to tell Louisa her job, but surely as PR woman, she ought to be out there rounding people up. 'You managed a good amount for Alex's party.'

'Yes, but I thought I could rely on you to get some worthier guests.'

Mallory was secretly rather flattered Louisa thought she moved in a world in which she brushed shoulders with 'worthy' famous people. Then Louisa brought her back down to earth.

'Well, not you, but I was sure Don would come through. I was hoping he'd at least know that Banksy person, or what about that man who sticks farm animals in formaldehyde.'

'Um, no, sorry.'

Louisa sighed. 'Mallory, I'm starting to think you're not taking this engagement seriously.'

'Oh, I am, but it's really far more about Nik's restaurant opening. Isn't it?' In fact, Mallory had often wondered why Louisa had insisted on tagging the two events together at all. Nik didn't seem to mind, but Mallory was slightly worried in case it looked as though her engagement to Don was going to overshadow Nik's great achievement, especially the way Louisa was carrying on.

'And what about the band?' Louisa demanded. 'You've not let me know their name.'

Truth was, Mallory had completely forgotten to do anything more about getting a band.

'You *have got* a band haven't you?' Louisa whipped off her sunglasses and Mallory couldn't help but do a double-take; usually so pristinely turned out, Louisa's eyes were uncharacteristically red-rimmed and puffy-looking, very much like she'd spent the entire morning crying.

Mallory immediately felt a pang of sympathy, she'd had no idea just how stressed Louisa had become over the opening and engagement.

'Are you okay?'

'Hay fever,' Louisa barked, hastily sticking the glasses back on again.

'In the autumn?'

'It's a rare kind,' Louisa said brusquely, obviously not wanting to admit weakness. 'The band was the one thing I asked you to do yourself! The music has to be particular for you and your fiancé! What's the point of me going out and getting someone signed, it won't mean anything to the two of you!'

'Yes, I know, don't worry, of course I've got a band,' Mallory said as convincingly as possible. 'I just can't remember the name! I'll text it to you as soon as I, um, locate their business card.' Mallory didn't think business cards were terribly rock and roll, but Louisa didn't pick up on it.

'The magazine has been getting rather worried about the event due to your lack of interest.'

'It's not lack of interest, I've just been busy. With the décor of the restaurant,' Mallory added lest Louisa had forgotten what her real, everyday involvement was.

'I don't know if you realised but I only managed to get such amazing coverage of Serendipity because of the high-profile engagement happening alongside it.'

Mallory would never have described her engagement as 'high-profile'.

'If, for any reason, the magazine thinks the evening won't be going off as planned, they'll pull out. And if they do that they'll probably print an unflattering revenge piece on everyone involved because of all the upset they've been put through and if that happens I doubt Nik's little venture will still be up and running by next summer. People just don't realise the power in a bad review or article.'

Mallory swallowed. If Nik got bad reviews and had to close Serendipity, he'd lose everything. As would Alex.

'You're sure everything is still on track?'

Mallory nodded, trying not to think of the disaster the previous night had turned into with Don.

'Good!' Louisa delved into her bag, producing a document. 'You won't mind signing this then.'

Mallory took it from Louisa. It was a contract stating that she and Don were having an engagement party on the date.

'Think of it as a pre-nup pre-nup. The magazine wants a little insurance.'

'But, but what happens if there isn't an engagement?' Mallory asked, suddenly feeling that familiar tightening of her chest and shortness of breath.

'You've assured me there will be,' Louisa said icily.

'I know, but what if... Don's flight is delayed, or, or I come down with food poisoning?'

'Magazine pulls out. No more restaurant.'

Mallory quailed slightly. If she didn't sign it or didn't come through on the night, she'd be responsible for the ruination of two people's lives.

But, of course why wouldn't she want to go ahead with it? It was what she wanted, after all. Things with Don were a blip. Once he was back permanently it would be fine.

'I need you to sign that and make damn sure Don is there on time and that nothing passes your lips except bottled water for the preceding twenty-four hours, which you should be doing anyway to avoid looking bloated in the photographs.' She handed Mallory a pen. 'And if you could try to rustle up at least *one* famous person involved in the arts, in the meantime?'

Mallory took the pen and signed the bottom line of the document.

Louisa took the pen and document off her again and gave her a thin smile.'Text me the band name by three pm today. They are well known, aren't they?'

Mallory had serious doubts she'd be able to magic up *any* band by three o'clock that afternoon, let alone a famous one! 'Um, they're more cool and edgy than famous.' Seeing Louisa's lips thin again, Mallory added, 'But very arty and hip.'

This seemed to satisfy Louisa and she wriggled off back to the car as fast as her tight suit and high heels allowed.

Now all Mallory had to do was find an edgy, cool, up-and-coming arty band. That was available to play at short notice. She pulled out her phone and rang Gregor and Stuart at Disco Divas.

CHAPTER 58

*M*allory got to Disco Divas just after lunch that afternoon.

'My God, they were quick to change Caz's shop weren't they?' she remarked to Gregor, breaking him out of his concentration as he looked through a dusty box of two-tone compilations.

He squinted up at her, pushing his glasses up his nose to see properly. 'Hi!'

'Is that who I think it is? Mallory Caine, salsa sensation! Stuart rushed up to her in a cloud of Tom Ford aftershave and kissed her on both cheeks.

'Recovered from the other night yet?'

He gave a shudder. 'Don't! Fish eggs are absolutely disgusting! Never again.' He nodded out the door towards Caz's old unit and folded his arms. 'So, have you seen her old shop? Fucking candles! Who needs a shop of wax? The new people are awful too.' His eyes narrowed. 'They're so *boring* and they *never* mix with anyone. They make their own sandwiches for lunch and bring them in Tupperware boxes.' He threw his hands in the air.

'How's he coping without Caz?' Mallory laughed as Stuart bustled away to serve a customer.

'Dreadfully. He doesn't have a gossip partner since she left.'

'How did you get on?' Mallory asked hopefully.

'It was a bit short notice but I called round a few of the numbers and there's a guy coming in who sounds quite promising.'

'You're such a star, thank you!' Mallory said. She'd nearly cried with relief when she'd phoned Gregor and he told her that bands left their cards up all the time, sometimes looking for bassists or drummers but sometimes just to advertise in the hope someone was looking for some live entertainment. Although she originally planned on getting something jazzy Don would like, she was just so pleased to have *anything* she wouldn't even have ruled out a marching brass band.

'The lead singer's due in anytime now. I think his band is your best bet; I've heard good things about them and he's in here all the time and seems nice.'

At that moment a guy in his early twenties appeared in the doorway, he had a mop of dark hair and was wearing such skinny jeans Mallory wondered if he sewed himself into them every morning.

'Ahh, Ted, this is Mallory, she's the one interested in hiring your band.'

'Cool.' Ted gave her a laid-back grin.

'I hope that's not too short notice.'

'Nope, I checked around and we're all free. I know you don't have time to come see us, but we've uploaded some of our gigs on YouTube, if Gregor doesn't mind…'

'Not at all.' Gregor turned his computer screen round to Ted.

'It's mainly our own stuff but we also do covers.'

'Sounds perfect. You can have access the day before to set up if you need.'

Ted nodded as he typed away on Gregor's computer. A few seconds later he and his band appeared. The film quality was poor as it was taken in a dark and dingy club but their sound was great.

They were covering a Rolling Stones classic and Mallory instantly fell for Ted's gravelly soulful voice. He then played footage of their own songs. She loved them. She also loved the fact they were available. She told them the amount Louisa had freed up to pay the band and Ted seemed more than happy.

'What's your band's name?'

'Phoenix.'

'Perfect!' Out of the ashes of her despair, a band had swooped in to save her bacon. She would text Louisa their name immediately, with two hours to spare on the deadline.

'Oh, just one thing,' Mallory added as she was about to leave. 'I've kind of agreed to do a song too. You don't mind if I get up on stage with you, just for one number?'

'Cool, what do you play?'

'Vocals. Badly.'

'It's true.' Stuart nodded beside her. 'She's awful.'

'Look, it's your gig,' Ted said with a shrug. 'We'll do the arrangement for you. We can hook up the day before when we're setting up and have a run-through if you like. What is it you're singing?'

Slightly embarrassed, Mallory told him.

'For real? That's no problem, but you don't mind if we play around with it?'

'I'm more than happy to be led by you, do whatever you think,' she said, running out the door to get the bus back to the studio where she desperately needed to work on the paintings. She'd even sing the blasted song backwards if it meant the whole evening would run smoothly.

CHAPTER 59

*M*allory lit the scented candles in the lounge then went through to the kitchen to check on the lasagne in the oven, satisfied to see the cheese bubbling and turning a rich golden colour. She sniffed the wine, a heady Barolo which had been decanting since the afternoon, and smoothed down the skirt of the dress she'd bought earlier that day. Short, red and strapless, it was like nothing she'd ever owned before and she still wasn't sure if she should go and change into her usual jeans and skinny rib top.

She sat at the kitchen table and nervously nibbled on a bit of ciabatta and stared at the clock, watching the second hand make a full sweep of the face.

Wine! That would help. She wanted to keep the wine in the decanter for the meal as she knew it would be perfect and she really wanted, no *needed*, everything to be perfect that evening, so instead she went to the fridge and poured herself a glass of the Gavi she'd also bought.

Described as being light and fruity with a crisp citrus finish, it could have been anything as she didn't even let it touch the sides, let alone ponder its merits as she took a huge big gulp of it. She topped up her glass and put the bottle back in the fridge.

She had another bit of bread as she didn't want to be passed-out drunk when Don appeared, which could be any minute. She'd worked out the journey time from when his plane touched down (which had been on time, she'd already checked online) to waiting for a taxi (allowing a fair forty minutes) and the journey back to her flat (considering Friday night traffic) which meant that he could arrive anytime...

She heard a knock at the door and Mallory jumped, most of the wine evacuating her glass and splashing on the table. Throwing some kitchen towels over the spillage, she teetered into the hall in the black high heels she'd found at the bottom of her wardrobe. It was ridiculous she felt so nervous about seeing him! He was her fiancé for goodness' sake!

She threw open the door.

He did a double-take as he looked her up and down appreciatively.

'Wow!'

Mallory beamed at him, telling herself it was lovely having Don, her fiancé, give her a compliment.

He stepped into the hall and gave a suspicious look to the coat stand which had managed to put a dampener on their previous romantic notions.

There was a moment's awkwardness before he engulfed her into a hug but just at the last minute she turned her head slightly to the side and his lips met her jaw. His mouth started a trail of kisses down her neck, but instead of enjoying the sensation Mallory tensed.

It's nerves, she told herself, as she extricated herself from his embrace.

'I'd best check on the lasagne.'

'Is that what I can smell!' he said appreciatively, following her into the flat. 'Since when did you start cooking?' His eyes lighted on the wine. He took a sniff. 'Wow! This isn't some cheap shit.'

'You're right, it isn't.' She'd spent nearly as much on it as she had her new dress.

'You do this all yourself?'

'Of course.'

He laughed. 'Come on, it's Sainsbury's finest, isn't it?'

'It certainly isn't.' She took a deep breath and reminded herself it was meant to be a romantic evening reuniting two lovers.

'So, all this is part of the new you, eh? I'm looking forward to getting to know more of this Mallory. Come here.'

He grabbed her hand and pulled her close, circling his hands round her waist.

'This is the only thing that has been keeping me going.'

'What, Italian food and wine?' she joked, but he silenced her with a kiss. Which was nice. Exactly as she remembered it being. She waited for the groin kick of lust or wanton desire. It wasn't that it was *un*pleasant, it just didn't knock the breath from her chest.

The timer on the oven rang.

'I'll go dump my bags and freshen up. We'll carry this on later.' He kissed the tip of her nose.

She waited until he'd gone before she wiped the moistness off on her oven gloves. This wasn't exactly going as planned. She'd half expected (as well as hoped) that as soon as she saw him, knowing he was back permanently, the same old feelings would kick in, but there was nothing apart from a slightly strained awkwardness. And not even the same awkwardness as a first date, because with that there was always the heightened sense of possibility and excitement.

Mallory took a deep breath, telling herself she was overthinking it all and downed the rest of her glass of wine, hoping it would help give her the desired aphrodisiac effect. It was most likely her lack of libido was due to her being so stressed with the final burst of activity before Serendipity's opening; with less than one week to go, she was still running around finishing off dozens of things at the one time.

It used to be so good between her and Don once, when just a look could turn her knees to jelly. The amount of time it had taken her to get over him was surely a sign of just how good it had been. And the wonderful thing was, she no longer needed to be over him. She had him back!

Later, after dinner, they sat together on the sofa drinking brandy. It had been a lovely meal and she finally felt as if she was thawing out. They'd laughed, reminiscing but also pussyfooting around anything that could be a reminder of a time when things weren't perfect.

She leaned back against his chest.

He kissed her neck and she closed her eyes. It was nice.

He continued to kiss her shoulders.

She gave a little sigh. Then a little shiver.

'Sorry, I don't mean to break the mood, but do you mind if I go and get a jumper or something,' she said.

'I know other ways to keep warm.' He resumed kissing her neck. She maybe wasn't completely turned on, but it was very nice to feel secure and loved.

'You know, you're not going to have to worry about the cold for much longer,' he murmured into her neck.

'Are you offering to fix the windows?'

He laughed. 'No, I'm thinking of a far more natural heat; the sun.'

'What? Solar panels?' Mallory didn't want to burst Don's

bubble but she didn't think an old building like hers would allow such a thing, there were surely planning permission loopholes they'd need to go through.

Don laughed again. 'Nope, just good old American sunshine.'

'I thought you were glad to leave. Do you really want to go back for a holiday so soon?'

'Uh-uh. Not a holiday, but to live.'

Her eyes snapped open. She sat up and wriggled round so she was facing him. 'What?'

He looked immensely pleased with himself. 'I've been dying to tell you for days, but I wanted to see your face; we're moving to New York.'

'What?'

'I've got an amazing new exhibition.'

She shook her head. 'But you're coming back to live here. That's what you've been doing all this time, you've been clearing up all the loose ends so you could come back here permanently.'

'That's what I went out to do originally, but then I got a call from my American agent. Turns out I was being a bit premature.'

'But you didn't like it out there.'

'I only said that when I thought no one liked *me*.'

Mallory could feel the vice-like tightness constricting round her chest again as a panic attack threatened. 'But now they do like you again, you're all ready to jump back over there?'

He nodded. 'Absolutely! It's a truly amazing place with so much opportunity.'

She looked at him and how his eyes glittered with excitement and realisation dawned; he was still the same Don, chasing the dream, the recognition and the adoration. 'And what about me?'

'You're coming with me obviously! I'm not making the same mistake twice. I'm not letting you out of my sight ever again. Being in different cities is hard enough, different continents? Forget it.'

'But I have a life here.'

'Times all that you have here by twenty, thirty, one hundred, and that's what it'll be like in the States. You can have it all.'

'What happens if I don't want it all? What happens if I only want a little, the bit I've worked at achieving right here?'

'Mallory! Just think about it, honey! It's an opportunity of a lifetime.'

'*Your* lifetime maybe!' She stood, folding her arms across her chest.

'Okay, maybe I shouldn't have pulled the surprise on you like that, but I genuinely thought you'd be behind it!'

'Why, because it's what you want and I'm automatically expected to fall in with whatever plan you've got?'

'No, because I thought you wanted us to be together and that this is an amazing opportunity for both of us. It's not as if you've got anything you can't leave behind here.'

'I don't? Oh no, just my family and friends and my career.'

'You don't exactly have anything you can't start somewhere else.'

Mallory was stung that he viewed her career as so transient. 'But I don't want to start anything somewhere else,' she fumed.

He held up his hands. 'Okay okay, I think we both need to take some time out and...'

'Oh, stop being so bloody Americanised!' Mallory shouted at him.

'Don't blame me for loving their culture and their mindset. You have changed, Mallory, but some of it isn't for the better. You used to be so amenable but now you're showing quite a selfish streak. And your negativity won't go down well in the States.'

She wondered how her murderous fury would go down!

Don, however, took her silence to be a sign she'd backed down. 'Don't worry about it. We could both do with a good sleep.'

Without another word Mallory stalked back into the kitchen

where she was met with the depressing sight of all the dinner dishes cluttering up the sink. Splashing hot water and a good squirt of Fairy Liquid into the sink, she got to work, taking great delight on attacking the dish of welded-on lasagne with a Brillo pad.

CHAPTER 60

*C*az waited as long as possible until heading off home and she pottered about the bar after closing time, wiping down the tables and cleaning the glasses until there wasn't anything left for her to do. She hoped she wouldn't catch Mallory and Don *in flagrante* in the hallway. Mallory had told her about their previous attempt which had almost broken their coat stand and made Caz look at their lovely IKEA rug in a new light.

Although she still disliked Don as much as ever, she was willing to be nice to him, for Mallory's sake. And it would be made much easier just by account of the great day she'd had. Her college coordinator for her counselling course had been in touch and it all suddenly felt real. She was finally moving on with her life.

And then, out of the blue, the bar manager had offered her the job of assistant bar manager, which she'd be able to do part-time when her course started, which would still give her a good amount of money to live off while she studied.

Having such a good day, Caz decided to forgo the walk home and after locking up and setting the alarm, flagged down a taxi, revelling in her little act of luxury.

Opening the door slowly, Caz quietly let herself in. Stopping off in the kitchen to make some hot chocolate she was surprised to see it pristinely clean. How did Mallory have the time to clean it, she wondered, when she was in the throes of reunited passion.

Taking her hot chocolate (with extra squirty cream and four chocolate-covered digestives to dunk) into the lounge she was startled to find Mallory asleep on the sofa, still wearing her new red dress, with her dressing gown thrown over her. She had a quick look down the side of the sofa in case Don had been on there too and had fallen off, but no, Mallory was very much the only person in the room.

Closing the door quietly Caz went into her own room. Their sleeping arrangements didn't seem a very good sign but Caz couldn't help have a small flutter of pleasure. She hated to see Mallory unhappy but she really thought that if she went through with the engagement she'd end up bloody miserable.

She said she loved Don, but Caz sincerely doubted it, especially after seeing Mallory and Alex doing their own dirty dancing at the salsa club. It had been going swimmingly well until Don had turned up and spoiled the fun.

Dunking her digestive into the huge frothy pile of cream, Caz wondered if there was any way she could bring them together. What they needed was to be left in a locked room until one of them broke and admitted their feelings. And for Don to bugger off out the way.

CHAPTER 61

*M*allory woke up early with a crick in her neck, feeling even more murderous towards Don than she had the previous night due to her having to sleep on the sofa. After the mammoth kitchen clean-up she'd gone to her bedroom only to find Don spreadeagled across her bed.

She tried shoving him over to the other side of the bed but he didn't budge. She thought about throwing cold water over him but knew she'd end up then having to sleep on a wet mattress and also risk them rehashing their last conversation again and she was just far too tired to be bothered.

She sat up as her mobile rang on the arm of the chair beside her.

'Hello?'

'Mallory, it's Alex.'

She sat up straighter. 'Hi.'

'Hi.'

There was silence. Then Alex cleared his throat. 'Are you okay?'

How she wished she could tell him the truth and say no, she was far from okay, she'd just discovered that her fiancé was probably as big a jerk as he always was but there was nothing she could really do about it because, as usual, she'd let things get so out of hand there was no turning back.

Instead she settled for an 'Uh-huh.'

There was a moment's silence.

'You've not seen the paper?' Alex asked.

She mentally slapped her forehead. She'd completely forgotten that that day's paper had the Saturday supplement special from his party.

'No, not yet, but Caz will have picked up a copy as she pops out first thing to get croiss–'

'I think you'd better go and have a look at it now,' he said in a low voice. 'It's not pretty.'

'What do you mean?' She was intrigued, had they written another sordid story about Alex?

'Just remember, people don't always believe the press, it'll blow over and I'm sure we can get them on defamation of character or something. Try not to worry about it.'

Suddenly Mallory felt queasy, the taste of the previous night's garlic ciabatta rising like acid in her throat. He was telling *her* not to worry! And mentioning defamation of character! Oh God, the paper must have found out about her false CV and ran an exposé on her.

'Alex–'

But he'd hung up.

She threw her dressing gown on over her dress and on shaky legs went through to the kitchen where Caz was already sitting with the paper in front of her. She looked up guiltily.

'Nice night?' she asked in a forced cheerful way.

'I'll tell you about it later. I think I need to read that. Alex just phoned me, told me to prepare for the worst.'

'I'll get you a coffee. Is Don about?'

'Still asleep probably.' Mallory would deal with him later but for now she wanted to read the article and get it over with. 'Is it bad?' Mallory asked, sitting down.

'It could be better.'

'Now everyone's going to know I'm such a liar,' Mallory whispered, running her clammy palms against her dressing-gown-clad thighs.

Caz frowned. 'What do you mean?'

'My CV! The paper's found out I've been lying!'

Still Caz frowned in confusion.

'I've been exposed!' Mallory exclaimed.

Caz turned the paper round for Mallory to read. 'Well, yes. But not in the way you think.'

It was bad.

In fact, by the time she'd got to the end of the article Mallory almost wished it *had* been about lying on her CV. Anything would have been preferable to the centre-page full-colour spread.

The headline was a real crowd-pleaser. 'Alex Won Over by Artist's Assets'.

And then it had *really* gone downhill.

Rather than an article on Serendipity, it was about Mallory and how she'd been picked to work on the project for her looks rather than talent. They'd managed to get their hands on nude photographs of when she'd modelled to make a bit of money while still at art college and the majority of the article focussed on her relationship with Don, insinuating that her success was purely on the back of his talent and she had used the same calculating approach to become embroiled with Alex and his new venture. There was even a grainy photo taken on someone's mobile of them together when their belts had been stuck at the salsa club.

'Where the hell did they get those photos?' Mallory said under her breath, covering the largest of the nudes with her mug of tea. The paper had made them out to be seedy but all the ones she'd sat for had been completely above board and it had helped fund her final year's tuition fees. She had no idea the photos even existed.

Mallory couldn't take her eyes from the paper as she rocked back and forth in her chair.

'Had you ever met this Fiona person before?' Caz asked. 'Because it reads as if she's got it in for you, like a revenge piece.'

'I'd never seen her before that night.' Mallory felt a wave of nausea wash over her. 'I even thought she was nice.'

'But how did she find out so much about you?'

'I think I must have told her.' That night at Alex's was still hazy, but Mallory did remember talking an awful lot; especially as Fiona had seemed so keen to listen. 'Caz, I feel really stupid.'

'Don't. The worst is you're too trusting and nice to think someone would turn round and stab you in the back like this.'

Mallory stared at the article again, reading aloud the worst bits.

"She was quick to point out she didn't have a drink problem, a little too quick... As the photographs suggest, Mallory's main commodity at art school was her face and body rather than talent and it's how she ensnared the world-famous Don Marsden... The restaurant's name isn't the only serendipitous thing, as the way Mallory fell into the job sounds more like a first date than an interview... She has obviously slipped effortlessly into his private life as she was at ease moving around his home. I just hope, for the sake of the restaurant, Alex's front of house is more professional than Alex acted as host at his own party, as Alex and Mallory slipped away for hours together to return drunk, unabashed to discover her make-up smeared over his shirt. Knowing Alex's reputation, she's far more likely to be a flash in the pan dish of the day, than a gourmet classic".'

Her voice wavered as she read the last bit. *"And he'd better count the cutlery at the end of the night as she can add kleptomania to her list of many talents as, I witnessed her steal an expensive Hermès scarf".'*

'It makes me sound like a talentless, social-climbing, thieving whore!' Mallory said, brushing away a large tear.

'I'm sure Alex's lawyers will be able to get a retraction. It's obviously all lies. I mean, Alex with your make-up over his shirt, disappearing off together?'

'That's true,' Mallory said sheepishly as Caz struggled not to look surprised, 'but not the way they make it sound though! We hid in a cupboard for a few minutes, to hide from Louisa and the photographer, and it was a small space and it must have happened then.' Now Mallory wished she *had* stayed in the cupboard all night.

'Fair enough but accusing you of stealing? Now, *that's* ludicrous!'

Mallory shook her head and Caz's mouth dropped open.

'I didn't steal it, but I *did* hide it. I got wine all over it and tried to wash it and ruined it and then Fiona came in and I didn't want to look like an idiot so I sort of hid it down the back of my belt, and then forgot about it, but I gave it back to Alex. But by that point everyone else had gone home!'

'Oh Mal. No matter, but the real ridiculous thing is the fact she's accused you of getting where you are because of Don and not your own talent. That's *obviously* bullshit.'

'Thank you, but I think the damage is done, don't you?'

Just then Don ambled into the kitchen, wearing nothing but a towel and a smirk.

'Morning gorgeous.' He kissed Mallory on the top of the head acting for all the world as if the previous evening's conversation had never happened. Mallory could feel her hackles rise as he plonked himself down at the table and took a swig of orange juice straight from the carton.

'Morning Caz,' he said as he poured an enormous bowl of Coco Pops.

Mallory was surprised Don didn't pick up on the daggers Caz was directing at him as he sploshed in some milk and started to wolf the cereal down. It was a toss-up for Mallory to know if Caz's death-look was because she hated Don or because it was her Coco Pops he was scoffing.

He glanced up at the paper, stared at the photographs then returned to eating his cereal.

Caz raised her eyebrows at Mallory.

She wasn't the only one surprised at Don's reaction. The photographs were good quality and even if you didn't bother to read the name of who they were of, anyone who even half knew Mallory would recognise her from them, even upside down.

'It would seem I've got my fifteen minutes of fame,' Mallory said dryly.

Don continued to crunch his cereal.

She tapped the paper. 'It's the article from the journalist who called you.'

'Ah. Don't let it worry you.'

Mallory inhaled sharply. 'Why did you say I shouldn't let it worry me?' she said lightly. 'Do you know what's in the article?' she asked, blood pumping furiously through her body.

Don stopped eating. 'Um, because you know what these journalists are like.'

'Enlighten me.'

Don threw his spoon into his bowl. 'Come on, Mallory! You know she phoned me to comment on the article. I was angry at you, thinking you were with another man. Which you were,' he added with an air of hurt pride.

'So, you thought you'd dish the dirt on me?'

'I hardly dished the dirt.'

'But you told her I did nude modelling.'

'I didn't know they'd make it sound sleazy. It's nothing to be ashamed of.'

'I know it isn't!'

'They wanted me to corroborate the stories. It was from you they got them in the first place.'

'And you just filled in the blanks?'

'Exactly!' He reached for the bread but Caz whisked it away to her side of the table.

Mallory had to take a few deep breaths to calm down. Caz made to get up from the table and leave but Mallory motioned for her to sit back down again. With someone else in the room she was far less likely to brain Don with the toast rack.

Don sighed. 'Look, the journalist told me that you and Alex were getting very close and it made me so jealous I came to get you. To win you back and prove my love for you. We've been through all this, Mallory.'

'But all this, this *crap* about me being successful because of you...'

'*We* know that isn't true.' He reached over towards her and it took all Mallory's willpower not to stab him in the back of the hand with the butter knife.

'But people reading it don't!'

'My agent told me it put me in a good light. He advised me to say as much as I could to turn the article round to being about me to get as much publicity as possible for the November exhibition.'

'You spoke to your agent about it but didn't think to consult me!'

'Mallory, please don't be like this. And I'm sorry about the photos.'

Mallory thought she was going to burst with fury. '*You even supplied them with the photographic evidence!*' She could feel herself start to hyperventilate.

'I hadn't meant them to go in. The paper wanted some photographs. My agent went through my laptop and sent them. I didn't know until it was too late. They're the ones from the first year we met, when we were loved-up and you posed for me for the...'

She held up her hand for him to stop. 'This is *not* the right time for a trip down romantic reminiscing lane.'

Don turned the paper round and quickly scanned the article. 'To be fair, it paints Alex in a bad light.'

'No, it *doesn't*! He's the young, free and single one, *I'm* the one meant to be getting engaged to you.'

'What do you mean "meant" to,' Don asked, running his hand over his closely-shorn head.

Mallory hadn't realised what she'd said. Was she actually saying out loud she didn't think they should go through with the engagement? Dozens of emotions flooded through her but anger was still front and foremost of the pack. 'If I were you, I wouldn't take anything for granted at this moment.' She took a deep breath and tried to calm down. 'I'm the one being painted as a scarlet harlot! It's always the same in the media.'

'Look, we won't have to be here long enough to read any more articles or to witness the fallout.'

It was Caz's turn to look up. 'Why?'

'We're moving to New York,' Don said.

'No!' Caz wailed and spread Nutella on a slice of toast.

'We are *not* moving to New York,' Mallory corrected Don.

'I really think it best if I left,' Caz said diplomatically, standing up, toast in hand. She paused a second before lifting up the jar of Nutella and taking it with her.

Mallory stood. 'I'm going for a walk to clear my head. Alone,' she added as Don made to speak.

Grabbing her jacket and bag, she left the flat, still wearing the red dress and heels from the night before. Aware she must look a fright with her hair unbrushed and her make-up no doubt smudged halfway down her face, she almost welcomed the sudden downpour of rain which completely ruined her shoes and half drowned her but at least turned her hair from frizzy bird's nest to sodden mop of corkscrew curls and washed the remnants of her make-up off.

Eventually she ducked into a café. After ordering a takeaway latte with two extra shots of espresso she wiped her face dry on a handful of the completely ineffectual paper napkins at the counter. Although she would have dearly loved to have sat in reading the papers – well, the ones that didn't have her as the reluctant centrefold – she didn't dare, in case Don tried to follow her.

She still couldn't quite believe what he'd done. And she didn't even want to think of the high-handed way he presumed she'd up sticks and bugger off to New York with him.

Leaving the café she wandered the streets, sipping her latte and squelching through puddles in her sodden shoes. The caffeine hit was like a bolt of clarity as she realised there was no way in hell she could be with Don.

She thought back to all those months she'd spent pining for him; what a waste of time and effort. Fair enough he'd been her first love, but he wasn't the love of her life. When he came back she'd been at such a low ebb that she'd donned her rose-tinted glasses remembering what had been and clung to the belief that he'd changed, but from the last couple of weeks it was obvious he hadn't changed in the slightest. Maybe he'd really tried to, but the old Don kept on making an appearance.

The remnants of the previous night's brandy and all her soul-searching about Don had caused her head to start throbbing and she looked about to see if she was near a chemist to buy some paracetamol. And that's when she noticed that without realising it, she'd been heading towards Serendipity.

CHAPTER 62

*L*uckily Mallory's coat had her keys in the pocket and she let herself in to Serendipity. Closing the door behind her she immediately felt safe, it was her little haven where Don couldn't reach her.

As she'd been working flat out in her studio she'd not visited the site for days and it looked as if the kitchen had suddenly exploded with life. There had been mountains of deliveries, and boxes sat opened, spilling with gadgets and she had no idea what they were for, but they all looked very technical and fancy. Every surface area was stacked with different-shaped crockery and boxes of glassware. A beautiful array of copper saucepans hung from the centre hooks like culinary bunting. It was all ready to be a real, live, working kitchen.

Suddenly a tsunami of sadness hit Mallory. She was almost finished working at Serendipity. In five days' time it would be open to the masses and her little sanctuary would be shared by all.

She went over to the fridges. Inside were tiers of plates of delicious canapés. Nik had been practising with dummy runs all week and had sent out a WhatsApp invitation to the staff to help themselves if they were in the building, as long as they let him know what they thought. Mallory's stomach practically snarled with hunger as she grabbed the top plate; a mix of miniature tuna and feta, prosciutto wrapped around pears with a blue cheese dressing and deep-fried crab cakes with wasabi.

She wolfed the lot down and felt instantly better.

So much better she was ready to go into the main part of the restaurant and have one last look at the interior while there weren't people cluttering up the room.

She pushed open the swing doors and an involuntary gasp escaped her lips.

The interior had been completely transformed in the few days since she'd last been in. All the scaffolding had been removed and the furniture was in place; simple and unfussy, it didn't detract from the rest of the décor.

Her frieze looked amazing, the gold leaf glinting luxuriously in the light streaming through the windows. The floor tiles were like ancient mosaics in rich azure and gold hues.

In the centre of the room there was a water feature of an urn with water trickling out into a pool of shimmering quartz, giving the effect of being in the best parlour of an ancient Greek mansion. In between each of the four long windows hung her paintings of the three Fates.

The first was of Clotho. Long brown hair curled on top of her head with tendrils hanging down her swan-like neck, she sat at her spinning wheel, looking out over an idyllic meadow, a dreamy expression on her face as she spun out the thread of life, light golden hues intermingling with darker shades.

Lachesis was on the next section of wall. Mallory had depicted her with short blonde spiky hair, modernising her look so she appeared far more edgy than she was normally portrayed. The diaphanous fabric of her dress was hoicked up over her thighs as she sat by the edge of a lake running the spun thread of life through her fingers, some sections thick, while other sections were thinned out and worn. Looking straight out of the painting with a mischievous twist to her lips, she looked very much as though she determined someone's happiness and disappointments on a whim.

The last painting was of Atropos. Instead of being outdoors, Mallory had depicted Atropos inside a dusty tower. Raven dark hair in stark contrast to her pale face, she lay draped over a table with the thread looping around her and onto the floor. Her beautiful face full of sorrow, Atropos held out a dainty pair of bejewelled scissors ready to decide where to cut the thread and end the life.

Mallory was incredibly proud of her paintings. She thought them among her best work. And she was just so glad they worked as well as they did in the space. At the far end of the room the wrought-iron spiral staircase had been finally put in place, giving access to the upstairs bar and bistro area.

Her eyes continued travelling upwards to the ceiling. To her very own Sistine Chapel. The builders and electricians had installed her final piece and she could at last appreciate the full beauty of what she'd created. Although she'd planned it out with painstaking care she'd never imagined it to be as breathtaking as it was.

The centrepiece of ceiling was lowered and she'd painted on a false sky effect of the most beautiful shades of blue blending into one another with streaks of hot pinks and oranges peeking through fluffy clouds like the most spectacular light-show of a dramatic sunset. She'd then painstakingly drilled dozens of holes in the painted MDF which she'd first plotted out on many pieces of joined-together parchment paper all ready for the electrician to thread individual fibre optics through.

And suddenly, as if by magic (well, more likely a time switch) the lights came on!

Mallory circled round, looking up in awe at the constellations twinkling down at her. There was Ursa Minor and the constant

Polaris; Camelopardalis, the giraffe; Cassiopeia; Andromeda clinging to her rock waiting for Perseus to save her. There was Ursa Major, Gemini and Hercules.

Hercules who, on completion of his twelve labours, had been rewarded for his bravery and placed in the sky.

There was a noise behind her and she turned round to see Alex emerge from the shadows at the bottom of the spiral staircase just a couple of feet away from her.

'I thought I was the only one here.'

'I heard you come in. I thought I'd turn on the lights and let you see how amazing it looks. I made sure you heard me this time just in case you attacked me with a bag of flour.' He smiled.

'Probably for the best,' Mallory agreed.

There was a moment's silence as Alex scuffed the toe of his shoes against the bottom step. 'Did, you, um, read the article?'

She nodded, painfully aware that Alex had seen her in the altogether. As would Nik and all the guys on-site she'd become friends with. And her neighbours. And her parents' neighbours. *Oh God, her parents!* Maybe moving away to New York might not be such a bad idea. It would certainly save her blushes.

'Are you okay?' Alex asked, looking at her in concern.

'I've had better days.'

'We can get lawyers onto it.'

Mallory shrugged but didn't say anything else.

'So, I take it everything's going to plan?' she finally said as cheerfully as possible, desperate to change the subject.

He nodded. 'Yeah. This place looks amazing.'

'Thanks. But you've all worked so hard on it.'

'Let's just hope to hell it works out. Nik's got so much riding on it.'

'So have you.'

'I suppose we all have, which is why we're all going to have to play nice with the journalists. Even me.' He gave a small laugh.

With a jolt, Mallory remembered the engagement contract

she'd signed for Louisa. 'Uh, is it possible the whole place would be ruined if a journalist prints a bad review?' Mallory asked, mouth dry.

Alex shrugged. 'They *can* be a vicious lot. Starting out as we are, it wouldn't do to piss anyone off, they all know each other and word gets around. But I really don't think Nik has anything to worry about, his cooking is amazing and the fact Irini is here too is a winning combination.'

But what if there was another reason, completely unrelated to the food or venue, which could cause the press to turn, Mallory thought miserably.

'I can understand your wariness of them though, you finding yourself in the papers like that and I was serious when I said we can get a lawyer and find out what went on. We can get a retraction and I'll speak out and explain it's all nonsense. We'll find out who sent in the photographs and–'

'It was Don,' Mallory said quietly before Alex got too carried away. 'Don spoke to the journalist and sent in the pictures,' she said, trying desperately to sound neutral and not to start blubbing in self-pity.

'He *what?*' Alex made to put his hand on her shoulder then, changing his mind, let it hang in mid-air for a moment before letting it drop by his side.

'Why did he do that? *How* could he do that?' He shook his head in confusion. 'What happened? What did you say to him?' He jumped about from question to question, obviously not quite believing Don could have been responsible. Pretty much how Mallory felt.

Mallory wearily went over and sat on the first step of the mezzanine staircase, suddenly struggling from the double whammy of her tiredness kicking in and the caffeine abruptly choosing that moment to vanish from her system.

'He was angry,' she said, wondering if that was, indeed, any justification for his actions.

'I can't believe it,' Alex said quietly, sitting down beside her. This time he did put his arm around her shoulder and pulled her into him. Resting her head against his chest Mallory was so exhausted and emotionally wrung out she wished she could just stay there for the foreseeable future, feeling his heart beat strong and steady through his shirt.

She didn't care if it was inappropriate but this time being so close to him had nothing to do with the strong kick of lust she normally felt around him, for the moment she just felt secure and that although she'd had the crappiest of days it was as if Alex's solid body was the physical embodiment of the phrase 'everything will be all right'.

His hand gently smoothed down her hair as she burrowed into him and she could have sworn she felt his lips brush against her hair.

'We can still get lawyers, sue him for defamation of character or whatever the hell it is, I'm sure there's something.'

'I can't afford a lawyer.'

'I can. Well, I can't, not at the moment, but this place will start paying its way and we'll get one.'

To her embarrassment, Mallory felt a large tear roll down her cheek then plop off the side of her face onto Alex's shirt. If she got a lawyer it would mean the end of the engagement and that would mean breaking the contract which would alienate the press which would wreck Serendipity's chances of succeeding, thus ruining Nik and Alex and then none of them would be able to afford a lawyer.

Mallory would have to go through with the engagement. She sniffed. 'I won't need a lawyer.'

'I don't think you'd manage to sue without one.'

'It's okay. I think he's genuinely sorry for it getting so far.' She could feel Alex's shoulder stiffen beneath her.

'It sounds like you're making excuses for him.'

'He's not an entirely bad person,' she said. No, he was also misguided, self-centred, thoughtless and a wanker.

'Mallory, tell me you've broken off the engagement with him.' His voice resonated through his chest.

'Uh, no.'

The comfort of his shoulder was abruptly removed.

'But you're going to?'

She couldn't meet his eyes. 'I can't.'

'That's the most ridiculous thing I've ever heard!'

She wished she could tell Alex about the contract but she knew he would try to talk her out of it and at that moment she wouldn't need a whole lot of convincing, but she couldn't risk wrecking his and Nik's dream. It was her mess and she'd be able to sort it out her own way.

'Look, I know what I'm doing, and I don't expect you to understand, or for anyone to understand really, but I... but nothing has changed.' She felt sick even just saying it, how was she going to manage on Thursday, at the actual event?

Alex stood and turned to look at her, raking his hands through his hair. He paced the floor in front of her for a few seconds, shaking his head.

'That's the most ridiculous thing I've ever heard,' he said again, looking at her incredulously.

Mallory couldn't help but agree.

'I really thought you were smarter than that.'

She opened her mouth to argue her point but shut it again when she realised there was nothing she could say in her defence that would sound reasonable.

'I really hope, as a friend you'll understand...'

'Friend?' Alex laughed hollowly. 'Is that honestly what you think we are?'

Mallory looked at him, chest constricting painfully. Just moments earlier, when he'd sat with his arm around her, stroking her hair, it felt like they were friends.

He stood looking down at the floor as if expecting to find inspiration from the tiles. Mallory didn't say anything, she didn't want to hear what he was going to say. Her insides ached hollowly.

Eventually he looked up at Mallory. 'I'm not playing this game anymore.'

'What game?' Mallory barely managed to whisper.

'This forced polite thing that we're doing. I can't keep up the pretence that we're friends. To be honest, the sooner Serendipity opens and we get through the hullabaloo associated with it the better, and then we don't have to see each other again.'

Mallory felt as if she'd been slapped. Without saying another word, Alex walked away and moments later Mallory heard the fire door slam shut as he left.

CHAPTER 63

*W*ith monumental effort Mallory managed to hold it together on the way home. The inner circle on the dusty underground carriage packed with buoyed-up football supporters heading to the game was not the place to have a full-blown mental meltdown.

She still held her composure as she let herself into the flat, hoping she'd manage to make it into the bathroom without having to face Don but the second she was through the door Caz bowled out of the lounge.

'It's okay, he's not here, he left not long after you.'

Mallory's shoulders slumped and her eyes started to fill. Caz immediately steered her towards the lounge and to the sofa and as soon as she sat Mallory dissolved into tears.

'I really think it's for the best, Mallory,' Caz said, handing her a tissue. 'I don't want him here in case I end up doing him some damage. I can't believe what he did!' she added, obviously thinking Mallory's tears were over Don's departure.

'He said we… we're not friends,' Mallory eventually managed to get out through wracking sobs as Caz dutifully handed her another tissue.

'Surely that should be *your* decision, not Don's and I don't think he's in any–'

'Not Don, A... Alex.'

Caz crouched beside her. 'What?'

'He said he... he'd just been pretending,' Mallory said, half hiccupping from crying so hard.

'You saw Alex just now?'

Mallory nodded. 'At Serendipity.'

'Sweetie, are all these tears over Alex?'

Mallory nodded. She drew in a shaky breath and pushed her hair back from her tear-soaked face. 'Oh Caz, it's been hell these last few weeks. I kept thinking and hoping it would be okay once Don was back but all the time I should have been thinking about him I was thinking about Alex. I've been feeling so guilty about it, which made me even more determined to feel something for Don. But it got to the stage with Alex that I was reading something into everything; every look, every conversation. That night at the salsa club I was so convinced there was all this chemistry between us.'

She stopped momentarily to gulp in some air. 'It was like I'd become obsessed. I thought I was going mad. Was it some sort of denial about Don? I was even going to ask you if there was a psychological term for my behaviour.'

'There is.' Caz nodded, helping to mop up Mallory's face with a fresh tissue. 'It's actually really common.'

'It is?' Mallory gasped and stopped crying. If she knew what the syndrome was she may be able to get therapy or even medication for it.

Caz sat back on her heels and gave Mallory a funny little smile. 'It's called "love". You're in love with Alex.'

Mallory slumped back on the sofa, while Caz fetched her a cup of tea.

'Could it not just be a crush?' Mallory asked Caz a couple of minutes later as she reappeared with two mugs of tea and the biscuit tin wedged under her arm. 'Just an ill-advised blip of insanity and next week, once everything's calmed down I'll be back to normal?' Mallory asked hopefully.

'Could be… but I doubt it.'

'But this makes it so much worse,' Mallory said quietly. 'Because all this time I've been, I've been…' she still couldn't bring herself to say the words, 'in love with…' which, looking back it was blatantly obvious that was what position she'd been in. 'He hasn't even liked me.'

Resting her hand on her arm, Caz asked, 'Mallory, did he actually say he didn't want to be friends with you? Because from what I've witnessed there's an entire periodic table worth of chemistry between you. Could you have picked up the wrong end of the stick? You do have a flair for the dramatic.'

Mallory shook her head. 'He told me he'd been pretending to be friends. It was as blunt as that.'

Caz sat back on her heels again. 'Hmmm. Well, at least if nothing else you've seen Don for exactly who he is now, so you can send him packing.'

Mallory took a deep breath. Caz was not going to like what she had to say. 'Thing is, I'm going to have to go ahead with the engagement. Louisa gave me a contract to sign which says there will definitely be an engagement between myself and Don. The paper asked for it as insurance in case one of us was tempted to pull out.'

'They must be mind-readers! Let's face it, you were suffering from such cold feet they were about to be amputated from hypothermia.' She offered Mallory a chocolate digestive. 'So, you've broken the contract, I doubt any court would hold you to it in light of what your "betrothed" did.'

'But if I don't hold up my end, the paper will withdraw its article and any good review. Word spreads fast and with enough bad-mouthing from the press, Serendipity could fold within months.'

'Oh Mal!'

Mallory knew it was preposterous to even think about going through with the party but she couldn't let Nik down. 'I can't be responsible for Nik going bankrupt and Alex has everything riding on it too.' Even saying his name caused such an ache in her chest she almost couldn't breathe. 'So, I've got to go ahead with the engagement.'

'But you don't love Don.'

'I know.' It felt such a relief for Mallory to finally admit the truth. It felt less of a relief knowing that she was still in an equally huge pickle. 'But I still don't want to make him look an idiot and with all the press and the attention our engagement is creating. A lot of it is my fault. Instead of stopping it weeks ago, I let Don think I was fully committed to our engagement. The least I can do is go through with it and then talk to him in a few days' time and break it off then, once there's no press about. It's the best way as Nik gets his review and Don doesn't lose face before the big event.'

'I can't believe you're still thinking about Don.'

Mallory shrugged. 'Old habits, I suppose.'

Caz crunched down on her biscuit, looking concerned. 'You're not going to relent are you?' she asked, spraying a mouthful of crumbs into her tea. 'I don't want to be having this same conversation in ten years' time when you're expecting your third kid!'

'No way, Caz. Never again.'

CHAPTER 64

*I*t was all very well for Mallory to say she would carry on as before, letting Don think the engagement was still going ahead, but another to go through the motions of being an active participant in their relationship. And she didn't think she could stand another round of evading physical contact.

Throughout the Saturday afternoon and evening Don bombarded her with phone calls, so many that her ringtone was getting on her nerves, but she didn't want to switch off her phone in case Alex called to say he'd made a terrible mistake and did want to be friends. She sat watching television clutching her phone, her heart leaping every time it rang only to crash to the ground when she saw it was Don.

Just before ten that night Don appeared at the front door. Caz was all for switching off the television and hiding behind the sofa until he went away but Mallory knew she'd have to face him at some point.

'Hi,' he said, a little breathless from running up the stairs. 'I'm so sorry...'

Mallory gave him a small smile. Despite being far too late to have it matter, at least he was *finally* apologising.

'But I'm having to head back down to London for a couple of days about this exhibition. There's been an issue with a light instalment.'

The smile froze on her face as Mallory looked at him, flabbergasted. 'London? You're sorry about *London*?' She clarified just in case she'd missed the part where he'd grovelled at her feet begging her forgiveness for being a shit over the photos and newspaper article.

He nodded. 'Yup, I know I said that was me back in Glasgow but they need me to sort it out and I don't trust the fools to carry out my wishes. Honestly, they've needed their arses wiped at every step. Anyway, I figured you'd be running around doing last-minute things before Thursday and be glad I'm out of your hair.'

He was right on that score.

'I just need to grab my bag,' he said, breezing past her into her bedroom and coming out seconds later with his holdall. 'Good thing I didn't bother to unpack my hand luggage!' he said cheerfully, not even the slightest hint that he'd spent even a nanosecond thinking about their earlier argument. 'You might want to check your phone's working; I've been trying to get hold of you all day.'

'To tell me you're going to London?'

He turned in the doorway. 'Ah no, that wasn't the only reason I wanted to speak to you.' He looked slightly sheepish and stared at the ground a moment before meeting her eyes.

'Oh?' Mallory waited, fair enough she'd had to drag the apology out of him but she'd feel slightly better when he showed *some* remorse.

'I've emailed you some visa forms you need to fill in. And...' he paused for effect, 'I've forwarded on some schedules on apartments we could rent, some even have a pool in the block! I'm desperate to see what you think of them.'

'For America?'

'No, for Bognor Regis! Yeah, of course for America!' He laughed.

Hardly the repentant Don she'd hoped for.

Mallory was about to launch into another long diatribe about how she wasn't going anywhere but managed to stop herself. There was no point in wasting her energy arguing with him because in a few days' time it wasn't going to be her problem anymore.

'I should be back on Wednesday; I'll see you then!' He gave her a peck on the cheek and he was gone, as if the article in the paper had never happened.

§.

Mallory stayed indoors all of the Monday. She'd spent all day Sunday checking her phone, so often that Caz threatened to remove it from her permanently unless she stopped turning it on and off just in case Alex had sent her a message which hadn't come through.

She didn't want to go out but lolling about in her pyjamas watching daytime television and phoning for pizza didn't hold the usual allure for Mallory. Normally when she'd finished a project and had nothing imminent to start she loved nothing better than to go into full slob mode for a day or two, but instead she wandered around the flat like a ghost, unable to settle to anything.

She tried meditating to clear her head but every time she closed her eyes she could see Alex standing at the bottom of the wrought-iron staircase telling her he couldn't keep up the pretence that they were friends.

She barely managed to sleep that night. Every time she nodded off she would dream about the engagement party with it invariably turning into a nightmare where she and Don were actually married and forbidden to divorce, and she would wake up with heart palpitations.

When Caz saw her at breakfast on the Monday morning she was so worried about Mallory's state of mind she offered to call in sick at the pub so she could stay home and look after her and Mallory had to practically bodily throw her out the flat, swearing that she'd be fine and agreeing to half-hourly phone call check-ins to prove she hadn't done anything silly. It was only on going to make herself a sandwich that she found Caz had removed all the knives from the cutlery drawer.

Mallory sat to an uninspiring lunch of dry bread and a Cup-a-Soup (the tin opener had also been removed though Mallory thought she would have to be pretty inventive to off herself with that, especially since it was a safety one).

Afterwards, to while away some time, Mallory had a bath and noticed Caz had gone through the bathroom cabinet and taken away anything that could possibly be of any harm: all paracetamol, aspirin, cold and flu remedies, even her oil of evening primrose tablets had vanished. To Mallory's great annoyance so had her razor and she had no way of shaving her legs.

Tuesday was spent in another mindless moping fug. At least Mallory had stopped checking her phone. She'd admitted to herself that Alex wasn't going to get in touch and she reluctantly allowed Caz to prise it from her grip and leave it on the hall table under strict instruction to only check it once every two hours. And when she did there was only ever a message from Caz ensuring she was okay. It only barely registered that Don hadn't even been in contact to see how she was.

By Tuesday afternoon, Mallory was fed up feeling sorry for

herself and went round to see if Olly needed help with painting the new shop unit he'd leased. It had come as a massive surprise to Mallory when he'd appeared one night at the flat to let Mallory and Caz know about his new venture, taking over the lease of the old Graphics shop. Never had Mallory seen him so excited as he unveiled his plans.

That afternoon, turning up in overalls and sporting a selection of paintbrushes, Mallory found Olly up a ladder painting the finishing touches to the name above the door: XANADU.

Inside, he'd boxed up all the previous stock and Irini was busy whitewashing the entire inside before they were going to start repainting the next day. Mallory found herself agreeing to paint a mural on the inside back wall over the weekend as she couldn't help but be caught up in Olly's infectious enthusiasm.

Later, splattered in paint and having thoroughly enjoyed her afternoon, Mallory joined Irini and Olly in having a beer to celebrate a job well done. Even with so much still to do, Olly didn't seem at all fazed.

Finishing off her beer, Mallory said goodnight, leaving Olly and Irini to it. She was delighted that Olly seemed so happy with Irini and there was no doubt Irini returned his affection. Happy that at least someone's love life was going well, Mallory walked home.

It was only on waking on Wednesday that Mallory remembered she had some purpose to her day. She had to go to Serendipity to meet Ted and go through the song together. She felt sick. The queasiness was partly down to her having devoured almost an entire chocolate cake the previous night in a burst of emotional eating, partly due to her having to sing in public, but also from the possibility she may bump into Alex.

She arrived as the band had finished setting up. The builders had erected a small, temporary stage near the kitchen door and Ted waved at her as he plugged in his guitar.

'You okay?' he asked as the drummer started to play some beats.

'I'm a bit nervous,' Mallory admitted as she got on stage and he handed her a microphone.

'You'll be fine,' Ted reassured her. 'I've gone over the number with the guys and we now just have to play about with it, find your range.'

'My range?'

'Yeah, the notes you can reach more comfortably, so you're not straining.'

'I strain over all the notes.'

Ted laughed, obviously thinking she was joking, because who would be mad enough to go on stage at a press-attended restaurant opening and engagement party and be completely tone deaf!

'Shall we start?' Ted asked. The bassist nodded and the drummer bashed his sticks together in agreement.

The rehearsal turned out not to be as bad as Mallory had feared. Ted had done a marvellous job of arranging the song, putting it into a key where she didn't sound as if she was a walrus in death throes. The band had played about with the iconic song and had turned the lovely, if rather cheesy hit into something wonderfully sultry and seductive. By the time they'd gone over it a couple of times Mallory was even looking forward to performing it.

She saw Nik arrive as they launched into their last rehearsal, and he stood watching them from the back of the room, giving them an enthusiastic round of applause and some whistles when they finished.

'That sounded great, Mallory,' Nik said, coming over to her as she hopped off the stage and Phoenix started up one of their own songs.

'Thanks. How's it all going? Nervous about tomorrow?'

Nik looked around him and smiled. 'More excited than nervous, I think; you?'

'Maybe slightly more nervous,' she admitted. She'd enjoyed singing with the band but knew doing it in front of a room full of people would be a very different matter.

'You can still pull out of it, you know,' Nik said.

'Oh no, I've spent so long memorising the lyrics, I'm definitely going through with it, and your ears didn't bleed, so that has to be a good sign.'

Nik took a deep breath. 'I wasn't actually meaning the song.'

Mallory looked at him in surprise.

'I know Louisa's railroaded you about this engagement.'

'Oh, but…'

'I just think, unless you're sure, you shouldn't go through with it.'

Mallory looked over at the band playing, wondering if it was obvious to everyone that she didn't love Don and they really shouldn't be together.

'There's a lot riding on tomorrow running smoothly,' Mallory said eventually.

'Not as much as some folk would like us to believe. I think there are some going to the party with their own agenda. I've seen you and Alex and–'

'But–'

'You need to talk.'

'We don't, we need to avoid each other as much as possible.'

'You two are both so stubborn.' Nik sighed. 'You can't tell me you feel the same for Don as you do Alex.'

'Didn't you once say I was far too sensible to get involved with him?'

'Yes, but since when has love ever been down to being sensible? I would have warned you off a quick fling with him, but I don't believe that's what's between you and Alex. And you and Don? Well...'

'We did love each other at one point...'

'Then you may be one of the lucky ones to experience that level of love more than once.'

'You make it sound so simple.'

'It is, when you break it all down.'

'Has Alex said anything?' Mallory tentatively asked, hope rising.

'To me? About his feelings?' Nik snorted with laughter. 'Don't be silly. We're men. I'm Greek and so I can get away with talking to you like this with my notions of romanticism. I'm happy to admit, when I met the love of my life, I knew she was the woman for me, instantly. If more people listened to their hearts, we'd all be in a better place.'

Mallory opened her mouth to speak, but she had no idea what to say. Just because Nik was a die-hard romantic and thought there was something between her and Alex it didn't mean Alex shared his sentiments. She also had no idea Nik had a girlfriend, and had assumed he was single as he'd not brought a partner to the weekend away, but before she could continue the conversation the kitchen door opened and Louisa stood in the doorway, holding up her hand to signal the band to stop playing which they dutifully did.

'We still have so much to discuss,' Louisa said, brandishing numerous pieces of paper all scribbled over and circled with neon highlighters.

Nik sighed. 'Can you just let me take charge of the restaurant as I see fit?'

As Louisa harangued Nik for not colour-coordinating the canapés for the photographs Mallory picked up her bag and coat as the band started playing a banging version of the Kinks' 'Sunny Afternoon'.

Walking into the kitchen, Mallory faltered slightly. Alex was draped over one of the counters, looking through another neon-highlighted list. He glanced up, his eyes momentarily fixing on Mallory's before sliding away as he returned his attention to the papers before him.

Mallory was about to retreat back into the restaurant when Nik came storming through with Louisa snapping at his heels. At the same time, Don appeared at the back door. In what felt like a double pincer movement, Mallory realised all escape routes had been blocked.

'I'm back,' Don said cheerfully to Mallory. 'And I'm taking you for lunch.'

Mallory bristled that he didn't even bother to ask, just presumed she wouldn't have anything else on. Which she didn't, but it was the principle that mattered!

And anyway, she was hungry. Too nervous about her impending vocal trauma, she'd not been able to eat breakfast and her stomach was rumbling loud enough to start competing with the drummer.

'Is everything organised for tomorrow?' Don asked, looking around.

Alex ignored Don, but Nik nodded and said, 'Yes, everything's great. There'll be a bit of running around getting the food ready but apart from that it'll be plain sailing.'

'My agent's organised a photographer to come along, get some snaps too.'

'Of course, not a problem,' Louisa said.

'It'll look good for my profile when we head back to New York with the engagement snaps.'

'You're going back to the States?' Nik said.

Don walked over and grabbed hold of Mallory's hand possessively. 'Yup, as soon as possible. Permanently.'

Alex continued to look through the papers before him. He must have heard Don's news, but clearly wasn't bothered by it, Mallory thought as they left Serendipity and she knew then there was no hope left for her and Alex.

CHAPTER 65

*L*unch was far easier to get through than Mallory had anticipated. Don's only topic of conversation was himself.

'I'm starting to regret agreeing to the exhibition over here in November. I should be focussing all my attention on America,' he moaned as he ordered two rainbow trouts without asking Mallory what she wanted.

'Excuse me!' Mallory said to the waiter before he walked away. 'I don't want the fish, I'll have the goat's cheese salad instead, thanks.'

'I thought you liked trout,' Don said.

'I do, but I also like exercising my ability to make decisions for myself.'

Declining wine and opting for a glass of water (Louisa's words about bloating had struck a chord) Mallory watched Don as he continually texted between gulping down his wine and munching on bread. Not once did he look at her, his beloved fiancée. Allegedly.

'So, what was it that made you decide you couldn't live without me?' she blurted out.

'Hmmm?' he said, his attention staying fixed on his phone.

She cleared her throat loudly to get his attention. 'What prompted you to phone me that night and ask me to marry you?'

He sent his text and laid his phone on the table.

'About two bottles of champagne and half a joint,' he joked. 'No really, I was at a low ebb.'

A low ebb? This was hardly the stuff of fairy tales.

He rasped his hand across his chin. 'More than a low ebb to be honest. You see, since we'd split up, things hadn't been going right for me. When we'd been together, everything always sort of slipped into place but when I went out there, on my own, it wasn't the way I'd planned it to be.'

He took hold of her hand across the table before she could move out of reach.

'I realised that all the good things that had happened to me happened when I'd been with you.' He took a deep breath. 'I called you that night to ask you to marry me to see if my fortunes would change. And it was the next day I got a call about a New York gallery interested in showing my work. Then, weirdly, nothing happened with it, I got no further forward. And then I got the call from the journalist about you and that waster. I was furious.

'For a moment I *actually* thought you might have gone and met someone else so I saw red and hot-tailed it up to see you. And, can you believe it but as soon as we'd agreed, face to face, to be together properly, my luck really started to change! On the way to the airport, I got a call saying that New York was almost definitely a dead cert. People were wanting to do interviews with me! A piece of my art went for a ludicrous amount of money and people were desperate for me to paint them!' He leaned forward and spoke in a hushed voice. 'My agent thinks I could be the next Lucian Freud! And it's all thanks to you, my little muse.'

Mallory couldn't quite believe it! He saw her as no more than a lucky charm. 'What if I'd said no?'

He gave her a cocksure smile. 'It was always inevitable we'd get back together. I was just waiting for the right moment.'

Yeah, when he'd hit rock bottom and had no other offers! She wanted to scream.

He continued. 'I knew I'd win you back. It was all planned. Part of my upcoming London exhibition is based on that one painting called *New Beginning*. My agent told me to start a bit of a buzz about it, so in interviews I hinted that I hoped we'd get back together again but I actually already had the piece *Reconciliation* finished. I knew you wouldn't be able to resist me.'

He sat back in his chair laughing, delighted at himself, and Mallory knew he wasn't joking; he really believed she'd never turn him down. He was going to get a shock in a few days' time. She didn't feel nearly as terrible for keeping him strung along as she had moments before.

His phone vibrated with an incoming text. He picked it up and tapped away on the keys in reply.

Mallory sank down in her chair, wishing she didn't have to spend another moment in his company.

On the bright side, she told herself as she snapped a breadstick in two, it was just another confirmation that she really was completely, one hundred per cent, no doubts remaining, over Don Marsden.

And in many ways, it felt quite liberating!

CHAPTER 66

*B*y the Thursday afternoon, Mallory had worked herself up into a frenzy of nervous energy at the forthcoming party. To take her mind off the evening ahead, she'd baked a batch of Madeleines, a Victoria sponge, some shortbread and meditated so much she didn't think her chakras would ever be out of alignment again. She'd even ended up cleaning out all her wardrobes and cupboards in a last-ditch attempt to find her missing Italian book.

After two fruitful hours she'd collected together four bags of old clothes for the charity shops but no book, which she figured must have dropped out of her bag without her noticing.

Luckily, the decluttering of her living space seemed to have had a knock-on effect to her head space and afterwards she sat in her tidy room with a wonderfully euphoric sense of achievement.

And she'd had a bit of a mind shift about the party too. For so long Mallory had been dreading it but with just three hours to go, she was starting to feel the first frisson of excitement about it! It was a party! It was a party celebrating an amazing restaurant opening. There was going to be champagne, canapés, a great band. And she had the most amazing dress to wear. She mentally skimmed over the bit where they'd be celebrating the engagement and she planned on having enough champagne flowing through her not to give a damn about getting up to sing.

She went to the back of the door where her dress hung. She reached out and touched the white satin, letting it slither between her fingers like the promise of the evening ahead.

She'd given herself three hours to get ready, which had seemed quite a generous amount of time. Any other given day and Mallory would have found three hours of spare time a substantial chunk in which she could have a couple of driving lessons, watch a film, have a yoga session, or fly to France (if she didn't count the waiting-around time in departures). She could even climb up and slither down a Munro in the space of three hours. But three hours to transform mortal Mallory to goddess Mallory was pushing it.

Thankfully Caz no longer deemed Mallory a suicide risk and had returned all the sharp implements she'd previously confiscated and now Mallory's legs could be fuzz-free again. Forty-five minutes down and she was shampooed, conditioned, exfoliated and moisturised and ready to start on her hair.

She laid out everything she'd need and the selection looked more like implements of torture than an array of beautifying aides.

After drying her hair, careful to give it enough lift at the roots, she straightened it then wrapped thick sections of it round heated rollers to set in heavy long loose curls. Waiting for them to cool she applied her make-up, copying the look of the screen sirens of the forties, with the wing tips of eyeliner on her top lids.

She slipped on the halter-neck dress, loving the way it whispered sensually over her skin, and stepped carefully into a new pair of completely impractical but oh-so-beautiful silver slingback high-heeled sandals encrusted with dozens of flashing diamanté crystals.

Taking out her, now cold, rollers she put her hair in a side parting and sculpted the front in a smooth Veronica Lake peek-a-boo style. She finished off the look with a slick of scarlet lipstick. Normally just a lip-gloss girl, the effect was quite startling but Mallory loved the way the colour zinged with her hair. It wasn't something she'd do on her way to Tesco for a pint of milk, but for making an impact it was perfect.

Caz took that moment to come crashing into her room. She took one look at Mallory and gave a squeal of delight. 'OhmyGodyoulookamazing!'

'Thanks!' Mallory felt fluttery with nervous excitement.

'And I'm running so late,' Caz wailed. 'I couldn't get away from the bar and now I'm going to make you late! And Olly is on his way round here too.'

'Don't worry about it. You take your time and get a taxi with Olly when you're ready, it doesn't matter if you're a bit late.'

'But do you not want some moral support?'

Mallory grabbed her clutch bag, so ridiculously small she wasn't able to fit anything other than her keys, phone, lipstick and some loose cash in it.

'You know what? I'm going to be fine.' And she truly believed she was as she gave Caz a quick hug goodbye and teetered downstairs to hail a taxi, making sure she didn't turn her ankle in her monstrously high heels.

❧

Mallory got to Serendipity a few minutes after seven and it was already crammed. She was only a couple of feet through the entrance when she saw the balloons and banners with her and Don's name intertwined with ribbons and hearts and her confidence wavered slightly.

Deciding Dutch courage was the way forward she helped herself to a glass of champagne and made a beeline for the spiral staircase, hoping to take cover in the shadows until the alcohol kicked in.

Over the heads of the people, she spotted Nik waving at her as he headed her way.

'Mallory, wow! Sorry, I mean, hi. You look amazing.' He kissed her hello.

'Thanks,' she said nervously, glancing around. 'I'm hoping tonight I won't get mistaken for the waiting staff.'

'No risk there.' He laughed. 'Have you had any food yet?'

'I've not been able to catch any.' She nodded over to another waiter carrying canapés being stopped by a group circling him as hyenas would a fresh kill.

'It seems to be going bloody well,' Nik whispered, crossing his fingers. He looked up at the ceiling twinkling down at them. 'But I guess our success lies in the hands of the Fates now.' He looked over at the panels of Clotho, Lachesis and Atropos then turned back to her.

'I think the success of this place will be down to your talent, rather than what may or may not be written in the stars,' Mallory said after a pause. 'Is your girlfriend here tonight?'

He looked at her. 'My girlfriend?'

'Yes, you were telling me how you knew instantly she was the one.'

'Oh yes, she is very much the one, but she's not my girlfriend. Well, not yet. In fact, we've only spoken once and I don't even know her name.' Nik grinned. 'But, when you know, you know!' He then became distracted by a woman walking towards them. 'Oh, I've just seen someone I need to go and chat to. She's a well-respected food editor with one of the nationals. Go forth and charm folk,' he added then melted away into the crowd.

Suddenly Mallory was left standing alone, clutching her almost empty glass to her chest. Leaning back into the cool wrought ironwork of the staircase, she lifted one foot at a time, trying to ease the throbbing pressure from her new shoes.

Then, all of a sudden, the flesh on her arms goose-pimpled as her instant Alex-dar began to pulse. Seconds later she caught his scent; that familiar whisper of verbena, leather and musk. She took a deep breath to compose herself.

'Mallory…'

She turned to face him, trying to ignore the kick of lust in her belly. He was wearing a tuxedo, with the tie and collar undone, making him look dishevelled and dangerously handsome.

'Hi.' She gave him a cool smile.

'Hi…' He looked as if he wanted to say more, but instead he took a sip of his champagne.

They stood facing each other for a few seconds, neither speaking.

'We should mingle,' Mallory said, breaking the silence. 'I think Nik wants us to schmooze with as many people as possible tonight,' she said, walking away with as much dignity as two burgeoning blisters and limited circulation allowed.

He caught up with her within three strides, as she got stuck behind a gaggle 'ooh-ing' and 'ahh-ing' over a platter of delicious-smelling seafood, which reminded Mallory she'd hardly eaten anything since the goat's cheese salad the day before. On the upside, her dress fitted perfectly.

'How are you?' he asked abruptly.

'Fine.' For someone who said he didn't want to be friends with her he seemed to be keen on monopolising her attention.

'Good.' His eyes flicked over her face briefly before fixing on a spot a couple of inches above her right shoulder. 'Have you spoken to Johan tonight?'

'No, not yet, I've only just arrived.' She didn't add that she'd also been trying to hide. 'Is he okay?'

'Yes. Yes, he's fine. I just wanted to let you know he's going to be doing an exhibition of my work. He loves my paintings.'

Mallory's heart soared for him. 'That's amazing. Well done.'

She stood awkwardly, thinking she should hug him, but not sure at all if the gesture would be welcomed.

'I just wanted you to know. I know you spend a lot of time with Johan, what with being his gallery assistant.'

The penny dropped. 'Ah right. Thank you!' she said, sounding very formal. 'I'll make sure I keep out of your way at the gallery. If you tell Johan in advance when you're in, I'll make sure I'm not working.'

She turned and managed to walk a couple of feet away before she felt Alex's warm hand grasp hers and pull her back round to face him and she nearly yelped in pain as the too-tight strap of her right sandal dug into the top of her foot, practically severing her toes.

'Wait. Please. I need to talk to you.'

'What for?' she said with more venom than she'd intended but the pain in her feet wasn't making her think straight. 'You've been incredibly clear with me. I didn't think you wanted any more *friendly* chats!'

He stepped back as if she'd stung him.

And then she became aware of someone calling her name. She turned to see Don pushing his way towards her.

And then everything seemed to happen at once – people pressing into her, the heat, the music… the throbbing of her feet. She stopped to try to loosen the strap on her sandal but somehow managed to catch the hem of her dress in her heel. As Don bore down on them, she kicked out her foot to free it from the fabric but instead of releasing her foot, she lost balance and started to fall, letting out a cry of anguish as she became horribly aware of the ground rushing up to meet her.

Luckily, Alex managed to catch her before she ended up knocking herself unconscious on the tiled floor and, as he helped her to her feet she was all too aware of his arms around her waist. He stooped down and managed to release her heel.

Mallory tried to laugh off her embarrassment. 'Sorry about

that, I'm not really a high heels kind of...' Her words dried up as she realised Don was next to them, as hawk-like and fearsome as ever.

She wished she maybe had knocked herself unconscious.

'What are you doing?' Don hissed at Alex.

'Don't you think you should ask if Mallory is okay before having a go at me?' Alex said.

'It just seems a little convenient you're always around.'

'Next time I'll let her fall on the floor in a heap, shall I?' Alex said, squaring up to Don.

'Will you both STOP it!' Mallory snapped. But even through her embarrassed discomfort she was aware of Alex's hand still resting on her waist, the heat of his skin searing an indelible print on her flesh beneath the sheer fabric of the dress.

Alex, as if suddenly realising too, dropped his hand.

Mallory turned to Don. 'I really hope there isn't another time that I almost fall the length of myself, but if I do I'll hover in mid-air until you can come and catch me, Don, okay?'

'Come on. Louisa's about to do her introduction,' Don said, turning and walking away.

Mallory fumed silently. Not only was Don quite unconcerned at her well-being, he was talking to her as if he expected her to carry out his every command like an obedient dog!

Alex took a step in front of her, blocking her. He then stared at her for a moment, looking hesitant, running his hand through his hair. 'I'm sorry,' he said.

'For what, catching me? You saved me a bruise.'

He shook his head. 'No, for everything else. I'm barely holding it together.'

He did look wretched.

'Are you nervous about tonight? If you can wait a few minutes Caz will be here and she always carries her bottle of Rescue Remedy with her.'

The look in his eyes told her he wasn't just suffering from

opening-night nerves. She'd seen that look once before, a few weeks previously, moments before they'd kissed.

'I don't want to avoid you at the gallery,' he said with a quiet intensity. 'I want us to be friends. I wanted more than to be just friends with you, but if friendship is all I can have I don't want to turn that down. You look beautiful tonight, I hope he appreciates you,' he breathed, barely audible above the noise of the restaurant. Then he bent down and kissed her very gently on the lips, his fingers lacing into her hair.

Mallory closed her eyes, her entire body zinging from the sensation, then he was gone.

She opened her eyes and tried to compose herself. Now, that was *definitely* more than just friendship. A handshake, high-five or buddy punch to the shoulder would have sufficed. But a lingering lip on lip? That was so overly friendly she was practically bouncing about with the bonhomie of it! But before Mallory could run after him and demand clarification on one of the most welcome, yet infuriatingly ill-timed actions ever, Ted and the rest of his band bounded on stage.

He grabbed hold of the microphone. 'Hi, we're Phoenix.'

And without further ado he launched into a rousing rendition of Jimi Hendrix's 'Foxy Lady'.

CHAPTER 67

*W*hile Phoenix played, Mallory searched frantically for Alex but the guests had created an immovable wall around her as they watched the band play and by the time she broke through the human barrier she couldn't see where he'd gone. The intensity of the way he'd looked at her, the kiss… She was still searching when Don came striding over to her, a man with a camera in tow.

'What the hell are you up to?' Don demanded.

'What do you mean?' she said shiftily. Had Don noticed her trailing after Alex? Had he seen the kiss? Part of her hoped he had so he would stomp out in a bad mood, ending their engagement once and for all.

But he was too concerned about himself to have noticed what Mallory had been up to. 'You've hardly spoken to me all evening,' he said petulantly. 'It doesn't look good.' He turned to the man with the camera. 'We're about to do the big engagement speech, okay?'

The photographer nodded as Don went off mumbling something about more champagne.

'The editor says the story will run in Sunday's paper,' the

photographer said cheerily. 'Bound to cause a bit of a flurry. Readers love a bit of drama, don't they?'

Mallory stopped scanning the crowd and turned to him. 'What do you mean? I thought this was just going to be a couple of photos about our engagement, for Don's agent.'

'And the rest!' The photographer gave a chuckle as he fiddled with the settings on his camera.

'The rest?'

He glanced back up at her, looking a little uncomfortable. 'Yeah, how Don managed to snatch you back from the clutches of the roving Lothario playboy.'

Mallory couldn't believe Don was willing to manipulate the truth to score points and get press coverage!

Any respect she'd had for him sputtered out like a dying candle. She'd planned on going ahead with the engagement to save him from public embarrassment then letting him down gently away from the press glare but looking at Don on the other side of the room necking a glass of champagne and texting someone, most probably his agent, Mallory couldn't bear to be in the same room as him let alone an engagement, no matter how brief she intended it to be.

She'd been so worried about misleading him, it hadn't dawned on her that he was using her too. Thinking about it though, it made sense. She wasn't the only one who'd neglected to tell her parents about the announcement; apart from a couple of friends of Don's, he hadn't invited anyone except press and those who could enhance his career.

He'd been full of apologies and remorse to Mallory when he thought his career was over but as soon as it had a Lazarus-like leap of revival, he'd reverted to the old, selfish Don.

All those months earlier when Mallory, Caz and Olly had burned candles and asked Aphrodite for help in sorting out their love lives, Mallory had thought she'd wanted Don but with all the annoying less-than-perfect bits removed. Well, she'd got that

Don for a little while but she knew now it wasn't what she wanted.

Even when he was playing the role of attentive fiancé she didn't truly love him; she'd moved on and outgrown him. What she once thought as masterful and experienced she now found controlling and bullying, his self-belief more like boorishness. Maybe Don did love her, in his own way, but it was very much *his* own way and that wasn't a way Mallory liked.

She was just debating making a run for it when Louisa sidled up to her. As always she was perfectly turned out, oozing elegance in a one-shouldered black evening gown, her blonde hair in a smooth chignon, make-up a flawless mask of disapproval.

'I'm going to do the official engagement announcement after the band finish this song.'

'Can we wait for a bit, please?' Mallory said.

Louisa narrowed her eyes. 'Why?'

'I... I... just need...' There was no point in sugar-coating it. She took a deep breath. 'I can't go through with it!'

Louisa steered her by the elbow towards a quieter corner. 'We had an agreement. You signed the contract. If you pull out now you'll be responsible for ruining Nik's dream.'

But if she didn't pull out she'd be ruining Alex's reputation and any way of possibly making things okay between them. 'I'll talk to the magazine and tell them I'm sorry for pulling out of the deal and...'

'You'll do no such thing!' Louisa hissed. 'I was worried you'd try to pull a stunt like this.'

'It's not a stunt, Louisa.'

'Do you know how much work has gone into this engagement party?'

'I realise that but–'

'That's why I thought I'd get a little insurance.'

'Great! You can get a reimbursement for the money you

spent.' Looking around, Mallory couldn't imagine a few balloons and ribbons costing *that* much.

'Oh, I don't mean *that* kind of insurance.' Louisa flashed her a triumphant sneer. 'I have your Italian book.' For a brief moment Mallory wondered if she intended on holding it to ransom but then remembered what else was in her Italian book; she'd marked all the pages of interest with bits and bobs of paper which included receipts for her cookery books and wine books, her riding lessons, her yoga classes and wine courses...

Louisa leaned forward to whisper in Mallory's ear. 'If you don't go through with this, I'm going to tell everyone here tonight you lied to get this job. Your CV is a complete work of fiction and I'm guessing you don't want your friends, colleagues, the press, Nik, Alex and potential future employers to know?'

Mallory swallowed.

'You need to play along tonight. Then you can bugger off. Away from Serendipity and away from Alex.' And Louisa stormed off, almost barrelling into Nik who was coming over.

'Everything okay?' he asked.

'Of course,' Mallory said, as brightly as she could manage.

Nik looked doubtful. 'You seem miserable. Don is networking, Louisa is hell-bent on ramming home the engagement party and as for Alex, rarely have I seen him looking as utterly dejected as he does tonight. Irini and I appear to be the only ones pleased that Serendipity is opening! Remember what I said yesterday. You don't have to go through with it.'

'I know, Nik. You're right. I don't want to go through with the engagement with Don. I don't even like him, let alone love him. But Louisa made me sign a contract and if I back out, the magazine will pull their coverage of the opening which could ruin your chances of making it a success and financially ruin you and Alex. Louisa also has something she can blackmail me with as extra insurance and if she lets slip what she knows about me, I'll look like a liar and a fool. And Alex didn't want to be friends with me, but I think he's just changed his mind and I really don't know what to do.' Mallory blurted everything out in a rush as Nik looked on, wide-eyed.

'Wow, there's a lot to unpack there. You do know that Louisa isn't always a rational woman when it comes to Alex? But despite all her attempts to get together with him, he's not interested. He pretty much spelled it out to her a few days ago. She didn't take it that well, to be honest.'

Mallory remembered the day Louisa gave her the contract to sign, she'd looked upset but had unconvincingly blamed it on hay fever.

'But really, you can't get engaged to Don out of some sense of misplaced loyalty.'

'But Serendipity...'

Nik smiled. 'There are many more people here than just Louisa's magazine crew. I've worked alongside these reviewers for years, remember. They're going to judge me on merit. It will be a success. Alex will not be ruined. You can't be blackmailed.'

'But I can...'

'You can't,' Nik said firmly and gave her a look.

'But...'

'It doesn't matter. You got the job here because you're a talented artist.'

Mallory let out a deep breath. Nik *knew*?

'Now, you need to go up on stage and break a heart. Just make sure it's the right one,' he added with a meaningful nod as Louisa marched back up to them.

'It's time. You know what you have to do,' Louisa hissed in Mallory's ear as she propelled her towards the band. Mallory walked over to the stage. Yes, she *did* know what she had to do.

Ted helped her up and gave her a wink. 'Do you want to do the song now?'

Mallory couldn't even contemplate it, knowing her voice would catch on every word. 'Not yet.'

As Louisa fetched a microphone Don turned to Mallory. 'I meant to say, your dress…'

Finally, he was going to redeem himself slightly by complimenting her! Too little too late but at least he'd noticed.

'I should warn you that white is fattening and the camera already adds a few pounds.'

Before Mallory could brain him with her clutch bag a hush came over the crowd as if everyone sensed an imminent announcement.

Mallory's mouth went dry as Louisa started her introduction, talking about Nik's new enterprise. Mallory zoned out, scanning the faces below, desperate to see Caz or Olly giving her a reassuring smile but they still hadn't arrived! Johan was looking up at her with a concerned expression.

Stuart and Gregor were at the back but Gregor wasn't wearing his glasses and was squinting to try to see the stage while Stuart was craning his neck to check out a celebrity a few feet to his right.

At the front, Nik stood smiling up at her. Beside him, Irini nudged him with her elbow. On Nik's other side Alex was too busy staring into his glass to look as if he was taking anything in that Louisa was saying. He didn't look up once as Mallory stood barely breathing on the stage. She needed something, some great big signpost to tell her what she was about to do was the right thing. She even looked up at her celestial ceiling but the lights just twinkled down merrily at her offering no guidance.

She was on her own.

Louisa prattled on and was getting closer to mentioning the engagement. Mallory couldn't allow her to get that far as, once it was spoken, it could never be retracted. She needed to stall the proceedings. She reached out and took the microphone from Louisa who was too startled at being interrupted mid-sentence to do anything.

'Um, hello,' Mallory said, far too close to the microphone as there was a squeal of feedback. 'Thanks for coming. I'm Mallory Caine. Before we go any further, I want to say a big thank you to the band, Phoenix.'

There was a round of applause and Louisa joined in as she carried on smiling, but in a rather unflattering rigor-mortised kind of way.

Ted, who'd been sitting on an amp jumped up and grabbed the neck of his guitar. 'Now?'

Mallory nodded.

He counted in the band and the opening bars of the well-known song filled the room. Mallory could see people recognising it but not being able to place it due to the change of tempo, key and rockier feel.

She mentally counted herself in before starting to sing the classic Elton John's 'Your Song'…

Her voice was shaky but she managed to hit the notes and to her delight, she didn't sound like a cat being strangled.

As she sang, Mallory dared to look out into the audience and at Alex who was staring up at her.

She knew, with every bar, she was killing off any shred of street cred that remained but she really didn't care anymore.

She sang loudly, her voice growing in strength. When she got to the chorus, Ted joined in, harmonising with her and to her ears it sounded great. She smiled over at him and he winked back.

She looked out into the audience. There was no way she was singing for Don; she was focussed on Alex who was starting to smile.

As the song finished and people cheered, Mallory knew what she had to do.

Her hands were so clammy she thought the microphone was going to slip from her grasp as she spoke.

'Before we continue celebrating the opening of Serendipity, I'd like to say a few words. Nik, the talent behind this most amazing restaurant is so lovely and generous he didn't mind sharing his one big moment in the spotlight with an engagement party… but before we carry on I have a confession to make. More than one, actually.'

Gregor had taken his glasses out of his pocket and had put them on to get a better look.

Mallory's legs were shaking so much her knees did actually knock together and she almost dead-legged herself. 'As well as being the, um, I suppose one of the guests of honour here tonight, I was also behind the design for the place. I did the mural and the ceiling and…' There was a smattering of applause which died down when Mallory silenced them with her hand. 'Thank you, but I'm not telling you this for any adulation. I'm worried I got the job under false pretenses.'

A murmur rippled around the room like a Mexican wave.

'You see,' her voice cracked and she cleared her throat which sent off another shrill squeal of feedback, 'what started off as a bit of a misunderstanding and a laugh ended up with me handing in a CV which claimed I could do a whole load of things which, at best I couldn't do, and at worst, scared the hell out of me.'

She could feel Louisa inching nearer towards her and Mallory held on to the microphone for dear life for fear it was about to be wrestled off of her. 'I got the job and I like to think it was also based on my merits as an artist and not just the fact I claimed I'd abseiled for charity.'

Feeling her face redden, she looked straight at Johan who was trying hard not to laugh. 'And I really don't know why I said that because I'm really not at all outdoorsy and I never want to abseil or gorge scramble or go parachuting. Maybe parachuting if the plane was going to crash and it was the only thing left to do to stay alive.'

Johan gently tugged at his goatee, trying to hide his mouth with his hand. Well, at least she was amusing one person. She didn't dare look at Nik or Alex.

'The thing is, when you start to lie it kind of engulfs you and takes over and before I knew it I was careering along trying to live up to the person I was claiming to be. Trust me, it was a full-time job. But I'd just like to say, in my defence, I've given being this CV person the best shot I could and I've had a lot of fun doing it and I, well, I guess I am pretty much that person now. Give or take an abseil and squash game or two.'

Unburdening herself, she was on a roll.

'You see it all started off a few months ago on Valentine's Day. Me and my two best friends made a pact because a couple of planets were in a certain position in the sky, my friend Caz can explain it to you when she arrives.' She looked up at the door, hoping that she would make a perfectly timed entrance. It stayed disappointingly shut.

'Anyway, I asked Aphrodite, the goddess of love, for help to find a direction in my life and to have more fun and to be able to get out there and do things and to shake it all up a little and you know, trying to learn everything off my CV has really given me that opportunity, as well as nearly bankrupting me.'

She was gratified to hear a couple of laughs.

'And I've realised that, along the way, I've gradually morphed into a new person, a stronger person; the sort of person who doesn't put up with crap. Which brings me to confession number two…' She focussed on Johan who nodded along in encouragement.

'That fateful night I also asked Aphrodite for help with love. My wish list was for a fabulous guy, one who wasn't temperamental or moody, who wouldn't place his career ambitions over me. I wanted someone trustworthy, handsome, passionate…'

'Don't we all!' a woman shouted from the audience.

Mallory smiled. 'And I've met that very person. The person I was dedicating the song to.'

There was a chorus of 'awwwws' around the room and people looked over at Don.

'Oh, but it isn't him.' There was an uncomfortable silence as she turned to Don, his face slack-jawed in shock. 'I'm sorry for doing this so publicly but I don't love you and I'm pretty sure you don't love me. I did in the past but we were different people then.'

She risked glancing down at Alex. He was looking back up at her with an unreadable expression. She faltered slightly, unsure if she should just cut her losses and run but she could see Stuart at the back giving her a thumbs-up sign. She carried on.

'I'd like to apologise to all you journalists at the magazine. I know you made me sign a contract to say there would be an engagement tonight and I'm so sorry, I just can't go through with it. And please don't write anything horrible about Nik or this place out of spite because me being a complete idiot has nothing to do with him or the cooking and he really deserves this place to work.'

'Who *is* this fabulous guy that you met?' someone shouted.

Mallory swallowed. Damn, she hadn't realised people would have listened so carefully. It was now or never. She'd already humiliated herself to the point of no return, she might as well carry on.

'It's...' she started before her microphone was abruptly pulled out the amp by a murderous-looking Don.

CHAPTER 68

*C*az was almost jumping up and down in the back of the taxi. Hitting every red light and going the strangest, not to mention *longest*, route to the restaurant, she half expected everyone to have packed up and gone home by the time they got there.

Olly looked at his mobile phone. 'It's from Irini. Mallory's doing a bit of an impromptu speech evidently.'

'Oh God! She's not a natural orator and we're not there to support her!' Caz wailed, trying to speed up the taxi with the power of her mind.

The taxi eventually pulled up and she left Olly to pay as she hurtled through the front door.

The place was packed but there seemed to be some sort of commotion as everyone was looking at everyone else in jaw-open surprise. At the far end of the room beside the kitchens was a stage and on it stood Mallory alongside the band and a furious, red-faced, Don. Caz watched as he suddenly let out a roar of animalistic rage and launched himself at Alex who was standing in the audience.

They hit the floor.

'This is your fault!' Don shouted as he and Alex scrambled to their feet.

Don pulled back his arm ready to land a punch but a man jumped in between them to stop them.

Then all of Caz's world seemed to slow down. It wasn't just any man trying to stop the fight. It was *her* man. Her very own Eros looking deliciously twinkly and dashing in a tuxedo.

And suddenly he was deliciously twinkly and dashing and lying in a heap on the floor rubbing his jaw as Don landed a punch on him.

Alex hunkered down low and took a run at Don, his head hitting Don square in the gut as he rugby-tackled him to the ground just a few feet away from her Eros.

Caz immediately ran forward, picking up a napkin and scooping her hand into an ice bucket and pulling out some cubes on the way. She fell down at his side.

He looked up at her in astonishment as she gently pressed the makeshift ice pack against his punched jaw.

'Are you okay?'

He stared at her for another couple of moments before saying, 'I think there's a very strong possibility I have concussion, I seem to be hallucinating.'

'And what do you seem to be hallucinating about?' She smiled, loosening his bow tie and undoing the top couple of buttons of his shirt.

'I could swear Florence Nightingale has just appeared before me in a red dress.' He laughed, sitting up.

'*And* Agent Provocateur underwear,' she said with a wink.

All around them chaos broke out as four security men ran forward, trying to get in front of the press who were delighted at the turn of events.

'I knew I'd see you again,' he said in delighted wonder.

'I'm glad you kept faith.' The ice she held against his jaw was melting fast from the intense heat bouncing off their two bodies as they devoured each other with their eyes.

'Tell me your name right now just in case something weird happens like a tornado hits or you disappear in a puff of smoke and we're separated and I have to go searching again. At least then I'll have a name!'

'It's Caz. Caz Lovatt.'

He laughed then winced as he fingered his jaw.

'What's so funny?' Caz asked, loving the way his eyes disappeared into tanned crinkly lines when he laughed.

'I've heard quite a lot about you already. My name's Nik. Nik Floros.'

&

After paying for the taxi, and scrabbling around for change for the tip, Olly got to the door of Serendipity as two burly security men were escorting Don out and Olly had to flatten himself against the door to let them past. Inside there was chaos. A few feet away Caz sat on the floor beside a rather dazed-looking Nik and Olly couldn't believe it when a moment later they started kissing! He knew Caz was a fast mover, but this took the biscuit – she'd only been three minutes ahead of him, max! No wonder Nik had looked dazed.

Irini hurried over to him, also doing a double-take when she saw her brother and Caz in what was fast becoming a steamy clinch.

'What's happened?'

'Apart from the world going mad? All I know is Mallory did a speech about lying on her CV and then she dumped Don because she was in love with someone else and then a massive fight broke out and Don got dragged off and *what* is my brother doing to your poor friend?'

'I've given up trying to fathom out what Caz gets up to! Trust me, it'll be *her* leading your brother astray.' They smiled at each other. Irini looked amazing in an emerald-green fringed dress which made her cute pixie face and haircut even more adorable.

He looked around. Clearly there was a lot of drama unfolding. Olly would normally try to help, to get involved and smooth the situation over, but there were silver trays of abandoned champagne bottles and the most delicious-looking food, although in such ridiculously small portions he'd need at least two platefuls for himself.

He nodded at the staircase. 'Where do they go?'

'The mezzanine bar area.'

'Come on!' Taking her hand in his and grabbing a bottle of champagne, he led her towards the stairs.

'What are you doing?' Irini asked, her eyes twinkling in delight.

'I'm seizing the moment,' Olly said as they ran up the stairs, giggling as the band started up a most satisfying cover of Led Zeppelin's 'Kashmir'.

§

Leaving the chaos behind, and knowing she was responsible for it all, Mallory jumped off the stage and ran into the kitchen, welcoming the sound being muffled as the service door closed. With all the staff out front watching the drama unfold, she had the kitchen to herself. She steadied herself on one of the counter tops, fearing she'd made a bad situation a hell of a lot worse.

The door opened and Alex appeared.

'You're bleeding!' she said, horrified at a livid-looking cut on his cheekbone.

He pressed the cuff of his jacket against it to stem the flow.

'Is it very painful?'

'Can't feel a thing.'

'You can stop with the macho bravado!'

'No, I really *can't* feel a thing, I'm numb from shock, and I don't mean from the punch to my face.'

'I'm so sorry...'

'I think we've more than fulfilled the brief for giving the press a good story but I realise you were cut off in your prime.'

'I was?' Mallory stood with her back to the cold steel counter top as Alex slowly walked towards her.

'Yes, you were just getting to the good part. Who is this man that you met?'

'I think you know.'

'I think I do.' With barely inches separating them, Alex gently brushed the hair from Mallory's face and leaned in to kiss her in a way that sent Mallory's stomach flipping and left them both breathless.

'I'm sorry for lying on my CV,' Mallory said as they broke off from the delicious knee-trembling kiss.

'It *hardly* came as ground-breaking news,' Alex murmured as he traced the outline of her collarbone with his lips, sending ripples of desire through her entire body.

Mallory tried to concentrate on what he was saying. 'Hmm?'

'I'm not stupid.'

Her eyes snapped open and she pulled back. 'You knew?'

He dropped a delicate kiss on her shoulder. 'Despite your valiant efforts I've never seen anyone quite so terrified at getting on a horse. And let's face it, you're not entering the Gumball 3000 rally anytime soon either. I think multiple countries in a week would be a bit of a stretch for someone unable to go any higher than third gear and who has issues with reverse.'

'But if you knew, why didn't you say anything?'

'To be honest I didn't see it as a big deal, and I didn't know if it was everything or just a couple of things. Who was I to doubt your proficiency at yoga? And I saw first-hand you can certainly salsa dance.'

'So, my CV had nothing to do with the job, it was all down to my talent?'

'Of course.' He cocked his head to the side. 'I had also pretty much fallen in love with you from around about the second glass of wine you threw in my face.'

She froze. He'd used the *love* word.

Alex realised he'd said it too. He gave her a lopsided grin. 'I think I'm well beyond the point of suggesting a chat over coffee to see if we've got anything in common.'

'I'd no idea.'

'I had no idea what you were thinking. One minute you seemed to like me, the next you were pushing me away. At first I tried to think of you as merely a business colleague. A very *sexy* business colleague.' He sighed, leaning in to kiss her again.

'When we went away for the weekend I was so sure there was something between us, and I'd already started to doubt the existence of your fiancé when, rather inconveniently, he turned up.'

'I only got engaged to him when I saw you with Louisa. I was waiting for Don to come out the shower to finish it with him when I saw you and her down on the patio.'

'And on seeing that, you ended up engaged to Don?'

She nodded. Now it seemed such a monumentally stupid reason to get engaged to someone; hurt pride.

Alex sighed again. 'I'm not proud of that. I felt so hurt and used. I wish you'd waited a little longer and watched me push Louisa off and walk away.'

'But the next day she was acting as if you two were together.'

'Acting. And I was in no mood to let you think otherwise. In fact, that's why I suggested you sing at the engagement party, I'd already heard you singing one day when you were painting the frieze and didn't know anyone was there. It was bad.'

'You wanted me to humiliate myself?' she said in mock anger.

'I wasn't in a good place.'

'I think you suffered enough with Louisa stalking you.'

'I tried letting her down gently, actually tried avoiding her, but that didn't work as she always managed to find me. I ended up being brutally honest with her the day after the salsa evening. Seeing you that night practically did me in and it took everything not to seduce you on that dance floor. When she dropped in on me the next day, I told her bluntly it was never going to happen.'

'That's when she came to see me with the contract for the engagement.'

'She did that?' He puffed out his cheeks and shook his head. 'I think she's got the message now. I saw her leave as Don was escorted off the premises.'

'Good riddance. If the papers do write a dreadful review because of me, I'm so sorry.'

Alex looked seriously at her.

'They're not going to be very happy,' Mallory added.

'You know, I have an idea how we can make it okay.' Grabbing her hand, he walked back into the main restaurant and picked up the microphone which had been dumped on the ground.

The band finished the song they'd been performing.

'Hello! Excuse me, can I have your attention please,' Alex said as he plugged the microphone back into the amp.

Mallory looked out into the crowd and at Nik who was standing, talking animatedly with Caz. Caz looked over at her and mouthed 'it's him' as Nik mouthed 'it's her' and it suddenly dawned on Mallory that Nik was Caz's Eros! And Caz was whom Nik had known was the woman for him.

She blew them both a kiss.

Alex cleared his throat. 'Does anyone have a pen?' he asked the crowd.

Ted reached over and handed him a Sharpie.

'Cheers. Some of you may be wondering what the hell is going on.' He pulled down a banner that had Mallory and Don's names on it. 'And I understand that you guys,' he gestured to the press, 'were expecting an engagement.' He scored out Don's name and scribbled in *Alex*. 'What do you say?' he said to Mallory.

'I say yes!' She laughed.

He waved the banner above his head. 'Seeing as we hate to disappoint,' he shouted as the photographers snapped away.

He turned to Mallory. 'I'm afraid we might have to wait a while until I can afford a ring!'

'I don't care!' she said, giddy with happiness and love for Alex, as the twinkling lights of the constellations shone down on their heads.

THE END

ACKNOWLEDGEMENTS

A big shout out to all at Bloodhound Books. In particular Betsy for saying yes, Morgen for her amazing and insightful editing, the wonderful Tara for all her hard work and patience, and Hannah for all the clever social media segments.

A NOTE FROM THE PUBLISHER

Thank you for reading this book. If you enjoyed it please do consider leaving a review on Amazon to help others find it too.

We hate typos. All of our books have been rigorously edited and proofread, but sometimes mistakes do slip through. If you have spotted a typo, please do let us know and we can get it amended within hours.

info@bloodhoundbooks.com

Ingram Content Group UK Ltd.
Milton Keynes UK
UKHW040634220523
422126UK00004B/66